PELELIU FILE

Dale Dye

"Dale Dye has a flair for telling stories and evoking images. His details about Marine life are accurate...Dye has the ability to draw the reader far enough into the story that the reader sees with the author's eyes and feels with his emotions...Dye's ability to tell a story the way it really happens is rare, and one sincerely hopes this book will not be his last...."

--Orlando Sentinel

"Capt. Dale Dye has done more than any other man alive to influence the way that America (and the rest of the world) views the U.S. military."

-- Lt. Col. Dave Grossman, USA (Ret.)
Best-selling author, "On Killing," "On Combat"

Dale Dye provides "firsthand knowledge...an inside view."

--Kirkus

Also by Dale Dye

LAOS FILE
RUN BETWEEN THE RAINDROPS
PLATOON
OUTRAGE
CONDUCT UNBECOMING
DUTY AND DISHONOR

PELELIU FILE

DALE DYE

WARRIORS PUBLISHING GROUP
NORTH HILLS, CALIFORNIA

PELELIU FILE

A Warriors Publishing Group book/published by arrangement with the author

PRINTING HISTORY
Warriors Publishing Group edition/November 2010

Warriors Publishing Group
16129 Tupper Street
North Hills, California 91343

ISBN 978-0-9821670-1-4

PRINTED IN THE UNITED STATES OF AMERICA

10 9 8 7 6 5 4 3 2 1

To our Skipper, Major Mordecai "Mawk" Arnold USMC (Ret) and to the weird, wonderful ISO Snuffies of the 1st Marine Division, Vietnam, circa 1966-1970.

PACIFIC OCEAN AREAS

Iwo Jima, Volcano Islands

The view from atop Mt. Suribachi was...

Well, sobering might work. An observer who did not have his historical sensitivity and combat experience might call it awe-inspiring or even spectacular. But Shake Davis saw too many blasted, broken and bullet-riddled specters on the black sand beaches below his perch to be impressed by Iwo Jima's desolate beauty. From the gummy, sulphur-scented terraces of the landing beaches, past the remnants of Airfield No. 1, beyond the quarry and north toward Hill 362-A which had been the focus of his attention for the past week, all he could see were ghosts.

It was the same every time he climbed the twisting trail toward the summit of the dormant volcano and ran through the sequence of the battle in his mind. From D-Day on 19 February through 26 March 1945, when the island was officially considered secure, more than six thousand American attackers and more than twenty-one thousand Japanese defenders died in just ten square miles of wind-scarred real estate. Standing near the very spot where a patrol from Easy Company of the 28th Marines had raised an American flag over Iwo on 23 February and created one of the most iconic images to emerge from World War II, he thought he could see all of them down below begging for recognition.

Turning to look over the rolling blue expanse of the Pacific toward mainland Japan some 600 nautical miles to the north, Shake hoped some Japanese bureaucrat was looking kindly on his request for at least another week prowling the island. He had some reasonable leads on finding what the samurai wanted him to find on Iwo Jima and some even better clues regarding his personal goal in probing the battlefields.

He'd sent the extension request for favorable endorsement through the same old friend that had gotten him a rare clearance to visit Iwo Jima in the first place. His pal was a modern samurai and a very senior officer in the Japanese military now but they'd gotten to know each other well while Shake was an active duty tactical advisor to the Japanese Maritime Self Defense Forces. They'd shared lots of time in rubber boats out on the Sea of Japan, festive dinners of squid and hot sake and an abiding interest in the Pacific campaigns of World War II. When Shake got the job that required him to poke around on Iwo Jima, he immediately contacted his old friend but permission for an extended stay on the island and freedom to nose around at will was no rubber-stamp deal.

He gave the big Marine memorial located on the summit of Suribachi a glance and smiled at the huge garlands of dog tags left on the edifice by Marines who visited the island by special permission once a year on the anniversary of the landings. There would be more added in a couple of days when the Battalion Landing Team from III Marine Expeditionary Force arrived from Okinawa to act as escorts for returning vets and families. The Japanese were bound by the 1968 agreement that returned Iwo Jima to their control to allow these visits but they didn't have to like it. There was pressure from high places in Tokyo to isolate the island and preserve it as a strictly Japanese enclave. The pressure had been sufficient recently to cause the government to officially redraw their maps and revise the name of the island to its original form: *Iwo To.* And surviving American veterans of the bloody fighting on Iwo Jima sure as hell didn't like that.

Shake picked up a piece of coral, wound up and heaved it as far as he could off the southern slope. It landed with a satisfactory plop among the breakers below and he hoped a ripple effect would carry up the North Pacific to somehow influence the decision-makers in Tokyo. He was close to his goals. He just needed a little more time...and some luck. But it was out of his hands and if the extension wasn't approved, he'd be leaving Iwo Jima on the same plane that carried the returning vets back to Guam and then Stateside. It was time to return to his digs so he started down the trail to the landing beaches six hundred feet below the summit of Mount Suribachi.

He trudged slowly across the third terrace of black volcanic sand above Green Beach and felt the familiar cloying tug on his hiking boots. The smell of rotten eggs rose to assault his nostrils with each step. There was no question in his mind why early explorers called this inhospitable flyspeck Sulphur Island. Every surviving veteran talked about that smell but after ten days on Iwo, Shake was slowly getting used to it. Climbing up onto the runway of Central Field, the only active airstrip on the island, Shake paused and stared down the long strip of crumbling concrete. It had been constructed over the southernmost of three airstrips built by the Japanese during the war. Shake nodded at a couple of Japanese sailors grooving their golf swings by knocking balls out into the surf. From what he'd seen during his time on Iwo, there were some serious PGA tour prospects among the four hundred or so Japanese troops who were stationed there. They had a hell of a lot more interest in golf, satellite TV broadcasts and videogames than they did in military history, which was just fine with Shake Davis.

They'd been curious about his mission at first, and then mostly ignored him. Shake had brought along his own rations and camping gear, so he was self-sufficient and no drain on the island's meager military resources. When he asked for help or borrowed tools, the Japanese island commander granted his requests with a smile and a nod. The commander on Iwo had a copy of Shake's permission letter from Tokyo locked in his desk drawer and that meant his *gaijin* guest was both political and well-connected. The less he knew about what the American was doing poking around the island, the better. And there was no indication in the letter that one of Shake's missions on Iwo—in fact, the reason high-placed contacts in the Japanese Self Defense Forces had granted it in the first place—was an effort to finally find out what had happened to the general who commanded Iwo's garrison during the U.S. invasion.

The remains of General Tadamichi Kuribayashi, the 53-year-old commander of the 109th Division and the Ogasawara Army Group on Iwo Jima had never been found. There was intense disagreement among historians. Some said he had committed hara-kiri late in the battle when it became obvious he'd lost the fight. Others swore he died while leading a last-ditch counterattack near Airfield No. 2 during the last days of the fighting on Iwo. Professional military men in Japan—led by a Japanese officer who was a close friend of Shake's—really wanted to find out the truth so the argument could be settled once and for all in the ultimate hope that Kuribayashi's remains could be located and taken to the Yasukuni Shrine in Tokyo, where he would rest with Japan's revered war dead. Given Japan's penchant for revisionist wartime history, conducting their own investigation was out of the question but Shake's request to nose around the island looking for American remains gave them a unique opportunity. And Shake's high-placed buddy assured all involved that the matter would be handled delicately. That did the trick and got him the OK to spend two weeks on Iwo Jima for "purposes of historical research of great interest to the government of Japan."

It also gave Davis too much to accomplish in too little time. The search for Kuribayashi was interesting and vital to his Iwo access but it leached time from the search for what he was really after: the remains of Marine Sergeant Bill Genaust. He expected to find that somewhere up ahead, past the remains of Motoyama Airfield No. 2 and the remnants of the old U.S. Coast Guard LORAN Station demolished in 1994. Somewhere near or on what appeared on wartime maps as Hill 362-A.

There were a lot of unsung and under-appreciated heroes of the fighting on Iwo Jima, but Bill Genaust, a Marine Corps motion picture photographer attached to the V Amphibious Corps for the assault, was unique. It was Joe Rosenthal, a civilian photographer for Associated Press that captured the hearts of Americans with his photo of the second and most impactful flag-raising on Iwo—one of the most iconic images in history. But what few Americans know about the flag-raising is that the entire sequence was captured in 198 frames of Kodachrome motion picture film shot by Genaust, who was standing near Rosenthal and cranking away with his 16mm Bell & Howell.

Genaust would not live to realize it, but his color footage was shown in movie houses across America and appeared daily for years as an overnight signoff segment on TV stations. Practically everyone has seen that sequence but only a few know who shot it. During the war, regulations did not provide credit to motion picture photographers although still images released to the public usually carried a credit. That was one reason Bill Genaust never got the recognition he deserved. The other reason was that Sgt. Genaust was killed on Iwo Jima and his body was never recovered. Shake Davis was digging around a collapsed cave on Hill 362-A in hopes of correcting that situation. He was bound to locate Genaust's remains and returning them to U.S. soil.

Eyeing the small dent he'd made in the mound of crushed coral, sand and lava rock where he'd been digging for the past week, Shake felt confident he was in the right place. Somewhere behind that mound, pushed into place by a Marine bulldozer to seal the entrance to the cave where Genaust and another man were killed searching for Japanese snipers, he'd find what was left of a fellow Marine who deserved a better hand than the one dealt to him on Iwo Jima. But as he shoved more shoring into the short tunnel he'd made in the base of the pile, Shake realized it was going to take more time than he had left to break through to the cave. If his extension didn't come through in the next two days, Bill Genaust would remain buried on Iwo Jima with all the other ghosts that haunted this island.

Shake Davis was on intimate terms with wartime ghosts. He'd spent a lot of years exorcising his own demons from combat tours in Vietnam and trying to shed some light on brothers listed as missing in action from a long and ultimately inconclusive conflict. That effort had kept him on active duty longer than he'd planned and nearly cost him his life a decade past, so when he finally left active duty he was determined to permanently retire Marine Gunner Sheldon Davis and find a good-old-boy name of Shake Davis spending his days somewhere between a barstool and a bass boat.

He should have known better. No master plan ever survives the first round downrange. And that round was fired by his wife, who emerged from the Betty Ford Clinic free of a debilitating addiction to vodka and ready to begin a new life divorced from all her old bad habits—one of which was Shake Davis. It was inevitable he decided when the lawyer plopped the papers down in front of him on the porch of Gus Quick's old cabin in the Ozarks. Fortunately, it was also amicable and his wife didn't want an oversize bite out of his retirement pay. She'd leave him enough to squeak by on, but the cabin willed to him by the old sergeant major and the bass boat had to go on the auction block. Daughter Tracey was on a seagoing sabbatical from her studies at the Naval Postgraduate School at Monterrey and working on research sponsored by the Woods Hole Oceanographic Institute, so she was self-supporting. His overhead was minimal but Shake still needed a job.

There were lots of folks out there—old contacts from his active duty or special operations background—ready to offer him one at sizeable salary but they all seemed to involve long tours in crappy locations or hustling hardware for defense contractors. He'd had enough of that so Shake cut expenses to bare bones, rented a little cabin on the Mississippi River in southeast Missouri where he'd grown up, and settled down to pursue his life-long hobby of reading military history with a particular—and perfectly understandable—emphasis on Marine Corps operations in World War II. Something would come along bearing a suitable paycheck and enough enticement to keep him from wasting the rest of his life drooling in a corporate cubicle.

He was living on a steady diet of fresh-caught, deep-fried catfish and bourbon whiskey when his cell phone buzzed and Chan Dwyer came back into the picture. Shake had been in semi-regular contact with her since the Vietnam thing and had seriously considered making a romantic run on Chan. But she was focused tightly on climbing to the top of the military intelligence heap. She'd left the active Army ranks for a high-level analyst slot at Defense Intelligence Agency and she'd been thinking about him lately. When Chan said she'd be delighted to see him any time he was Back East it got Shake to thinking of how lonely he'd become.

She also said she had a lead on something that might interest Shake if he had time to drive up to St. Louis and meet with Ken Moore, who ran an independent organization called Moore's Marauders, which specialized in finding the remains of wartime MIAs and returning them to their families. Moore had been probing around intelligence circles for years searching for information on MIAs from World War II, Korea and Vietnam. He was well-respected for his willingness to undertake search missions that the U.S. government couldn't—or wouldn't—handle through the Pentagon's Joint POW-MIA Accounting Command.

It was Moore who got Shake interested in Bill Genaust. He couldn't offer a big salary but he could support travel and expenses. What Moore needed was someone well-versed in Marine Corps history who would be capable of focused investigation. That person would need connections in Japan to be able to gain access to Iwo Jima. Chan Dwyer had told Moore that Shake Davis might be the perfect fit and after he and Moore shared a few beers in a downtown St. Louis pub, Moore knew that Chan was right. The mission came together in short order after that initial meeting.

Shake made his contacts in Japan and discovered he'd have to decline Moore's offer of high-tech ground-penetrating radars and staff archeologists to assist on the mission to Iwo. Given the General Kuribayashi angle that was driving Japanese cooperation, the trip would have to be strictly low-key and involve low-tech grunt work. Shake didn't realize just how much pick-and-shovel would be involved until he started kicking around on the island. After twelve days, he had nothing more than a six-foot hole in the side of Hill 362-A to go along with some credible hunches about what happened to the Japanese general.

When he spotted an ominous layer of dark clouds headed for Iwo from the east, Shake dug into his rucksack for a snack, slung the pack, picked up a sensitive mass spectrometer and headed toward the remnants of an old sulphur mine near the northeast end of Airfield No. 2. His best guess from research and tidbits that had been gleaned from the few Japanese soldiers taken prisoner on Iwo was that Gen. Kuribayashi's remains probably lay in a mass grave where 300 of his soldiers died in a very effective, focused and deliberate counterattack against elements of the 5th Pioneer Battalion and Navy Seabees who were working on the airfield. That action on the night of 25 March was nothing like the last-ditch banzai charges that Marine veterans of earlier action in the Pacific had come to expect. Shake had found a rare transcript taken during interrogation of two Japanese soldiers who had held out and survived on Iwo until sometime in January 1949. They both swore that their commanding general had personally led that attack and was killed in the resulting combat. Given what Shake knew about the atypical nature of the action and Kuribayashi's distaste for wasteful banzai charges, it seemed likely the general was involved. From one old soldier's perspective on another, Kuribayashi just didn't seem like the ritual suicide kind of guy.

He'd gotten some solid near-surface readings indicating an underground mass in the area. It could be old ordnance or the remains of a tank or amtrac. On the other hand, it could be a bunch of Japanese soldiers buried where they were killed with their weapons and equipment. A little digging in just the right place would provide the necessary hints one way or the other but Shake felt he was onto something here. He was waving his detector over an area of scrub brush on the west side of the old runway when the rain started failing. He was cursing the weather, convinced that it would curtail his efforts for the day, when the satellite phone in his rucksack began to chirp.

Caller ID told him it was daughter Tracey but he'd guessed that before digging the bulky handset out of his pack.

Only three people had the sat-phone number. He'd spoken with Moore to provide a progress report yesterday morning and made embarrassing small-talk with Chan Dwyer that night, so neither of them was likely to be calling. That meant Tracey was on the line—or "on the bird"—as she liked to say, calling from somewhere in the Pacific where her ocean science team was conducting research. They'd been trying to hook-up ever since Shake announced he was headed for the area on this job but she was living aboard a research vessel and hard to find. Shake punched the transmit button hoping Tracey had landed some place where he could spend a few days with her if his extension request was denied.

"Send your traffic, girl."

"Daddy, how the hell are you?"

"Substandard to shitty as usual. Better question is where are you? Send PosRep."

"You're not gonna believe this, Dad..."

"If that tub you're sailing ran aground and you need rescue better call your squid buddies. I'm stuck out here on Iwo Jima."

"And I'm stuck on...guess where. You're gonna love this!"

"Wherever it is, it can't be more god-forsaken than Iwo Jima."

"Oh, yes it can, Gunner Davis. How about Wake Island?"

"You're on Wake?"

"I am indeed, Daddy. And gainfully employed in significant scientific research, I might add."

"There's nothing left on Wake..."

"Except me and my team...and a great little bar called the Drifters Reef."

"Tracey, you stay out of that place. I've been there. It's a snake-pit. Horrible stuff happened to me last time I fell in there. It was back in the bad old days and we were doing a transpac on a C-130. Damn thing lost an engine and we were stuck on Wake for a week...maybe more...I don't remember."

"Bet you remember sitting on that old porch watching the sun go down and feeling the tide flood in over your feet. There's some serious South Pacific mojo out here, Pop."

"That part I do remember. What the hell are you doing on Wake, girl?"

"We're tracking some sort of fish-kill phenomenon, Dad. It's really weird stuff...Pacific salmon washing up dead on beaches...serious impact on the goony bird population in the mid-Pacific. Meat and potatoes for us science wonks. We're gonna be here for another two weeks at least. Any chance of a hook-up?"

"Depends on what happens in the next two days, Tracey. I've asked for an extension but no word yet. If it doesn't come through, I'm headed home. I could maybe meet you on Guam but there's no way to get to Wake...unless you're some highly-paid and under-employed geek on a research grant."

"I know. We're stuck out here until the ship gets back. Wake is one of those rare places where you can't get to from anywhere. Just our luck."

"I'd really like to see you, sweetie..."

"Me too, Dad. It's been too long."

"Heard from your Mom?"

There was a long stretch of satellite static before Tracey Davis replied. It wasn't lost on her father.

"Mom's fine. She called from Palm Beach. Seems to be doing OK."

"Sober?"

"Far as I could tell. She's...well, she seems to be keeping company with somebody that's kept her entertained."

"You don't need to soft-pedal it, Tracey. She's got a right to look around for happiness. I damn sure didn't provide much."

"Can we skip that and change the subject before we lose the bird here?"

"Sure, it's starting to rain like a fat cow pissing on a big flat rock out here and I need to seek shelter."

"No chance of a hook-up on Wake, Dad?"

"Don't see how, honey. Are you good? Anything you need?"

"Need to have a beer with my Dad at Drifters Reef. Other than that, I'm OK."

"Let me work on it. Maybe we can rig up something on Guam or Saipan. I've got a few bucks to spare."

"OK. I'll stand by. How's your health?"

"Superlative for a guy that checks in at four days older than dirt. I'm good to go and looking forward to giving my best girl a hug and a kiss."

"We'll get it done, Dad. Stay tuned. I love you."

"Bye, honey. Love you."

Rain was bucketing down by the time he punched off the connection with his daughter. His tent and a meager meal was a mile away but he didn't mind a long, wet walk. Brothers who fought and died on Iwo Jima suffered much worse and he owed it to them to continue the march. Tracey was fine. He was frustrated but still excited by his quest here. If the extension didn't come through, there would be a next time, a next trip and a next effort. He had time one way or the other. Neither Bill Genaust nor Tadamichi Kuribayashi was going anywhere.

Sulu Sea

Making minor engine turns and dragging a sea anchor aft, the big yacht wallowed in the Sulu Sea just south of Jolo. All the running lights were doused to avoid detection by Philippine Armed Forces coast-watchers and to make it easier for the crew to spot the signal they were looking for from the beach half a mile north of their position. The sophisticated nautical GPS system aboard the vessel indicated they were smack on the designated mark and they'd been holding position for the past twenty minutes. Someone ashore was late, compromised or simply stupid. They couldn't keep the big yacht drifting for much longer without risking discovery by a patrol boat.

Jolo—like all the other islands strung out along the Sulu Archipelago in the Autonomous Region of Muslim Mindanao—was a primary focus of Philippine military activity these days. That was understandable. Abu Sayyaf *jihadis* had been on a rampage of killings and kidnappings lately in an effort to raise money and sustain their fight with the government in Manila and any other handy infidels. With these believers, if you weren't willing to tolerate or propagate Islam worldwide, you were the enemy and there were no affordable holds barred. That's what made them so attractive to the movement's leadership. Muslim separatists in the Philippines, the Moro National Liberation Front and various off-shoots of that group, focused mainly on creating a Muslim state in Mindanao totally divorced from the infidel government in Manila but the leader of Abu Sayyaf on Mindinao had a greater global vision. What he didn't have was means to realize the vision. That might be remedied tonight if all went according to the plan developed before they put to sea from the port of Dubai six weeks ago.

Sayed Abdullah focused the binoculars and swept the shoreline once again for the prearranged signal from the Abu Sayyaf contacts. Hopefully, they knew more about the science involved in the mission than they did about keeping schedules.

His team stood on the brink of one of the most ingenious and potentially devastating strikes on the enemies of Islam ever attempted but he wished they were working with more sophisticated allies. Admittedly, the Abu Sayyaf military commander had conceived the plan and sold it to his superiors and the financiers in Saudi Arabia but the science involved in the mission was something else entirely. That's why the first stop they made in the South Pacific was at Jakarta to pick up the Indonesian researcher now safely billeted in one of the yacht's luxurious staterooms. His two scientific compatriots ashore on Jolo had failed to meet deadlines and drawn unwanted attention, so they were changing venues. Once he had the scientists and the Abu Sayyaf leader aboard, they were headed for a place where the American intelligence apparatus did not reach, a place where the people controlling the spy satellites would never think to look.

Abdullah handed the infrared sensing binoculars to the chief of his fifteen-man Quds Force security detail and headed toward the bridge to check on radar contacts. If patrol boats were in the area, he needed as much early warning as possible, so he'd ordered the captain to keep the air and surface search radars rotating. Those orders and all others on this operation were issued in English. With Arabs, Indonesians and Filipinos involved and so much at stake they could not afford language misunderstandings, misinterpretations—or secrets—within the team. Everyone involved would be competent in English and speak it at all times. That had been one of Abdullah's first demands when he accepted the mission outlined weeks ago by the Iranian Quds Force mission commander aboard this very yacht in Dubai.

Climbing toward the blacked-out pilothouse, Abdullah pondered the enormity of what they were attempting. If it worked as planned, his place in heaven was assured and his life on this earth would be as heavenly as the staggering fee he was being paid could provide. But it was such a long-shot and he'd known that from the moment his Quds Force handler contacted him in Damascus. He was a veteran of several wild and wooly clandestine operations around the world but he really wanted no part of what he considered a gaggle of amateurs here in the South Pacific. The fight was for the cradle of Islam, cleansing the holy places, striking blows against infidels worldwide and putting his native country in a position of leadership in the inevitable Fourth Caliphate. That was the long-range plan and Abdullah believed they'd do well to stick with it.

That's what he thought when the messenger found him in an Al Qaeda safe house but it certainly wasn't what he said when he was ordered to proceed to Dubai for an important meeting. The Quds Force handler said go, he would be joined by a QF mission security team in Dubai. The man issuing the summons was a very rich and very influential member of the House of Saud who had funded a number of QF missions in the past and this one was to be viewed as a cooperative effort. Orders from the Saudi prince were to be obeyed as if they had come from the Supreme Council in Tehran.

He didn't require much persuasion. Sayed was on the run anyway. He'd been hiding in the Syrian capital from intense scrutiny by the Americans and their various puppets who correctly suspected—but couldn't yet prove—that he was both chief bag-man and primary show-runner in a series of spectacular attacks on targets ranging from Kabul to Karachi and into the belly of the beast. A number of bombings were planned for the U.S. mainland. It was wise to keep moving and enough money had been spread along the route to insure he'd slide safely across international borders between Damascus and Dubai.

On the bridge, a nervous captain reported both radar screens clear. He was equally anxious to get this part of the mission underway and kept switching his attention between read-outs from the GPS navigation station and the radar repeaters. The Lebanese Muslim sailor was a trusted operative and a veteran of many cruises in support of QF missions so he was prepared for the worst. If patrol boats were in the area, they would run for international waters to avoid contact. If he was stopped and boarded, the captain had valid international papers that would pass initial scrutiny but not much beyond that. The Philippine Navy was on high alert and they'd be more than a little suspicious of a yacht with Middle Eastern registry cruising off a string of islands infested by rabid separatist gangs. And then there was the arsenal of weapons stashed below decks that the QF security chief insisted was vital to the mission.

Abdullah thought it was an unnecessary risk. As far as he was concerned, the only conventional weapons needed on this trip were the ones already loaded in the Zodiac tied up alongside, waiting to go ashore and into the hands of the Abu Sayyaf on Jolo as part of the bargain. The Zodiac could be scuttled and abandoned quickly if they were discovered but there would not be enough time to dig out the collection of personal weapons—including RPGs, grenades, land mines and machineguns—which, for some paranoid reason, the security detail considered vital. QF Security Teams were never very sophisticated but they were responsible for mission safety, so the weaponry would remain aboard and he would just have to accept the risk.

Abdullah ducked out of the pilot house, glancing over the side where the small boat was tied up to the yacht and bobbing in the chop. The security guards were at their posts; one forward and one at the controls of the muffled outboard engine, and the two big crates of weapons and ammunition were lashed firmly in place. When the signal was finally made, he could quickly grab the valise full of cash and get aboard the boat for a quick trip ashore. They'd be three men going in and six coming back, but with the weapons and ammunition offloaded there would be plenty of room in the Zodiac.

It was the cash that worried Abdullah. There was a lot of it in various currencies easily negotiable on Mindanao. He didn't like carrying cash. It was incriminating and hard to explain in an era when business deals involving big sums were almost always done via electronic transfer. It was clean and hard to trace that way but the Abu Sayyaf cells didn't keep bank accounts. They insisted on cash for cooperation plus an extra infusion of arms and ammunition to cover the trail of operations on Jolo. The upside was the diversion Abu Sayyaf would provide once they had a fresh supply of funds and sophisticated weaponry. While the mission team worked in seclusion to the east of the Philippines, local *jihadi* cells throughout the archipelago and on Mindanao proper would run a bloodbath that would draw attention away from the real hammer being forged elsewhere.

Back inside the pilothouse, the yacht's captain reported no radar contacts and still no signal from shore. He had an annoying habit of sucking noisily on an empty pipe when he could not smoke openly and the gurgling got on Abdullah's frayed nerves. He gave the radars a quick glance and left the bridge along the companionway that led aft past a row of staterooms and out onto the weather decks. One of the doors on his left cracked open and he noted the bulging, bloodshot eyeballs of Dr. Susilo Nasuton sweeping the passageway. If there was anyone aboard more worried about the mission than Abdullah, it must be Nasuton, the lavishly-paid and internationally recognized geneticist and microbiologist from Jakarta. For a very senior and supposedly dedicated member of Indonesia's Jemaah Islamiya, the man seemed insufferably whiny. Abdullah suspected it was simply because the scientist was not used to field work. At any rate, he was vital to the mission and therefore had to be not only tolerated but placated.

"Why haven't you gone ashore, Sayed?"

"No signal as yet. It will come soon. We aren't dealing with people who keep precise schedules here. It's nothing to worry about."

"My compatriots need to be recovered quickly, you understand? There is still much work to be done and this relocation will set us back weeks."

"And whose fault is that, my friend?" Abdullah tried hard to keep his tone friendly and patient but they'd had this discussion in one form or another every day since they left Indonesian waters. If the two scientists working for Nasuton on Jolo hadn't made stupid mistakes they would not need to move out of the Philippines. And Abdullah would not have been called to oversee the project and get it back on track.

"The science is not exact. I've told you that before. We are in experimental territory here and...."

"Yes, Susilo, and some of those experiments have drawn unwanted attention. You saw the reports. The Americans have a scientific vessel investigating. Even Greenpeace is looking into it. How long will it be before the rest of world's ecological alarmists get on the case?"

"They will find nothing that could not occur in nature. That's the purpose of all this!"

"The purpose of all this, my friend, is to punish the infidels for their outrages and to further establishment of the Fourth Caliphate. You would do well to remember that."

Susilo Nasuton blinked rapidly and chewed on his thick mustache. It was past time to change the subject. "Even if they trace the source to the southern Philippines, they will find nothing incriminating."

"And we keep it that way, Susilo. That's why we are moving. We've been through all this many times."

Abdullah patted the scientist on the shoulder, shoved him gently back into his stateroom and pulled the door shut. At the rear exit of the passageway Amin Faraz, the QF security chief, waved the infrared binoculars and pointed toward the shore.

"We picked up the signal. They appear to be a few hundred meters east of where they are supposed to be."

"Was the code correct?"

"It was. Two long, two short. All infrared. Do you want to get underway?"

"Immediately. I'll be in the boat in three minutes."

Abdullah ducked into his own stateroom, unlocked the storage bin beneath his bunk and grabbed the satchel of cash. With just a little more luck, they'd be underway to a new and secure location in less than an hour. If the scientists did the job they were so-well-paid to do, the attack could be launched in a matter of weeks, perhaps even less. It would, of course be the last effort they made on this earth but the scientists didn't need to know they were martyrs just yet.

Wilkes Island - Wake Atoll

Tracey Davis stood knee-deep in the gently lapping surf southwest of the beach on Wilkes Island and scooped another bloated, goggle-eyed casualty into her net sample bag. About three hundred meters north of her position, up around Kuku Point, Woodrow Cheeley was on a similar mission collecting dead gooney birds, but he'd be pissed if she used that term to describe what he was doing out here on Wake Atoll. He'd show that crooked, condescending smile and point out that he was collecting specimens of black-footed albatross (*Diomedea nigripes)* for dissection and research into unexplained deaths among the tiny mid-Pacific atoll's transient bird population.

Woody was like that: Cute, sensitive, intelligent and a wonky pain-in-the-ass sometimes. They'd been flirting on the cusp of a shipboard romance for three weeks but it never seemed to get quite hot enough for consummation. If Tracey hadn't eavesdropped on a couple of Skype conversations he'd had with a cutie he kept on a loose leash in his hometown of Asheville, North Carolina, she could be convinced that Woody was gay. But Woody was straight. He was also overly-focused and often oblivious to the romantic elements of cruising—all expenses paid—through the exotic South Pacific with a young, vibrant and consistently horny crew of Navy and civilian scientists who didn't have a care in the world beyond their various academic fields. The guy needed appropriate stimulation and Tracey was hoping the bikini she'd bought in Honolulu would provide it.

With the research vessel off tracing migration patterns to see if they could determine a nexus for whatever was killing fish and birds in a sort of ocean corridor running from somewhere in the vicinity of the Malay Peninsula across the Pacific in an easterly direction, the research team on Wake had the freedom to conduct its own research in a more relaxed manner. It was all fairly focused and tight-ass aboard the RV Seascope, so the stay-behind team of young scientists on Wake didn't complain much despite the spartan living conditions on the tiny island.

It would be two weeks or maybe three before the ship returned to pick them up and assess the results of their wildlife research. The vessel was owned by the National Oceanic and Atmospheric Administration and carried a scientific team from Woods Hole to look into what appeared to be a new pattern of fish and sea bird deaths in the South Pacific. Wake came into the picture when scientists began to plot migration patterns among the affected fish and bird populations and discovered that casualties were piling up on the three islets of the tiny atoll. Wake seemed to be some sort of mid-Pacific cut-off as affected wildlife populations moved west to east. That movement pointed like a diseased finger at Hawaii and the U.S. West Coast, so while the international scientific community was mildly curious, the U.S. government was distressed enough to write a big check and re-direct NOAA assets.

As alarmists in the scientific communities were tuning up to start banging the drum about yet another man-made ecological disaster, certain paranoid elements in the U.S. intelligence community smelled something more rotten than dead fish and birds. They were monitoring the research closely and all reports to the NOAA and Woods Hole were being copied to the National Counter-Terrorism Center. Tracey Davis was unsure where she should stand on that issue, but her concern just now as a Navy ocean scientist on loan to the research team was to gut some fish and see if she could tell what was killing them. And that would keep her right at Woodrow Cheeley's elbow, shoving slides under the sophisticated microscopes in the modular lab they'd set up on Wake's main island.

Tracey plopped another specimen of *Oncorhynchus* into her bag and wondered once again why the dead fish they'd been finding on Wake and elsewhere in that imaginary sea corridor were almost exclusively varieties of Pacific salmon. If there was really something nefarious behind the phenomenon, it was directed at one of the world's most-popular food fishes.

On the other hand, salmon were notoriously susceptible to various naturally occurring diseases and parasites. They'd have a better feel for the situation when the dissected specimens, slides and cultures were ready for examination.

She heard her name called and turned to see Woody walking into the surf-line carrying a burlap bag bulging with what she presumed were dead gooney birds. He was waving a Motorola portable radio and eyeing her tan lines above and below the bikini.

"Janis called. She wants everyone back at the lab for a dinner meeting. Said she's got some early data and wants opinions from all area reps."

"Thought she said we weren't going to start processing cultures until tomorrow."

Woody shrugged and made a valiant attempt to unglue his gaze from Tracey's chest. "You know the notoriously anal Dr. Janis Fielding, P-H-fucking-D and microbiologist to the stars. Right now is too late."

"Our fearless leader has probably whipped out Occam's razor and sliced us off another theoretical model to work on." Tracey started splashing through the surf-line, heading in the direction of the modular lab array they'd constructed near the end of Wake's semi-active airfield. Woody fell in just a step behind her which gave him a good view of her butt.

"You gonna change or risk offending Doctor J with your feminine pulchritude?"

"Why would she be offended?"

"Two reasons: It may have escaped your notice but Doctor J is, how to put this delicately, built like a boy? Also she's a bit light in the frivolity spectrum."

"Since when is a bikini frivolous?"

"Since you stepped into that one this morning. Doctor J is unlikely to admire its subtle charm."

"So I'll change into my geek outfit prior to the meeting." Tracey shrugged and pointed toward the ramshackle building on the horizon near the airfield. "You up for a beer or two at Drifters Reef tonight?"

"Long as the patio's open. All those war toys in the bar make me nervous."

"There's some serious military history in those artifacts, Woody. And you'd know that if you ever read anything besides ornithology papers."

Jolo Island, Autonomous Region of Muslim Mindinao

Sergeant First Class Dave Martinez scratched viciously at his crotch and wondered whether his promotion would come through before the chiggers finally chewed the balls completely off his body. The Special Forces operator asleep next to him in the jungle hide was the team's senior communications NCO, who had told him yesterday morning that Marty was on the list for promotion to master sergeant. SFC Tony Labella was a wild card in the team deck on occasion, but he was wired into the Army system tighter than a popcorn fart. If Fat Tony said he made the promotion cut, then it was gospel. And it meant Marty would likely take over as team sergeant of ODA One Four Charlie when the incumbent executed his transfer orders back to The Schoolhouse at Ft. Bragg.

That would please the shit right out of SFC Martinez, who had just about enough of these overnight surveillance missions after three months on Mindanao and the other southern islands as part of Joint Special Operations Task Force - Philippines. Between the Moro National Liberation Front, Abu Sayyaf and all the other Muslim separatist splinter-group assholes in the southern Philippines, there were so many High Value Targets that it would take every operator in 1st Special Forces Group to keep Mark I eyeballs on all of them. And night ops were both the norm and the worst with chiggers and spiders and snakes and leeches and mosquitoes big enough to stand flat-footed and shit in the back of a six-by and...

SFC Martinez forgot his discomfort and re-focused on the trail they'd been assigned to watch until dawn. Something was moving through the bush to their right rear. He flipped the night vision goggles down over his eyes but there was nothing to see on the trail. It was still and quiet in the direction of the AS camp they'd been over-watching for the past three days and just as lifeless in the other direction toward the beach. Still, his highly-tuned bush sense was tingling and his ears told him they were about to have company. He carefully touched Fat Tony and gave his shoulder a slight squeeze. SFC Labella responded immediately and silently as he always did when the familiar signal was given.

"Got something?" Labella barely whispered as he hit the power switch for his NVGs and swept the trail for movement. Marty pointed at his ear and nodded in the direction of the AS base camp. Labella closed his eyes and shifted focus to his ears. He heard the familiar shuffle-slap of sandaled feet moving through the jungle underbrush. It took him less than a minute to assess the sounds.

"More than two...maybe five or six...and they've got a load on."

Martinez nodded agreement. It could be a routine patrol. Could be a ration detail checking fish-traps along the beach. In that case, they could go back to scratching chiggers. Or it could be the HVT they'd been looking for heading for some kind of meet with AS elements who regularly came ashore from other islands in this area. If that was the case, they were most definitely interested. That terrorist piece of shit had a rap-sheet longer than a dinosaur's dick and he was the reason they were on Jolo in the first place. Seems whatever Colonel Ibrahim did was of great and abiding interest to the higher-ups in their chain-of-command. Ibrahim was a senior military commander of AS forces in the southern PI. He was also harder to find than a PFC in the Pentagon.

Martinez and Labella scrunched down even further into their over-watch position and then froze as an AS party came into sight around the bend in the trail that led to the beach. Fat Tony was right as usual. There were six people in the party. The point man was a barefoot little bush-beast who carried an AK-47 like he knew what he was doing. Next came three men, followed by two women, both of whom carried what looked like equipment cases. That likely meant the AS were sending something off the island or receiving something on the beach that needed to be transported in those cases. Marty thought the former was more likely and focused on trying to estimate from size and construction what might be in the cases.

Fat Tony nudged him gently as the party approached to within about eight feet of their position. Marty shifted his gaze and caught his breath. No doubt about it. The second man in the file was the infamous Col. Ibrahim, strutting along like he didn't have a care in the world. There had been no sign of him even being in the area recently. Marty briefly considered aborting their reconnaissance mission and snatching Ibrahim. It would be a relative piece of cake unless the party had flankers out or another detail following farther down the trail. Either way, they could probably get away with it. On the other hand, it didn't pay to second guess orders when you were stuck out on the shitty end of the stick. In the murky business their detachment was conducting in the Philippines, you never knew for sure what the Intel geeks were up to from one day to the next. Orders were to conduct surveillance and report activity. Going beyond that might fuck all over some master scheme being run by either J-SOT or the Philippine Constabulary. Better just follow orders and keep eyes on the prize.

Martinez felt another nudge from Fat Tony and focused on the two men following Ibrahim. They were unarmed and didn't appear to be AS fighters. It was hard to tell for sure but he suspected they weren't even Filipinos. Their clothes were cleaner, the facial structures were different and neither man walked like he was comfortable in the bush. That was interesting enough to make Marty study both men intently as they passed his position. His best guess was that they were Indonesians. They'd been seeing a few of them on Jolo and elsewhere in the archipelago where surveillance was being conducted by either Special Forces or SEAL teams working the area. Feedback from J-SOT indicated most of them were bomb-making specialists imported by AS to improve their IED efforts. That might explain the equipment cases but the AS on Jolo were usually receiving rather than sending when it came to bomb-making gear.

When the trailing females were well past their position, Martinez motioned to Fat Tony and began to collect his gear. They'd melt back into the bush and run parallel to the trail until they found another over-watch position where they could observe the stretch of beach near the AS campsite. "That was fuckin' Ibrahim, no doubt about it. We gonna call it in?" Labella was digging in his rucksack and fiddling with his lightweight AN/PRC-119A SINCGARS encrypted radio.

"Not just yet, Tony." Martinez was stabbing at his PLGR-96 GPS to mark the exact location of the sighting. "Let's get eyes on the beach and see what they're up to first." SFC Labella nodded, jerked the straps to close up his rucksack and shouldered the load. In thirty seconds after they'd sanitized their over-watch position, both SF soldiers had disappeared into the dense jungle of Jolo Island.

* * *

"You sure it was him?"

"No doubt in my military mind, sir." Martinez and Labella were kicked back in a pair of folding chairs sucking on lukewarm bottles of San Miguel beer inside the ramshackle rattan structure that served as Operations Detachment Alpha - One Four Charlie's team house on the Zamboanga Peninsula. "The sleazy little sonofabitch passed close enough we could have reached out and strangled him. In fact, Captain, I gave some serious thought to doing just that."

Captain Bob "Killer" Killen, the detachment commander, grinned and reached into the battered Styrofoam bucket that held their rapidly-dwindling weekly beer ration. "Good thing you didn't do that, Marty. Otherwise, you wouldn't have picked up what you did on the beach. Any thoughts about what he was doing or where he was going?"

SFC Labella ran his beer bottle across his sweaty forehead. It didn't help. "One thing's for sure, sir, Ibrahim ain't in our AO anymore. We waited four hours after the Zodiac left with him and those other two aboard. He didn't come back. At least he didn't come back to the beach area where they usually come and go from the base camp area."

"We requested UAV over-flights at first light to look for anything suspicious offshore. No word on that as yet." Killer Killen didn't say so but he doubted the J-SOT element on Mindinao had even launched one of their precious few Unmanned Aerial Vehicles to check out suspicious vessels south of Jolo. Mission time was hard to come by on the few U.S. air recon assets doled out to the Philippines from the massive commitments in Iraq and Afghanistan.

"Could be he's off visiting some of his outfits on the other islands." Martinez scratched at his chigger-bitten crotch and wondered if the team medic had any clear fingernail polish left. It was the only thing that seemed to work on the irritating bites. "We need to pass the word to be watching for him all over the AZ."

"Already done." Capt. Killen consulted the notes he'd made in the earlier, more formal debrief. "We sent flash traffic soon as we got your initial report. We'll just have to see if the turd shows up anywhere in the Autonomous Zone. Meanwhile, I'm interested in the boat. You guys ever see AS use something like a Zodiac before?"

"Pretty pricey gear for the locals," Martinez admitted. "It looked new and definitely a military-style rig. Had a muffled engine; the whole shot. Three men aboard when it landed. They off-load a couple of crates. There's some conversation but we were too far off to hear any of it. One guy from the boat hands over a satchel of some kind to the point man and that guy split back up the trail toward the base camp."

"Then the two dudes and Ibrahim are in the boat with those equipment cases and they shove-off straight out to sea." Labella picked up the narrative. "The two females sit down on the crates and about a half hour later a whole bunch more females and a couple of guys carrying AKs show up with rope and bamboo poles. They rig up the crates for carrying and head up the trail. Whatever was in those boxes was heavy. They were struggling."

"Gotta be weapons or demo, right?" Martinez polished off his San Miguel and stretched to snag a replacement. "We probably just saw a resupply run. And the Indonesians or whatever they were? My guess is they were Mike Charlie in this area and headed for someplace else to do their thing. Probably had bomb-making shit in those cases."

"Yeah, it feels like some kind of swap-meet deal." Capt. Killen had sent the team's HVT spot-report up their dual reporting chain as a flash priority without added comment or speculation. Now the three soldiers were thinking out loud as they tried to connect the dots and get a feel for what it might mean.

"AS gets whatever was in the crates and the guys in the boat get whatever was in the equipment cases," Killen speculated. "Plus Colonel Ibrahim and a couple of Indo bomb experts who are mission complete on Jolo. We're continuing the surveillance on the base camp so we'll know what they got on this end. But who the hell were the guys in the boat and what was in those cases? That Zodiac's got my attention. What if it was sent from some bigger ship out at sea and they took Ibrahim and his pals completely out of the area? Now we got a missing HVT. That ain't good."

The routing on the HVT spot report had included the Philippine Constabulary and the Philippine Navy command that was running maritime patrol operations in the Sulu Sea. As usual there had been no acknowledgment from the Filipinos. There was no way of knowing whether they even got the message traffic much less took any action on it.

Fat Tony Labella stuffed his lower lip full of Copenhagen and spit into his empty beer bottle. "If that's what happened, Captain, the defecation's gonna hit the oscillation. Ibrahim suddenly disappears and we were the last ones to see him? We're gonna wind up searchin' every island southeast of Mindinao tryin' to find his sorry ass."

"There it is," Martinez assented. "And if we don't find that little fucker...well, down-time is gonna be in mighty short supply." There was silence for a few minutes as they all pondered that possibility. Army Special Forces assets were stretched painfully thin in the southern Philippines.

"Not much we can do about that, gents." Killer Killen stood and gathered his notes. "Those are the breaks in the special warfare community." He grinned at his two NCOs and headed for the door of the team house. "If it was easy, everybody could do it. Finish off the beer if you want. We're due for a resupply sometime tomorrow."

When the officer disappeared out the door, Martinez examined the four remaining beers floating in the bucket of tepid brown water. "You want another bottle of this horse piss?"

"You drink the rest." Labella rubbed his rumbling stomach and stood to stretch the kinks out of his muscles. "I'm gonna see if I can find something to eat that don't make me puke and then fire up a couple of rockets for transmission."

Martinez raised his eyebrows over a fresh bottle of beer. "When you gonna learn to stay in your own pay grade, Fat Tony? Every time you start generating message traffic outside the chain, Killer starts to shit little blue BBs."

"I'm sick of this right-hand, left-hand stuff, Marty. You keep information like this over-compartmentalized and someone drops a big shit-ball in our laps. You know that. You've seen it happen. There's so many fucking spook outfits on the grid you can't even count 'em anymore. Way I see it, the more they all know about what we know the better off everybody is."

"Your funeral, pal." Martinez shrugged and drained half the beer in the bottle.

"There it is." Fat Tony Labella headed for the door of the team's hooch. "And if you keep calling me Fat Tony, I'm gonna tear your fuckin' head off and shit in your shoulders."

Wake Island

"Our little mid-Pacific sojourn may have taken an ominous turn." Dr. Janis Fielding was in melodrama mode as she passed out copies of the spreadsheets she'd downloaded from counterparts aboard the RV Seascope. "This data just came in and I made copies for everyone. Take a few minutes to look it over and then I'll want opinions from all disciplines."

Tracey Davis scratched at a patch of skin that was starting to peel under the modest khaki safari shirt she'd tossed on over her bikini top and began to scan the rows of figures. Fielding was a bit of a drama queen but some of this stuff did look disturbing. Seated to her right, Woodrow Cheeley tossed his copy of the print-out on the table and sat back with his hands folded on his stomach. She elbowed him and pointed at the printed material.

"You under-whelmed or just don't give a shit?"

He shrugged and popped the tab on a Diet Coke. "Not my thing. No data on birds. It's all fish stuff, right?"

Tracey riffed quickly through the pages. There was nothing in the material relating to avian studies. Apparently, the scientists working at the more sophisticated labs on the ship had limited their studies to fish they'd harvested after leaving Wake. It didn't take long to see the bottom line. The people manning the spectrographs and electron microscopes aboard the Seascope were drawing no definite conclusions as yet, but the evidence was pointing toward *Clostridium botulinum.* Tracey thought that couldn't—or shouldn't—be right but these early readouts looked convincing.

"You should have a feel for the figures by now." Dr. Fielding returned to the conference table from a sideboard where she'd made herself a peanut butter and jelly sandwich. "Let's just go around the table and get your takes on this. Chemistry?"

"Out of my wheelhouse." Dr. Stanley Radicoff, the breezy research chemist from UC Berkley was slathering yellow mustard on the cold cuts he'd piled onto a flour tortilla. "Our bad boy doesn't appear to be chemical in nature. Looks more like something you and Andrew should handle." Radicoff nodded to his right where Dr. Andrew Merman, a microbiologist on loan to the team from MIT was poking around in a plastic bowl of Ramen. "That said, I can't fault the discipline. It looks like they followed all the appropriate protocols and did the right tests."

"Just not enough of them." Merman slurped a spoonful of noodles and chewed for a moment as he ran a finger across a printed page. "We need a bunch more data and independent verification. What if our samples don't yield similar results? It's too early in the process to panic and put all this down to botulism. It doesn't make sense anyway. You find *botulinum* in fish all the time but it doesn't kill the host."

Fielding punched up a screen on her laptop and studied it for a moment. "Unless someone somewhere is messing around with the genomes. There's a report here that says the Soviets tried it out on some unpronounceable island in the Aral Sea in the early '70s..."

"C'mon, Jan," Merman complained as he poked at his noodles. "What are you looking at? That testimony from Alibekov, the former Soviet bio-weapons guy? Read on. He says they were trying to splice the toxin gene onto other bacteria to come up with a contagious form of *botulinum.* They failed. It was way too hard."

"That doesn't mean someone isn't out there giving it another try." Dr. Kimiko Fukihara of the U.S. Army Medical Research Institute for Infectious Diseases had been convinced from the day she came aboard the RV Seascope that they were facing a serious threat. As an internal medicine specialist in infectious diseases and epidemiology, she'd studied any number of botulism outbreaks in her native Japan that were traced to seafood of one type or another. "You want to remember that *botulinum* toxin is the most poisonous substance we know of. You introduce it to a food source, and millions would die, especially if you could come up with a contagious form. I'm not saying that's what we're looking at here, but we shouldn't write it off."

Woody seemed a little more interested in the direction the conversation was taking. "That's a fairly long stretch isn't it, Kimiko? I seem to remember something in the literature about bad jalapeño peppers or something a couple of years ago...somewhere in the Southwest? Bunch of people got sick but nobody croaked."

"Limited universe on that one, about sixty people give or take. And they were all treated with anti-toxin. We knew what we were dealing with and we dealt with it. This could be different."

Tracey held up her hand and got the nod from Dr. Fielding. "As the resident fish guru, I think we need to go back to what Andy said earlier. *Botulinum* doesn't kill the host. It kills people who eat the host. Or people who eat the host before heating it up to around one-eighty-five Fahrenheit anyway. I think we need to be taking a closer look at environmental issues. Could it be something in the habitat? Could fish in the flow we're studying be picking up something in the water that stimulates growth of bacterial spores?"

Sarah Kellerman, the ocean science and atmospherics specialist from Woods Hole, shrugged and consulted her notebook. "There's nothing unusual in local waters or in the algae-plankton world around Wake. I'm waiting for read-outs on samples the folks on Seascope are taking as they back-track along the counter-current flow. I'll be able to give you a better opinion then but for right now, if there's something in the water, it's not in these particular waters. Could be something closer to the nexus – wherever that turns out to be. More when I get the data dumps."

"That's probably a dead-end," Doctor Fielding said as she tapped at her laptop's keyboard. "It says here no cases of waterborne botulism have ever been reported."

"Don't misinterpret that," Dr. Fukihara warned. "That means the toxin doesn't normally survive in water but it doesn't mean it can't...especially if some element of the genome has morphed or been altered. It's not that far-fetched. *Botulinum* occurs in seven categories depending on the strain. We need to know more about what we're dealing with here. Is this Type A, the kind of stuff they purify and use in botox injections, or is it one of the others, B through G?"

"We start on that early tomorrow morning. Let's recap unless we've missed something." Dr. Fielding cut a glance at Woodrow Cheeley who was casually checking his watch and wondering if he could talk Tracey Davis into an outrigger canoe trip across the Wake lagoon before the Drifters Reef opened for nightly business. "Woody, any input from the wonderful world of birds?"

"Nothing yet, mainly because I haven't done any dissections, but it's not hard to see the cause and effect. Fish carry toxin. Birds eat fish. If toxin is the sort that's lethal to avians, birds die. I'll clean that up for you starting tomorrow."

"OK, tonight we take some more time to examine the data from Seascope. Cross-disciplines and confer as intellectual curiosity impels you." Dr. Fielding ran a pencil down the checklist she'd prepared during the meeting. "We'll take a reverse-research approach to this thing. First thing is to verify the data from Seascope. Are we really looking at *Botulinum*? If so, what strain? From there we can start to speculate on causes and pass the data on to Seascope and research assets back home."

She snapped her leather file folder closed and swept her eyes over the Wake research team. "A couple of thoughts before I cut you all loose for the evening: Remember we're doing basic research here; looking for information. I don't want anyone going all Dr. House, MD on me. Just do your research and assemble the data. It's way too early to engage in wild speculation about mutant genetic experiments or terrorist plots. And finally, remember what Kimiko said earlier. *Botulinum* is deadly stuff; serious poison and potentially lethal. Starting tomorrow, we work with specimens under strict haz-mat protocols, masks and gloves at all times. If you don't know the drill, talk to Kimiko and she'll get you snapped in on procedures. The stuff normally doesn't penetrate intact skin but I want all of you to use extreme caution with any kind of sharps. Cuts, scrapes or open wounds of any kind, see Dr. Fukihara."

Sulu Sea

They were 34 nautical miles south of Jolo Island, making a leisurely sixteen knots on an easterly heading by the time Abdullah managed to get the principals assembled in the yacht's dining room. He'd offered the AS operational commander a private stateroom where he could shower and relax prior to their meeting but the man he knew only as Col. Ibrahim didn't seem interested. Seated as they were, elbow to elbow around a green-baize table pouring tepid tea into enamel cups, Abdullah sincerely wished the AS mastermind had followed the others into the showers when they'd returned from the pick-up point on Jolo. The man reeked of jungle rot and body odor.

The two Indonesians seated on either side of Dr. Susilo Nasuton were clean but clearly uncomfortable as they watched the senior scientist pore over their notes. They would be considerably more uneasy when Abdullah started the project review for which he'd called the meeting.

"Dr. Nasuton, we will begin when you are ready."

Nasuton nodded without looking up from the notes he was taking from the pile of charts he'd downloaded prior to the meeting. Abdullah nodded and reached for the teapot in the middle of the table. He offered a refill to Col. Ibrahim who placed a hand over his cup and glared at Abdullah.

"I wish to discuss the command structure for this operation," Ibrahim said.

Abdullah replaced the teapot and breathed deeply to bring his temper under control. All he got for the effort was a cloud of nasty stink and a strong desire to slap the Filipino leader across his filthy face. The man seemed bound to make things difficult but Abdullah had been assigned this mission to insure it went smoothly. And that meant finding a way to get along with the man who had come up with the scheme and convinced Abdullah's commanders that it might just work.

"Of course, Colonel Ibrahim, what troubles you?"

The guerilla commander glared around the table, pulled a plastic bag out of his pocket and deftly rolled tobacco into what looked like a cornhusk. Abdullah shoved a book of matches in his direction and watched as the man lit his cigarette and exhaled a plume of rancid smoke. Fortunately, the yacht had an efficient air-conditioning system.

"This is a military operation. I am the senior military commander. The operation will be initiated and conducted under my command."

Abdullah waited for more but that seemed to be all Col. Ibrahim had to say on the matter of operational command of one of the most audacious strikes ever attempted in the name of the great Islamic uprising. The man puffed angrily on his smoke, scratched at his scraggly beard and stared at the ceiling.

Abdullah was saved from further confrontation when Nasuton looked up from his notes and nodded that he was ready to begin reviewing the scientific elements of the operation.

"We will discuss command relationships later and in private, Colonel. For now, perhaps, we can focus on the status of our scientific efforts?" Ibrahim waved a hand but continued to stare at the ceiling. Abdullah bit his tongue and nodded for Nasuton to begin.

"Much of what we have to report is technical in nature. Perhaps it is best to review our efforts from the beginning so that we can all be clear on the objectives. For the past three months my colleagues and I have been working to develop a weapon that can be used to advance our worldwide struggle against the enemies of the faith. In simple terms, we have been attempting to splice the toxic *botulinum* gene onto bacteria occurring in a number of human food sources. We have been working from data gleaned from early experiments conducted by Russian geneticists and microbiologists and using advanced techniques developed by myself and my colleagues at the Islamic University of Riau..."

"And whose idea was it to develop such a weapon?" Col. Ibrahim mashed his homemade cigarette into an ashtray and pointed a grimy finger across the table. "Let us not forget that I brought the concept to the leadership and convinced them to fund the effort. Without that, you scholars would still be staring at bugs and we would not be on the verge of an ultimate strike."

Having made his point, Ibrahim busied himself rolling another smoke. Abdullah took another deep breath and signaled for Nasuton to continue. It was inconceivable to him that this smelly little jungle-fighter had the brains to generate any idea much beyond loading a rifle. He'd have to do some research on this Col. Ibrahim. There must be something beyond the obvious. His mentors were not likely to expend huge amounts of time and money on wild schemes brought forward by grimy little fanatics.

Nasuton caught the cue and shuffled his notes. "As I was saying, the leadership funded our research but ordered us to move the experiments out of Indonesia for, uh, security reasons when difficult questions were asked about the nature of our work and the source of our funding. We moved a fully-equipped laboratory to Jolo where we could continue under the protection of Col. Ibrahim and his forces from Abu Sayyaf. The focus of our work was on species of Pacific salmon, as these fish make up a significant portion of the food source in many targeted areas of the world. Assuming success in these experiments with salmon, we feel confident that the toxic gene in communicable form could easily be transferred to other food sources in target areas."

Abdullah nodded and stared at the two scientists sitting at Nasuton's side. "Obviously, something went wrong. Or the people who study these things wouldn't be probing around throughout the Pacific. What happened?"

Galan Wahid, the Indonesian geneticist Nasuton had dispatched to Jolo, raised his hand and got a nod from his boss. "We believe it was the, uh, the detritus from our experiments that caused the problem; not the work itself. You see..."

His partner Ahmed Suharto, the microbiologist on the Jolo field team, picked up the cue from his obviously flustered partner. "We were working under strict protocols and took every precaution to hide the nature of what we were attempting." He seemed just as nervous but a little more forthright about what happened on Jolo. "As Dr. Nasuton had foreseen, there was a need to eliminate failed specimens and cultures that did not meet our criteria. We regularly handed this material over to Colonel Ibrahim's men who were instructed to take it to sea and dump it well offshore."

Col. Ibrahim finally seemed interested in something besides his cigarettes and the ceiling tiles. "My men did precisely what we were instructed to do. All this material was taken by boat to the specified area north and east of the Mindinao where it was dumped. We took pains to make it look like we were simple fishermen dumping bait. It was all according to the master plan."

Nasuton shoved a couple of his charts across the tabletop where Abdullah could see the Pacific Ocean currents described in colored arrows across latitude and longitude lines. "I believe that may be the cause of our concerns." He tapped a pen on a circular pattern inscribed in red and running in a circle to the east of the Philippine archipelago. "This is the basically circular pattern inscribed by the South Pacific and South Equatorial current flows. Our plan was for the experimental detritus to be dumped in this area where it would simply circulate with the current and be confined to this area, assuming it had some sort of toxic effect, which we did not expect."

Abdullah was becoming short-tempered and anxious to get to the bottom of what was clearly a scientific glitch. "It is clear your precautions were not sufficient, Doctor. If they had been, the Americans and all the others poking around in this area would not be here. Do you have an idea about what happened?"

"Two problems, I believe." Nasuton consulted his notes while chewing on his mustache. "We were likely mistaken in demanding that the detritus from our experiments be disposed of at sea, an understandable methodology given that we were working with fish, but there was clearly some unexpected effect on surrounding populations. We are looking into it. Having made that initial miscalculation, I believe we also erred in dumping it in this area."

Dr. Nasuton pointed at the charts and tapped a yellow arrow that ran straight from west to east along the equator. "This yellow arrow represents the Equatorial Countercurrent. I believe some toxic material was carried out of the designated area by this current. When phase two of the mission begins, we will require the regular assistance of a specialist in oceanography."

Abdullah leaned across the table to get a closer look at the current flow. "And the material carried by this current killed other fish? And those dead fish showed up further east which caught the attention of the scientific community and brought them to the South Pacific on a fishing expedition?"

Abdullah's play on words was lost on Nasuton who glanced at his colleagues and nodded glumly. "I suspect that is precisely what happened, Sayed."

Abdullah shoved angrily at the charts. "A potentially costly miscalculation, doctor." This mission was beginning to look as if it might be beyond effective control. And now he was faced with having to recruit yet another scientist into the fold. He knew from past experience that the more people who knew about a mission, the smaller the odds that it would be launched undetected. Discipline would have to be tightened. If the infidel scientists traced the source of the contamination to the southern Philippines, they would find nothing incriminating. He had ordered that track to be well covered. But their paranoia knew no bounds these days. They would not give up easily if they smelled something manmade or unnatural.

"Is this fish-kill situation likely to continue? Can we limit the damage to what has already been done, at least until we are ready to strike?"

"It's our opinion that this is a limited situation; confined to a specific area and a specific population." Ahmed Suharo said as he glanced at his partner for confirmation. "Of course, there is some movement of contaminates due to the countercurrent flow that Dr. Nasuton mentioned, but we have not yet fully succeeded in the gene splicing element of the experiments. We believe the damage will be limited and determined to be caused by a naturally occurring phenomenon."

Dr. Nasuton picked up the thread of his colleague's speculations. "This is why we are moving, is it not? The situation will be investigated but the infidels will conclude it is an isolated occurrence. Granted it's mysterious and unexplained, but it will be eventually written off as just another of the contaminations that occur regularly in the ecosystem, more fodder for those who are convinced the earth is doomed."

Abdullah was weary of the waffling. "You understand the importance of secrecy here?" He fixed his most intimidating glare on the scientific team. "This mission will not succeed if we are hounded by infidels who suspect anything beyond the hand of God in what they are seeing. Your job is to insure that is what they suspect—and all they believe—when the mission begins. Can you assure me something like this will not happen again before we are ready to strike?"

"I have designed new protocols for our continued experiments." Dr. Nasuton reached into his briefcase and handed a document across the table. "The specifics are contained in this directive. We will no longer dispose of any materials at sea. From now on, we bury what doesn't work and only experiment in limited, fully-confined areas at our new location. We will confine our experimental population with the barrier nets stored down below. It will look like what we say it is: A series of simple experiments in aquaculture or fish-farming."

Abdullah nodded slowly, chewing on the problem and pondering the bulky stack of documents stored in his stateroom. The permission to conduct those fish-farming experiments in the Republic of Palau where they were headed had cost his QF mentors and the Saudi backers more money than the Republic of Palau had seen since the islands gained independence in 1994. And there was more where that came from if Abdullah and his team ran into any blackmail from Palauan bureaucrats. With God's help and some strict discipline, he could make this work despite the early blunders.

"Let us have no more missteps or miscalculations." Abdullah said as he stood and nodded at the scientific team. "Doctor, please give me a written synopsis of your experimental findings to date—in plain language. Colonel Ibrahim, we should meet after dinner to discuss your concerns."

Iwo Jima

Shake Davis had his gear staged and ready to load aboard the airplane that brought the returning veterans to Iwo Jima. His request for an extension had been denied by Japanese government authorities. His buddy in the Japanese Maritime Self Defense Forces apologized profusely when Shake called him to see if there was a way to get around the situation and stretch the visit. Absent some dramatic breakthrough which Shake had failed to produce, he was going to have to bow to Japanese sensitivity and leave Iwo Jima's ghosts where they had rested for more than 60 years. The only bright note was that his Japanese military contact seemed confident he could get Shake back on the island next year, perhaps for a longer stay and with a larger research team.

Shake watched the old vets, all escorted by energetic young Marines, wander in small clumps across the landing beaches and around the base of Mt. Suribachi. It had been a real treat and a huge motivational kick to see these active duty Marines lined up as a guard of honor when the vets climbed down from the aircraft. Many of the old warriors were hobbling on canes or being supported by family members, but they all straightened up and marched like Marines when they passed through the cordon of youngsters in camouflage uniforms standing rigidly at attention. *The skeptics can kiss my ass,* Shake thought as he noted the awe and respect one generation of Marines showed for another, *the legacy of the Marine Corps is a living, breathing force.* He'd been a part of that force for nearly thirty years and there were times when he'd felt all the emphasis on teaching history was a distraction. But you see something like this out on a crappy little Pacific flyspeck and you know for sure it's the history that shapes the future. In a military outfit reliant on individual motivation for success, that kind of thing is not only valuable, it's vital.

Shake had spent most of the morning after the veterans arrived talking to as many of them as he could. Unfortunately, he had discovered nothing new about Genaust. Some of the old gents claimed they knew him vaguely. A few remembered seeing Marine Corps photographers covering actions they were involved in, but no one had any specific insights. One old former corporal from Waukegan, IL, said he'd seen Genaust shooting motion picture footage around Hill 362-A and heard from a buddy that the photographer had been killed poking around one of the caves in that area. Nothing more useful surfaced after almost a full morning of questions.

The Japanese factions backing his search for General Kuribayashi seemed satisfied to wait for another day. Patience was part of their cultural make-up, he supposed, and what was another year after more than half a century of unanswered questions. On the other hand, Shake wasn't anxious to make the call to the States in which he'd have to tell Ken Moore that the Iwo search for Genaust was a bust and he'd have to raise more money if he wanted to continue next year. He headed for the landing beaches carrying a Mason jar he planned to fill with Iwo's infamous black sand. When he got home, he'd decant some of it into the glass cigar holders he'd been saving and give it away to Marine buddies who'd never had the chance to visit the hallowed ground of Iwo Jima. It wasn't much but it was all he'd be bringing back from this trip.

As he was digging on the beach just above the high water mark, Shake was startled by the squeak and scrape of a landing craft beaching just below his position. He looked up to see a Navy LCM-8 lowering its bow ramp with its engines burbling and snorting as the coxswain struggled to keep his landing craft from broaching in the rolling surf. He thought it must be a load of sailors from the Amphibious Ready Group wanting to set foot on Iwo, but when the bow ramp finally smacked down on the sand Shake saw the vessel carried a lone passenger. A Navy officer in wash-khakis stepped off the ramp and stood looking up and down the beach. When he caught sight of Shake, the officer waved.

Shake stood and squinted as the man approached. There was nothing familiar about the handsome, clean-shaven black face. He was a full lieutenant and wore the aiguillette of an admiral's aide, so he was obviously from the flagship offshore. Shake was positive he didn't know the guy but it became quickly apparent the aide recognized Shake Davis.

"You'd be Gunner Davis, U.S. Marine Corps, Retired." The aide stuck out a right hand weighted down by a U.S. Naval Academy class ring. Shake shook the hand still trying to figure out how this young hard-charger knew him. He'd likely retired while the guy was still a midshipman at The Boat School.

"Guilty as charged, Lieutenant. Do I know you?"

"Lieutenant Jim Hardy, sir. I'm Admiral Ault's aide. He sent me ashore to ask you to join him out on the flagship."

Shake eyed the officer up and down and decided he liked the man's bearing. It wasn't hard to understand why he'd been tapped as a flag aide. And the guy was clearly no backwater dog-robber from the gold surface warfare qualification badge he wore on the left breast of a well-pressed shirt that had obviously seen some time in shipboard laundries. And then he reran the conversation.

"Admiral who? Did you say Ault?"

"Yessir. Rear Admiral Jeffrey Ault is commodore of the ARG." He pointed seaward at the largest of the ships holding position offshore. "His flag is out there on the Makin Island. He said you'd probably be shocked to hear his name."

"Well, that significantly understates the case, Lieutenant. Your admiral and I go back a long way and into some tough times."

"That's what I hear, sir." Hardy laughed, reached into his pocket and produced an old snapshot of Shake and then-Lieutenant Commander Jeff Ault sitting in a Hanoi bar, surrounded by beer bottles and obviously having a great time in the belly of a former enemy's beast. "The admiral said you'd have a hard time believing he was anywhere besides some Stateside brig."

"He's a good man, and I say that from personal experience. You're lucky to be his aide."

"Couldn't agree more, sir. You ready to go?"

"Well, as much as I'd like to spend some time with the admiral and borrow some water for a shower, I'm due to leave on that aircraft back there in a couple of hours."

"Admiral Ault said it was important, sir. In fact, he said something like 'you bring Shake Davis back out here to the ship and don't let him give you any shit about it either,' or words to that effect."

"I really can't afford to miss that airplane, Lieutenant."

"No sweat, sir. One thing about being an admiral...they've got helicopters and ships and all kinds of ways to get a man where he's going. And, just between you and me, Mr. Davis, I think the admiral has some kind of important info for you. He was on a sat-phone link for about twenty minutes this morning and your name was frequently mentioned."

"In that case, I'd better go retrieve my gear before it goes someplace I'm not."

USS Makin Island (LHD-8) - Off the Volcano Islands

The coxswain nestled the Mike-8 deftly up against the platform of an accommodation ladder that had been rigged amidships on the port side of the USS Makin Island, a nearly new Wasp-class amphibious assault ship. The sailor serving as the landing craft bow-hook took a turn of his line around a stanchion to keep the bobbing landing craft snugged up to the massive ship that Shake had been told displaced more than 41,000 tons. Shake stared up at the haze-gray wall of the ship's hull and figured it was at least a half-mile climb to the quarter-deck somewhere up above. The climb was one thing but he was more concerned with the first big step from the gunwale of the rolling landing craft to the accommodation platform. It had been some time since he'd done that dance.

"The bow-hook will give you a hand, Gunner," Lt. Hardy said as he gently shoved him toward a set of steel rungs that would allow Shake to get up on that narrow gunwale and—hopefully—make a dry transfer from landing craft to flagship. "We'll bring your gear up right away."

Trying hard to look like he did this kind of thing every day, Shake climbed up and got a firm grip on the bow-hook's shoulder. The young sailor nodded at the accommodation ladder: "Easy does it, sir. Soon as we get an up-roll, just step on across." A wave lifted the landing craft and Shake watched the platform descend in his field of vision. When he was level with it, he made the jump and grabbed at the rail of the accommodation ladder with both hands. The grinning sailor gave him a thumbs-up and pointed upward toward the flight deck. Shake began to climb on unsteady legs.

As his head and shoulders cleared to the quarterdeck level, Shake heard the shriek of a bosn's pipe and noted that side-boys in pressed blue coveralls had been mustered on either side of the rail. He paused and looked below him at the empty accommodation ladder. If they had prepared this kind of official reception party, there should be at least an admiral preparing to board. The Navy didn't muster side-boys for broke-dick retired Marine Gunners.

But apparently they did. As he continued to climb, Shake heard the clanging of bells and an announcement over the ship's 1-MC public address system. "CHIEF WARRANT OFFICER, UNITED STATES MARINE CORPS, BOARDING." The bosn's pipe trilled again and the side-boys snapped up a salute. Shake faced aft and saluted in the direction of the national ensign. He wasn't sure it was appropriate since he was wearing civilian clothes but the habit was impossible to control in his state of shock over the pomp and ceremony. He spotted the officer of the deck inboard of the saluting party, strode past the side-boys and offered a second salute.

"Permission to come aboard, sir."

Before the OOD could respond, Shake heard a familiar growl from the shadows of a nearby ladder leading topside. "Let that old warhorse come aboard, Lieutenant. He's got more salt in his seabag than most of our sailors have in their skivvies." While he was still holding his salute, Shake Davis found himself wrapped in a bear-hug and face-to-face with Rear Admiral (lower half) Jeff Ault, his old Navy buddy from the hunt for the Laos File which had nearly gotten them both killed a few years earlier.

"Looks like we're gonna be shipmates for a while. You've been shanghaied!"

* * *

"Sorry I can't offer something stronger, Shake." They'd spent a half-hour catching up on life and times earlier but Ault wanted to get his old friend showered and set up with a state-room in officer's country before they discussed anything more serious. When Shake was squared away aboard the Makin Island, Lt. Hardy escorted him to the admiral's sea cabin for coffee and a cigar. "Of course, there might be something alcoholic down in the chief's mess, "Ault grinned at his old friend, "but I wouldn't know about that."

Shake grinned and took a sip of the strong coffee, savoring the familiar taste. "Navy coffee's fine, Jeff, and a damn site better than the stuff I've been brewing for myself on Iwo."

Ault settled into a comfortable chair across from his old friend and offered a cigar and cutter. "How'd that go? You find what you were looking for?"

"No such luck. I tried to get the Japanese to give me an extension but they wanted to keep it all low key. There's a possibility I can come back next year with more gear and more people. Hope it works out that way. I'm not certain about Kuribayashi, but I think I can find Genaust."

Ault sucked on his cigar and blew a plume of smoke toward a ventilator in the ceiling. "Just as well, Shake. I've got a feeling you're gonna be busy with other things for a while."

"Yeah, your aide mentioned my name came up in a phone call this morning. All this got something to do with that?"

"I'm not for sure but I'd bet it does. You remember a guy who called himself Bayer?"

"Bob Bayer, senior spook when we were working on the Laos File deal. He the one that called?"

"Affirmative. He's now the director of the National Counter-Terrorism Center. He didn't want to tell me a lot of details, but he's damn sure anxious to talk to you."

"What's he want with me? I'm not in that game. Never was except by accident anyway."

"These days nothing drives the bus faster than counter-terrorism efforts, Shake. Those guys have very deep pockets and all kinds of weird shit working all over the world. My guess from what Bayer said is that he's got something he wants you to look into for him."

"Jesus. That would be scraping the bottom of the barrel. Haven't they got enough operators in uniform and spooks on payroll?"

"I'm just guessing here, Shake, but maybe he's looking for something with a deeper cover. Maybe there's something he thinks you can investigate for him without raising suspicions. See what I mean? Who's gonna suspect an old retired fart is working an active intel operation?"

Shake grunted and pulled on his cigar. "Maybe...and I wonder how Bayer's gonna react when I tell him to stick that right directly up his ass?"

"You'll have a chance to find out." Ault checked his watch and then glanced at the world time display on the bulkhead of his sea cabin. "You're due to talk to him on the sat-phone in about twenty minutes."

* * *

"I'm fine, Bayer, having a ball here aboard ship with my old buddy Jeff Ault. Congratulations on the new job. And what the hell is this all about anyway?"

"Shake, we need some help with what I think is a very serious situation. I can't tell you a lot about it on the phone but we need to meet."

"Some very weird stuff happened the last time we got together. I'm not sure I want anything to do with you or whatever the hell you're so worried about. Is that clear enough?"

"I wouldn't ask if I didn't think you were the man to help us out on it. I don't want to be overly dramatic here, Shake, but I think you'll understand my concern if we can meet and I can brief you in person."

"Well, I assume you're somewhere inside the Beltway and I'm smack dab in the middle of the Pacific Ocean aboard a Navy ship. It might be a while before we can find a Starbucks and have a chat."

"I'll come to you, Shake. That's how serious I think this situation is. You ever heard of a little island out there called Wake?"

Shake Davis nearly strangled the handset. It all seemed a little too convenient. "I suppose it comes as no surprise to you that my daughter happens to be out on Wake right now doing some scientific research?"

"Truthfully, I didn't know that...but it works in my favor, right? I'll fly out to Wake, brief you on the situation and you can spend some time with your daughter as a bonus. How's that?"

"No promises, Bayer. If I don't like what I hear, you made a long damn trip for nothing."

"If that's the way it is, your call. All I'm asking for is a chance to pitch you an idea that's really important to national security. That's not hyperbole, Shake. I mean every word of it."

"OK." Shake couldn't dispel the feeling that he was about to stumble into a very large basket of shit, but at least he had a choice. And the deal included a chance to spend time with Tracey. "I'll meet you on Wake Island. Wait, how the hell do I get there from here?"

"Admiral Ault's got his orders, Shake. You should be steaming in that direction right now. He'll drop you off. I'll see you on Wake in a couple of days."

Philippine Sea

Abdullah turned from his laptop and saw Col. Ibrahim hesitate before stepping out of the yacht's dark interior. The AS commander glanced up toward the security man leaning on the rail one level above the sun-deck and glared. The sentry stared back for a moment and then turned his attention to the horizon. Abdullah snapped his laptop closed and stood.

"I have been in contact with the leadership and received some guidance in regard to our situation." He'd planned their meeting for the open air of the yacht's weather decks to avoid having to suffer Ibrahim's body odor but the man surprised him by arriving freshly showered and surprisingly clean-shaven. In Abdullah's relatively limited association with Filipino Muslims, he'd found them proud of the scraggly facial hair that passed for beards among their faithful. He decided to count his blessings and not make an issue of it.

"I was not aware you needed further guidance." The man's hands were shaky and he seemed slightly unsteady on his feet as he rolled one of his rancid cigarettes. Abdullah put it down to shaky sea legs. "It seems straightforward to me. I am in command and will make all decisions relating to the mission when it is time to strike." Col. Ibrahim waved his hand at the QF security guard on the deck above them. "I should also remind you that I will oversee security once we reach our destination. Do you have questions about that?"

"The security team will need no supervision," Abdullah said. "They are veteran fighters and quite capable. I've worked with them before on missions like this one."

"There has never been a mission like this one! And these men are Iranians. Do you think I don't know that? They are used to open deserts, tanks and conventional forces. We will be working on islands surrounded by water. We will eventually strike from the sea. What do they know about that?"

"You underestimate their capabilities, Col. Ibrahim." Abdullah forced himself to remember that his orders included pacifying this annoying firebrand and keeping him in check as the mission developed. "They are well-trained special forces soldiers, trained as combat divers and possessing other valuable skills. Their assignment to us is a mark of the high-priority the leadership places on our mission."

Col. Ibrahim busied himself with rolling another cigarette and then turned his back to guard his match from the breeze blowing over the after-decks. Abdullah waited patiently and then continued. "Your advice on security matters will be most welcome. But there is much work to be done before we begin the strike phase of the mission. The scientists must be free to do their work without interference. And there is the unavoidable contact with the Palauan government. I will handle that. The less you are seen at those times the better it will be."

Ibrahim spun to face him, stepped in close and jabbed a finger into his chest. "You do what is required in support of the mission, but never without my knowledge. And let there be no misunderstandings. I will not tolerate any changes in the plan."

"Why would there be changes?" Abdullah returned the man's glare still attempting to get a sense of this strange individual. "Assuming the scientists succeed, we introduce the weapon into North American waters..."

"No!" Ibrahim cut him off and gave his chest another painful jab. Abdullah took a step back wondering if the man might attack him physically. "We *test* the weapon first, specifically in Philippine waters off Luzon. The first use must be in the Philippines. It was agreed!"

In truth, the business of a test strike on Luzon had been discussed during his briefing in Dubai but he was unaware of any agreement in place. That would have to be clarified. The mentors had suggested it might be a prudent test of the weapon, but there had been no guarantees made as far as Abdullah knew. And Abdullah left Dubai firmly believing the mission's main objective was always to use the weapon against the

Americans. He had very detailed instructions about carrying out that strike when the time was right.

"Of course, should a test strike be necessary, we will conduct it against Luzon. The science team will know what's required when they have finished their work."

Ibrahim smiled and flicked his cigarette butt over the side. "Luzon...Manila...and then you may do what you wish with *my* weapon." And then he turned abruptly and scrambled down a ladder, heading for the hatch that led to the interior of the yacht.

Abdullah found a seat and fired up his laptop. He tapped a few keys, opened an encrypted file and found the necessary address indicator group for his handler in Tehran. The message he sent was a simple query: **"Should it become necessary for effective accomplishment of the mission, do I have authority to eliminate Pineapple?"**

The answer came after only fifteen minutes. He'd expected a quick response since his site was monitored around the clock. What he did not expect was the response he got: **"Under no circumstances. Pineapple must survive. See to it."**

* * *

Three hours after his confrontation with Col. Ibrahim, Abdullah stood once again on the after-deck watching a blood-red sun sink into the Philippine Sea. He was trying to make sense out of the disjointed bits of information he'd managed to glean from his queries over a satellite phone and an encrypted email program. In all the years of covert work he'd done for the Quds Force, he had never hit such an intelligence black hole. Incredibly, it seemed the leadership and the Saudi bankers were willing to spend huge sums and take even bigger risks on a man they didn't know much about. Either that or his mentors were unwilling to tell him what they knew. That was beyond dangerous; it was potentially lethal.

When Abdullah made that very point to his controller in Tehran, he got a firm reminder that he was there in charge of the mission to insure things went smoothly. That effectively muted Abdullah's urge to simply toss the man overboard and be done with the irritation. His follow-on query about the test strike in the Philippines drew an equally vague response. More guidance would be provided when the weapon was ready to use.

A few more useful items came from his contact with a trusted Jemaah Islamiya intelligence operative he'd worked with in Jakarta. The man had told him that Ibrahim was a former officer in the Philippine Marine Corps and had been in on anti-government military mutinies in 2003 and 2006. That explained the military rank the man seemed so proud of, but it also posed more questions that Abdullah was still laboring to answer. Were Muslims allowed to serve in the Philippine Armed Forces and become senior officers? At this point Abdullah was certain only that Col. Ibrahim was not exactly what he claimed to be.

There was the sudden clean shave and the faint odor of alcohol on his breath. And there was the sense in his gut that Col. Ibrahim was somehow a dangerous poser. He'd find out one way or another, sooner or later. In the meantime, Abdullah would continue his research and accept the risk of further communications with various sources. He was too experienced and much too cautious to tolerate unknown elements in a field operation. Caution kept him alive and he wished to remain that way. Martyrs were to be revered but the fact remained that they only fought one battle and never knew victory beyond that.

Jeddah, Kingdom of Saudi Arabia

"What news of our business in the Pacific?"

Prince al-Azizi swept his arm toward the pillow-strewn conversation nook in the corner of his office suite. His visitor, just off an executive jet flight from Riyadh, shook his head, pointed at his ear and strode toward the towering glass doors that led out onto a massive marble patio. Even in a royal residence, surrounded by security and swept regularly for clandestine audio or video monitors, it didn't pay to take chances.

Fresh tea and pastries were in place as they always were any time day or night on the prince's broad patio overlooking the busy inshore waters of the Red Sea. His visitor nodded toward a glass-topped table shaded by a fringed velvet sun umbrella and waited until his sponsor was seated comfortably. The prince waved off a pair of hovering servants and reached for the urn to pour glasses of his favorite green tea. He nodded at a chair opposite his position and slid the first glass toward his visitor.

As he folded himself into the lounge chair, the visitor removed a metallic device about the size of a paperback novel from his briefcase, placed it on a marble banister and flicked a switch. The low-frequency white noise generated by the device plus the ambient background clutter would foil any attempt to monitor their conversation with long-range directional microphones. As a senior operative of Re'asat Al Istikhbarat Al A'amah, The Kingdom's General Intelligence Presidency, he understood that in the ongoing battle for influence and advantage waged by competing factions in the convoluted corridors of the House of Saud, only the cautious survived.

"As ordered, work on the project is being relocated. All assets have been removed from the Philippines. The Iranian team leader, the security force and the Indonesians are aboard the yacht. They are a few days away from the Palau Islands and we will be contacted when they are working again. I foresee no immediate problems."

"And the longer range problems, my friend? You have more experience with the Persians than I do. Have we made a deal with the devil?"

"The enemy of my enemy is my friend." The visitor shrugged and sipped tea. "The Iranians have the motivation and the expertise—especially the Quds Force operatives—but they lack the leadership, the organizational skills in the long run. When the panic spreads and the Muslim world looks for salvation, they will not turn to Tehran."

"We must keep our hands clean in this." The prince made a vague gesture toward the west.

"There will be no connection with you or the House of Saud, no matter what happens elsewhere in the world."

The prince rose, walked to a sideboard and returned with a copy of the International Herald Tribune. "What of this?" He tossed the paper down in front of his visitor and stabbed at an article with his finger. The visitor glanced at the newspaper briefly. He'd seen the story earlier and had been following the reporting on Internet sources.

"The Iranian indicates it was a matter of unintentional and unexpected contamination. The scientists say it was limited to a small area but spread by the current flow. It continues to attract attention within the scientific community but I'm assured it will all seem like a natural occurrence—the will of Allah, blessed be his name—when they have finished poking around in the Philippines."

"And what will they find when they poke around in the Philippines?" The prince plucked a candied date from a bowl and chewed delicately as he watched a small fleet of fishing boats retrieving nets offshore, the scales of their catch glittering like gems in the brilliant sunlight. He marveled that such innocent creatures could play such a big role in God's plan for the faithful.

"If you are referring to the scientists and the environmentalists, they will find yet another unexplained contamination of a fish population. That is the reason the scientists chose the botulism toxin. Contamination happens all the time in nature. They will suspect nothing more and busy themselves arguing about what manmade ecological disaster caused it."

The prince waved his hand airily. He'd heard all these arguments and justifications when the Saudi Secret Service man and his Quds Force counterpart had brought the original proposal to his attention. "The key, my friend, is the scientific work. If the Indonesians succeed in creating a mutation of this toxin, we have a truly effective weapon to use against the Americans and their infidel allies. That is the goal."

The visitor lit one of the gold-tipped filter cigarettes from his mentor's silver tobacco box and turned to watch the offshore fishing fleet. "You understand, of course, that some, perhaps many, of the faithful might also be killed when a contagious toxin is introduced into a food source?"

"*Insh'allah.*" The Saudi prince slouched in his chair and folded his hands across his stomach. "There are always friendly casualties in any fight worth having. I am weary to death of these constant, uncoordinated struggles for survival of the faith. Iraq, Afghanistan, Taliban, Al Qaeda sniping at the enemy, a bomb here, another bomb there, martyrs on airplanes. It is time for a strike that will suck the breath out of our enemies, my friend. If some of the faithful must die in this final battle to force the infidels to pull in their claws, then so be it. *Insh'allah.*"

There was silence on the patio for some time while the visitor smoked and the prince studied the fishermen in the Red Sea. Both men pondered the enormity of the thing they had set in motion. If it worked as planned, the nature of the world they knew would change once and for all. The faithful of God's earth would rapidly ascend through true parity to ultimate power. But there were so many unknowns, so many variables.

"Abdullah informs me that our Pineapple is insisting on a test strike in the Philippines, assuming the scientists succeed in their work. It will add significantly to the cost and to the mission profile. Are you still in favor?"

"The cost is one thing, the profile is another." The prince leaned forward and snatched a cigarette from his silver salver. The GIP man lit it for him and waited for the rest of the thought.

"You have managed to cover our expenditures well so far. The Muslim charities and relief organizations we set up are excellent funnels. The money is not a problem. Consider the situation if our Pineapple is allowed to introduce a contagious toxin among his sworn enemies in the Philippines. On the one hand, we get a very good look at the result of such a strike and a gauge of the reaction to it. It would all be very valuable information for use in the strike on the ultimate target. On the other hand, we must not underestimate the intelligence of the infidel doctors and scientists. They might conclude that the Philippines had been the subject of a biological attack and be on guard."

The GIP man smiled, squashed his smoke in an ornate silver ashtray and lit another. The beauty of an operation like this was in the twists and turns, the subterfuge and diversions. "And that is why we have our Judas goat, our disgruntled Colonel Ibrahim, veteran of the Philippine insurrections, avowed enemy of the Manila government. They may not know *how* he did it, but we will ensure that they know he did it. The presumption would be that his objective was achieved in the Philippines and there is no danger to the rest of the world."

The prince chuckled remembering the report he'd gotten when the impostor had been secreted off Mindinao and into Jakarta for a meeting with the GIP and Quds Force representatives. "To give the little apostate credit, he knew how to play his cards. The Abu Sayyaf cover got him to Jemaah Islamiya, then to the scientists, and then to us, the only ones with enough money to fund his scheme. We should convert him to the true faith."

"Perhaps." The GIP operative was clearly enjoying an ultimate irony. "If we approve the test strike on Luzon, it will be revealed that the mastermind behind the attack is not a Muslim at all. The guilty party is a Christian, a Catholic, I believe, born Ignacio Felodon, and posing as Abu Sayyaf to cast guilt on innocent Muslims in the Philippines. He will, of course be a casualty of the attack, so the Pineapple will provide no further information regarding the weapon or his funding."

"Perfect!" The prince chuckled and glanced at his Blackberry. He had another meeting scheduled with the medical doctor who would begin manufacturing an antidote as soon as the biological attack team delivered specific requirements. "A Christian posing as a Muslim in an attempt to blame the faithful? Our indignation will be loud and righteous."

Bolling Air Force Base, Washington, D.C.

When the land-line on her desk buzzed for attention, Chan Dwyer glanced up from the stack of field reports she'd been scouring and studied the caller ID. She didn't recognize the number but an icon on the screen indicated it was from a government phone so she reached for the handset.

"D-One Four Oh Four," she said giving her department and desk number as required by Defense Intelligence Agency protocol for calls from outside lines. "This is an unsecured line. Can I help you?" In the background she heard the DIA's central system click in to record the call.

"Hey, Chan, it's George Wilson over at NSA. How you doin'?"

"Pretty good, George, I'm kind of liking the new assignment." She'd met the mid-level National Security Agency employee at an intel community mixer in Georgetown shortly after she'd left the Army and gone to work for DIA. Some flak from the Department of Homeland Security had decided the way to improve interdepartmental communication was to invite the worker bees to regular cocktail parties. Wilson was a recently divorced linguist and cryptanalyst who'd been hitting on her regularly ever since. "China desk was getting a little crowded. What's up?"

"Well, for one thing, I'm still wondering when you're gonna let me take you to that new Thai place over in Arlington."

"It's an unsecured line, George. And just because I'm half Thai doesn't mean I like Thai food."

"OK, I won't take up much of your time here. I ran across some stuff that I thought you might want to see. Involves the Philippines and I remembered that was your new gig. Want to take a look?"

"Depends on what it is. If you've got something that's more than back-channel chatter, yeah, I'd like to see it."

"I'm not really sure what it is, Chan. Our filters picked it up. Normally, this stuff is close-hold in-house. You know the drill. But I remembered you said you were looking at some HVTs and an up-tick in AS activity in the area and...what the hell? They've been screaming about sharing info. Should I send it over?"

"Sure. Standard encryption and send it to the D-1404 address I gave you. Mark it for my attention."

"I'm about to hit send right now. And if you don't like Thai, I know a great little steakhouse over on 19th and K."

"Give it some air, George. I'm still getting oriented. New game, new players. You know how it goes."

"Yeah, yeah, but I don't give up easily. If you make any sense out of the stuff, just return the favor. Share and share alike, OK?"

"I'll do it, George, and thanks for thinking of me."

Chan re-cradled the phone and checked her encrypted server. Nothing new, so she turned back to the reports she'd been reading. From her own military experience she knew the Army Special Forces NCO who scatter-shot the field report to a long list of addressees in the intelligence community was probably in for an ass-chewing for jumping command channels but she was grateful for the information. If she could put something valuable together about the HVT her department was focused on, she'd have to be sure the Army knew that SFC Labella, serving somewhere in the southern Philippines, contributed valuable information.

She re-read the narrative covering Col. Ibrahim's departure from Jolo and wondered where he might have gone. And aboard a Zodiac with a couple of guys the report speculated were Indonesian bomb designers? What was that all about? And, more importantly to the supervisors who assigned her to the Abu Sayyaf watch desk, who the hell was this guy? Ibrahim was obviously a nom de guerre. In an adjacent pile of paper were query responses from the Intelligence Directorate of the Philippine Armed Forces. She'd been through them all dozens of times and got nothing more valuable than a grainy surveillance photo and some insider speculation. The picture resembled others she'd seen of scraggly, paramilitary AS fighters in the bush. Nothing jumped out as a key to positive ID but the guys in the field swore it was him and she trusted their judgment. The most insightful thing the Filipinos had contributed was that Ibrahim was "presumed to have some military tactical and technical expertise." That was like saying the man was a dangerous asshole: True, but not very helpful.

Chan called up a message screen and typed in the address of the J-2 section of the Joint Special Operations Team—Philippines. She was tempted to suggest that the SF shooters in the field just find the little shit and whack him. That might be enormously gratifying but it wasn't the smart move just now. If they could find Ibrahim and follow around long enough, they might be able to help the Philippine military fix and eliminate most of the major AS cells in the Sulu Archipelago. She took a frustrated breath and began to hammer at the keyboard of her government-issue Panasonic Toughbook computer: "Expend all effort to re-locate HVT and reinstate continued surveillance. We are analyzing field reports and SIGINT in attempt to provide you with actionable information."

She stabbed at the send key and noticed a flashing icon was awaiting her attention, indicating the items from George Wilson had arrived. Calling it up on her screen, she began to scroll through the material. The first few pages were mostly snippets of phone conversations between a sat-phone transceiver and...she scanned the attached analysis...a cellular phone...number not in data banks...that involved Arabic language trigger words including "mission/attack/scientist" and a list of other terms that NSA computers had been programmed to detect.

Party One on the sat-phone was apparently asking for instructions or clarifications concerning some mission involving science or scientists. Most of the responses from Party Two were either absent or indecipherable. One-sided as it was, it was enough to trip the NSA program triggers but there didn't seem to be much more, other than an interesting reference to something or someone called "Pineapple." She made a note to have the NSA SIGIINT guys add the word to their trigger list if they hadn't already done that.

The translated decryption of the email traffic Wilson sent was even sketchier. Party One, presumed due to co-location of sending sources to be the same person who made the sat-phone calls, was seeking background information about "Pineapple" again. Unfortunately, most of the response was simply blocks of cyber-gibberish. Whatever program the queried source was using had defeated the NSA's initial decryption screen. She made another note to have Wilson work on that and then kicked back in her desk chair wondering if all this somehow tied into AS and Col. Ibrahim, her department's most-elusive HVT.

Fooling with the mouse to move copy around, she noticed what looked like two sets of map coordinates sent to the monitoring agency by the KY intelligence satellite that made the intercept. And then her intelligence analyst senses alerted. She turned to the desk-top computer that tied her into the DIA mainframe, called up the geographic information page and typed in the first set of coordinates. It took a while, but the screen eventually told her those coordinates were located in the Sulu Sea. Bingo! Chan asked for more information and in a few seconds, the screen lit up with a map of the southern Philippine Islands. An icon was blinking over a spot south of Mindinao about fifty nautical miles offshore.

Chan Dwyer's eyes widened. The sending source had to be a sat-phone and a computer on a ship. Bouncing back and forth between her desktop and laptop machines, she highlighted the pertinent information and saved it to her secure working files. Then she scrambled around in between the two screens and found the field report from the ODA that had been watching Col. Ibrahim. Bingo again! The HVT was reported as departing Jolo aboard a small craft that the SF guys thought might have been sent from a larger vessel at sea. But was Col. Ibrahim "Pineapple?" Or was he the sender asking about someone code-named Pineapple that AS was doing business with in the area? No way of knowing right now, but it was a tantalizing line for further investigation.

Chan struggled to control her excitement as she punched in the second set of coordinates. The mainframe chewed for a little longer on her query but finally told her that the second computer involved in the email exchange was located somewhere in Jakarta, Indonesia. She frowned, chewing on that revelation for some time. If she assumed the seaborne source was their HVT bad guy, what was he doing talking to someone in Jakarta? And what did that mean if anything? Suddenly it seemed like a no-brainer. The Special Forces backgrounder had mentioned Indonesians accompanying Col. Ibrahim. And Indonesia was the home of Jemaah Islamiya. She picked up a pencil and scribbled on a notepad, letting her brain connect the dots.

Ibrahim...Pineapple...AS...Jakarta...JI???

And then she picked up her phone and punched the speed-dial key that connected her with the DIA's section chief for the Southern and Western Pacific.

Wake Island

As Shake Davis leaned out the starboard access door, the big CH-53E Super Stallion helicopter banked and made a low-speed sight-seeing pass over Wake Island. It looked almost exactly the way he remembered the place from years ago except for the cluster of temporary modular structures on the western end of the runway. Those would belong to Tracey's science team. He could see a number of them shading their eyes and staring up at the camouflage-mottled Marine helicopter droning overhead.

There wasn't a lot to see on a mid-Pacific atoll that measured only about six square kilometers in total acreage. Three small islets—Wake, Wilkes and Peale—surrounded a stunning aqua colored lagoon. There were a few old rusted-out WW II Japanese shore defense guns slowly giving way to wind and weather, but Shake focused on a clapboard building just coming into sight as they turned on final to land on Wake's runway. He keyed the microphone switch on his headset.

"See that ramshackle old building?" Shake reached across the fuselage and tapped RAdm. Ault, who was leaning out the opposite door watching as the vaguely horseshoe-shaped atoll passed beneath the aircraft. "The one with all the junk piled up around it? That's Drifters Reef. Best damn bar and grill for a couple of thousand miles, east or west. Beers are on me tonight. You won't believe that place."

Jeff Ault grinned and gave him a thumbs-up. They'd made arrangements prior to lift-off from the USS Makin Island to spend the night in transient quarters on the island. The civilian caretakers who maintained Wake's limited facilities were puzzled but pleased to have company. Lt. Hardy had a briefcase full of cell phones and computer gear that would allow his boss to stay in touch with the ARG as it steamed beyond the horizon so they could afford an extended historical tour while Shake took care of business. Before taking off from the Makin

Island, the CH-53's crew had been less than enthused about the prospect of an extended stay on Wake until Shake had reminded them about the lore of the little atoll and its significant role in WW II Marine Corps history. At that point the five Marine airmen fired up their laptops and began researching Wake Island's defenders with an understandable emphasis on fellow fliers of Marine Fighter Squadron-211 who had bravely but futilely dueled marauding Japanese in the skies over Wake back in December 1941.

As the helicopter reared and settled into ground effect for a landing, Shake spotted his daughter standing by the old island FAA terminal and waving wildly. He waved back but Tracey had already turned to shield herself from the big bird's rotor-wash. There were no other aircraft visible around the terminal or the transient hangar and Shake reasoned Bayer had yet to arrive on Wake. Hopefully, that would give them all time for a walk around before he had to deal with whatever the spook was selling on this trip.

When the crew chief lowered the access stairs, Shake shouldered his rucksack and charged out into the tropical heat and glare. Tracey was headed in his direction with her arms extended for a hug. She looked terrific, tanned and healthy in shorts and a cut-off sweatshirt that said FISH NAVY on the front. A couple of what he presumed were research teammates smiled and waved in the shade of the terminal building as Tracey bounded into his arms. He gave her an extended hug and then pushed back to study the lovely woman his daughter had become. She was a stunner and as smart as she was beautiful.

"Oh my God, Daddy! Can you believe this? You look great! How long can you stay?"

Shake draped an arm over her shoulders and steered his daughter toward the terminal as the helicopter's crew began shutting it down. "Couple of days, I guess. Depends on a guy I'm meeting out here. We'll see once he arrives."

Tracey introduced her father to Janis Fielding and Woodrow Cheeley who welcomed him to Wake and had kind words to say about his daughter's value to their research efforts. They were joined in the terminal building by Adm. Ault and his aide who were caught between gawking at a wall full of squadron and unit stickers from outfits that had transited the island over the years and admiring Tracey Davis. When Shake introduced her to the admiral, he was proud to see Tracey go serious and snap into a modified position of attention before shaking Ault's hand. She might be running with a loose crowd of scientists and relatively unsupervised on a lonely little island, but she was still a Navy officer.

"Good Lord, Shake! How did this happen?" Ault poked him in the ribs while Tracey was meeting Lt. Jim Hardy. "Something that gorgeous can't be carrying any of your genes. There must have been some kind of mix-up at the hospital."

"Bred in base housing and born at the U.S. Naval Hospital Camp Pendleton, pal. If there was some kind of mistake, your Navy medical weenies made it. I'm really proud of her...really, really proud." Shake was getting choked up and full to bursting with the impression his daughter was making on everyone she met. "Why don't you and Jim Hardy get the aircrew squared away while I check on Bayer's flight? We'll grab something to eat and then I'll give you a little tour of wonderful Wake Island."

* * *

According to the air terminal advisory system, they had at least three hours, maybe more, before a U.S. government Gulfstream 5 tail number Tango Sierra Niner Seven Zero, out of Washington, D.C., was due to land on Wake. That meant time for chow and a quick tour so everyone headed for the island's dining facility. Over a simple and surprisingly delicious meal, Shake and Tracey did some catching up and he explained what little he knew about why he wound up on Wake for a scheduled meeting with the director of the National Counter Terrorism Center. Tracey reminded her dad of how close he'd come to getting killed when he'd undertaken a mission for Bayer in

Vietnam. Shake shrugged it off and promised that if he didn't like what he heard, he'd tell the spook unceremoniously to go piss up a picket-rope. They were all looking forward to a big night at the legendary Drifters Reef, Wake's only watering hole, and Shake was determined not to let anything Bayer might pitch put a damper the party.

They started on Peale Islet and examined the remains of a Japanese shore battery emplacement. It featured a rusting five-inch naval gun that bore Royal Navy markings. Shake told them it had likely been captured and brought to the island by the Japanese after the fall of Singapore. Then they moved on to the main islet of Wake, where they poked around the command bunker that had been occupied by Marine Major James P.S. Devereux and Navy Commander Winfield S. Cunningham who lead a relative handful of Marines, sailors and civilian construction workers in holding out for two weeks against the Japanese invaders. The inevitable surrender had been ordered from here after 109 men died in the fighting to defend the outpost. About 1,600 surviving defenders went into the bag as POWs, but the Japanese attacking force took a seriously bloodied nose in the fighting. They lost a thousand men, two destroyers, one submarine and 21 aircraft. It didn't seem like much in the early scheme of things, but Wake's Marine defenders sank the first two Japanese warships lost in World War II.

The visitors broke out digital cameras and snapped pictures of each other standing next to the tall memorial to the island defenders that constituted one of two major attractions for Wake's few visitors. Atop a granite spire was a weather-beaten eagle, globe and anchor to commemorate the sacrifice of Devereux's 1st Defense Battalion and the men of VMF-211—known thereafter and to this day as The Wake Island Avengers—including Major Henry Elrod who became the first Marine aviator to be receive the Medal of Honor during World War II. As they reached the second attraction on Wilkes islet near the edge of the lagoon, a battered VW bus caught up with them and an airfield messenger informed Shake that the expected aircraft was inbound and estimating less than an hour to touchdown on Wake.

Shake checked his watch for a time-hack and then pointed at what had become known as "98 Rock" or sometimes "POW Rock." On his first extended stay on Wake, Shake spent quite a bit of time sitting near that landmark and contemplating the determination of one American to insure someone in the distant future beyond his own inevitable death would know the fate of his comrades on Wake.

"Don't know who carved this," he said as he ran his fingers over the inscription and recalled the tragic history of the Americans who were held on the island by the Japanese conquerors as slave laborers, "but I've always remembered the story. Two years after they invaded Wake and carted most of the survivors off to mainland prison camps, the Jap commander out here realized he was in the backwater of a losing fight. So he ordered that the 98 American civilians still on the island be executed. One of them escaped but knowing there was no way to get off the island, he found a coral rock and carved this epitaph for his buddies." It read simply and starkly: 98 US PW 5-10-43. "Whoever the guy was, he had balls the size of watermelons. They caught him and cut his head off. He had to know it was inevitable but he wanted to leave some kind of record, and here it is."

While the tourists snapped more photos, Jeff Ault tugged at Shake's elbow and pointed at the horizon. A Gulfstream 5 was barreling in toward Wake on final approach.

* * *

Bob Bayer looked pretty much the same as Shake remembered him from their initial meeting in Quantico where the hunt for the infamous Laos File had begun. A little less hair; a little more spread around his middle, but there was no mistaking the carriage and cold, clear gaze. The guy regularly traveled the corridors of power and knew his way around them. All that was no surprise as his visitor climbed down from the executive jet and headed toward Shake with a smile and an extended hand. The shocker was the guy who bounded down the steps in Bayer's wake.

The last time he'd seen Lieutenant Colonel Mike Stokey was in a post-operation debriefing in Hanoi. It was during that event that Mike pulled Shake aside and explained that his involvement with the MIA search in Southeast Asia was only a cover. At the time he was what intel veterans called "sheep-dipped" or drafted from the active duty ranks to work under cover for the Central Intelligence Agency. Given the company the stocky red-head was keeping on this trip, Shake was fairly sure his old friend was still hip-deep in the game.

Shake shook hands all around, showing much more enthusiasm for Stokey than for Bayer and then led them to a borrowed conference room where he'd asked the island caretakers to set up coffee and sandwiches. During the half-hour they took to eat and relax, Shake found out that Bayer had been tapped to head the nation's central clearing house for counter-terrorism information with a specific mandate: Knock down the partisan barriers to information sharing that hindered efforts to stay at least one step ahead of the multiple bad guys seeking to do the nation harm. It was a tough nut, Bayer told him, because America's plethora of spook outfits had been keeping secrets for so long that it had become more of a lifestyle than just a method of operation. Secrets were secrets and meant to be kept no matter who was seeking access—foe or friend. It was a difficult, dangerous and delicate balance keeping the various good guys in the loop and the various bad guys out of it.

Stokey revealed that he'd gotten his promotion to full colonel and spent a relatively placid few years in the Pentagon before finally retiring and going to work for the CIA full time. He was still unmarried—or "available for guilt-free liaisons" as he described it—which Stokey saw as a good deal since his duties as an at-large field operative kept him on the move around the world pretty much full time.

"Which brings us..." Stokey concluded and began digging around in an old leather briefcase on the floor next to his chair. "...to this little meeting here on Wake Island."

"Yeah," Shake learned forward in his chair and grinned at his visitors. "I can't help feeling like MacArthur when Truman ordered him to Wake for a come-to-Jesus meeting back during the Korea thing. As I recall, El Supremo got his ass handed to him."

"Different times and different problems, Shake." Bayer snapped open a file, scanned some information contained in it and then looked up over the rims of his reading glasses. "Here's the deal...and what we say here, stays here." Shake glanced over at Stokey who was still shuffling papers. He nodded assent and motioned for Bayer to get on with it.

"We have what we consider solid information that some bad guys we've been watching for some time now are cooking up a major attack. That's nothing new these days and normally wouldn't cause us to do much more than re-tune the radar. But this is a different matter. We're seeing some evidence that it's going to be either a chemical or biological event."

After a few long moments while Bayer and Stokey just stared at him silently from across the table, Shake's mental circuits began to click. It didn't take him much longer to complete the connections. "I should've known you wouldn't pack up and fly all the way out here just to draft me into some spook scheme." He shook his head and pointed a finger at Bayer: "You could have done that after I got back Stateside. Whatever the hell you're talking about has got something to do with the stuff Tracey and her pals are researching here on Wake, doesn't it?"

Bayer shrugged as if to say Shake should have known that. "Yeah, but before you get your knickers in a knot, let me assure you I had no idea your daughter was part of the research team and neither she nor any of the others is privy to details. We monitor the information they send but it's a one-way street; strictly a need-to-know deal. Obviously, the scientists know we're interested, but they don't know why beyond a general security concern. It's going to stay that way, and that means you can't tell her anything about all this."

"That won't be hard." Shake shrugged and reached for his coffee cup. "So far all I know is that you guys think there are people—most likely some flavor of Muslim wing-nuts—fooling around with chemical or bio weapons. Read a few radical blogs and you know that much."

"Fortunately, we know a little more than that. At least we think we do. That's where you may be able to help." Stokey pulled a pile of photos out of a folder, found the one he wanted and shoved it across the table. "Recognize this guy?"

Shake studied the grainy enlargement: Mean-looking little bastard, wiry and underfed, wearing a bandana on his head with a floppy bush-hat crammed over it. The man was definitely Filipino but fairly nondescript. High cheekbones and a relative flat nose but those were common ethnic features. The man had a thin mouth with virtually no visible lip-line that made the hand-rolled cigarette he was smoking look as if it had been jabbed into his jaws. And the jaws were covered with patches of scraggly facial hair. *Most likely a Moro guerilla fighter*, Shake thought, looking at the ratty GI surplus webbing the man was wearing. There was something vaguely familiar about him but that was no surprise. Over the years he'd served in the Philippines, Shake had seen a hundred men who looked like the one in the photo.

"Can't say I know the gent..." Shake tapped the photo and then reached for his coffee cup. "My guess is he's probably MNLF from the gear and beard."

"AS, actually, and he calls himself Colonel Ibrahim, commander of Abu Sayyaf forces in the southern Philippines." Bayer nodded and began to shuffle through the pile of photos on the table. "Same game but much more serious players. They've got solid hook-ups with Jemaah Islamiyah in Indonesia and Al Qaeda worldwide. Now see if you recognize this guy."

Bayer placed a much clearer photo on the table next to the first one. It didn't take Shake more than a few seconds to recognize the man in the official military portrait. He scrutinized the Philippine Marine Corps uniform and the rank insignia to be sure, but he knew this guy. Could the man in the uniform of one of his country's most elite military formations be the same man in the guerilla-fighter gear? Didn't seem likely despite what he was obviously supposed to think.

"Well, this guy I know." Shake tapped the official photo. "He's a light colonel in the photo, but he was a lieutenant when I knew him in the Subic Bay area. Felodon's the family name. Can't remember his first name, but he was one of the Philippine Marine officers assigned to my mobile training team. Pretty good one as I recall." Shake looked at the men across the table and saw them exchange a look. "You two trying to tell me Felodon and this other guy are the same man? That dog won't hunt."

"Why not?" Stokey rose, retrieved the aluminum coffee pot from a sideboard and poured into their empty cups.

"Well, shit, Mike, that ought to be obvious." Shake reexamined the side-by-side photos and shook his head. "For one thing, outfits like the Moro National Liberation Front and Abu Sayyaf and the like...they're all devout Muslims, right? And I'm fairly damn sure from watching him go to mass most Sundays that Felodon is a Catholic. Seems to me a bunch of Muslim separatists aren't going to enlist some infidel who used to be a Marine officer fighting against them and just hand him an AK. It doesn't work that way in my experience."

"He could have converted." Bayer shrugged and stirred sugar into his coffee. "Weirder things have happened."

"Maybe..." Shake reexamined the photos. "But I don't see it. When I knew him, this guy was a rock-solid true believer; capital T and capital B. You don't just shit-can all that and suddenly become a devout Muslim, Cat Stevens and a few others being the exceptions that prove the rule."

"And again, why not?" Stokey plucked a folder from his briefcase and waved it in the air. "This is his personnel file. It turns out Colonel Ignacio Felodon of the Philippine Marines was hardly your upstanding, loyal officer late in his career. He was a big player in the so-called Oakwood Mutiny against the

Arroyo government in 2003. He got locked up on that deal and then they cut him loose when he promised to behave. Three years after that, he's a ringleader in the Manila Peninsula anti-government riots in downtown Makati."

"OK, I copy your point, Mike." Shake help up a hand to cut off the recitation. "Let's say for the sake of argument that this guy in the bush configuration is Felodon. And let's say he's either converted to Islam or bullshitted his way into the Abu Sayyaf somehow. You think he's now got something to do with this chemical or bio deal?"

"There it is, Shake." Bayer slouched in his chair and scratched at his chin. "We're working with bread-crumbs admittedly; mostly NSA intercepts, Intel reports and SWAG, but we think he's a prime mover in whatever is going on in the Pacific."

Shake nodded and grinned, remembering just how much of the military intelligence information that impelled him through one crisis after another in his active duty time was nothing more than SWAG—Simply Wild Ass Guesswork. "OK, so all this involves me how?"

"We need to know a bunch more about Felodon, Shake. You served with him; knew him fairly well and you're still pretty well connected in the Philippines..."

"Wait a minute, you guys. What makes you say that? That whole mobile training team thing with Felodon and all that was a long time ago."

"We keep tabs on our pals too, Shake." Stokey help up another folder and grinned. "It says right here that you were back in Manila eighteen months ago to receive..." Stokey scanned the file and then looked up to see Shake staring daggers at him from across the table. "...the Ancient Order of Sikatuna...awarded for distinguished service in the field of foreign relations."

"That had to do with something that happened a long time ago." Shake felt himself getting sucked into a wormhole. "They just took a while getting around to giving it to me."

"Endorsements on the award are from some serious players, Shake...Secretary of National Defense, Chief of Staff of the Armed Forces and, let's see...one, two, three, four general officers. I'd say you're still pretty well thought of in the PI."

Shake leaned his elbows on the table and scrubbed at his eyes. "So you want me to go to the Philippines and look around for Felodon. And then what?"

"We'll be working on what he's up to, Shake." Bayer was poking a little plastic stylus at his PDA. "What we want you to do is get us some background on Felodon. Talk to some sources and ask some questions. Confirm for us that Colonel Ibrahim is Ignacio Felodon. There's a big hole in our information on him between 2004 and 2005. Where was he and what was he doing during that year? Anything in his background that makes you think he's got the gear or the expertise to be involved in something like a chemical or bio attack. We need answers, Shake, and we need them in a hurry."

Shake pondered for a moment feeling like a largemouth bass contemplating a lure: There's a hook in there even if I can't see it right now. "Drop the other shoe, Bayer. Why the time crunch? What is it you aren't telling me?"

"It looks like maybe whoever is behind this deal, and that's presuming it is what we fear it might be, is onto something really dangerous. We think it might involve botulism and that's about as serious as it gets. If somebody has managed to turn that shit into a weapon, we are in very, very serious trouble around the world, Shake. And that's no exaggeration."

"I don't get it." Shake was still waiting for the hammer to fall. "As far as I know, there's no outbreak of disease or rash of deaths anywhere. Press would be all over that like a cheap suit. Tracey says they're examining dead fish and birds. Are you thinking what's killing the fish and the birds out here is part of the attack?'

"Could be. And if it is what's next? They get something deadly into a worldwide food source like salmon or tuna and people start dying in a hurry. And what about if they manage to make the stuff communicable or contagious...or if they develop a new strain that we can't counter? This thing could be worse than loose nukes, Shake, much worse."

"You've been through the training, Shake." Stokey swept his background material into a briefcase and locked it. "You know what this stuff can do. This is an all hands evolution. We need you."

"I need a couple of days to think about it," Shake responded. "And maybe spend some time with Tracey."

Bayer nodded and extended his hand to shake. "Fair enough. We've got to debrief the science team and see what they've got for us. Then I need to get you certified and funded, but I can do most of that while I'm airborne. I'll launch for Jakarta tonight and drop Mike off so he can get to work and we'll send the plane back for you on Tuesday. That's day after tomorrow. How's that feel?"

"That's as good as it's gonna get, I guess." Shake shook the outstretched hand. "Assuming I say yes, I'll need a bunch of background, everything you've got, everything you even suspect or think you know."

Bayer fumbled in a coat pocket and came out with two small computer thumb-drives. "The one marked Alpha is an encryption/decryption program. You'll need it to read the one marked Bravo. That's the entire intel dump. You've got a computer, right?"

"I've got one...but I'm still not sure where to fix the bayonet on the damn thing."

"Once you've downloaded Alpha, destroy the drive. That leaves you with an encrypted shield on your machine that can't be accessed without your password or the correct prompt from another machine with the same program. It includes an email program. We'll communicate that way while you're in the field." Bayer nodded, picked up his gear and walked out of the room.

Shake looked at Stokey and shook his head. "You guys came out here pretty damn sure of yourselves, didn't you?"

"What was it Dr. Gonzo used to say, Shake? When the going gets tough, the tough get weird? Now get your ass down to the PI, get us some good information and stay out of the whorehouses. I'm gonna be doing the same thing in Jakarta—except I won't have the whorehouse problem."

* * *

Shake Davis sat quietly on the rambling beachfront veranda of the Drifters Reef watching one of the most gorgeous sunsets on earth. Normally when it came to simply appreciating the spectacular confluence of sun and horizon, he was strictly a morning kind of guy. Some of the most beautiful sights he'd ever seen involved a majestic blob of lemon yellow sun rising in stately grandeur to spread arcs of dazzling light over verdant jungle canopies. He'd watched sunrises all over the world and snatches of the 23rd Psalm always came to mind, especially the part about restoreth my soul.

There was a cold bottle of Heineken at his elbow and warm Pacific wavelets lapped at his bare feet as the sun sank into the horizon. The reflection of crimson sunlight on the surface of the Pacific Ocean had awed and comforted seamen for centuries. *Red sky at night, sailor's delight.* He generally detested the over-used and abused word, but it was hard to think of this display as anything but awesome. Shake blinked slowly a time or two using his eyelids like a camera shutter, clicking images into his memory banks.

He'd seen a lot of beautiful things in his very active life—in and out of uniform—but the sunset viewed from Wake Island was a special touchstone that never failed to make him smile. Shake had never been a very religious man but he believed there was something in universes both known and unknown that surpassed the physical. You could argue science all day long but watch a sunset like this one and it was hard not to credit the hand of God in something so beautiful. Conversely, he'd also seen a swivet of really ugly things in a lifetime of running to the sound of guns and it was often difficult to believe a loving God would countenance such brutality. That led him to polish off his beer and head inside the Drifters Reef for a replacement. While he appreciated nature's magnificence Shake Davis was a pragmatist given to grabbing the bull by the tail and facing the situation. His world, molded by God or formed by microbes from the Big Bang, was no place for navel-gazing. You dream in one hand and shit in the other. See which hand fills up first.

He'd left the steak-fry and barbecue staged for their visitors by the Wake Island caretakers early so he could catch the sunset from the veranda. Tracey had promised to break away as soon as she could when Shake whispered he'd like to have a little private time with her before the crowd hit the bar. He checked his watch, expected she'd be along in a few minutes and pointed at a dusty bottle of the coconut-flavored rum she favored. The Filipino, who doubled as bartender when he wasn't maintaining the island's fresh-water catch-basin filtration system, grabbed the bottle and wiped it clean on his shirttail. Shake slipped a twenty across the polished teak bar and told the man to guard it until he gave the nod.

Fresh beer in hand, Shake ambled through the ramshackle interior of the Drifters Reef. Everywhere he looked there were marks of passage from visitors of one ilk or another. Walls, tables, chairs, stools, stanchions and nearly every other kind of flat surface were festooned with unit stickers, decals and patches from all branches of the military, foreign and domestic. There were bills of worldwide denominations, usually signed by the people who left them behind. There were hats of all descriptions—usually bearing a military logo—tacked or stapled all over the bar's sagging ceiling. It was a quasi-tradition in the Drifters Reef that anyone who entered wearing a hat bought the house a round of drinks and sacrificed the offending cover to enshrinement on the ceiling.

He knew the feeling and the philosophy behind the symbols. When you find yourself in a rare and esoteric place, there's an impulse to leave a mark for posterity, knowing you are so far off any beaten track that your mark will likely be there forever, appreciated only by those few who make a similar trek. It was something like a dog finding the fire hydrant at the farthest edge of his world and pissing on it to let the rest of the pack know an intrepid explorer had passed that way.

Shake stepped outside into the last light of the setting sun and walked slowly around the shabby exterior of the building. It was like poking through a vintage military junkyard. For years, visitors to the island and those who had the unenviable fortune to be stationed there when it featured an active Air Force contingent and a fully manned U.S. Coast Guard navigation station, had wandered around picking up wartime detritus and nautical junk that washed up on Wake's shores. Whatever they found was traditionally brought around to the Drifters Reef and unceremoniously dumped on the patch of sand that surrounded it.

Over the years, the stuff had come to form its own structure and it now seemed like the walls themselves were composed of old rusted machineguns, deck plates, lifeboats, antiaircraft mounts, nets, floats, life preservers, rusted rifles and ammo cans. Nothing the Pacific waters or the island sand surrendered was too big or too weird to become a part of the bar's motif. A wave-battered twenty-foot wooden lifeboat someone had found years before Shake made his first visit to Wake was still perched precariously above the entrance to the building where it formed a sort of crude frame for the bamboo splits that spelled out Drifters Reef...just in case someone might mistake the place due to acute inebriation.

He was admiring the rusted remnants of a Japanese Type 92 heavy machinegun when a raucous belch interrupted his musing. He turned to see his daughter striding up the path from the beachside barbecue area. He grinned and waved remembering how they used to play at belching across the dinner table at each other when she was a teenager thus driving her mother to disgusted distraction.

"Sounds like you enjoyed the meal."

"Good Lord, Daddy," she said as she gave him a quick hug and then backed away to clear a path for another stentorian belch. "I haven't eaten that much in years. And they just kept piling it on. The rest of the crew will be a while. The admiral is personally grilling everyone's steaks to order and no one wants to piss him off."

"Well, let's have a little pop." He gave his nearly empty beer bottle a shake. "I'm about ready. And I found a bottle of that girly rum you like."

They took their drinks to a table that gave them a spectacular view of Wake's central lagoon and access to the salt-scented sea breeze that blew in through an open window. Tracey sipped her drink and stared at the warm glow of the bar's yellow light reflected off the gently rolling surface of the water. "It's really beautiful here, isn't it?"

"It's got an ugly history." Shake clinked his beer bottle against his daughter's glass and grinned at her. "But there's no denying it's beautiful at times. Did you catch the sunset?"

"Oh, my God, wasn't that something?" Shake winced knowing what was coming. "It was awesome!"

"So how's the research going? You guys find anything interesting besides dead fish and birds?"

Tracey Davis grinned at her father who was doing his usual bad job of looking casual and disinterested. "You know what we're finding, right? Or what we think we're finding?"

Shake shrugged and slugged at his beer but his daughter was having no part of it. "C'mon, Dad, the math here is fairly easy to do. All our data is being copied to the national security people and suddenly a couple of wheel-horses from the government show up...on Wake Island of all places? Someone in the counter-terrorism business is thinking this is all somehow connected to a plot by person or persons unknown who are fooling around with chemical or biological weapons. I've been to the lectures."

"You're a scientist as well as a naval officer, what do you think?"

"You mean do I think we're seeing something that could be a terrorist attack? Well, it could be, I guess. On the other hand, we're dealing with botulism of one variety or another and lots of that occurs naturally, especially in certain fish populations. It's hard to say at this point but I hope to hell it's just some naturally-occurring phenomenon. *Botulinum* is really nasty, the most lethal stuff on earth if our resident infectious disease expert has got it right."

"You guys are being real careful, right? I trust you, girl, and I'm in no place to second guess the scientists, but that kind of thing scares the bulldog shit right out of me."

"Full hazardous material protocols, Dad. Nobody's convinced this is somehow manmade but nobody's taking any chances with it either. For the most part, we're used to working with the creepy-crawlies that live inside fish and birds, and some of that stuff is enough to gag a maggot."

"You got a mouth on you like a Marine." Shake signaled for refills from the bar and heard the first overtures of a noisy mob approaching along the beach. "Just promise me you won't take any chances, Tracey. No risky stuff, OK? Promise me?"

"I don't think it's me that needs worrying about." Tracey Davis leaned across the table and stared into her father's eyes. "You're in on this deal somehow, aren't you? Those guys you met with today didn't just drop in to say hello and how are you. What have they got you doing?"

"Nothing right now..." Shake saw the suspicion in his daughter's expression. "And that's the truth. I haven't agreed to anything."

"But you will, Dad. I know you. So just out with it before the party starts and I have to get you drunk enough for field interrogation."

"They want me to snoop around in the Philippines and look up a few people I used to know out there. Just background information on some guys they're interested in, that's all."

"And no cloak-and-dagger, Force Recon, hide-and-slide, snake-eater stuff? That didn't work out so well last time. And you're the only Dad I've got."

Snake glanced out the window when he heard his name shouted. Admiral Jeff Ault was leading a staggering contingent up the beach. It was almost party time at the Drifters Reef.

"I reckon the shit-storm is about to start, Tracey. Let's make a deal here. No more about this tonight. You've got the number of the satellite phone, right? It belongs to the guy I work for but I'll reimburse him for the charges. Let's set a call date and time. I'll fill you in on what I'm doing and you'll know I'm OK, and vice versa. You let me know how you are and keep me clued in about anything you find in your research."

"If you're just checking on some old buddies in the Philippines..." Tracey waved at the approaching mob and held up her drink. "How come you want to know about our research?"

"Tracey, just do your dad a favor, OK? Just keep me posted on what you find."

Playtime was over in the next minute. When the crowd of sailors, Marines and scientists exploded into the Drifters Reef the serious party machine kicked into overdrive. Survivors swear that Dr. Janis Fielding's rendition of the Dance of the Flaming Asshole on the teak bar was the capstone of a memorable night. Others claim that RAdm. Ault's mandatory abandon ship drills requiring all hands to leap from the roof into Wake's lagoon was the highlight. And there are those who swear that Gunner Davis demonstrating the shrapnel effect of an 81mm mortar round by dropping his body on a proper trajectory into a four-foot stack of empty beer cans marked the acme of the evening. No one can say for certain.

Gulfstream TS-970, Westbound over the Pacific

Tracey was right on the money. Shake Davis closed his eyes and relaxed into the plush seat of the aircraft headed from Wake to a scheduled late afternoon landing in Manila. *I am so goddamn predictable.*

Even Bob Bayer, stretched out prone on one of the airplane's bench seats up forward, had known he would accept the mission to the Philippines. Fifteen minutes after Bayer returned to Wake, he found Shake standing by the Marine memorial. Bayer nodded and pointed toward the runway. "C'mon, Shake. Let's go."

No greeting, no questions and no doubt about it. Shake Davis was back in the ballgame—as he was expected to be by everyone but himself. Couple what the intel wonks thought might be happening and what the scientists predicted might occur if it was, and there wasn't much choice. If some dedicated and motivated bad guys staged a serious biological attack somewhere—regardless of the where, when and how—the resulting panic and paranoia would literally freeze nations and disrupt commerce worldwide.

And if said bad guys managed to somehow come up with a bug that was contagious, there might be no way to get that deadly genie back in the bottle before millions died. What if an unseen, unknown bug that couldn't be killed with bullets and bombs started eating into populations around the world? What if the one insidious threat to human survival that really, truly scared the crap out of everyone started killing millions like the Black Plague that devastated Medieval Europe? *Really bad shit* didn't half cover it.

Given what he'd read in the intel dump now stored and tightly encrypted on his laptop, Shake was fairly certain they could ignore the chemical threat. He'd read the research reports, spent some time with the experts on Tracey's team and asked some guarded questions. If there was a threat being planned or in progress, it was biological in nature. And that meant a worst-case scenario if someone was trying to turn kindly old Mother Nature into a raging, disease-ridden hag. He'd searched around the Internet and tried to remember all the creepy, mandatory classes he'd taken on biological warfare. It all came down to the same thing: Turn the bugs loose and everyone's ass is grass just standing tall and waiting for the inevitable lawnmower.

You may direct your biological attack at a specific target but the bugs are equal-opportunity killers always threatening to rampage out of control. There's a reason this kind of nightmare is a favorite haunt of horror storytellers and moviemakers. There's a reason mankind's worst enemy is one he can't see and often can't control; one that indiscriminately invades, then conquers and kills without warning or mercy.

Of course, it could all simply be what the scientists kept reminding everyone was a distinct possibility. Maybe it was just post-9/11 paranoia manifest in spooks shitting peach pits and imagining the worst in anything out of the ordinary. Maybe it was simply part of an inevitable variance in all living things; some zig in the normal zag pattern that results in a brief, lethal threat to humans in one form or another. Maybe all we've got here in global terms is a metaphorical fart in the evolutionary whirlwind. *Maybe that's all it is,* Shake Davis told himself, but there's a whole hell of a lot riding on a bet like that.

So let's give the devil his due. Shake closed his eyes and felt sleep creeping up on the edge of his consciousness. *Let's say the bad-guys are about to stage a bug attack on the good guys. What the hell does that have to do with Ignacio Felodon of the Philippine Marines? And assuming Felodon is now one of the bad guys, what the hell is he doing fooling around with his former Muslim enemies in the southern Philippines? And how does a straight-ahead guerilla fighter like Felodon know diddly-squat about biological warfare? Inquiring minds want to know. And if there's anybody can get some answers, I probably can. Folks in the PI owe me a thing or two.*

Mindoro, Philippines—Then

"Lieutenant, let me tell you something." Marine Gunner Shake Davis popped a lemon-lime Charms candy into his mouth and chased it with a swig from his canteen. "I'm more than a little disappointed. This patrol leader of yours couldn't find his ass with a ten-man working party."

"We didn't get what was promised." Lt. Ignacio Felodon paused in rolling one of the homemade cigarettes he smoked with cull tobacco wrapped in a bit of cornhusk. "We asked for the best men and the unit commanders sent us their problems." Shake's Philippine Marine counterpart on the Mobile Training Team had more to say but the discourse was interrupted by a raging torrent of Tagalog from deep in the bush to the right of their position.

"Sounds like Sergeant Mariano is ripping off another piece of the corporal's ass." Shake pulled a plastic bag out of his pocket and checked his training schedule. The deep reconnaissance team they were trying to form was three events behind for the day. "Maybe it'll do some good. We're way behind the power curve."

"He'll be lucky if the sergeant doesn't cut his balls off." Felodon heaved himself up off the ground and massaged the knots in his thighs. Following a lost patrol up and down steep, jungle-covered hills was tough on everyone's legs but the students needed to learn in a hurry. The constabulary command wanted a deep reconnaissance unit ready for active service in less than two weeks. "Do we still transition to night operations? Or do you want to hold off for another day or two?"

"We better go ahead and get into the night stuff, Ignacio." Shake re-checked his sweat-stained schedule. "If the P-L doesn't cut it, we'll just have to send him home and hope we get a better replacement."

Felodon nodded and started into the bush to retrieve the patrol but Shake caught him with an additional thought.

"Ask Sergeant Mariano to come see me—after he's done removing the patrol leader's balls." Felodon chuckled and disappeared into the green.

Shake was in the process of re-jiggering their Mindoro training schedule when he caught the squelch break on his radio. One of the two veteran U.S. Marine infantry NCOs he'd sent to conduct area reconnaissance for the night phase of their training program was calling from somewhere below the hill. He stretched for the handset and jammed it up against a sweaty ear.

"Tango Six. Send your traffic."

"Tango Four Charlie, Six." Staff Sergeant Steve Wyatt was calling, which meant he and Gunnery Sergeant Dick Liccardi had likely completed their area recon. "We've got two solid positions plotted. Alpha is a beach recon about one point five clicks from the harbor site. Bravo is a night ambush along that trail we spotted about two point five clicks out. Gunny and me are all set to play bad guys tonight with Sergeant Mariano. Which one you want to do, Boss?"

"Four Charlie, Six, we better go with Alpha. We send this patrol out any further and they'll wind up in downtown Manila sucking *balut*."

"Is it that bad up there, Boss?"

"Nah, we'll get it done one way or another." Shake looked around to be sure none of their Filipino cadre or students were within hearing. "But our little brown brothers are a couple of grid squares away from making a solid deep recon unit."

"Copy all, Boss. We go with Alpha tonight. We'll use the IBS and see if we can land without getting caught."

Shake turned to replace the radio handset and found himself looking up at Sgt. Jubal Mariano of the Philippine Constabulary Special Action Force. The veteran commando was smiling down on him from no more than a foot away with his razor-sharp bolo bush-knife dangling from his right wrist. The guy moved like a snake in the bush. Shake pointed at the bolo and nodded.

"No blood on your blade. I guess our patrol leader has still got his balls?"

"Not for long if he doesn't improve." Mariano squatted on his heels and accepted the cigarette Shake offered him. "You wanted to see me, sir?"

Shake could hear the hapless five-man recon patrol returning with Lt. Felodon loudly alternating between lecturing and hectoring. "You're a really good man, Sergeant Mariano. I've never seen anyone as good in the bush. I mean that." Mariano bowed his head slightly to acknowledgement the compliment and waited silently for the other shoe to drop.

"Lieutenant Felodon is not gonna like losing you from the training team, but I'm going to recommend that you become patrol leader when this unit goes active. Is that gonna be a problem?"

"I go where I am needed, sir." Mariano shrugged and looked over his shoulder in the direction of the returning patrol. "It's probably for the best if this new unit is to be of any use against the Moros in the south islands."

"OK, Jubal." Shake smiled and remembered what he'd told his two NCOs after they got a good look at Sgt. Jubal Mariano working in the bush. If the Constabulary SAF had a couple dozen Sgt. Mariano clones, there wouldn't be a guerilla problem in the south islands. "Keep this between us for right now. I'll let Lt. Felodon know when the time is right."

When the patrol broke into the clearing, Shake noticed that the patrol leader looked like a man who had been shot with a powerful shit pistol. Much more failure coupled with the impressive ass-chewing Felodon and Mariano delivered and the poor corporal would be suicidal. He turned to Felodon and nodded. "Lieutenant, please have Sergeant Mariano take the point. We'll run a compass march back to the harbor site." Shake broke out his lensatic compass and map. "Base course will be two-eight-zero magnetic. Tactical formation and flank security all the way."

Felodon nodded at Mariano who preset his compass bezel to the designated azimuth and motioned for one of the patrol members to move out as marker. The disheartened patrol leader moved to fall in at the rear but Shake caught his elbow. "Let's you and me work a parallel course, Corporal Velasquez. I'll give you a hand and see if we can beat them back to the base." The Filipino NCO smiled for the first time since he'd been working with the mobile training team.

Halfway down the mountain after some gentle coaching, Shake was gratified to note the SAF corporal seemed to be getting the hang of walking on a compass heading, circling around obstacles in their path and then returning to the base course. Sometimes it was just a matter of teaching them to keep the compass needle aligned and forget about the theory behind it all. The corporal seemed to be the kind of guy who could master the technique if he wasn't bothered about why it worked.

Confident that they'd eventually find themselves emerging close to the objective, Shake just followed the man's lead and let his mind wander back to the time when he'd been ordered to report to the commanding officer of the 31st Marine Expeditionary Unit on Okinawa.

A mission that looked like a political turd in a military punchbowl had just landed on the colonel's desk. Someone high up in the Philippine government wanted a special unit trained quickly, competently and very, very quietly. The objective was a unit of the Philippine Constabulary's Special Action Force able to work deep and dark tracking Moro insurgents who were causing the Manila government more than a little international heartburn.

"You know the ropes down there, Gunner." The colonel had been a student when Shake was a resident instructor at the prestigious Philippine Jungle Warfare School. "Pick yourself a couple of good staff NCOs, get down to the PI and get it done. And keep it off the radar."

When the selected team stopped by the G-3 Operations shop on Okinawa for a detailed briefing, they discovered the reason for that final caution. There were elements in recently elected Philippine President Gloria Macapagal-Arroyo's government still smarting from the economic impact of the U.S. pullout of the Philippines in 1991. It was a self-inflicted wound primarily caused by economic blackmail and exorbitant rents on U.S. bases in the country but that didn't keep the politicians from blaming everyone but themselves for the nation's crumbling economy. And these days, Arroyo's not-so-loyal opposition was even claiming the recent upsurge in Muslim separatist atrocities was proof that the arrogant Americans had left their loyal Filipino allies in a dangerous lurch.

What made it all worse was a rash of kidnappings that had recently spread from Mindanao as far north as the main island of Luzon. The Philippine military had been searching for a trio of American Christian missionaries taken by the Moro National Liberation Front at Baguio for weeks with no luck and no leads. International pressure—especially from Washington—was building and President Arroyo wasted no words in accusing her generals of everything from insubordination to incompetence. Frustrated with finger-pointing and backbiting in her regular military establishment, she decided to create a dedicated unit of national police trackers and reconnaissance specialists to feed her unfiltered information that she could act on quickly and directly. President Arroyo wanted an outfit that could out-guerilla the guerillas and she didn't care how that unit got trained and fielded.

Her generals thought they were going to be publically humiliated as a bunch of incompetent, Third World stumblebums who couldn't defend the population. Calling on the Americans to save their collective bacon didn't do much for their national pride and made it look like the whole business of tossing the Yanks out of the Philippines was a monumental blunder. They had to go along with the President's program, but the generals and the admirals in Manila would be just as happy if the whole idea swirled down the crapper and took the Arroyo government with it. Enter Gunner Davis and his mobile training team, which spirited selected men over to the sparsely-populated island of Mindoro where they could work away from prying eyes.

Shake was so distracted chewing on that knotty political situation that he nearly ran over Cpl. Velasquez, who was kneeling at the edge of a clearing and grinning like he'd just gotten a meritorious promotion. The man snapped his compass shut with a decisive click and nodded for Shake to take a look through the tangle of brush at their front. No need for that. Shake could hear Gunny Liccardi's shortwave radio droning away on the other side of the clearing. They were within spitting distance of the training team's harbor site.

"Very good, Corporal!" Shake wrapped an arm around the delighted SAF trooper and decided he'd give the guy another shot at leading tonight. "You did an outstanding job...but you must be able to do it every time and all the time. Can you do that?"

"Yes, sir, it's not so hard if you trust this," Velazquez looked at his lensatic compass as if it was the Rosetta Stone and then tapped his temple. "And this."

"That's right." Shake poked him in the stomach. "Like the aviators always say, trust your instruments and ignore your gut."

At dusk a much more confident Cpl. Velasquez led his patrol on a compass heading toward an isolated stretch of Mindoro beach. Assuming that they reached the designated spot, the recon unit would set up in three linear positions to observe the beach and watch for aggressor activity. Sometime in the early hours before dawn Gunny Liccardi, SSgt. Wyatt and Sgt. Mariano would paddle ashore in a rubber boat and try to slide by the observers onto the beach. Assuming the Velasquez patrol managed to spot the aggressors, they were to track them covertly to an objective inland where Shake and Lt. Felodon would be waiting to spring a blank-fire ambush. The two officers had spent a good part of the afternoon rigging a deadfall, a Malay gate and a bamboo whip as nefarious surprises for the patrol to either discover or trigger along the route.

It was inky black in the jungle by the time Shake and Felodon reached their planned ambush site. A quick, coded burst transmission on the Filipino net told them the patrol was in position where they thought they should be near the beach. Shake was snuggling into his poncho liner for a nap when his radio demanded attention. He checked the luminous dial of his watch. It was too early for the Gunny and his team to be calling.

"Tango Seven, Six. Send it."

"Gunner, we're about a mile offshore. There's what looks like a fishing boat out here and the guys on it are rowing for the beach, right toward our landing area."

"Copy all, Seven. Let 'em come. We'll see what kind of spot-rep we get from our guys."

"Might not be a good idea, Gunner. I think these guys are packing serious heat. They passed right by our pos and we saw a bunch of AKs and other gear."

Shake's pulse began to pound and he whispered for Felodon to dial up the American tactical frequency on his radio so he could monitor the conversation. "Interrogative, Seven. Did they spot you?"

"That's negative, Gunner. Too dark out here and we were laying low in the water. Mariano got a good look and counted eight people and maybe five weapons. He says he thinks these dudes are bad guys for real. How copy?"

"Copy all. Wait out." Shake turned to Felodon now sitting just a few feet away from him in the pitch dark. "What do you think?"

"I think maybe our training exercise has just become a combat operation, sir." Felodon snapped on a red-lens flashlight and examined the frequency dials on his radio. "I also think we should call up the PC unit here on Mindoro and report the landing. I'm trying to remember the frequency..."

"Where's the nearest PC station on this island?"

Felodon took a moment to think. In the glow of the flashlight, Shake could see by the set of the man's features that he'd shifted into combat mode. "Calapan City...maybe fifty kilometers northwest."

"Can you reach them on the radio?"

"Maybe." Felodon used the red light to read a list of emergency frequencies he'd pulled from his map case. "I don't think we can reach the central station from here, but they've got patrol vehicles with radios. Maybe I can raise someone on the guard frequency."

"Give it a shot..." Shake was in no position to take chances with an armed band of guerillas. His guys had weapons but all their ammo was blanks. A firefight would be distinctly one-sided and lethal for them. "But before you do that, get Corporal Velasquez on the horn and tell him what's up. Under no circumstances is he to reveal himself or his people to these guys if they land in his area. Tell him to just report what he sees and sit tight."

"Tango Seven, Six." Shake keyed his handset and tried to compute how long it might take a crew of what had to be MNLF guerillas to row a mile from sea to shore. He didn't have much time to avoid trouble. "We've alerted our guys on the beach to sit tight and stay out of sight. Have you still got a visual on that boat?"

"Roger." Gunny Liccardi's voice was barely a whisper in the handset. "We're behind them and off to their right. They're pulling for shore and not checking Six."

"Stay with them, Gunny. After they land and start inland, you guys police up our team and head for the harbor site. We'll meet you there and figure out what to do about all this. Be quiet and be careful. We don't want this thing turning into a fight."

"Copy all, Six. We'll push you on this freq when we're ashore and secure."

Shake gathered his gear and tried to work out an effective solution to their new problem while Felodon attempted to contact a PC patrol on the guard frequency. He was having no luck. Patrols normally monitored their own command frequency and only checked the alternate guard frequency occasionally. Felodon would keep trying to catch one of the few patrols on Mindoro but they needed to come up with a plan in case that failed. Contact between the training unit and the guerilla landing party was a losing proposition that would likely get some people killed. Best bet would be to let them pass unmolested, and then send some men to interdict one of the island's few main roads where they'd be likely to run into a constabulary motor patrol. Then they could turn the problem over to people with real rounds in their weapons.

They were about halfway to the harbor site with Felodon regularly barking into his handset when the distinctive crack of AK-47 fire broke the stillness from the direction of the beach. Before he could retrieve his handset and ask for a report, Gunny Liccardi came up on the net. "Six...we've got problems. Either they spotted something or..." The rest of the report was lost in the roar and rattle of an M-60 machinegun. Unless the guerillas had one of their own, Velasquez' machine gunner had fired a burst of blank ammo and it was probably going to get him killed in the next few minutes.

He heard Felodon shouting into his handset in Tagalog. Either he'd managed to contact a constabulary patrol or he'd switched to the tactical frequency and was talking to their men on the beach. As the firing dribbled off to isolated AK pops, Felodon provided an update on the situation.

"Corporal Velasquez reports one of the Moros nearly stepped on one of his men. He believes that man and one other in the same position are dead. He ordered the machinegun to fire to cover his withdrawal. Velasquez and two others are running for the harbor site. The Moros are pursuing..."

"Shit! I was afraid of that." Shake chewed on the problem for a moment and then decided Cpl. Velasquez had made the right move. The guerillas didn't know the patrol was firing blanks and that gave him an idea.

"Tell Velasquez to find a good hide and lay chilly. We'll stage a diversion and pull them off his back." As Felodon relayed the instructions, Shake grabbed his own handset and began to transmit to his team bobbing offshore in the rubber boat.

"Tango Seven, Six. Our patrol is moving out in the direction of the harbor site. They think they've got two KIA on the beach and the bad guys are in pursuit. We need to take the heat off of them. How far offshore are you now?"

"Six, Tango Seven is just off the surf line. You want us to pursue?" Gunny Liccardi didn't sound anxious to set off chasing armed guerillas with nothing but blanks in their magazines.

"It's on you guys, Gunny. Get on the beach ASAP and see if you can make 'em think they're being chased from behind. Once you've got 'em stopped..." This was the hard part. Shake understood he was asking his veteran guys to engage in a firefight in which they couldn't do any damage and could easily get killed in the effort. "Don't take any unnecessary chances, but see if you can get them to chase you in the direction of our ambush site. Use that admin trail you found on the scout so you can move fast and get well ahead of them. I'll have the lieutenant meet you on the trail with a chem light. Keep me advised as you can. How copy, over?"

"Copy all, Six. We're headed for the beach now. Tango Seven out." If it worked as Shake planned, Liccardi, Wyatt and Sgt. Mariano would distract the Moro element and set them on a tail chase away from Cpl. Velasquez and what was left of their training unit. What happened at that point Shake was still trying to work out as he led Lt. Felodon in the direction of their ambush site. The booby traps they'd prepared for Velazquez might serve to slow the bad guys down and maybe by that time they could feed this whole shit sandwich to the local Philippine constabulary. Felodon was back on the guard frequency, transmitting on the run and trying to reach a roving patrol.

They broke out of the bush and onto an open path that led in the direction of the ambush site. During the day, Shake and Felodon had rigged boobytraps along this trail hoping to teach their students an object lesson about taking the easy way in approaching an objective. It was one of Murphy's most reliable laws of combat: *The easy way is always mined or booby trapped.* If Velasquez and his patrol had used the speed trail on the exercise they would have run alternately into a deadfall, a Malay gate, and a bamboo-whip, all traps that Shake had learned about the hard way in Vietnam and then taught to students in the Jungle Warfare School. Of course, the versions he and Felodon had rigged along the trail were minus the deadly barbs and other trimmings that made them lethal, but if he had enough time that might be able to remedy that tonight. It would be tight and they could use an extra set of experienced hands.

"Tango Seven, Six. Stay status, over."

"Six, we are off the beach and heading northeasterly. We can hear the bad guys thrashing around up ahead but no more firing so far. We're gonna find a place where we can hit them in a flank and then run like hell in your direction, over."

"Roger all, Seven. You and Wyatt handle that. Send me Sergeant Mariano on the double. Tell him to use the speed trail."

"Roger, Boss." Gunny Liccardi didn't sound happy about losing the help when he came back on the air about a minute later. "Mariano just left. He's inbound to you somewhere along the trail. We'll take a whack at these guys as soon as we can and then follow in trace."

At a bend in the trail just ahead, Lt. Felodon was huddled over his radio, aiming a hooded flashlight at the Mindoro map spread on his knee. As Shake joined him, the Filipino Marine signed off and smiled. "I raised a mobile patrol. They are pulling in reinforcements now. Then they will head in our direction. They have requested we try to maintain visual contact with the Moros until they arrive."

"How far out are they?" Shake didn't mind doing a little real-world recon for his allies but these guys in the landing party were now on high alert and knew they'd been discovered by the military. That much would be obvious to them from the encounter on the beach.

Felodon did a quick map study using his thumb to measure road distance to the nearest possible intercept point. He didn't look happy with the result. "Maybe two hours, maybe more, it depends on how long it takes them to get moving in our direction."

"Tell them to move with all possible speed, Ignacio." Shake thought it chancy at best and more than a little dangerous for his basically unarmed guys to track an armed, alert enemy to some unknown point for two hours. "We'll do what we can once I'm sure our guys are safe."

Felodon reached for his radio handset but Shake grabbed his elbow. "You wait here and make the call. I've got Sgt. Mariano headed this way on the run. Meet him and then both of you join up with me..." Shake snapped a green light stick to start the chemical reaction and then stuck the glowing cylinder in the low branches of a nearby shrub. "We're gonna re-rig those boobytraps and see if we can do these guys some damage."

Shake was working on the trail-sweeper deadfall, jamming sharpened bamboo spikes into a heavy ball of congealed jungle mud, turning an unpleasant object lesson into a potentially lethal surprise for the Moro guerillas, when he heard the first tinny bursts of M-16 rifle fire. Liccardi and Wyatt had found their spot and would now try to lure the guerillas into a very deadly game of bumper tag in the jungle. His ears told him they were less than a kilometer away. It would be tight but the game was on for real now.

He finished work on the deadfall and began to pull it back up into the treetops that formed a canopy over the trail. What had originally been a heavy but relatively harmless ball of mud was now something more akin to the spiked head of a medieval war club. It was rigged so that an encounter with the vine holding it aloft would send the barbed ball plunging down parallel with the trail and hopefully impale one or more people along its deadly path.

Just as he was re-tying the tripwire over the trail he heard footsteps at his rear and turned to see a greenish glow bobbing in the dark. Ten seconds later, Sgt. Jubal Mariano appeared on the trail leading Lt. Felodon toward the spot where Shake waited to keep them from running into his tripwire. Mariano had his blank-adapted weapon slung across his back and his bolo in hand. The chem-light was gripped between his teeth and cast a pale, eerie glow on his chiseled features. Both Filipinos slid to a knee, panting and listening to another burst of gunfire that rattled in the bush well off to their left. Both AK and M-16 fire this time.

"The Gunny and Staff Sergeant Wyatt will pull them onto the trail." Shake pointed down the path and spit out a staccato burst of orders. "You two help me re-rig these booby-traps so they'll do some damage. Ignacio, you take the Malay Gate. Get as many spikes into it as you can. Jubal, you've got the bamboo whip just up the trail from the gate. Same deal, spike it and rig it low. Maybe we can..."

Sgt. Mariano nodded but held up a hand to interrupt. "They have hostages, sir!"

"What?" Shake suddenly saw a bad situation getting immeasurably worse. "What kind of hostages?"

"One man...two women." Sgt. Mariano stuck the light stick into a pocket of his uniform and took a deep breath. "All white. They are in pretty bad shape from what I could see."

"They must be the ones from Baguio," Felodon added. "It is no wonder we couldn't find them on Luzon. They were moved off the island."

"Shit! Can it get any more fucked up?" Shake was trying to decide whether or not to go on with his original plan. Civilians complicated matters considerably and he didn't want to take a chance on getting them killed in some sort of high-speed, one-sided war game. "You guys got any suggestions, now's the time to hear 'em."

"The hostages are slowing their speed." Sgt. Mariano stared off in the direction of another burst of gunfire from the bush to their left. "That works in our favor."

"When they hit the traps, maybe we can cut them away from the Moros." Felodon didn't sound very confident. "Maybe we could hide them until the PC patrol arrives."

"Any update on that?" Shake was running down the potential courses of action. He didn't much like any of them.

"They are moving in our direction at high speed. One hour, maybe a little more."

"It all sucks, gents. Let's stick with the original plan. Jubal, find a place to intercept the Gunny and Staff Sergeant

Wyatt. Be sure the Moros hit the trail and then start in this direction. Ignacio, you and I will do the re-rigs on the other traps and then try to run parallel with them as they move up the trail. If it looks like the hostages are in any kind of danger, we move in quick and see what we can do to rescue them."

Shake waited for a nod of acknowledgement. There were no challenges to his command or his ideas. "If that happens, Jubal, you and the other two Marines come running and we all pile on. Questions?"

There were none. They all knew the long odds they were facing.

* * *

Waiting on his belly with his heart pounding in his chest, Shake Davis heard a few rounds of AK fire crack through the darkness. His trained ears estimated the range of the trigger-pullers to be less than a hundred meters down the speed trail to his left. He was in position at the fulcrum of the deadfall's intended swing with Sgt. Mariano just behind him with his bolo at the ready. Lt. Felodon was to his right about thirty meters up the trail near the Malay gate he'd rigged with bamboo spikes and suspended over the path. The idea was to try to corral the hostages and shuttle them off into the bush during the confusion after one or more of the boobytraps were sprung. It wasn't much of a plan, but it was all they had right now.

Off to his left, Shake could just make out the dim glow of the chem-light he'd planted as a signal for Gunny Liccardi and SSgt. Wyatt to keep them from running into the traps. He could hear their pounding footsteps intermingled with short bursts of blank fire from their rifles. Suddenly, the chem-light disappeared and he heard SSgt. Wyatt's coarse whisper.

"Last man!"

That meant his two Marines had policed up the light and turned off into the jungle. As their pursuers sent a ragged burst of ball ammo up the trail in his direction, Shake turned over his shoulder and felt for Sgt. Mariano's bolo. "Give me the blade, Jubal. You grab for the hostages and get them gone in a hurry. You'll do better with them in the bush." Mariano didn't argue or discuss the matter. He released his grip on the blade and acknowledged the order with a tap on Shake's leg.

The Moro point man came into sight at a bend in the trail and slowed his rush, listening for sounds from the people he was pursuing. Shake could barely make out two more guerillas behind the point and suspected that the hostages would be somewhere around fourth in line with two more armed men behind them if Liccardi's count was correct. If they got lucky and the deadfall took out the lead man, he'd have to deal with the guys walking slack and drag behind the point while Mariano did what he could to hustle the hostages off the trail. That meant the two guerillas walking tail-end Charlie in the formation would be a major problem, but there was little he could do about that now.

Firing from the hip, the lead Moro sent a burst up the trail, said something to the men behind him and then began to advance. Shake silently gathered his legs beneath him ready to spring as the guerillas approached his tripwire. This guy was no amateur, but he wasn't expecting booby traps and his attention was riveted straight ahead. He never even looked down as his foot snagged the vine Shake had rigged to trigger the deadfall. The point man froze as he heard the rustle in the branches that formed a canopy over the trail but he was too slow to avoid the forty-pound ball of mud that smacked him directly in the chest, driving two bamboo spikes through his ribcage.

Shake sprang from the bush swinging the bolo like a meat-axe and caught the slack man in the neck with the blade. His victim fell hard dragging Shake down on top of him as the next guerilla in line triggered a burst from his AK-47. Shake heard the rounds snap past his ears as he struggled to regain his footing. He whipped the bolo around with a roundhouse swing and felt the blade bite into wooden fore-grip of the third guerilla's rifle. With the bolo out of play, Shake made a grab for the guerilla to keep him from getting his rifle back into action. Off to his left he saw Sgt. Mariano thrashing his way into the bush with what looked like two females; one under each arm. The third hostage was lying on the trail curled into a protective ball, either hit or playing possum while the deadly action swirled around him.

Grabbing his wheezing opponent by the throat, Shake pushed him violently backward and toppled onto him as they stumbled over the prostrate body. That body moaned and squirmed, which let Shake know he still had one hostage left to rescue even if he managed to dispense with the current problem before the remaining two guerillas caught up to the ambush. He could hear their shouts as they pounded up the trail headed in his direction, but he was locked into a lethal struggle with his current opponent and it was all he could do to keep the wiry little bastard under some modicum of control. Even as he groped for a weapon to fill his free hand, Shake understood he was likely to die in the next few seconds or become a fourth MNLF hostage.

"Gunner, haul ass out of there!" Gunny Liccardi's shout was almost lost in the deafening bark of two M-16 rifles ripping through thirty-round magazines on full-automatic. Within seconds, their blank fusillade was answered by long, crackling bursts from AK-47s firing the real deal. Liccardi and Wyatt had bought him some time by initiating a firefight with the two trailing guerillas but they couldn't stick around and trade rounds. He had to act fast.

Shake jammed his free hand into the tight space between his body and the guerilla's, looking for some way to retrieve the bolo or come up with some other weapon that would end the struggle decisively. His fingertips jammed painfully against the AK's curved magazine and he wedged his hand in deeper, feeling for the magazine release while he tried to keep the desperate guerilla pinned to the ground. Finally, he found the paddle-shaped lever, tugged at it and felt the magazine pop free of the weapon. He jerked it free of their embrace and jammed the sharp edge of the magazine into the guerilla's face.

The man thrashed violently as Shake kept jamming the magazine into his face. To escape the punishment, the guerilla turned his head. Shake spotted a target of opportunity and delivered a stout blow to the temple. He felt the man go slack, pushed away and looked around him for the third hostage. He was about halfway into the trailside bush, doing a low-crawl and yelling for Dora and Audrey in a panicky, adrenaline-choked falsetto. Shake grabbed his ankles and hauled him back onto the speed trail.

"U.S. Marines! We gotta get you out of here! Let's go!" Shake gripped the stunned hostage at the elbow and started him up the trail. It was like hauling an uncooperative drunk out of his favorite bar. The man kept shouting that he wouldn't leave Dora and Audrey. Above the babble, Shake could hear shouted orders from down the trail. The remaining guerillas were getting reorganized to take up the pursuit. He was about to throw the struggling man over his shoulder when Lt. Felodon suddenly appeared. He was pointing up the trail.

"Take him and go!" He made a dash for the middle of the path where the point man lay bleeding out with the deadfall still locked to his chest by the bloody bamboo spikes. "Sergeant Mariano is waiting for you with the two women where the trail meets the primary road." Felodon grabbed the wounded man's AK, retrieved the magazine and quickly chambered a ready round. "I'll take care of the rest."

Shake whirled the male hostage around and tried to inject some element of calm into his voice: "There you go, see? My friends have got Dora and Audrey just up the trail here. They're safe. Now let's go join them." The hostage turned docile and nodded. There were still live booby traps on the trail, so Shake pulled the man into the bush where they could run a parallel course toward the juncture. Felodon now had a weapon loaded with live ammo and he was more than capable of either killing or capturing the two remaining guerillas.

By the time he'd carefully worked the exhausted hostage past the Malay gate position, Shake heard two short bursts of AK fire; same weapon, no return. Apparently, Felodon opted for the former course of action over the latter, a good move given their circumstances. He stepped out onto the trail, sat the hostage near a tree and handed over his canteen. The man chugged greedily from it.

Shake was reaching for his radio handset to call off the dogs and reassemble his forces when a small caliber shot came from the opposite side of the trail, tore through his left hamstring and sent him spinning to the ground near the hostage. The pain was intense, but Shake knew from first-hand experience it wasn't lethal. He shoved at the hostage trying to get the man out of the line of fire but any escape was cut off by the guerilla that emerged from the bush aiming a Makarov pistol at them. The right side of the Moro's face was bruised and swollen. Dried blood was caked along his scalp line and his right ear was mangled. *One fuck-up is all it takes*, Shake thought as he watched the man he should have killed in the initial struggle walk toward him, clearly intent on not making a similar mistake.

The guerilla seemed puzzled for a moment as he stood aiming the pistol at Shake's head. He kept cutting glances at the missionary apparently trying to decide whether it was better to kill the man who'd maimed him or recapture the hostage. Shake averted his eyes, figuring he could do without seeing the trigger squeeze and muzzle blast that ended his life. Just to his left he saw the three stones they'd piled alongside the trail to mark the location of the bamboo whip, the last of the pre-rigged booby traps they'd prepared. Just to the right of the marker he spotted the vine that kept the green bamboo branch bent back under pressure. If he was very lucky and had just a few seconds left before the guerilla made up his mind, there might be a way out of this fix.

Shake held up his hands to signal surrender and struggled painfully to stand. As he had expected, the guerilla backed away out of arm's reach and right into the center of the trail. Shake bent low as if to help the hostage to his feet and kicked hard with his good leg to snap the tripwire. The bamboo whip whirred viciously over his head and caught the wounded guerilla right in the throat. There had been no time to re-rig the trap with spikes but the brutal impact of the bamboo was enough to knock the man off his feet. Shake stamped hard on the guerilla's right wrist and twisted the pistol out of his hand. As the surviving guerilla lay gasping on the ground he looked up into the muzzle of his own weapon.

The encounter had been over for 45 minutes when the Philippine constabulary patrol rolled up to the road juncture in three jeeps that bristled with weapons. An officer jumped out of the lead vehicle and stood staring at the four dead guerillas Gunny Liccardi and SSgt. Wyatt had lined up neatly alongside the road. Lt. Felodon trotted over, grabbed the officer by the elbow and steered him toward the surviving guerilla who sat opposite his dead buddies, his hands and feet tightly bound. Also on that side of the road, Cpl. Velasquez and his surviving men had laid out their slain comrades covered with ponchos.

Shake sat with the other survivors—three missionaries who had been run rough-shod all over the northern Philippines by their MNLF captors for the past six weeks—and tried to explain what had happened to set them free. Given his orders to maintain a low profile, he was doing a lot of weasel-wording and trying to decide how much information to provide. He was saved by the throbbing chop of helicopter rotors. A pair of Philippine Air Force Huey's blew low over their heads and wheeled into pedal-turns looking for a suitable landing zone. He could tell by the polish and paint that they carried VIPs. Shake had the uncomfortable feeling his low-profile mission had just emerged blatantly onto the international skyline.

It didn't surprise him all that much when the guy who crashed through the bush from the landing zone to the road junction wearing a suit and tie introduced himself as the military attaché to the American Ambassador to the Philippines. "What we have here, Mr. Davis," said the attaché, "is a bit of a sticky wicket."

* * *

During a hushed meeting at the Presidential Palace in Manila, the hostages were debriefed prior to a press conference. They were all God-fearing, patriotic Americans so it wasn't hard to convince them that it was in the interest of their country if they credited the entire rescue to Philippine forces. In fact, warranted the President of the Philippines and the U.S. ambassador in the name of his president, if the presence of American Marines during their dramatic rescue was kept secret for the next fifty years, the missionaries could be guaranteed official support of their worldwide mission for at least that long.

President Macapagal-Arroyo was satisfied with granting her generals and their Special Forces soldiers full credit for tracking the guerillas and rescuing the hostages. Her generals were delighted to accept the credit, quit making public noises about coups and throw their wholehearted support behind her administration. They were, after-all, clearly capable military superstars now that they'd shown their mettle in the hostage rescue. Lt. Ignacio Felodon and to a lesser extent Sgt. Jubal Mariano, became instant international heroes of the all-important counterinsurgency game. Their photos and suitably humble quotes were flashed around the world.

Gunner Shake Davis, with yet another bullet hole in his hide suffered in service to his nation, policed up GySgt. Dick Liccardi and SSgt. Steve Wyatt from isolation in Quezon City and swore them to secrecy. The next morning at zero-dark-thirty they were whisked back to Okinawa in an unmarked aircraft. Before they left Manila, the Philippine president sent an emissary with classified letters of commendation and four cases of cold San Miguel beer. She also sent her promise that someday in the future she would call them back for appropriate recognition by a grateful nation.

Manila, Republic of the Philippines—Now

A splendidly uniformed field grade officer of the Philippine Marines met Shake at the immigration counter of the Ninoy Aquino International Airport and waved a dismissive hand at the officer who had been curiously examining Shake's passport, which did not contain a visa. Apparently, his luggage had already been retrieved from the Gulfstream and was stuffed into the trunk of the highly-polished staff car waiting for him at the airport curb, surrounded by four Philippine Marines standing at rigid parade rest. In less than twenty minutes after Bayer had shooed him off the airplane, Shake was nestled into the backseat of the sedan and headed for a meeting in Quezon City with the chief of staff of the Philippine armed forces.

Bayer's in-flight phone calls had set it all up for him. Now all Shake Davis had to do was nose around starting at the top with the brass hats and eventually maneuvering his way down the chain to Jubal Mariano. There would be the official story about Ignacio Felodon and then there would be the real story hopefully related by the man who knew him best. If a man like Felodon had truly gone rogue there was a reason and if there was a reason—good or bad—it might lead to some vital information that Bayer and his boys could use to prevent an attack that would make 9/11 pale by comparison.

Babelthaup, Palau Islands

It was a rough trip back over the twelve miles of rain-soaked road between the nominal capital of the Palau Islands at Ngerulmud and the Koror harbor slip where their vessel was being refueled and resupplied. Despite Sayed Abdullah's best efforts the little rump-sprung Peugeot they'd rented for the trip to the government center seemed to find every pothole and the wipers wanted to quit if their speed fell anything under full bore through the driving storm. It was an ugly day on Babelthaup, but neither Abdullah nor Dr. Susilo Nasuton, who sat next to him wiping away at the condensation on the inside of the windscreen, was bothered by it.

The scheduled appointment with the man in the capital who bore the impressive title Minister of Cultural, Agricultural and Scientific Affairs had gone well, with virtually no questions asked once the Palauan bureaucrat confirmed the hefty deposits wired into his official and personal accounts. Locked in Abdullah's briefcase on the backseat was a sheaf of official-looking documents that authorized them to conduct aquaculture experiments on Peleliu with full government cooperation. Waiting for them once they reached that island would be a team of anxious and well-paid natives who would provide anything and everything they might need, according to the bureaucrat who wished them all the luck in the world with their scientific endeavors. For 5,000 extra dollars, which Abdullah covered in cash from his pocket money, the Palauan minister also promised to keep them alerted to any inquiries about their work, which he would either deflect or divert. The man had not seemed at all suspicious about that aspect of the deal and bought Dr. Nasuton's explanation of the need to protect details of their experimentation with nothing more than an understanding shrug.

If the irascible Pineapple and his security force had managed to carry out their assigned tasks and obtain required supplies without flashing too much money around the impoverished waterfront at Koror, they would be underway in a day—two at most—for their final destination: the island of Peleliu. Nasuton assured Abdullah they had all the scientific equipment required in the two large containers stored aboard the yacht. In less than a week they should be conducting experiments again and that much closer to developing the ultimate weapon required for the mission.

Abdullah had done some Internet research during the voyage from the Philippines to the Palaus. Peleliu had a bloody military history but it had been largely ignored and rarely visited since the end of World War II except by adventurous parties of scuba divers. It had been more than sixty years since that island had been a battlefield. All that would change soon. The next world war, the conflict that would mark the birth of the inevitable Fourth Caliphate, would be launched from Peleliu.

Quezon City, Republic of the Philippines

The direct approach was failing miserably. The brigadier general who'd ushered him past a spit-shined honor guard and into his private conference room claimed he was honored to welcome a holder of the Ancient Order of Sikatuna, and would do all he could to help, but he'd never heard of a Lieutenant Colonel Ignacio Felodon. Shake was quickly and cordially passed up the convoluted chain of command at Camp Aguinaldo, headquarters of the Philippine armed forces, but the glad-handing cooled considerably every time he mentioned Ignacio Felodon and he quickly found himself bundled off to another suite of offices.

By the time he finally reached the inner sanctum and met the chief of staff, he'd decided to make a more circuitous approach. After an obligatory shot of vintage Tanduay rum with the nation's most-senior military officer and compliments on the fine crop of local sugar cane that produced it, Shake steered the conversation around to his days on staff at the Philippine Jungle Warfare School. Half an hour later, with several more shots of rum down the hatch, Shake Davis and the general were just two old warhorses rehashing the good times when they were both young studs out there on the razor's edge.

"The Negritos we had assisting at the school were fantastic. There's none better in the bush, if you ask me." Shake watched the general pour rum into crystal glasses and decided there was no way he could refuse another shot of the stout liquor.

"We drafted several of them to give us a hand down in Mindinao." The general handed over a glass and settled into a roomy leather armchair with his own drink. "After you trained the first deep recon unit, we decided it was definitely the way to go after the Moros, so we pulled out all the stops. The Negritos were very helpful. We're still using some of them but they're mostly attached to the PC these days."

"I had a really good friend in the PC Special Action Force back in those days. He was excellent in the bush. We'd never have rescued those hostages if it wasn't for him."

"I remember..." The general sipped his drink and seemed to be searching for a name. "I believe the constabulary gave him a medal and a promotion right away. What was his name?"

"Mariano. Sergeant Jubal Mariano."

"That's it! He was in all the papers. And you weren't." The general seemed to get a big kick out of that and reached for the rum decanter.

"It's the deal we made with the president, General. It wasn't something we needed to take credit for, and we were lucky to have good Filipinos with us on the training team. You have any idea where I might find Sergeant Mariano these days? I'd really like to see him again."

"I can find out very quickly." The general walked to his desk, picked up a phone and began a long-winded conversation in Tagalog with someone on the other end. Shake sipped his drink and tried to decide whether or not to push his luck. He'd drawn blanks concerning Ignacio Felodon so far, but the chief of staff would likely have been a contemporary; maybe even a colleague.

"Good news for you, my friend." The general topped off their drinks and plopped himself back down in the armchair to consult a sheaf of notes. "Your friend is now Sergeant Major Mariano and he's still very much on active duty. The constabulary says he's down in Mindinao right now, attached as SAF liaison to the Joint Special Ops Team down there."

"Suppose I could get down there to see him, General? Or is that a restricted area these days?"

"I think we could make it happen," the general said raising his glass in salute, "for a man who holds one of my country's highest decorations."

Shake raised his glass and decided to take the plunge. "Just one more thing, General, and then I'll stop taking up your valuable time."

The chief of staff nodded, placed his glass on the coffee table and folded his hands across his stomach. "I was wondering if you would get around to it. The commander of my honor guard said you were asking about Felodon."

"Yes sir. He was a good man to have at my side when we did that hostage rescue. I'd like to know what happened to him."

There was a long silence as the general closed his eyes and tilted his head to catch the warm breeze from his office ceiling fan. "I'm trying to decide how much I should tell you. It is not a pretty story."

"I'd really like to hear it, General. If you're willing to share it with me."

"I suppose we owe you that much." The Philippine chief of staff sat up in his armchair and placed his hands on his knees. He was suddenly dead sober and dead serious. "We made national heroes out of Mariano and Ignacio Felodon after that hostage rescue thing on Mindoro. That may have been a mistake but we needed Philippine military heroes at that time and there were political considerations.

"Both men were very high profile here in our country, with the Philippine people and also with the Moros of the MNLF, the HUKs and the New People's Army. In the case of Sergeant Mariano it was less of a problem. He was unmarried and easy to transfer out of danger. In the case of Ignacio Felodon, it was a difficult situation. We promoted him to lieutenant colonel, kept him in the headlines and touted him as an example of the quality, loyalty and dedication of our military officers. He was celebrated—and protected." The general shook his head and reached for his glass.

"Unfortunately, we did not take similar precautions with Felodon's family: a wife, two sons and his parents, all of them living in an apartment somewhere in Pasig City."

"That doesn't sound good, sir."

"It wasn't." The general sipped, sighed and continued. "We sent Felodon on a speaking tour of our military bases. While he was away, Moros of one brand or another—no one knows for sure—killed his family...all of them. Broke in, shot the parents, the wife and the kids. And then they burned the entire apartment building. No survivors."

"Good God! How did he take it?"

"How would any man take the loss of his family? He was crushed. Unfortunately, he blamed us, maybe with some reason. At any rate, he became involved in anti-government activities. You may recall some of the problems we had with the so-called Oakwood Mutiny in 2003? And the anti-government riots in Makati? Felodon was in the middle of it all. Some say he was the ringleader."

"Was he arrested?"

"He was. But how could we prosecute a certified hero who had lost his family to the Muslim rebels? How would that look? Many of the local people believed he had every right to hate the government and strike back at those who couldn't protect his family. It was ugly, my friend, very ugly."

"What happened to him, sir?"

"You must understand that Felodon was very bitter and calling for the violent overthrow of the government."

"Yes, sir, that's understandable."

"We had no choice, Mr. Davis. Ignacio Felodon was stripped of his citizenship and exiled."

"Exiled? Do we still do that to people?"

"We did it with Ignacio Felodon. He was flown out of Manila in early 2004, never to return. And his name was placed on a watch list among all our allied nations."

"Do you have any idea where he is now?"

"Probably in Hanoi or Ho Chi Minh City."

"He went to Vietnam?" Shake was stunned and fumbled with his glass as the general rose and extended his hand.

"Felodon's choices were limited. Allied nations in the Pacific Rim didn't want a potential radical. The Vietnamese agreed to take him...and he went. End of story. Now I must ask you to excuse me. See my aide and we'll arrange for you to visit with Sergeant Major Mariano on Mindinao. Please come and see me again before you leave the Philippines. There is still some rum left."

Aboard RV Seascope, Near Johnston Atoll, Mid-Pacific

The captain spotted the U.S. Coast Guard KC-130 turboprop on a low, slow approach to the island's runway and sent word for his flight crew to launch the ship's resident Bell Jet Ranger helicopter. It wasn't part of his brief to know why, but he'd been ordered to waste no time in getting two VIPs aboard the Seascope as soon as possible after they arrived on Johnston Island from Honolulu. When the helo pilot successfully lifted the four-passenger aircraft off his fantail, the captain picked up the phone and got Dr. Janis Fielding on the line.

In an air conditioned conference room below decks, Dr. Fielding got the message, hung up the phone and turned to the scientific staff she'd selected to brief the visitors. "They're on the way. Should be here in less than a half-hour. Let's go over it again. No panic, no wild speculations, right? We report what we found from a strictly scientific perspective."

"These guys are from Homeland Security, right?" Dr. Andrew Merman, the microbiologist looked up from a pile of spreadsheets. "Any chance they'll even understand what we're talking about?"

"If Mr. Goodall has trouble with the science, I'm sure Doctor Jerardi will explain it all to him." Janis Fielding punched keys on her laptop and began to review the slides they'd prepared to illustrate their findings on Wake Island and in the sophisticated research labs aboard Seascope. It was not a pretty picture and had all the potential in the world for getting a lot uglier.

Makati, Metro Manila, Republic of the Philippines

A room with a balcony view of Intramuros and the bay was pricey but Shake Davis was assured by the officious desk clerk that all fees and incidentals had been paid for the duration of his stay at the historic Manila Hotel. *What the hell,* he thought, as he stood on the balcony of his ornately-decorated room and stared out at Corregidor, the once defiant guardian of Manila Bay. If it was good enough for General Douglas MacArthur to call home for six years, it was good enough for a retired chief warrant officer on an overnight stay. He had an early pick-up scheduled for tomorrow when a staff car would take him to meet a military flight from Luzon to Mindinao, so he'd probably have to pass on a sightseeing trip out to The Rock. But there would be time for a look around after dark for a few of his old haunts in Makati's back streets.

Meanwhile, he wanted to light some fires in the intelligence community and see if he could establish a track on Ignacio Felodon, in Vietnam of all places. He checked his watch and decided Chan Dwyer was likely to be home in bed. He needed her advice and felt fairly sure she wouldn't mind the late call. He powered up his satellite phone, waited until it acquired the link to a bird and then punched in Chan's home phone number. She answered after the third ring.

"I've been wondering when you'd call."

"How'd you know it was me?"

"Caller ID, Shake. I don't have that many friends packing sat-phones these days."

"Sorry about the hour."

"No sweat. I'm used to it. Where are you?"

"Manila. At the Manila Hotel, in fact. But they wouldn't give me the MacArthur suite."

"You'd just get delusions of grandeur." Her throaty laugh was delightful and he realized how much he missed her.

"What are you doing in the Philippines? Last I heard, you were out on Iwo Jima."

"Does the name Bayer ring any bells with you? If not, how about Mike Stokey?"

"Uh-huh, sounds like somebody we know has been drafted again."

"Yeah, sort of. They've got me looking into something out here—someone actually—and that's where I could use a hand."

"Let me get a pen." There was a noisy pause as Chan Dwyer dug in her nightstand and Shake wondered how much he could safely say. He'd probably have to follow the phone call with an encrypted email to let Bayer know he was asking for DIA assistance.

"OK, fire away. What can I do to help?"

"There's this guy, former Philippine Marine officer by the name of Ignacio Felodon." Shake spelled the name for her and then confirmed the read-back. "I knew him fairly well when we ran a mobile training team over here. Anyway, he got into some serious trouble, mostly anti-government demonstrations and things like that, and got his ass kicked out of the country—with serious prejudice. My sources here say he was exiled, P-N-G, no passport, never to return, the whole shot."

"Where did he go?" There was a note of suspicion creeping into Chan Dwyer's voice. "Or is that what you want me to find out?"

"Are you still in touch with any of our old contacts from Vietnam?"

"Your guy went to Vietnam?"

"So I'm told. I'd start with Hanoi and then look into Ho Chi Minh City."

"Got it. I'll initiate a search tomorrow...but I'll probably need some sort of tag to hang on the queries. Can you give me some idea of why I'm asking?"

"Chan, I hate to talk about something like this on a sat-phone. It might have to do with the situation down in Mindinao. This guy could be involved. I can't say much more."

In the bedroom of her efficiency apartment in suburban Maryland, Chan Dwyer finished her notes and hung up the phone. Her intelligence senses were throbbing and she was unlikely to sleep much more tonight. She decided to shower, dress and get an early start at the office. Whatever Shake was after in the Philippines or Vietnam, Chan was nearly certain it would tie-in somehow to her current case. Her gut told her so...and good intel officers never ignored a gut-feeling.

RV Seascope, Near Johnston Atoll, Mid-Pacific

As the last slide in her PowerPoint presentation faded, Dr. Janis Fielding hit the conference room light switch and looked at the visitors for reaction. Jerry Goodall, the hard-nosed former Director of the FBI who now headed the Department of Homeland Security, was hard to read. He merely nodded and reached for a pen to make notes in his briefing folder. Dr. Joe Jerardi, the president's science advisor, had a more discernible reaction. He looked stunned.

"That's a brief overview of our findings, gentlemen." Dr. Fielding dropped into her chair and took a deep breath. "We'll be happy to take questions?"

"Well, you seem to be moving away from a naturally occurring phenomenon." Dr. Jerardi nodded at Tracey Davis and raised his eyebrows. "Is that safe to say, at least as it concerns the fish you examined?"

"As you know, Doctor, *botulinum* is found fairly regularly in certain species of fish so we initially thought this might simply be an outbreak among Pacific salmon. Dangerous if consumed by humans, but controllable through fishery alerts and the like. But the strain we discovered in dissected specimens was different than anything we'd seen before. It seems deadly to the host whereas naturally occurring strains don't usually affect the host. In other words, this stuff has either morphed naturally or been modified."

"And it's not just the fish." From his seat at the far end of the conference table, Woodrow Cheeley chimed in despite a stern look from Dr. Fielding. "Whatever has happened to this strain is communicable...at least one step up in the food chain. All the birds I dissected out on Wake were killed by this stuff contained in the fish that make up their primary diet."

"I got all that from the briefing." Jerry Goodall looked up from his notes and reached for a coffee cup. "Any chance this isn't botulism? Could it be something else entirely?"

"It's *Clostridia botulinum*, no doubt about that, but it doesn't equate with any of the previously identified strains." Dr. Kimiko Fukihara set her Diet Coke can delicately on the green baize tabletop and picked up the conversation. "It's just different from anything we know about standard strains A through G. It tends to kill the host...which for clinical purposes is good news—unless people around the world start eating dead fish."

"Or unless this thing somehow morphs further, adapts to the host and learns to survive." Dr. Andrew Merman, the microbiologist, was convinced the newly-identified strain of *botulinum* was merely the tip of a very deadly iceberg. "That's what tends to happen in nature. These organisms always seem to find a way to survive and thrive. It's the nature of the beast, so to speak."

"Suppose that happens." Goodall swept his gaze over the assembled scientists. "Then what?"

"Then we've got a very dangerous situation on our hands, sir." Dr. Fielding punched up a slide showing the proportion of the world's populations that regularly depended on fish or aquatic food sources as a major portion of their diet. "You can see from the chart here that should this stuff in a survivable form somehow infiltrate the food chain in many parts of the world—including the United States—we'd be facing a pandemic. I don't think that's overstating the case."

"That's the rub, isn't it?" Jerardi ran his finger down a string of data on the pile of reports in front of him. "I see that this strain seems to survive in water which is not generally the case with *botulinum*."

"That's correct, Doctor." Kimiko Fukihara rose and pointed at an adjacent string of data on the charts in front of Jerardi. "And you'll notice that it retained a better than seventy percent toxicity rate when heated at or above one hundred eight-five degrees Fahrenheit, or normal cooking temperatures. This thing is a survivor."

"Well, we need to start working on an antidote, right?" Goodall seemed frustrated and anxious to get started doing something concrete about this new threat. "And we need to get the word out to world health organizations, fishery alerts, that sort of thing."

"It may be too early for that, Jerry." Dr. Jerardi leaned back in his chair and stared at the population chart. "I think Dr. Merman's point is germane here. This thing will probably morph into a more stable form and until that happens, we really can't develop an effective antitoxin. Strains of *botulinum*, whatever they may be, can only be treated with antitoxins specifically directed at that strain. There is no blanket antidote that works across the spectrum of toxins. Best bet would be to put out a subtle warning through our global health services network."

"Let's stop dancing and deal with the 800-pound gorilla in the room." Goodall checked a vibrating cell phone and hit the switch to turn it off. "Is this just Mother Nature in a particularly bad mood? Or is someone fooling around with the genetic makeup of this stuff?"

"That's impossible to say for sure." Dr. Fielding had been hoping the question wouldn't be asked. "What we know is that this strain of *botulinum* has never been seen before in nature. That's unusual, but not unimaginable. We know this strain is deadly. Our projections indicate as little as point seven to point nine micrograms would be lethal to humans. I don't like to project but if Dr. Merman's theory is correct and the bacterium finds a way to survive in an aquatic host without killing the host, then we've got a very serious threat to human life on our hands."

"That's not what I asked, Dr. Fielding." Goodall folded his hands and stared at the scientist sitting across from him. "I asked if you all thought someone might be working with the genetic make-up of this thing in order to turn it into a weapon. Let's drop all the scientific cover-your-ass stuff. Is that possible—or likely?"

"It's certainly possible." Dr. Fielding turned to Andrew Merman who had expressed his views earlier in the pre-briefing. She knew what was coming.

"And, frankly, I think it's more than a little likely." Merman rose and handed an envelope to Dr. Joe Jerardi. "The details are contained in my report. I'd direct your attention to the conclusions at the end of the data analysis. I've been working with gene-splicing most of my professional career. And this strain we've discovered has a lot of the distinct earmarks of that sort of experimentation. Bottom line: I think someone—for some unknown reason—is screwing around with the *botulinum* genome. If that's the case, and the reason is an attempt to weaponize the strain, then the next step would be to make it communicable among humans. That would be a very bad situation."

"Thank you all for your time and efforts." Jerry Goodall stood and nodded at the scientific team. "I don't have to tell you that all of this is strictly classified. You are not to have any contact with the press or answer any questions from any source without my prior approval. As of right now, we are extending all of your contracts so you can continue to study this thing. If that presents personal or professional problems, let Dr. Fielding know and we'll see what can be done to help."

Tracey Davis held up her hand and stood. "Sir, I'm on active duty...detached from my command for this expedition..."

"Not anymore you're not." Goodall smiled reassuringly and motioned to a nearby aide. "We'll make a call today. From now on, you are working for the Department of Homeland Security until we say otherwise. There's still a whole bunch of questions here and I want answers."

As they emerged onto the Seascope's weather deck and headed aft for the waiting helicopter that would take them back onto Johnston Atoll and then by fixed-wing aircraft to Honolulu, Goodall turned to Dr. Jerardi and handed over his phone. "Number one on the speed dial, Joe. Call the President's Chief of Staff directly and set up a full briefing with NCA. Make it urgent priority and schedule it for just as soon as possible after we get back to Washington."

While Dr. Joe Jerardi waited for a connection with the White House switchboard, Goodall pointed at the Blue Tooth transceiver plugged into his aide's ear. "Get Bayer on the hook right away. Tell him I said he was right on the money. I want a full-court press on this thing beginning now."

Fairfax County, Virginia

Chan Dwyer pulled her car off the Georgetown Pike at the Langley exit and wheeled into the parking lot of a nearby Starbucks. Traffic had been surprisingly light on the national capital beltway and there was time for coffee before the meeting at CIA headquarters. She had at least an hour to sit on a fern-bedecked patio, sip the trendy caffeinated concoction du jour and review the hailstorm that started yesterday morning when she'd submitted a multi-base intelligence search request for information on Shake's person of interest with the DIA's Vietnam desk. Running a POI search was usually a no-strain; routine deal but the request for background, location and current activity on Ignacio Felodon had instigated a shitstorm of monumental proportions.

She was barely back at her desk just down the hall when her section chief called, told her to dump everything on the Pineapple HVT project onto a thumb drive and report to his office. "I'm not sure what one thing necessarily has to do with the other," the DIA's Southern and Central Pacific team leader said, "but there's a link between this Colonel Ibrahim thing, your search request for info on Felodon, and something that's got Homeland Security's skivvies twisted into a serious knot." It didn't take long for the two intel veterans to figure out it was likely that Col. Ibrahim, Pineapple and Ignacio Felodon were either one person or possibly two people working in concert on some imminent threat to U.S. security. They were in the middle of speculating on that when the phone chirped and Chan's boss was informed that the director of the National Counter-Terrorism Center was on the line. The conversation was short and fairly one-sided. When he hung up with a curt acknowledgement that he would do what he'd been ordered to do—and right away—the section chief shook his head and turned to Chan Dwyer sitting across the desk from him.

"So...you're an old pal of Bob Bayer, the NCTC director. I didn't know that."

"I wouldn't say we're old pals." Chan shut down her laptop and removed the thumb drive containing all her working files on the case she'd coded AS/PI/PINEAPPLE. "I was on a mission he was running in Vietnam years ago when I was still on active duty. Only met him the one time when we debriefed the Laos File thing."

"Oh, yeah, the MIA deal. That was a coup. You were in on that?"

"I went along as an adjutant but I was wearing an M.I. hat all the way. I was a rear-ranker for the most part. I'm surprised Bayer would remember me at all."

"It's got something to do with the search request you submitted on this guy Ignacio Felodon. Bayer wants you and all of our background material in his hands before lunch today. Download anything that's not on your thumb drive, organize it by level of reliability, leave out any speculation and get what you need from your desk. Looks like you'll be working out of McLean for a while."

When she got to the NCTC two hours later, the man called Bayer met her personally outside his office, made small-talk about old times for a minute or two and then welcomed Chan to Task Force Pineapple. He noted the surprised look on her face and explained that they'd been connecting the intercept and intelligence dots in parallel to her own investigations. There was little doubt at the NCTC that Col. Ibrahim, Ignacio Felodon and Pineapple where the same guy and he wanted everything she had that might help find him in a hurry.

"And you've got Shake Davis poking around the Philippines looking for this guy?" Chan was a little dazed by it. "Why draft Shake into all this?"

"Turns out Shake knew the guy fairly well way back when. They worked together on a mobile training team in the Philippines. Shake was in on a hostage rescue of some American missionaries and eventually got decorated for his actions by the Philippine government. We figured he could call in a few favors, nose around a little on the extreme inside and see if this Abu Sayyaf guerilla leader might just be Ignacio Felodon working for the bad guys down around Mindinao. We got a report from him this morning. He thinks his guy is our guy."

"Well, that's valuable intelligence, but why the flap? What's Colonel Ibrahim or Felodon up to that's got everybody wrapped around an axle?"

"That's what Task Force Pineapple is working on right now." Bayer grabbed Chan Dwyer by the elbow and led her toward a conference room at the end of the hallway on the executive level of the building. "Let's get you briefed and download what you've been able to find on your own. This is scary stuff, Chan, and I'm asking for best efforts from everyone involved."

All that was yesterday and at the end of a long and tiring day, some task force principals were ordered to re-convene the following morning at CIA headquarters in Langley. Apparently, Task Force Pineapple was struggling to move from analysis to action. High-level and highly classified briefings were being given to government heavyweights all over town but the center of gravity seemed to be the CIA, where the National Clandestine Service had been alerted for imminent action.

Chan Dwyer drained her coffee cup and checked her watch. She needed to get back on the road. She was pre-cleared for entry at Langley but the process was never slick or short. She wanted to be on time and at her best for this meeting. If she knew anything for sure about how The Company worked in these situations, it wouldn't be long before an action brief was developed and agents were headed for the field. She was determined to be one of those agents. Chan Dwyer was primed for action and the rush running through her system had nothing to do with the coffee drink she'd just consumed.

U.S. Embassay, Jakarta, Indonesia

Mike Stokey followed the sergeant from the Marine Security Guard Detachment into the embassy's secure communication facility and plopped his notebook on the horseshoe-shaped table that formed the centerpiece of the stuffy room. "Any chance for a cup of American coffee, Sergeant? I've had about all the green tea I can stand for one lifetime."

"No sweat, sir." The sergeant nodded sympathetically and headed for the door. "The Gunny can't stand that shit either. He makes us keep a pot of Maxwell House brewing 24/7. I'll get you a pot and a cup."

Stokey eyed the sophisticated telephone console at the far end of the table: "When you get back with the coffee, I'll need you to show me how to load and fire on this telephone thing. I need a secure line to the States and no interruptions."

While he waited for coffee Stokey flipped through his notes and decided his initial conclusions were correct. He'd been poking around Indonesia for a week but he could have saved himself a lot of trouble and gastric distress if he'd just trusted his instincts and called Bayer earlier. There was no doubt in his mind that he'd found a link after just two days among the students and staff at the Islamic University of Riau. He had missing scientists of the True Believer persuasion and the right specialties. He had a Philippine connection and maybe even the beginnings of a trail. He should have just called it in and headed out to sniff around the track but the undercover intel game wasn't played that way if you wanted to survive it. His cover as the visiting administrator of a worldwide scientific scholarship fund required him to spend the extra time listening to endless pitches for the big bucks he was purportedly ready to disburse among worthy Indonesian scholars. That done and the links established it was time to bring Bayer and the staffers up to speed.

Stokey was frowning at the phone console when the Marine sergeant arrived with a pot of coffee and condiments on an aluminum tray. "It looks like something out of Star Trek, sir, but it's pretty straightforward." The NCO pointed at a red button at the top of a long row of buttons on the console. "This line is direct to the State Department operator in Washington. You give 'em a number and priority code and they hook you up scrambled and secure. Nothing goes through local trunks or the embassy switchboard. Comm guys check it daily and sweep the area for bugs. Think you can manage?"

"Well, I'm just barely competent on a standard cell phone." Stokey poured coffee and then picked up the handset. "But I'll give it a shot. Where will you be if I need help?"

"Right outside the door, sir." The sergeant plucked a pager off his duty belt and laid it down beside the phone console. "If you need me, just press the button and I'll come running."

It took the Washington operator a couple of minutes to verify his priority code and connect him with Bayer wherever he was Stateside at this hour. Stokey was into a second cup of coffee when he finally heard Bayer pick up and initiate a scrambler on his end. Following a series of electronic squawks and beeps, Bayer came through loud and clear as if he was sitting in the same room. Stokey stabbed at a button on the phone console marked with a speaker icon, slumped back in his chair and lifted his feet onto the table.

"Hey, Bob, I think we've got a handle on the players. Three top guys at the university are MIA: one bio-chemical department head, one microbiologist and one geneticist." Stokey checked his notes and found the page he wanted. "Break out your ink-stick and stand by to copy: Susilo Nasuton, Ahmed Suharo and Galan Wahid." Stokey spelled each of the names and then fell silent while Bayer took his own set of notes on the other end of the line.

"I'll run 'em right away but given the disciplines, it sounds like they'd be involved in something like this. And all devout Muslims, right?"

"Roger your last. And sources tell me they are all members of the university's Muslim Brotherhood organization. That's the surface story. These guys are also big-time members of Jemaah Islamiya. You know what means."

"Uh-huh, the science arm of the worldwide movement. Nerve gas research, explosive-formed penetrators on IEDs, the whole shot. Any idea where they went?"

"Philippines. No surprise there, I guess. Puts 'em in Ibrahim's ballpark. I got two separate sources who say they left aboard a yacht out of Jakarta. Supposedly they are all working on some sort of aquaculture project. If that don't set your alarms off, you ain't listening."

"You have any trouble getting people to talk?"

"Nah, the university administration was under some pressure over the work these guys were doing. Seems they were fooling around with stuff that scared the shit out of certain parties in the government. I couldn't get specifics but it doesn't take a genius to figure out what it was. Scary stuff—read botulism—and even the mullahs weren't happy with that. They were anxious to convince me that nothing like that was allowed on their campus and no scholarship money would be spent in that area of research. The cover worked like a charm. That's the good news."

"And the bad news?"

"The bad news is that my same two sources swear their missing colleagues were intending to continue their research and experiments in the Philippines. And they had money to burn from sources unknown with very deep pockets. That pretty well nails it, I'd guess."

"Shit." Bayer exhaled in frustration and Stokey heard the springs in an office chair on the other side of the world squeak loudly. "So now we've got three scientists, likely to be fooling around with botulism, in the Philippines where they are reported to be consorting with known Abu Sayyaf operators."

"Has Shake found out anything over there?"

"He's fairly sure Colonel Ibrahim is Ignacio Felodon, one and the same. Interesting back story there. I'll send it to you in an email. Anyway, we're confident they aren't in the Philippines anymore. They key question is where are they now."

"I might have a lead on that." Stokey flipped through his notes to a page containing the results of an interview with one of Galan Wahid's former lab assistants. "But it doesn't make much sense."

"Whatever it is, it's better than what we've got right now, which is zip-point-shit."

"I talked to one of his lab assistants, female, who I think has the hots for her boss and maybe vice versa. She got a post card from Galan Wahid—one of those touristy things from Koror. That's in the Palau Islands. When I finish up here, I'm gonna make my way out there and poke around a little."

"Hold off on that, Mike. Let's take it a step at a time. You meet up with Shake in the Philippines and debrief him on this Felodon thing. I think that guy is the key here. I'll talk to Langley, get it cleared and let Shake know to expect you soonest."

"Where is he? Manila?"

"He's down on Mindinao trying to verify what he's found out so far. Meet him there and do the debrief. We get a handle on Felodon and we can start taking it apart one piece at a time. This is no one-man band. So, what's the hook-up between Felodon and these missing scientists? Who's footing the bill? What are they planning? I think Felodon's the answer to those questions."

"What about the Palaus deal? If they're out there somewhere dicking around with bio weapons, we need to get on 'em in a hurry and shut it down."

"It's all about time and resources, Mike. You know that. A postcard from Koror is interesting but it doesn't mean they are set up and operating out there. They've got a fucking yacht, for Christ's sake. They could be anywhere. You got any details on the boat?"

"Not much. It was apparently big and luxurious, kind of like some rich guy's plaything. Nobody knew anything much about it and I didn't want to press too hard. You could check with the Coasties or Pacific Fleet. My bet is you'll find something that fits with a Middle Eastern registration."

"Yeah, could be. I'll get onto the International Maritime Organization. A thing that size would be hard to hide but there's a lot of ocean and a lot of big boats out there. Maybe I can get the Navy to over-fly the Palaus and take a look for us."

"OK. I'll head for Mindinao...but I still think I'd be more useful following up on the Palaus thing."

"Leave it with me, Mike. We're ginning up a task force from Clandestine Services and special ops assets in the area. If the trail leads to the Palaus, we'll be on 'em in a hurry."

Stokey sat up and poured himself another cup of coffee. "Bob, I work for Clandestine Services. Remember? I am one of those assets and I'm damn near in place out here."

"You'll be closer in the Philippines than you are in Jakarta. If these assholes are fooling around with bio-weapons in the Palaus, we'll know it before long."

"I read the reports from the science team and the action brief from your boss. We may not have much time to fart around with investigations and cross-checks. We need to nail these fuckers before they find a way to poison a lot of people."

"I'm on it. Call me from the Philippines after you've talked to Davis."

"I want in on this thing, Bob. Don't try to cut me out of the action."

"Shake Davis said something similar in his last report. You guys are a pair to draw to. Head for the Philippines. I'll be in touch."

Stokey broke the connection, picked up the pager and mashed the call button. The Marine sergeant pushed through the security door in seconds and walked over to check the level of coffee in the pot.

"More coffee, sir?"

"Yeah, but let's get it in the cafeteria. And then you can introduce me to whoever handles travel arrangements around here. I need to be on the road early in the morning."

Jolo Island, Autonomous Region of Muslim Mindinao

He was older now, a little slower and more deliberate in his movements, but SgtMaj. Jubal Mariano still slithered like a snake through the jungle. Shake Davis smiled and tried to keep up with his old friend who was wearing well-worn civilian clothing and headed for a village less than a click inshore from the beach where the Philippine Navy PT boat had dropped them off a half hour earlier. Mariano was certain they'd find a lead to Felodon, aka Col. Ibrahim, in that village. His source was a devout Muslim. He was also a hard-headed merchant who never passed a chance to turn a buck regardless of source, creed, race or religion. And SgtMaj. Mariano had a pocket full of JSOT bucks from the command's slush fund used to buy, bribe or suborn sources throughout the southern archipelago.

Thrashing around in militant Muslim badlands seemed a little risky when Mariano suggested it two days ago at Davao, but the veteran guerilla fighter insisted it was vital if they wanted to get a feel for what Felodon might have been up to on Jolo. The trip was strictly a Philippine Constabulary Special Action Force deal, but before the JSOT signed off on it, two Army SF troopers were assigned to go along as gun-guards. Green Beret SFCs Tony Labella and Dave Martinez knew the lay of the land on Jolo. They also knew how to handle the weapons they were carrying loaded and locked at Shake's back as the patrol approached the Muslim village. In exchange for an intel dump on their observations while tracking Col. Ibrahim on Jolo, Shake told the two NCOs everything he knew about what might be at stake.

When Mariano signaled a halt to do a solo reconnaissance on the outskirts of the village, Shake automatically stepped off the trail and took a knee facing outboard. Old habits were impossible to break under the circumstances but he felt a little silly with nothing in his hands but an old machete. He turned to see Labella and Martinez also on a knee forming a three-point security perimeter with him. They were in the same alert posture, but they had M-4 carbines to point in the direction of potential threats.

He heard a chuckle and looked over his shoulder to see Martinez grinning at him. "Hey, Mister Davis...you can take the soldier out of the bush..."

"But you can't take the bush out of the soldier," Labella chimed in from across the trail. "Some fired-up Tango comes screaming out of the ville, you just go prone, sir. We'll pop his ass and then you can use that blade to cut off his ears."

"That's what Marines did in the Nam, right sir?" Martinez picked up the thread and tugged at an earlobe. "We've seen all the stuff on the cable about you bad-ass Jarheads back in the day." Both NCOs were grinning and waiting for Shake to take the bait. They'd been on his case in the Doggies versus Gyrenes mode since they got underway from Zamboanga headed for Jolo.

Some things never change...nor should they, Shake thought, as he ran a thumb along the sharp edge of the machete and fixed the soldiers with an evil leer. "You fucking green beanies just don't get it. Ears rot and stink. We used to just cut off their balls...and eat 'em."

Shake turned his attention back to the village but there wasn't much to see. Mariano had disappeared inside a cinder-block building that looked like some sort of general store at the center of a group of surrounding makeshift structures. Somewhere inside he hoped Mariano was exchanging cash for information he wanted badly. He let his mind wander and reviewed the conversation he'd had with SgtMaj. Jubal Mariano in the bar at the JSOT compound shortly after Shake arrived on Mindinao from Luzon. They'd spent four San Miguel beers catching up on lives and times and then focused on Ignacio Felodon. The more Shake revealed about what U.S. intelligence sources suspected, the more Jubal Mariano seemed to confirm that the infamous Col. Ibrahim could be involved.

* * *

"He was a very angry man, sir. Very angry, and he blamed the government in Manila for what happened to his family."

"That's understandable, Jubal. And I guess you can sort of understand why the government would kick him out of the country. The only other option was to put him on trial and deal with all the stink that would involve."

"So he ended up in Vietnam. I heard a number of things from various refugees and Vietnamese sources who travel back and forth from Hanoi to the Philippines. In fact, when he left Vietnam, I was the first one to know about it. I reported it to the National Command Authority but there was no...what do you call it? No feedback?"

"He left Vietnam? OK. Where did he go? Back here to Mindinao? Is that when he started this Muslim militant deal?"

"Oh no, sir, he didn't come back until later, maybe a year later, and nobody knew he was here on Mindinao. At least nobody that knew Lieutenant Colonel Ignacio Felodon was Colonel Ibrahim, the Abu Sayyaf chieftain. I tried to tell them what I suspected, but they were more interested in other things. And no one wanted to believe the Moros would accept a Christian man like Ignacio as one of their own."

"How did he pull that off?"

"The Moros needed a leader with military experience and Ignacio proved himself quite capable in a number of skirmishes with government forces. In my opinion, the Abu Sayyaf cells knew he was not a Muslim but they were happy to go along with the charade as long as their Colonel Ibrahim kept winning fights for them. In the end, he had the same motivations they do. Why argue with that? Among the Moros down here, an infidel who fights at your side is as good as a True Believer."

"Jesus, Jubal. We never learn, do we?"

"We learn when we get burned, sir. That's the way it is. You know that."

"Yeah, I do. And when we get burned we wonder why nobody saw the fire. But the guy we knew doesn't seem like the type who would get involved in biological war stuff. That's pretty sophisticated. And he's a fairly simple, straight-ahead soldier. He knows that's bad mojo that can get out of control in a hurry. You don't fuck around with it no matter what your motivation is."

"Sometimes your gut overrules your common sense, sir. And you know that as well as anyone."

"OK, Jubal, but there's a lot of science involved. Your standard soldier doesn't understand all that stuff. He doesn't know how to develop bio-weapons, right?"

"Yes, unless someone teaches him, sir, unless someone suggests a way that a simple soldier can employ the germs as a weapon."

"And who would have done that with Felodon? Someone in Vietnam, is that what you're suggesting here?"

"Ignacio Felodon was turned over to the Russians, sir."

"He was what?"

"And from the Russians to the Iranians...the Quds Force, I believe. And they have been working on biological warfare for years. I think if Ignacio is involved in something like this, he got his education—and his ideas—from Tehran. It makes sense to me."

"Jesus Christ, Jubal! Did you report any of this?"

"Of course I did, sir. But I am an enlisted man here in the Philippines. The big dogs rarely hear the barking of the little dogs. And there was no reason until now to believe Col. Ibrahim was anything more than just a skilled Moro fighter causing local troubles."

"Jubal, I really need some hard information here. What do you suggest?"

"I suggest we visit Jolo, sir. I have a source there that I've used many times."

"Is he reliable?"

"He's very well-connected, sir. He was the one who told me about Ignacio's involvement with the Russians and the

Iranians. He loves to talk when it is safe for him to do so. And he's a greedy bastard."

"What's your guess, Jubal? Is Ignacio Felodon, or Colonel Ibrahim, capable of or likely to try something like a biological warfare attack?"

"He is both motivated and capable. And his target would be the Philippines."

"Maybe his initial target would be, but this kind of thing can get out of control in a hurry. This is bigger than just a threat to the Philippines, Jubal."

"If you wish to know what I think..." Jubal Mariano stared out a window and pondered the sliver of moon rising over Mindinao. "There are too many ignorant people with their heads buried in the sand. I can show you copies of the reports I submitted on this man and my suspicions about him. Three times I reported these things and no one wanted to believe me. I could have found Ignacio Felodon and killed him a year ago and we would not be facing this situation."

Shake simply nodded his understanding and acknowledged Mariano's resentment. It was yet another example of the hubris that infected top flights of the intelligence community, with self-centered bureaucrats ignoring red flags simply because they were waved by low-level guys down at the bottom of the pecking order. He'd seen it before and there was no excuse for it.

"And I'll tell you something else I think, sir. Whatever he is doing now, Ignacio Felodon is no longer the avenging angel. He is simply a tool, you understand? He is being used."

"You're probably right, Jubal. But the guys who sent me out here are listening now. That's for damn sure. If there's an attack coming, the bigger questions are what, when and how?"

U.S. Central Intelligence Agency, Langley, Virginia

It took nearly two days of marathon meetings among players from all elements of the intelligence, security, law enforcement and military special operations communities but they'd eventually managed a draft of what was called an "action initiative." Most of that time was spent in finger-pointing, badge-thumping and jurisdictional disputes but none of the representatives at the table were arguing that the threat wasn't real or pressing. They'd all pored over the scientific findings, heard the hypotheticals from the Centers for Disease Control and pondered the field reports on the suspected roster of players. They'd listened with growing apprehension when the military biological warfare experts from the National Interagency Biodefense Command at Ft. Detrick, Maryland, were brought in to make their what-if predictions. The consensus was clear. Something serious and significant had to be done in a hurry. The question now before them was what, and by whom?

There had been some early arguments for an international task force given the potential worldwide nature of the threat. Bayer and several others who had been through that ponderous and contentious drill quickly nixed the idea. Where they might be helpful, allied intelligence services would be briefed on the situation. No one wanted the U.S. accused of withholding critical information, especially if a serious biological weapon was triggered despite best efforts to keep it from happening. On the other hand, given what they all now agreed needed to be done, American assets were available and reliable.

By the end of the dinner break on day two, a Presidential Finding arrived by courier from the White House. Given what he'd heard from his National Security Advisor and the Secretary of Homeland Security added to the reports from various agencies concerned, the chief executive pulled the trigger on a fully funded and totally covert operation with a simple mission: Find these guys, confirm what they are doing and put a prompt stop to it...under control of the NCTC, with full access to required assets of the CIA and Special Operations Command. Bayer now had the ball and full authority to call the play.

He promptly adjourned the full council and called for a sidebar with the agency's chief of Clandestine Services and a Navy SEAL captain from Special Operations Command. In less than an hour, using nothing more sophisticated than secure cell phones and a couple of yellow legal pads, they formed a dedicated task force and developed an initial plan of immediate action. Bayer fed the draft of the action initiative into a nearby shredder and headed for the door. He had some serious mountains to move but at least they were out of the locker room and onto the field.

Chan Dwyer caught his elbow before he could reach the executive elevator. "Mr. Bayer, sorry to bother you, but I was wondering, who do I have to sleep with to get my name on the go-list for this thing?"

Bayer showed a grin that rapidly turned into a belly-laugh. "Chan, you're a piece of work." He felt the tension of the past two days rushing up through his system and hoped he didn't appear hysterical. "What makes you think there's a go-list?"

She nodded toward the other end of the corridor where the senior SEAL and the man from Clandestine Services were comparing notes with cell phones glued to their ears. "You blew off all the suits. Those guys are the grunts, or at least the guys who own the grunts. We're going after the assholes and I can help."

"How so? And better be convincing. This has got to go down quickly with minimum fuss. There's no room for excess observers."

"OK, sir. Bullet-points only: I've been on this Colonel Ibrahim thing up to my eyeballs for months. I know the major player and his teammates. I'm hard-wired into the nexus for rapid intel from all sources, military and civilian. I'm also a graduate of the chemical, biological, radiological and nuclear officer's course at Fort Leonard Wood—emphasis there on biological. And I'm an experienced field agent. You might not remember me, but I was on the team that recovered the Laos File."

"I read the reports, Chan. Shake Davis and Mike Stokey spoke very highly of you and your efforts in Hanoi and points south."

"There's another bullet-point, sir. I know the players on both sides."

"I'm too tired to argue this right now..."

"Then don't, sir. Just put me on the list. I'll pull my weight. That's a guarantee."

Bayer checked the fire in Chan Dwyer's dark eyes and then checked his watch. "Let me think about this overnight. I've got to get out of here and set some things in motion. You'll hear from me in the morning, one way or the other."

He'd just managed to nod off as his driver negotiated nighttime traffic between Langley and McLean when a vibrating phone in his shirt pocket brought him out of the fog. He checked the caller ID and shook his head. She was nothing if not persistent.

"Chan, I haven't even gotten back to my office yet. I said I'd call you in the morning."

"Sorry, sir, but it's not about that. We just got a hit from that recon flight you ordered yesterday. I thought you'd want to know about it soonest."

"Did they find the boat?"

"Looks like it, sir. Fits the description you gave. It was apparently milling around west of the Palau Islands."

"Great. Assuming the Navy got hull numbers or whatever yachts carry, ask them to find out who owns the thing."

"I did that, sir. Response came in just before I called. It's a 74-meter yacht named Al Calipha, Saudi flag, registered owner is PanArabia International out of Jeddah. Last port of call was two days ago in Koror."

"What the hell is PanArabia International?"

"Also ran that before I called you, sir. It's a mega-conglomerate involved in construction, real estate and—what else—petroleum exploration and production. And here's the kicker, Mr. Bayer: One of the principals is Prince Mohammed al-Azizi, a member of the royal house and a big player in the radical madrassa game. We've had him on the radar for quite a while."

"Nice report, Chan. Thanks."

"It's what I do, sir."

"Yeah, I guess so. Pack lightly, Chan. You'll be hearing from someone in my office before noon tomorrow."

Jolo Island, Autonomous Region of Muslim Mindinao

Sergeant Major Jubal Mariano appeared as he intended as he left the village store carrying a nylon-mesh bag full of fresh fruit, a carton of local smokes and a few other items that might be in short supply on a fishing boat anchored offshore. Unless you knew better or suspected something unusual, the man strolling away from the village was just another of the local fishermen who visited the merchant occasionally to restock supplies before heading back out for the deep-water fishing areas south of Jolo.

Mariano was an old hand at this kind of dicey undercover work. He'd even gone so far as to smear himself with fish oil before heading for a meeting with his source in the village so he'd smell like a working fisherman. Apparently the ragged, salt-encrusted clothing and stench of gutted fish wasn't enough this time. As the constabulary NCO made a right turn onto the path where Shake and the two SF soldiers waited, he neither paused nor looked left or right. He drew abreast of the patrol, made a quick take-cover hand signal that could have been confused for swatting at mosquitoes and whispered a warning.

"Two following. Snatch mission...beach where we landed."

Without missing a step, Mariano hitched his bag onto the opposite shoulder and kept walking. At his back, Shake Davis and SFCs Labella and Martinez melted into the jungle and began a silent speed-run on a parallel path.

By the time SgtMaj. Mariano broke out of the jungle onto the beach, Shake and the SF NCOs had caught fleeting glimpses of the two guerillas following him from the village. They appeared to be Abu Sayaaf standard trigger-pullers; comfortable in the bush, silent and savvy with the folding-stock AK-47s they carried at the ready like veterans. Both guerillas took a knee in the palmetto shrubs where the jungle gave way to a stretch of pristine white sand. They were silently watching Mariano who stood just inshore from the surf line and appeared to be searching the horizon for his boat. After a minute or two, Mariano tossed his bundle on the sand and began to stomp up and down the beach cursing magnificently in Tagalog just like a luckless fisherman whose buddies had abandoned him for some unknown reason.

Keeping a steady eye on the watchers, Shake, Labella and Martinez maneuvered silently as close as they could get to the beach, carefully stopping at a spot where they had a clear view of both Mariano and his two trackers. They settled in about twenty meters to the rear of the two AS guerillas. Labella and Martinez automatically shouldered their carbines and squinted through ACOG sights, instinctively taking up solid sight-pictures. Shake saw their right thumbs moving toward the safety levers and motioned to get their attention. He shook his head vehemently and mouthed the words: “Snatch, take ’em alive.” Both SF NCOs nodded their understanding but kept their weapons shouldered. With the drop on his adversaries and two weapons aimed in on them, Shake was about to shout a challenge when the AS fighter beat him to it.

Keeping their AKs leveled at the hip and pointing directly at Mariano, the two AS fighters stepped from cover and advanced on Mariano, who did a credible shock-take and fell to his knees as ordered with his hands behind his head. Things had just gotten considerably more complicated. There was now about thirty meters between the good guys and the bad guys who were both pointing their weapons at opposite sides of Mariano’s head with fingers on triggers. Martinez leaned over to whisper in Shake’s ear.

“Better pop ’em, sir.” The shouting on the beach was getting dangerously loud and it looked like the AS folks weren’t buying Mariano’s protestations of innocence. “Two head-shots, easy range from here.”

Shake pondered and rejected the suggestion. Even with two solid hits, there was a good chance one or both of the guerillas might spasm on a trigger. He didn’t want to chance it with his old friend. “Let me see if I can distract them.” Shake moved toward the spot closer to the beach that had been recently vacated by the men now screaming questions at Mariano. “If it looks bad, take your shots.”

He found a small rotten coconut in the palmetto patch and hefted it to judge what it might take to splash it into the surf line. These guys were clearly edgy. If he created a noise from one direction and then a distraction from another direction, there might be a chance to take them down without having to kill them. For some reason, Mariano thought they should be taken prisoner and that was good enough for him. He checked the two soldiers at his back and noted that they'd moved to give themselves a clear field of fire. And then he heaved the coconut as hard as he could.

As he'd hoped, both men whirled seaward when the nut splashed into the water. At that moment, Shake stood up and screamed. “Drop your weapons or you're dead!” Also as he expected, both AS fighters spun toward him at the sound of his shout.

What he didn't expect was that both of them would cut loose and empty their magazines in his direction. Fortunately, neither man had bothered to unfold the stock on his weapon and fired without aiming. Shake dropped flat and gritted his teeth as twenty or thirty rounds of 7.62x39mm ammo chopped into the palmetto and showered him with vegetation. Despite the ringing in his ears, he clearly heard a single pop from an M-4 at his rear and the sound of meat thudding into meat from the direction of the beach.

With no more rounds incoming Shake slowly stood up to assess the situation. One guerilla was sprawled on the sand leaking blood from what looked like a high chest or shoulder hit. He was alive. The other man was flat on his ass and staring defiantly at the muzzle of his own weapon which was pointed directly at his nose and aimed by SgtMaj. Jubal Mariano. Labella and Martinez, weapons at the high ready, advanced by the palmetto patch and stepped onto the beach. Labella stripped flex-cuffs out of a pocket and moved to hog-tie the guerillas while Martinez and Mariano kept them covered.

"This one will make it." Labella examined the wounded guerilla and reached for a bag of instant clotting powder in his first-aid kit. "Assuming you want him to survive. It's your call."

"Patch the asshole up best you can, Tony. And let's get these guys moved off the beach. We're gonna need a new plan here."

* * *

"My source was not there." SgtMaj. Mariano sucked on a cigarette and pointed at the two prisoners who were propped up on either side of a palm tree in a clearing they'd found deeper in the jungle. "These two were hanging around watching me from a back room."

"Did you get anything at all?"

Jubal Mariano smiled, plucked a mango from the mesh bag and began to peel it. "I got some very nice fruit. You should try some." When the three Americans selected a piece of fruit and began to eat, he continued the story.

"It was difficult to push too hard, but I did get some interesting information from the merchant's daughter. She's running the store now."

"What happened to her father?"

"Dead. Apparently from some mysterious illness. He died suddenly and in great pain about three days ago, right after his dinner."

"Oh, shit!" Davis cut a look at Labella and Martinez. "Tell me it wasn't a fish dinner."

"It was." Mariano finished his mango and tossed the remnants at the pair of guerillas who were stoically ignoring the conversation. "And whatever killed my source also killed his son. Fortunately, for the daughter and her mother, the men always eat first. When the women saw what happened, they decided to go hungry that evening. The daughter told me there is a big problem in villages along the coast. No one will eat fish."

"That doesn't sound right, Jubal. That's not the way this stuff is supposed to work."

"The daughter told me one last thing, sir. She said the fish that killed her father and her brother came from a small lagoon near her village. It's a place, she said, where fish were trapped and easy to catch, even by hand."

"That fits. Can we take a look at this lagoon?"

Mariano rose and walked over to the unwounded AS guerilla. He jerked the man to his feet and placed that familiar bolo beneath his chin. In minutes they were following the man through the bush and headed west of the village.

* * *

The lagoon was more like a small tidal pool that had been netted with nylon mesh to keep what was inside from getting outside and into open water. Shake could see half a dozen dead fish floating belly-up in the still water. Easily visible below the surface were about a dozen live fish moving in sluggish and erratic patterns. It certainly wasn't a place where he'd go searching for an easy meal, but apparently the locals weren't so squeamish.

"Those are some really fucked up fish, Mr. Davis." SFC Martinez squatted next to the pool and watched the fish for a few seconds while Mariano interrogated the wounded Abu Sayyaf fighter and SFC Labella scouted the surrounding area. "You think they've been infected with that botulism shit?"

"Most likely, Dave." Shake thought it over for a few seconds and decided he didn't know enough about this deal to safely take a sample. "You ever done any frag-fishing?"

"Heard about it; never tried it."

"Time to expand your field experience. You got any grenades?"

"I got three M-67s." Martinez touched a dump-pouch hanging from the right side of his webbing. "I think maybe Fat Tony's got a couple more."

"I'll go find him. Then you guys frag the shit out of this pool. Fish should all float to the top. When we've got 'em all, we'll scoop 'em out of the water, dig a hole and bury 'em."

"Copy all, Mr. Davis, but I think I'll make some kind of gig out of the bamboo around here. I'm not real anxious to be handling these fucking fish."

SFC Labella was standing near the wreckage of a Honda generator using the toe of his boot to move bits and pieces around on the ground. "This was the power source, Mr. Davis. Here's the transformer and the wires run to a tin-roof hooch right past that stand of bamboo."

Shake followed Labella through the bamboo and did a quick search of a long, screened structure that reminded him of the standard hard-back SEA huts so familiar from base areas in Vietnam. At least three men had lived in this structure. Shake spotted the bamboo-sprung sleeping platforms inside and three banyan stumps neatly-arranged around a fire pit to the left hooch. He was snapping some digital photographs of benches that had obviously served as platform for equipment of some kind when Labella stuck his head inside the door.

"Found this out near the fire pit." Labella showed a small aluminum case secured with a snap-latch. "It's got slides inside. Same kind of stuff we used in high school biology. That tell you anything?"

"Tells me whoever was fucking around out here knew how to use a microscope. You find anything else?"

"Some smashed up Petri dishes and other lab type stuff that I didn't want to handle. Also found five positions in a semicircle anchored on the water; standard security perimeter. I'd say no more than ten people here at any time. And a dime will get you a dollar that two of 'em were the dudes we saw leaving Jolo with Ibrahim."

"How come you guys never spotted this place?"

"Too much ground, too few people, who the fuck knows." Labella handed over the box of slides and shrugged. "We were focused on HVTs and that meant Colonel Ibrahim.

Every time he was spotted, we put a recon tail on him but as far as I know, he never came near this area while he was on Jolo."

"He's a savvy sonofabitch. He was when I knew him and it looks like that didn't change when he switched sides. Likely he knew you were on his tail and he avoided this spot to keep you from finding what was going on here, at least until the day they decided to get the hell out of Dodge."

"Yeah, likely I guess. And that means whatever was going on here was pretty important to him. Don't look good does it, sir?"

"Looks like something we need to report in a hurry, Tony. Let's get that fish farm destroyed and then you can call our ride. I need to retrieve my laptop and write up a report on all this stuff."

While Labella and Martinez dumped hand grenades in the water and gigged dead fish, Shake consulted with Jubal Mariano on the result of his interrogation. After they'd been given a close-up look at Mariano's bolo, both AS guerillas decided a long stretch in a Philippine prison was the lesser of two evils and sang like jungle macaws.

"Both of them were on Felodon's payroll, sir. They don't know exactly what was going on but they know it involved fish. And they know there were two Indonesians here for a couple of months. Sometimes they were assigned to security and sometimes they were with patrols that kept people away from the area. About a week ago, they were told the place was to be abandoned and they got paid extra to clean it up, smash everything left behind. Then kill any fish in the pool and bury them."

"How come they didn't kill the fish?"

"The wounded one said they took one look and decided they wanted no part of that. When the merchant and his son died from eating one of those fish, they spread the word to stay away. That's what they were doing at the store in the village."

"OK, Jubal. I'm gonna send a serious rocket up the chain of command as soon as I can get a secure circuit. They damn sure won't ignore it this time. Get both of those bad boys ready to travel. Pick-up boat will be here in about an hour."

Naval Air Station North Island, Coronado, California

Chan Dwyer found the hot-spot in the terminal waiting area and fired up her Toughbook laptop. She was anxious to re-read the report from Shake Davis in the Philippines and she had at least an hour according to the sailors who were loading two large containers of SEAL equipment into a Navy C-40A Clipper parked inside a nearby hangar. Much of what Shake included in his encrypted flash email from Zamboanga was stuff they already knew, so it was clear that Davis was outside the information loop to some extent. Maybe that was intentional; standard need-to-know protocol. Or maybe Bayer intended to just send Shake home with a pat on the back now that they'd moved beyond the initial intelligence gathering phase of the operation. *Good luck with that*, she thought. Shake Davis was as likely to walk away from something like this as he was to appear in public wearing a pink tutu and ballet slippers.

She grinned trying to conjure up that image as she waited for her computer to boot and looked around for Lieutenant Commander Janet Dewey, the only other female on the Task Force go-team. Dewey was a stunning Nordic blond who looked like she'd be just as comfortable in horned helmet and armored breast plate as she was in the Navy working coveralls she wore to last night's pre-deployment briefing at the Naval Special Warfare headquarters on the Coronado Navy Base.

She'd made it difficult for the ten buffed-out bruisers from SEAL Team 1 to pay attention as Lieutenant Kerry Dale Hunter, the SEAL team commander, issued his terse frag order for the trip from North Island to Guam, where they were all apparently going to meet up with a ship that would take them to the Philippines and then on to the Palau Island group. Janet Dewey was the go-team's bio-warfare expert and she'd been impressive during a brief presentation on the bio-hazard protocols that might be required at their destination.

She had also been impressive when Chan introduced herself; mentioned her own military background and speculated that the biggest bio-hazard they might be facing was testosterone overload. "No sweat," Janet Dewey said with a wink. "We get to screwing around with bad-ass bugs and their balls shrink up to the size of BBs." That was clearly not the prevailing situation around the terminal coffee urn where Dewey was currently chatting with all ten of the enlisted SEALS. Presumably, Lt. Hunter was elsewhere supervising the loading of their gear.

Chan was skimming page two of Shake Davis' report when her phone buzzed. Caller ID told her Bob Bayer was calling on his classified office number at NCTC in McLean. He'd promised to call when she'd had a chance to digest the field report from the Philippines.

"Hey, sir. You caught me at North Island. We leave shortly."

"Did you get a look at Shake's report?"

"Yessir, I got a kick out of the dateline: Zamboanga. Couldn't help flashing on Lee Marvin singing that song in the John Wayne movie, *Donovan's Reef*."

"What's that?"

"You know, Lee Marvin is on this tropical island and he sings that song: 'The monkeys have no tails in Zamboanga. The monkeys have no tails; they were bitten off by whales...'"

"Never saw it. What do you make of the Quds Force thing?"

"I'm a little stunned to tell you the truth. It's no big secret that those guys are in the business of exporting terrorism. We found their fingerprints all over the area in Iraq. And we know for a fact that they've been messing around for some time with bio war stuff. But that's all been buried under the hoopla over the Iranian nuke program."

"In your opinion as an intel analyst, could it be that this guy Felodon is working for them? I mean, do they find a shit-canned Filipino, pick him up, school him on bio warfare and then send him out to carry out some grand scheme?"

"I don't know, sir. He'd provide a whole bunch of deniability if they had something like that in mind, but this is way out of their normal ballpark. It's the other side of the world and, well, you could connect them in the overall effort, I guess. You know, worldwide *jihad* and all that garbage. And he would be a very credible cut-out when and if the finger-pointing started."

"What about the Saudi connection? Is there something to that? It's this thing with the yacht that's got me intrigued. Could the Iranians be in bed with the Saudis and they got together and drafted Felodon to conduct an attack? And if so, why? Given motive, means and opportunity they could just do this deal on their own."

"I don't have the answers to all that, sir."

"Well, you're the intel guru on this thing, Chan. We need answers. Whatever else you do out there, stay on this and let's get something formulated. What we do and how we do it is gonna depend on what we know. We'll stop this thing in its tracks, but I want the bastards behind it. That's the long-range goal."

"I'm on it, sir. I'll keep you posted."

"Do that, and do it regularly and often."

Chan Dwyer was poring over page six of Shake Davis' report from Zamboanga when one of the SEALs told her she might want to make a final head-call. They were finished loading now and expected wheels up in twenty minutes.

Peleliu, Palau Islands Group

The Palauan bureaucrat on Babelthaup was apparently as good to his word as money could buy. When Sayed Abdullah and Dr. Susilo Nasuton arrived on Peleliu via the yacht's runabout boat, they were met at the Camp Beck dock by the island's governor. He promised full and enthusiastic support for the aquaculture experimental team he'd been told would be resident on the island for several months. He was also visibly disappointed when Abdullah informed him that none of their team members would be staying in the three or four local establishments that offered lodging on Peleliu. His disappointment was assuaged by an envelope full of cash which, Abdullah informed the governor, was the first of regular weekly payments he'd receive. And there were assurances quickly made that a similar amount of cash would be spread around the island in purchasing supplies and paying for local labor.

The workers from the nearby settlement of Dibel were all paid cash to help unload Dr. Nasuton's equipment. They hauled it to a secluded cove just up the island's west coast, north of Peleliu's three World War II landing beaches. By nightfall on the day of their arrival, a scientific base camp was established. Abdullah briefed the operatives and then turned them all loose to explore the island's five square miles and spread a little cash around Peleliu. Part of the Quds Force security team would keep an eye on the scientists and the rest would conduct an area reconnaissance of the high ground to the rear of their campsite.

It was marked on their satellite maps as the Umurbrogol Massif, a collection of jungle-covered, coral ridges and valleys where some of the bloodiest fighting on the island took place during World War II. Over the private protests of the Quds Force security team leader and in an attempt to keep Col. Ibrahim pacified, he put the Filipino in charge of that mission. The *Humlet*, or village chief of nearby Dibel, assured him that the generators would be fueled and functioning before dark. Dr. Nasuton wanted access to the island's local power, so Abdullah forked over some cash to hire a local electrician and pay for the necessary connections.

By 2130 local time he was able to signal the Al Calipha to stand off and commence their pre-planned leisurely cruising in a steady circle around the Palau Island group. In the morning local fishermen and divers would emplace the trap nets and the scientists could commence their experiments. Inside a tent, by the light of a bright lantern, he constructed his wireless antenna, established an Internet connection and began to compose his initial progress report to Tehran with an info copy to Riyadh.

Camp Navarro, Zamboanga, Mora Province, Philippines

In the steamy messhall that fed the rear echelon troops of the Philippine Constabulary's 1st Scout Ranger Regiment, Shake Davis and Mike Stokey sat sipping sweet pineapple juice and nibbling on remnants of an excellent lunch. SgtMaj. Jubal Mariano had arranged for them to stay at the headquarters of the Western Mindinao Command while they waited for reaction to the report and the evidence sent stateside by official courier from the embassy in Manila.

"Good chow." Stokey fingered a morsel of *lumpia*, dipped it in a spicy sauce and popped it into his mouth. "Beats the shit out of monkey-meat on a stick."

"You're spoiled rotten, Mike." Shake had insisted on a couple of dodgy shish kabobs from a street vendor late in their pub crawl through the seamy side of Zamboanga City last night. "We could have gone with the seafood dinner, but I'm a little put off on the whole fish deal these days."

"Think positive, Shake. We've got a pretty good handle on this deal now. We know the major players and we've got a fairly good idea what they're up to. It's just a matter of finding 'em and shutting 'em down."

"Any word on that?"

"Usual bullshit from the bureaucrats." Stokey checked his phone for messages and shrugged. "Stand by to stand by was the last I heard from Bayer, but nobody's gonna be dragging feet on this thing."

"You really think they're somewhere in the Palaus?"

"Could be, I guess, but it doesn't seem likely. My money's on the yacht. Fucking boat like that would be a perfect floating platform to launch some kind of attack, right? They just motor offshore of a selected target and dump their shit, nobody's any wiser. We'd know a bunch more if Bayer had sent me out there to look around instead of fucking around with you in the Pee Eye."

They were walking toward their assigned rooms at the Camp Navarro Visiting Officers Quarters when SgtMaj. Mariano roared up in an old U.S. surplus M-151 jeep. He jammed on the brakes and motioned for them to get into the vehicle. "There's an aircraft inbound from Guam. You are ordered to meet it at the air base."

As the jeep cleared the main gate of Camp Navarro, Stokey felt his phone vibrating and picked it out of his pocket to read a text message. "Nice of 'em to let us know," he shouted at Shake over the wind blowing through the open jeep. "The aircraft's full of operators from SEAL Team 1. Apparently somebody's got a plan."

* * *

Shake and Mike Stokey watched a Navy C-40A approach, gear and flaps down, on final for a landing at Edwin Andrews Air Base, which served the Philippine commands based around Zamboanga. They were sipping rancid coffee from paper cups on the observation deck of the arrivals lounge while SgtMaj. Mariano paced behind them with a cell phone pressed to his ear. The aircraft was just over the runway threshold when he snapped the phone shut and joined them.

"Thirteen passengers, two of them females." The sergeant major punched out a number on his phone and waited for a response. "I'm told they will be staying here overnight. I'm calling for rooms at Camp Navarro. Will that be OK?"

"Sure." Stokey watched the C-40A pilot grease a landing and roll out past lines of Philippine Air Force OV-10 Warthogs lining the active runway. "Do we meet them here or what?"

Mariano broke off his phone conversation and pointed at a van rolling toward them. "The aircraft is being put inside a hangar on the far side of the field. We meet them there."

The van fell into formation with a checkered follow-me truck and crossed the duty runway. In the distance through the heat-shimmers rising off the airfield taxi apron, Shake and Stokey watched an aircraft tug push the Navy transport into a remote hangar. There was a squad of Philippine Constabulary sentries taking positions around the building as they got out of the van and strolled inside the darkened hangar. A set of air-stairs had been rolled up to the fuselage and they could see figures milling around inside, but their eyes were still adjusting to the light change and it was hard to distinguish details.

"Gunner Davis and Mister Stokey?" A tall, stocky individual dressed in khakis and a nondescript polo shirt approached with his hand extended. "I'm Lieutenant Kerry Dale Hunter, gents, Detachment OIC from Team 1 at Coronado."

They shook hands and watched the remaining passengers sort through the personal baggage being unloaded from the plane. Shake introduced SgtMaj. Mariano who reported that their accommodations were ready at Camp Navarro and inquired about gear or cargo that might need to be offloaded.

"My guys will handle that, Sergeant Major. I'm told there's a secure lockup right here in the hangar?"

"Yes sir. And the hangar will be guarded around the clock. I'll direct your men to the security area." Mariano trundled off toward a waiting forklift operator and Lt. Hunter turned his attention back to the two Americans.

"I've got a team of ten shooters and two specialists," Hunter made a vague gesture toward the dark interior of the hangar. "And I have a mission brief for you, Mr. Stokey, whenever and wherever you say."

"Call me, Mike," Stokey grinned. "And I'd guess the best time for that would be after you folks have had a chance to clean up and ingest a cold beer. We'll arrange a secure area out at Camp Navarro."

Shake was about to question his status in all that when a shout from the far side of the aircraft interrupted. "Holy shit! I know that voice."

"You'd *better* know it!" Chan Dwyer dashed across the hangar floor and wrapped her arms around Shake. "How the hell are you?"

"Well...dazed and confused pretty well covers it." Shake pushed her away gently and took a good look at the woman who had been on his mind and out of his life for so long. She was as gorgeous as ever; an enticing mix of genetic strains that resulted in an exotic beauty imbued with tensile strength. Chan gave him a kiss on the cheek, hugged Mike Stokey and then stepped away to examine them full-length. "Well, the years take their toll...except on you two." She ran her hand through Shake's crop of white hair and smiled. "Maybe a little more snow on the mountain top, but you both look like you can still go the distance."

"You are as gorgeous as ever, Chan." Stokey chimed in to cover for Shake who was clearly in a state of shock. "What are you doing here with all these snake-eaters?"

"I'm the intel officer on this deal. And have I got some information for you guys. As they say in the biz, you're not gonna believe this shit."

"Let's save that for the brief." Lt. Hunter moved off toward his SEALs who were supervising the unloading of two large cargo containers. "In fact, as of now, we don't discuss anything unless we're in a secure location." He stopped, turned and pointed a finger. "That would be in the nature of a direct order, Chan."

Chan Dwyer nodded and followed him to the pile of baggage where she picked up her personal gear and followed the SEALs into a waiting bus. Shake Davis and Mike Stokey piled into the step-van and followed when the bus wheeled away from the hangar. Stokey made small talk on the way back to Camp Navarro, but Shake didn't catch much of it. He was dealing with a confusing jumble of memories and emotions. Assuming they didn't screw the pooch on this mission and all die of some horrible disease, he was determined to find a way to make Chan Dwyer a more permanent part of the rest of his life.

* * *

Less than two hours after touchdown on Mindinao, the Operation Pineapple Task Force was fed, watered and headed for a briefing area secured for them by SgtMaj. Mariano as the last act of his temporary additional duty assignment. The veteran Philippine Constabulary NCO was ordered to report back to headquarters in Davao City, where his commanding officer and a contingent from Manila were waiting to hear the results of his investigation into the identity and recent activities of the infamous Col. Ibrahim. Shake Davis and Mike Stokey went along to see him off at the Zamboanga air base.

"Something tells me they'll be listening to you this time." Shake gave his old friend a hug and a gym bag full of hard-to-find goodies they'd picked up at the base canteen. Stokey had stuffed an envelope full of spare Philippine pesos into the bag that amounted to more than Mariano earned in a year of service pay. It would be nice surprise for the veteran guerilla fighter and his family.

"If I know what comes next, it won't make much difference," said Mariano as he climbed into the Philippine Air Force UH-1N warming up on the ready pad. "It's an American problem now and my seniors will gladly close the file on Ignacio Felodon." Jubal Mariano buckled himself into the web seat and smiled. "He's a dangerous man, my friend. If you come into contact with Felodon, don't hesitate to kill him."

* * *

There were two Philippine Marine sentries cradling M-4 carbines outside the double-door entry to a secluded cinderblock structure as the jeep carrying Shake and Stokey back from the airbase cleared the razor wire perimeter surrounding the classified corner of Camp Navarro. Lt. Hunter was outside the entry conferring with his senior petty officer who had just finished a security sweep.

"Area is clean, Boss, and all hands are inside except for Mr. Stokey and Gunner Davis." Chief Special Warfare Operator Frank "Lurch" Wiley jerked a thumb over his shoulder at the two Americans getting out of a jeep pulling up to the curb. "And here they come now. You got anything else for me?"

"Nah, this will be a quick and dirty frag order. We'll be out of here in a half-hour, shakedown the gear and then wheels up for Guam in the morning. No liberty for anybody, Chief. We're in full lock-down as of now. You can take the jeep and get 'em a case or two of beer, but nobody drifts outside the wire for any reason."

"Aye, aye, sir. How you gonna handle Gunner Davis?"

"Very delicately. You go back inside and check to see everybody's got their shit together."

Chief Wiley nodded at Shake and Stokey as they approached and then ducked inside the building. Lt. Hunter stepped out to meet them holding a lanyard with a classified area visitor's pass which he handed to Stokey. The lack of a second pass wasn't lost on Shake Davis.

"You're one short on those things, Lieutenant. Or are you trying to tell me something?"

Lt. Hunter tapped a sophisticated mobile phone in a holster clipped to his belt. "It's nothing personal, Gunner. You know how it goes on these deals. I checked with higher and they said absolutely no access for anyone not officially assigned to the mission."

Stokey saw a familiar red blush creeping up Shake's neck and put a placating hand on his friend's elbow. "Easy, Shake, he doesn't make the rules."

"Well, maybe he should. Maybe it's high time the operators on the ground made the rules instead of playing cover-your-ass and calling the bean-counters in the rear." Shake shook off the restraining hand and stepped into drill instructor range of the SEAL officer, who was standing his ground but showing a distinct backward lean.

"Lieutenant, it would be rude of me to remind you I've got more time on a firebase crapper than you've got in combat. It would be unbecoming of me to point out that I've got more time on a medevac slab than you've got in the Navy. In fact, I don't want to embarrass you by saying that I was doing sneaky-pete, snake-eater shit while you were still learning your alphabet. So I won't do that. What I *will* do is ask you to get on that high-dollar cell phone of yours and punch up whatever asshole in your chain-of-command told you I'm not going on this mission."

While Lt. Kerry Dale Hunter fumbled with his phone, Shake retrieved his satellite transceiver and handed it to Stokey. "Bayer is number four on the speed dial. Get him on the line and tell him to stand by for a fucking ram."

In less than thirty seconds, Lt. Hunter had reached a Navy captain at Special Warfare Command Coronado and informed him that Chief Warrant Officer-5 Sheldon Davis, United States Marine Corps, Retired, wanted a brief word with him. Shake smiled his gratitude and snatched the phone to his ear.

"Captain, this is Gunner Shake Davis. I won't bother you with my background or qualifications. You've probably got the whole file up on your laptop right now anyway. What I will bother you with is a demand to rescind the stupid-ass order that excludes me from this mission. And before we begin a pissing contest here, Captain, I've got Bob Bayer, the director of the National Counterterrorism Center, on another line right now. As soon as we've had our little chat, I'm gonna have him give you a call and square this bullshit away officially. Is all that in accordance with your understanding and approval?"

Shake listened for a few seconds still smiling at Lt. Hunter who looked more than a little awed at the flavor of the conversation. "No offense taken, Captain. And I assure you that I am in absolutely splendid physical condition. There's not a goddamn thing your SEALs can do that I haven't done a time or two while they were still shitting boot camp chow. I might be a little slower these days but I can still hack the fucking load. In fact, why don't you confirm that with Lt. Hunter here while I carve off a piece of Director Bayer's ass?"

He tossed the cell phone back to the SEAL detachment commander and grabbed the satellite phone out of Stokey's hand. "Bayer, this will be a one-way conversation. I'll talk and you'll listen. I don't know what the fuck is going on back there but I will be on this mission. You owe me that and a lot more, and I'm calling in my chits. You know good and goddamn well that we're gonna need someone out here on the ground that knows those islands. I've spent years studying the fight for Peleliu and Angaur. I know the terrain like the back of my hand. And if you'll check the record, you'll find out I was just out there last year crawling the old battlefields for three weeks, so I've got the most recent, first-hand knowledge of current conditions. Now, you just hang up and get that squid four-striper out at Coronado on the phone. He's waiting for your call."

Shake mashed the button to disconnect and turned to Lt. Hunter who had just flipped his phone closed and re-holstered the instrument. The SEAL officer grinned and made an inviting gesture toward the entrance to the building. "Welcome aboard, Gunner Davis. I think we can call this an interim clearance."

* * *

"You've all met Chief Wiley here." Lt. Hunter was completing introduction of his enlisted operators as his senior enlisted man spread a large-scale map of the Palau islands across the conference table. "And that short-round over there with the growth beneath his nose is our leading petty officer, Chris Grey."

A relatively short SEAL with wiry muscle bulging beneath a Bruce Springsteen souvenir sweatshirt stood and ran a finger across a neatly trimmed mustache. "Just call me Dubbya Dee, which the rest of these guys will tell you stands for Whistle Dick." He got the expected chuckles and sat back down at the conference table. "The story behind that is not suitable for mixed company."

"Obviously the first thing we've got to do is find these guys." Hunter reclaimed the floor and waved a hand over the map. "Dubbya Dee will be leading the first in a series of insertions on the most likely islands to do our initial recon. We'll be inserting two men at a time plus Lieutenant Commander Dewey and a package of sensors. The idea is to get in there, spot our targets if we can, sniff around a little for bio-hazard and then extract. More details on that later. Gunner Davis has been in the Palaus most recently and he'll be conducting a map study with the insert teams."

Shake took a look at the map and tapped the southern sector of the island group. "There are about 200 islands in the Palaus but only eight of them are inhabited. We can probably ignore Babelthaup—too many people and too much traffic. Best bet is either Peleliu or Angaur. I've been on the ground on both islands. I'd suggest we order up some large scale maps of those places and start there."

Lt. Hunter made a note and nodded at his detachment chief who reached for a cell phone and strolled out of the conference room punching numbers. "OK. The chief is on it. Maps will be inbound to us soonest. There are two more phases of the operation that will be going on simultaneously with our initial inserts. Mike Stokey will be heading for Babelthaup from Guam to do some sniffing around the island bureaucracy, such as it is..."

Stokey tapped Ngerulmud on the map near a block of black on the largest of the islands. "The seat of government is here. I'm not sure how to pronounce it, but they tell me it's something like Ner-el-mood. Anyway, I'm going in as advance man for a major phosphate mining conglomerate, if you can believe that shit. There are deposits all over the islands so it shouldn't raise any red flags for me to be poking around out there. Credentials, cash and a letter of introduction are waiting for me on Guam. If I get lucky, maybe I can narrow the search for you. I'll be in touch all the way and feeding you updates."

Hunter checked his watch and pointed at Chan Dwyer where she sat at the end of the table scrolling through material on her laptop. "You all have met Chan Dwyer from DIA. She's our intel slash comm officer on the mission. She'll be digging around the netherworlds for leads on who is behind this deal and keeping us in touch with higher. Any Intel we pick up gets fed to her directly. Any questions?"

There were none so Lt. Hunter began to refold the map. "We're operating on Alpha time out here, so be sure to reset your watches if you haven't done that already. I'm told there's chow laid on for us at the camp officer's mess. A bus will be outside the VOQ at 0500 tomorrow morning. I want to be wheels-in-the-wells at zero six. We're due aboard the Independence by 1500 tomorrow."

"We're going aboard an aircraft carrier?" Shake paused in his maneuver to corner Chan Dwyer before she could leave the conference room. "That seems like overkill."

"That was the old Independence, Gunner, back in the day. This one is a brand new littoral combat ship. They rushed her out from Pearl at better than 40 knots. She's a hell of a special ops platform and we'll be using her as our floating CP for this operation."

Shake noted the grins on the faces of the SEALs filing out of the room and guessed they were looking at him as the out-of-touch old fart he felt like at the moment. Fair enough. He was going to have to hack a fairly heavy load to build trust with these guys. He shrugged it off and caught Chan as she was stuffing her laptop into a padded briefcase.

"It looks like we're going on a romantic, all-expenses-paid cruise through the South Pacific. Does that romantic part do anything for you?"

"Why Gunner Davis..." Chan smiled and poked him in the ribs. "Whatever are you suggesting?"

"You make it hard to focus, girl. I've been thinking about you a lot...and missing you badly."

"Let's take it slow, Shake."

"OK. How about you be my dinner date at chow tonight? I'll introduce you to *lumpia* and other exotic delicacies. We'll see where it goes from there."

National Interagency Biodefense Command, Ft. Detrick, Maryland

"They're close." The Army colonel pointed at the enlarged depictions of material found on the slides rushed to Ft. Detrick from the Philippines, where Shake Davis and his team had found them in the rubble on Jolo.

"How close?" The man called Bayer had just sat through a full-scale scientific briefing on the weaponization of botulism and was still not sure what he'd heard. What he felt was that there was a loud and dangerous clock ticking somewhere out in the Pacific and they needed to smash it before the alarm went off and people started dying in droves.

"You heard what the science guys had to say." The colonel commanding the military's top biological warfare research team snapped on the projector and looked around the briefing room. Until the past week's revelations, he'd been fairly confident the genie would remain in the bottle and he'd be able to retire quietly without ever having to face a situation like this one. "There's not a whole lot I can add."

"I heard the briefing, Colonel." Bayer walked to a sideboard and twisted the cap off a bottle of water. "And that's all fine for the lab rats." He drank deeply and then examined the bottle critically through muted fluorescent light, trying to imagine killer microbes swimming around in the liquid. "But I've got the President, his National Security Advisor, the Secretary of Homeland Security and everyone else in the loop demanding to know where we stand. I need a soldier's perspective."

"OK, from a soldier's perspective..." The colonel folded his hands across his ribcage and twisted one of the brass buttons on his uniform blouse. "Whoever is screwing around with this stuff is on the brink of developing a weaponized variant of one of the most deadly toxins known to man. When I say weaponized, what that means is a form of the stuff that can survive on its own in various hosts and various mediums, which means it can be effectively introduced into human populations. From what we've seen of their work, they are trying to make a variant that's communicable between humans. In other words, they're trying to come up with a bug that jumps from person to person and kills indiscriminately...like the Black Death in the Middle Ages. You get that and you've got the ultimate first-strike weapon. You simply turn this stuff loose on a target population and wait for them to die. No particular risk to yourself."

"Why not? If this stuff is communicable, the people employing it would be at risk also, right? How the hell can they control something like that?"

"Once again, from a soldier's perspective, Mr. Bayer, you don't employ a weapon like this without thinking through a defense. Once the weapon is developed, the first thing you do is muster the scientists and make damn sure you've got something in hand that will keep it from killing your own people. It's like the bad old days when we were stockpiling nerve gas agents. We had every soldier on the battlefield trained to use atropine injectors."

"What if this is just a gaggle of terrorist lunatics who don't give a shit if they die in the effort? There's been a lot of that going around since 9/11."

"Then you've got a big problem, Mr. Bayer. That said, I've been studying this stuff for twenty years now and my experience is that it scares the hell out of everybody, even the lunatics. Going up in a blaze of glory at the wheel of a VB-IED is one thing. That's respectable in some circles; makes you a martyr and all that nonsense. But thrashing around on the ground with bugs coursing through your bloodstream, dying in agony and choking on your own puke, that's another thing entirely. I'm betting there's somebody out there involved with this effort that's working on an antidote. I'd be pulling out all the stops and looking for people or organizations working on botulism antitoxins."

"You guys are plugged into that world, right? You can dig around without setting off alarms?"

"We are and we can. But I wouldn't rely on us completely. Most of our sources are military types and this doesn't feel like a state-sponsored effort. I'd open up the whole can of alphabet soup, if I were you, Mr. Bayer, FBI, CIA, DIA, NSA, the whole shot."

"Back to my original question, Colonel: How much time have we got?"

"Wish I could give you a definitive answer, sir, but I can't. They could strike out completely after a few more weeks and write it all off, but I don't consider that likely. They're too close to success from what we've seen. Or they could hit it right in the next couple of days. In which case, it would be a matter of finding them and putting a stop to it before they can launch an attack. What worries me most is the nature of the beast."

"And by that you mean what?"

"I mean Mother Nature. These toxins and organisms are built to survive. They sometimes find a way to do that despite our best efforts to control them. What worries me is that this variant they're working on takes on a life—or a form—of its own and kills a shit-pot full of people before we even learn what it is much less how to counter it. These guys, whoever they are, are most definitely playing with sweaty dynamite here."

In his SUV headed back toward Washington, Bayer chewed on a sack of greasy french fries and waited for his executive assistant to get the Chief of Staff of the U.S. Air Force on the phone. It didn't take long. The senior Air Force officer was on the shortlist of military people privy to Operation Pineapple information.

"General, I need your best long-range UAV for a recon mission. It has to do with Pineapple."

"That would be our Tier Two-Plus RQ-4 Global Hawk, Bob. We've got two squadrons controlling them out of Beale Air Force Base in California."

"Can they work over water, say in the South Pacific?"

"They can work anywhere in the world. We can launch on command, refuel and do systems checks at Hickam and then at Andersen on Guam. Should be no problem, but I'll need details to come up with the right mission package."

"Give me a name and number at Beale, General, and tell them to expect me out there before noon tomorrow."

U.S. Navy Base, Guam, Northern Marianas Islands

Shake Davis, Chan Dwyer and LCdr. Janet Dewey stood on the edge of the Navy base admin LZ and watched an MH-60 Sea Hawk helicopter approach on a low pass over two Los Angeles class fast-attack submarines moored alongside a tender in Apra Harbor. That would be their ride out to the USS Independence steaming somewhere out over the horizon and waiting to receive the final three members of the Operation Pineapple task force.

Recalling the time he'd spent doing underwater launch and recovery drills as a member of a Marine Force Reconnaissance Company, Shake nudged Chan and pointed at one of the boats that was taking on a sling-load of cargo from the tender's midship crane. "At least we're not working off a submarine. Closest I ever came to drowning was doing an underway recovery aboard one of those things. It was some kind of malfunction in the forward escape trunk. I swear they had to pump forty gallons of South China Sea out of me on that deal."

"You're gonna love the Independence, Shake." Janet Dewey grabbed at the aluminum case containing her portable sensor kits as the inbound helo began to descend. "I was aboard her for the shakedown cruise late last year when we were evaluating various mission packages the ship might carry. Independence can be rigged for all sorts of close inshore operations. She's a Marine's dream and SEALs swear by the concept."

Shake shouldered his gear and watched the helo settle into ground effect over the center of the landing pad. "Can I ask you a personal question, Commander?"

"You can if you call me Janet."

"How do you feel about that old Navy thing? You know, calling a ship 'she' and all that. I'd have thought the PC Nazis would have put the kibosh on that."

"She for a ship doesn't bother me a bit. In fact, I kind of like it; preserves Navy tradition, you know? And tradition says sailors look at their ship like a mother or a lover and that's why they refer to it in the female gender. I'm good with the mother thing and I think the PC Nazis are afraid to tackle the lover aspect for fear of offending lesbians."

Shake heard Chan Dwyer's hoot of laughter over the roar of rotor blades and decided he liked Lieutenant Commander Janet Dewey a lot. If the U.S. Navy had more female officers like her coming up the hawse pipe or out of The Boat School, they'd be OK in the struggle for sea power. That would be a very good thing for his daughter if Tracey decided to continue her military career.

USS Independence (LC-2), Philippine Sea

Lieutenant Commander Janet Dewey asked the aircrew to do a pass over the ship prior to landing so Shake and Chan Dwyer could get a look at the sleek new vessel that was rapidly becoming the show pony of the surface Navy. As the helo circled and banked they could see by the turbulence at her stern that the ship was making considerable speed but didn't seem to throw up any bow wake at all. Dewey explained some of that over the headsets the helo crew chief had provided for the passengers.

"It has to do with her configuration. Independence has a forward bow thruster so you don't see that old 'bone-in-her-teeth' deal when the ship is at speed. And she can do upwards of forty knots all day long."

"That's what, more than fifty miles per hour land speed?" Chan Dwyer had spent most of her military time in the air or on land and this thing cutting cleanly through the chop down below was an impressive sight.

"That's right. She's the fastest thing afloat of this size and maneuvers like a Maserati."

"Weird shape." Shake craned to keep the vessel in sight as the pilot flew aft and set up for a landing on the spacious flight deck where a crew waited with chocks and chains to receive the helo. "Looks kind of like a banjo, or an anteater with that big long nose."

"It's a trimaran, Shake, all aluminum with three keels in the water. She can plane just like a ski boat. I'll ask the skipper to give you guys a tour once we're aboard and squared away."

The Sea Hawk settled smoothly on the after flight deck with barely a bump as the pilot expertly matched his airspeed with the speed of the Independence. They climbed out of the aircraft and recovered their personal gear as an officer wearing tailored blue coveralls under a high-visibility flight deck vest motioned for them to follow him toward a hatch in the vessel's superstructure.

When they made their way through a maze of passageways and reached the wardroom, they found Lt. Hunter poring over charts with a tall, rawboned officer wearing a pair of reading cheaters perched on a nose that looked like it might have come into contact with a fist or two in the past. Their escort introduced him as Commander Doug "Diesel" Bland, commanding officer of the Independence. The ham-sized hand he stuck out to shake sported a Naval Academy class ring.

"Welcome aboard Independence, folks. If any of you smoke, I'm afraid you're gonna have to go cold turkey on this cruise. We're all aluminum and smoking aboard is a fire hazard."

Bland seemed all business and serious as a heart attack for a few seconds and then reached into the hip pocket of his coveralls to produce a can of Skoal. "If it gets too tough, we've got plenty of chew aboard." He smiled and stuffed a pinch of tobacco into his lower lip. "Just remember not to spit into the wind on the weather decks."

"There are accommodations ready for you but space is limited." Hunter helped himself to a dip and tucked it into a cheek. "Chan, you'll double up with Commander Dewey. Shake, it's you and me. I'm calling an update briefing here in the wardroom right after noon chow. Does that work for everyone?"

"How soon before we get to the Palaus?" Shake could see the officers had been studying the nautical charts of surrounding waters before they arrived. There were course projections leading toward the southern islands, so they'd taken his advice about Peleliu and Angaur.

"Three days max, but that's one of the things we need to hash out at the briefing." Cdr. Bland tapped the chart with a pair of dividers. "We don't want to come roaring up over the horizon and spook the folks you're looking for. And I want to find that damn yacht before they spot us on radar. We're gonna have to do some creative navigation once we make the rendezvous with the Seascope."

"We're meeting up with the Seascope?" Shake was stunned. "My daughter's aboard that ship."

"Not for long..." Lt. Hunter reached into his pocket and unfolded a message form. "This just in from CNO...Lieutenant Junior Grade Tracey A. Davis USNR is ordered aboard USS Independence, LC-2, for temporary additional duty in connection with Operation Pineapple. Rendezvous with RV Seascope and cross-decking will be conducted ASAP...and yada, yada, yada. Looks like this is gonna be a family affair, Shake."

"What the hell is that about?" Shake wasn't at all sure he was happy with having his daughter along on what could turn out to be a very dangerous mission. "She's not a line officer, for Christ's sake. Tracey is a scientist in uniform."

"Well, she's coming aboard regardless." Hunter handed over the message form and pointed to a paragraph. "She's officially assigned TAD to Operation Pineapple as science advisor to me and back-up for Lieutenant Commander Dewey as detachment CBRN officer."

"I thought that was Chan's deal. She's had the training."

"She's gonna be a little too busy for that collateral duty," Cdr. Bland reached for a stack of baseball caps bearing the USS Independence command crest and began handing them out to his visitors. "We just got word the Air Force is putting up a Global Hawk UAV over the area to help us get a fix on that yacht. Ms. Dwyer will be monitoring direct feeds from the bird around the clock."

* * *

Shake was standing on the flight deck shaping his new Navy ball cap into a respectable combat crush when he saw the Sea Hawk flying up the stern wake on final and carrying his only daughter to her new assignment aboard USS Independence. The ship had slowed from her normal flat-out cruising speed to conserve fuel and recover the resident helo. The ship's navigator, the stocky female full lieutenant standing next to him, said that wouldn't last long on a "high-speed, low-drag, kick-ass vessel" like the Independence and promised they'd be closing Palauan waters in under 72 hours.

There wasn't much on Shake's personal schedule until then, so he intended to have a talk with his offspring and give her a few well-chosen words of fatherly advice about staying the hell out of the line of fire, should one develop during this mission. He was running over that lecture in his head when the helicopter settled onto the deck and Tracey jumped out wearing the Navy's new gray, blue and black mottled camouflage combat uniform.

"Looks like my new roomie's here." The navigator strode across the flight deck to greet the new officer that would be sharing her stateroom for the cruise but Shake just stood and stared. The sight of his daughter in a uniform that suggested she might be up for a fight rather than screwing around with fish had him stunned. This wasn't at all what he'd bargained for when Tracey announced she was going to graduate school on the Navy's dime and accepting a commission that carried at least six years of active duty payback time. Ocean science was one thing but service aboard a littoral combat ship—emphasis on combat in this case—was a whole different deal.

"Permission to come aboard, sir?" Tracey plopped her seabag and a large metal case marked with bio-hazard stickers at his feet and rendered a respectable salute. She was all smiles, beaming the same way she used to as a kid when she dragged him aboard gut-wrenching rollercoaster rides at pricey theme parks.

Shake brushed at his forehead briefly and then wrapped her in a bear hug. "Permission granted...I guess."

"Sir, you two can catch up over coffee in the wardroom." The navigator picked up some of Tracey's gear and nodded toward the hatch leading to the interior of the ship. "We need to get Lt. Davis squared away in my quarters. And the Skipper wants to kick it in the butt as soon as we get the helo secured."

Shake followed his daughter and the navigator inside the ship. As they passed the wardroom, he stopped and put a hand on Tracey's shoulder. "Meet me back here soon as you can. We need to talk."

"I'm a big girl, Dad..."

"Yeah, I know that. And you're playing in the Big Leagues on this thing. That's what we need to talk about."

Shake was reading a full-color brochure from General Dynamics extolling the virtues of their LCS design when Tracey returned to the wardroom thirty minutes later. She was wearing one of the USS Independence ball caps but it looked box-stock and freshly minted. "Let me fix that cover for you." He snatched it off her head and began to work it into salty shape. "You don't want these black-shoe swabbies thinking you're a boot."

Tracey poured coffee for herself and slid into a chair opposite her father in the ship's small wardroom that was about to become more cramped with what were now four extra officers in addition to the eight the ship normally carried. "This ship is so cool! I mean, if you gotta go to sea, this is definitely the way to do it."

"Listen, Tracey." Shake inspected the crushed ball cap and handed it back. "This is a combat vessel and we're on what I'm afraid might turn out to be a combat mission. The guys we're after out here don't play nice. This is the kind of deal where shots may be fired, if you get my drift."

"I get your drift." She tried on the hat and gave it a few of her own tweaks. "I also understand that part of being in military service is going where shots may be fired. I'm doing my duty, Dad. And right now my duty is to be aboard this ship and help out with whatever happens. That's the way it is. And I'd expect you to understand that. I really don't need—and I really don't want—you trying to babysit me out here."

"It's not that. It's just..." Shake was trying to figure out what in the hell he was really trying to say when he was saved by Chief Wiley who stuck his head inside the wardroom door.

"Hey, Gunner...the Boss and Commander Bland need you up on the bridge. Those maps we ordered are downloaded.

And Lieutenant Davis, Chan Dwyer is looking for you up in comm spaces."

"Where's that?" Tracey stood and drained her coffee. "I'm gonna need a GPS or a road map."

"It's just aft of the bridge, Ma'am. I'll show you. We're headed that way."

* * *

"That's the Seascope." Chan Dwyer tapped a fingernail on an LED screen showing the sea space surrounding the Independence as detected by the ship's Sea Giraffe 3-D radar. "They've been ordered to stand by west of the Palaus in case we need scientific help after we find our targets."

"Glad I'm here rather than there." Tracey looked around the dimly-lit comm suite where sailors wearing headsets were manning a bank of sophisticated consoles. There was a low murmur of jargon-filled phrases as communicators sent and received messages from and to spaces throughout the ship. It all appealed in a visceral way that made her feel martial and more truly involved than she'd ever felt in her relatively short Navy career.

"You might not be after you've had a chance to digest this stuff." Chan Dwyer moved to a remote computer console that had been set aside for her exclusive use on the Pineapple mission. She picked up a thick envelope full of downloads and handed it to Tracey. "This is the latest from the people at Ft. Detrick. It's what they found on those slides your Dad sent from Jolo. Mr. Bayer wants you to become intimately familiar with it and then brief Janet Dewey on anything she needs to know." Chan scribbled on a Post-It note and stuck it on the envelope. "Any questions about the material, you're to call this guy at Ft. Detrick. I can arrange the call anytime."

Tracey took the envelope, but made no move to look at it or leave the area. She just stood looking at the electronic displays and listening to the murmur of sailors at their duty stations. One part of her mind told her she was aboard the

Independence. Another more fascinating part had her aboard the Enterprise with Captain Kirk and Commander Spock. Chan Dwyer rolled a spare chair up to her desk and Tracey sat without looking.

"I'm sorry...a little overwhelmed, I guess. This is the first real ship I've ever been on...you know...a man-of-war and all that."

"Me too." Chan smiled. "And I've got to admit it is pretty cool."

Tracey chewed on a lip for a few seconds and then decided there was no time like the present to get it off her chest. "My Dad's acting like a butthole about it."

"Nothing new there." Chan laughed and rested her chin in a hand; staring idly at the wallpaper on her computer screen. "Your Dad's a free-wheeling kind of guy but he's like a Papa Bear about you. I heard that first time I met him."

"The Laos File thing. He still talks about that—after a few beers."

"So you know all about that?"

"Yeah...mostly he talks about you."

"Me?" Chan checked to see if Tracey was serious and apparently she was.

"He's had a crush on you for years. Is this the first clue?"

"Actually, it is, at least it's the first serious clue." Chan was somewhere between stunned and delighted; unsure which way the ball might bounce. "I mean, Shake...your Dad...kids around sometimes. You know, he flirts kind of...but I was never sure how to take that."

"Because he's an old fart?"

"No, not at all! I've never thought of him in terms of his age, or the difference between his age and mine. That makes no difference."

"So, you'd consider hooking up with him?"

"Tracey, is there a reason you're sounding like little Miss Match Maker here?"

"My Dad needs someone in his life, Chan." Tracey leaned in and laid a hand on Chan Dwyer's forearm. "He spent most of his life giving everything he could to me and my Mom, not to mention the Marine Corps. It drained him and he needs something—someone—to fill him back up again. That's a tall order, but my impression is that you're the kind of woman who can fill it."

Tracey leaned back in her chair and crossed her arms. "If I'm out of place here, I apologize. But I love my Dad. He's a good man and he deserves a good woman. That's it, all I've got to say. Thanks for listening."

Chan Dwyer took a deep breath and wondered how to respond...to Tracey, much less to Shake Davis. "I'm gonna need someone to relieve me on the scopes when they get the drone airborne. Let me show you how that works."

Beale Air Force Base, Marysville, California

There were three partitions inside the long building that housed the mission control center for the 12th Reconnaissance Squadron. Each compartment was called a cockpit but they looked more like standard work station cubicles found in typical corporate office suites. The air inside the structure was dehumidified and air-conditioned to protect the sophisticated electronic equipment while the lighting was color-corrected and kept intentionally dimmed to avoid glare on the LED screens that seemed to be everywhere either streaming video or scrolling data.

The Air Force brigadier general who commanded the reconnaissance group at Beale pointed to the right-hand cubicle and steered Bayer in that direction. "That's your mission, designated Hawk Three Zulu. Captain Dee Kulacz is flying right now. She's one of our most-experienced RQ-4 sticks. We usually have a camera operator and an analyst on crew for Global Hawk missions, but we've eliminated those slots per your instructions."

Bayer peered over the cubicle wall and saw a petite woman with broad shoulders and cropped brown hair wearing a headset, staring intently at a large flat-screen display and using her left hand to gently manipulate a set of controls that looked something like a high-tech videogame console. She was dressed in a tailored flight suit and seated in a chair that looked like it might have been lifted from an F-15—minus the restraints and ejection gear.

"We try to make it look and feel as much like a standard aircraft cockpit as we can." The brigadier handed Bayer a headset and helped him adjust the lip microphone. "We want our pilots to feel like they are flying a real world mission and not playing videogames."

"Where is the bird right now?" Bayer peered at the screen over the pilot's shoulder but all he could see was an expanse of water showing whitecaps and what he thought might be a school of dolphins. The brigadier turned to check a repeater console and stabbed at the attached keyboard.

"Hawk Three Zulu departed Andersen on Guam thirty-six minutes ago with a full fuel load. While the bird was on the ground the mission techs installed the requested package for you. It's carrying the synthetic aperture radar array and transmitting real-time images and data via satellite link. What you're seeing on the screen is what the bird is seeing on look-down mode. Captain Kulacz can direct the view from directly below the flight path to out along the horizon in any direction just by manipulating the controls on her console."

"Can I talk to Captain Kulacz?" Bayer fumbled with a button on his headset cord. The brigadier keyed his own mike and nodded at the pilot. "How ya doin', Dee?"

"Level at two-four thousand and just under 300 knots indicated, sir." She raised her right hand showing an extended thumb but never took her eyes off the console which displayed aircraft status, heading and position data via boxes inset on the screen. "Just ran the diagnostics and all systems are on line."

"Captain, this is Bob Bayer, director of the NCTC." Kulacz glanced over her shoulder and smiled briefly before returning her attention to the displays. "This is our mission you're flying."

"Yes, sir, I got the full brief yesterday morning before we launched. We're tracking and on course for the Palaus. We got the up-check from the Independence an hour ago and the down-link is established. They're seeing what we're seeing in real time."

"So, you got the material from the National Reconnaissance Office?"

"It came through early this morning, sir." Capt. Kulacz tapped an adjacent screen and a full-color picture of the Al Calipha moored in a very pricey slip at Dubai popped into view. "This is what we're looking for, right? I've uploaded a high-res image into the bird's onboard computers. The radars are doing regular panoramic sweeps out to return limits looking for anything that matches the profile."

Bayer pulled a leather-bound notebook from his pocket and scanned a page. "Can you pull up a map of the area?"

Kulacz tapped her right-hand screen again and the Al Calipha disappeared to be replaced by a map of the Palau Islands. She expanded the view until a tiny diamond appeared to the right of the islands. "That's us," she said pointing to the tracking icon, "about one hundred eighty-five nautical miles due east of the target area. My flight profile calls for a northerly course correction in about twenty minutes and then set up an orbit over the area."

"I've talked to the people out on the Independence." Bayer reached over the pilot's shoulder and indicated the southern portion of the island group. "They think we'd have better luck concentrating here to the south around these two islands."

"Well, that's helpful, sir. If we can tighten the search area, I can fly lower and get us a better look once we find the target."

"Let's do that, captain. Forget about the northern area. Just set up your search orbit and focus on the waters surrounding Peleliu and Angaur."

"Copy all, sir. We should be orbiting that area in just about an hour from now."

Over the Northern Pacific, Approx. 7°01'N 134°15'E

The new instructions sent from Capt. Kulacz to the navigation computer aboard the RQ-4 Global Hawk at 20,000 feet over the Palau Islands put the UAV into a tight left-hand turn about ten miles southeast of Peleliu. Radar returns from the last scan over the island of Angaur indicated a target matching the profile in the onboard reference file was located about twelve miles due west of the landmass on a heading of 270 degrees magnetic.

More inputs from the pilot brought the wings level, locked the navigational radar dead on the bearing and sent the aircraft into a shallow descent that would put it directly over the nautical bogie at an altitude of not less than 18,000 feet AGL with cameras rolling and real-time images streaming. Assuming the bogie was indeed the object it was told to search for out here in the vast reaches of the western Pacific, a signal would send the Global Hawk into a preprogrammed set of passes that would provide excellent views from various altitudes and angles.

Aboard Al Calipha, South of Angaur, Palau Islands

The captain sent a plume of fragrant pipe smoke into the breeze blowing across the bridge wing and scanned the easterly skies with his binoculars. There was nothing immediately visible beyond a scudding cumulus cloud bank in the direction of Angaur but the search radar indicated an aircraft was approaching from that direction at an altitude of between eighteen and twenty thousand feet on a bearing that would intercept the yacht's current course. That wasn't particularly unusual. The yacht's expensive air-sweep radar had regularly picked up commercial airline traffic in this area, headed one way or another between various population centers.

What had the captain concerned was the altitude of this contact. It was too low for an international flight. Those commercial heavies normally made their Pacific transits well above thirty thousand feet. He gave the sky another sweep and then knocked the dottle out of his pipe bowl and stepped inside the wheelhouse. He checked the radar repeater and noted the contact was still approaching on the same course as when they'd first detected it. He hung his binoculars on the arm of his bridge chair and turned to his first officer with a reassuring grin.

"It's most likely an interisland commuter at that altitude. Probably out of Koror and headed for Angaur." He checked the sailor on watch at the radio station for messages from the team on Peleliu. There had been no traffic since the morning communication check, so the captain decided to get a late breakfast and an update on repairs to an evaporator that had been giving them trouble lately. He was two steps down the accommodation ladder when the first officer shouted for his attention.

"Captain, lookout reports visual on an aircraft approaching off the starboard beam."

Hopping back up the ladder and grabbing his binoculars on the fly, the captain ducked back out onto the starboard bridge wing and swept the sky above the clouds. He still couldn't spot the aircraft, so he climbed the ladder to the flying bridge above him and motioned for the lookout to give him space at the eyepieces of the high-magnification, electronically-enhanced glasses that were tied to a bearing repeater at the yacht's conning station. He spotted the aircraft almost directly overhead but he couldn't see much detail. It was smaller than a commercial commuter with a v-tail, a bulbous nose and a slate blue paint job. The captain was unable to identify the aircraft type, but his instincts told him it was military. He considered making a radio report to the team on Peleliu, and yet he didn't want to create unnecessary alarm or draw attention to his vessel.

He climbed down the starboard ladder and reentered the wheelhouse. "Steady on our current course and speed. Tell the lookouts to ignore the contact. We don't want to look like we're concerned." He was still wondering whether or not to take a chance on an intercepted radio call when the decision was made for him. The first officer reported that the mysterious aircraft was executing a lazy left turn onto a reciprocal bearing. That could mean they were either looking for his vessel or simply interested enough to make a second pass. Either way, he had to report the situation to Sayed Abdullah and that pushy little pretender on Peleliu.

USS Independence (LC-2), Philippine Sea

"Did you see it?" Bayer's excited voice came through loud and clear from the UAV mission control station in California. Lt. Kerry Dale Hunter grinned at the team crowded around Chan Dwyer's computer console and keyed his headset. "Crystal clear on this end, sir. We spotted the name on the transom and even caught a lookout giving us the hairy eyeball from the flying bridge. That's Al Calipha."

"And you got a good position and course?"

Hunter glanced at Commander Bland and got an affirmative nod. "We got it: south of Angaur and on a northerly course. We're headed in that direction." He was about to continue when Chan Dwyer slapped a Post-It note on the screen and tapped it to get his attention.

"Uh, sir, Chan Dwyer is suggesting we call off the UAV. If we spotted them, it's likely they spotted us. We got indications from the bird that they painted it with some pretty heavy-duty air search radar."

There was a period of silence before Bayer came back on the air. "That's negative. I don't want to lose that vessel before you can get into the area. The Air Force guys back here are going to adjust and get out of their radar sweep. They're telling me they can fly far enough away to not look nosey and still keep an eye on the Al Calipha."

"Copy all, sir. We'll continue to monitor here."

"Yeah, do that. And continue on a course to intercept those guys ASAP. Seems to me given the yacht's position you ought to concentrate on Angaur. Is that what you're thinking?"

"Yes, sir. Unless the vessel heads for one of the other islands or we get better intel, we'll put the first recon element onto Angaur sometime tomorrow morning. We're set to make an insertion via helicopter from over the horizon and then put our team ashore via SDV."

* * *

In the small stateroom she shared with Janet Dewey aboard Independence, Chan Dwyer stifled a yawn, adjusted the web-cam and waited for NCTC Director Bayer to come up on the video link. She'd been working through the night trying to glean information from the material the NCTC had forwarded from NSA intercepts. It was all partial and piecemeal. The analysts speculated that the target was using alternate programs that kept them from obtaining full readouts and locking in on precise locations for both sender and receiver. They were working the problem but in the meantime, Chan, Bayer and everyone else concerned were in the wonderful world of SWAG—Scientific Wild Ass Guesses.

"Hello, Chan. How goes it out there?" Bayer looked gaunt and about as tired as Chan felt when he came up on the link. She couldn't tell where he was, but she could see he hadn't been getting much more sleep than she had.

"Pretty good, sir. I've been going over the intercepts and it's fairly clear that there's an Iranian connection. I'd say the major players are elements in Tehran and Saudi Arabia."

"Yeah, CIA is working that now. They've got their eyes on a Saudi prince who's been moving big bucks around lately. He's number one with a bullet in the SWIFT program and, check this, he's a principal in the conglomerate that owns the Al Calipha."

"That's probably the moneybag in this deal. What worries me is the Tehran thing."

"Yeah, that got everybody's attention. We're worried about nukes and those guys are messing around with bio-weapons. If they're active players —and I think they are—it will be a Quds Force deal and that means you're up against some genuine bad actors out there. Be damn sure Hunter and his guys know that."

"Yes, sir. I'm due to brief them in about an hour."

"There is some good news. NSA reports they've gotten a pretty good intercept on some scientific stuff. Apparently, it was a report of sufficient size that they managed to get most of it. It was sent to an address in Jeddah which fits the Saudi connection. The people at Ft. Detrick are looking at it and they think it was sent so that someone on the other end could start work on an antidote. We're doing the same thing but that's playing catch-up ball, Chan. I want these bastards hammered before they can launch an attack. That order is going out to Hunter through the chain of command right now."

"Is that material something for Lieutenant Commander Dewey and Lieutenant Davis?"

"Absolutely. I'm sending it out encrypted as soon as we sign off. Be damn sure they see everything and talk it over with the people at Fort Detrick. Anything else for me?"

"Just one thing, sir. I've been trying to figure out this connection between the major players we think we've identified and Ignacio Felodon."

"And?"

"Well, sir...if we presume this is some sort of radical Muslim cabal bent on international jihad, where does Felodon fit in the picture? According to Shake, he's been playing at being an Abu Sayyaf Filipino Muslim for the past year or so. But Shake believes the AS people knew all along he wasn't a true believer and I've got to figure the Saudi and Tehran players would know that also. So, why fool around with him at all? Unless they're looking for a scapegoat to take the fall when they launch a biological attack, they just don't need this guy."

"Did you run this by Shake?"

"Yes, sir. He's convinced Felodon is being set up to take a fall for someone. It makes sense to me. Let's assume for a moment that the target for the weapon might be the Philippines. We know they're in the area and it would be no stretch to introduce a weapon like this into the Philippine food chain via the Al Calipha. And according to what Shake said in his report on Felodon, there's plenty of motive. When people start dying, it would be a credible slam-dunk to just point the finger at Felodon and say he was extracting revenge."

"And that would deflect any attention from the real villains. Interesting stuff, Chan. I'll chew on this for a while but we need to lay hands on the people cooking up this mess out there. If there's radical Muslim players involved we'll need to prove it. Bottom line: I don't much care right now about motivations. The clock is ticking. We stop it before it starts and then worry about the rest."

"I'd say that's at the top of everyone's priority list out here, sir."

"So, how's Shake getting along?"

"Pretty good, I guess. He's not very happy with the Navy bringing his daughter into the mix but she's not taking any crap from her Dad." Chan smiled into the camera thinking about the regular bull sessions she'd been having with Tracey Davis. "And I think the SEALs have adopted Shake. Kindred spirit from the same tribe, you know?"

"He's hard to ignore," Bayer chuckled and reached for the keyboard on his end of the connection. "That Navy captain at Coronado is still wondering what hit him."

The screen went black and Chan Dwyer looked longingly at the bunk along the wall of the stateroom. A nap before her scheduled briefing would be nice but she had to download the scientific intercepts and relieve Tracey Davis up in the comm shack.

Peleliu, Palau Islands Group

"Under no circumstances are you to approach this area unless you hear otherwise directly from me. Do you understand?" Sayed Abdullah was fairly certain from the captain's description that the Al Calipha had been observed by a military drone of some sort but he was determined not to panic.

"I understand. We will adjust course and stay well south. The aircraft has disappeared from our radar. I will contact you if it reappears."

"Do not contact me by radio unless there is an emergency." Abdullah knew only too well how vulnerable communication on open frequencies could be and they did not possess a scrambler on the maritime sets. "Use the computer program to send regular reports." At least the programs on their email server were encrypted. "I will monitor that and send you instructions as necessary."

The captain of the Al Calipha signed off and left Abdullah wondering if he should continue or pack up and prepare to move once again. He dropped the radio transceiver into a charging console, ducked out of his tent and strolled along the stretch of white sand beach where Dr. Nasuton and some locally hired help were harvesting fish for dissection. They were reporting significant progress; perhaps as little as one week more and they might have the answer. Initial reports on the weapon had already been sent to Jeddah and Tehran where other scientific teams would be working feverishly to absorb the nature of the new toxin and develop an antidote.

Only yesterday evening Nasuton had experimental work moved into a sterile prefab structure and ordered his assistants to perform their procedures in bio-hazard suits. That required them to work at night to avoid scaring the locals who dropped by regularly during the day asking for jobs or just poke around out of curiosity. It also robbed Abdullah of badly needed sleep. Fortunately, he'd been able to keep the man he now thought of as Ignacio Felodon at bay by allowing the irritating bastard to flail around the jungle-covered hills building useless defensive positions and stocking them with the heavy weapons they'd brought ashore in sealed boxes marked as laboratory equipment.

The other thing that had been robbing him of sleep for the past four days was a flurry of messages from his mission director in Jeddah via three randomly alternating encryption programs. It was a laborious process to establish effective and secure communication links and his controllers were being obstinate about sharing information. They'd leaked a little about Col. Ibrahim and then told him a little more each time he'd responded with questions. After three or four exchanges, Jeddah had signed off with orders to ask no further questions and limit his communication to status reports and data from Nasuton's team of scientists.

Abdullah had operated in the shadows of international intrigue long enough to understand he was going to elicit no further information. His controllers had decided he had no need to know beyond what he'd been provided in response to his complaints about Col. Ibrahim. At least he now knew who the imposter was and it wasn't hard to figure out what his handlers intended for the man after the attack was launched. No wonder he'd been ordered to keep Felodon safe and satisfied. The man was a perfect scapegoat, what the westerners called a patsy or a fall guy. He had to admit the long-term scheme was brilliant.

He plopped down on a coconut log and watched the surf roll in while he waffled between discretion and dedication. It might not be a bad idea to inspect those positions in the Umurbrogol Massif rising off to his right just across the island's west road. He'd agreed to give the Filipino a free hand and even assigned most of the Quds Force security detail to help with busy work mainly to keep Felodon out of his hair. The effort would pay dividends beyond distraction only if it came to a fight here on Peleliu.

But why should it? Abdullah wondered as he scratched idly at the sand flea bites on his ankles. There was nothing sinister about a luxury yacht cruising lazily off any islands in the western Pacific. Rich people around the world owned such ships in order to take cruises to exotic locations. And so what if the Americans took a close look at a ship cruising these waters? It had to be Americans if the aircraft they'd spotted was indeed a drone. And of course they'd be interested in a vessel with Middle Eastern registry. Their paranoia knew no bounds. But so what? As long as they stayed away from Peleliu, the mission could continue unmolested. And the machineguns, RPGs and sniper rifles could rust up in those rugged hills for all Abdullah cared. The real weapon that would damage the infidels far beyond bombs and bullets was swimming around in that secluded lagoon up the beach.

No, they were too close to success now. The weapon would be ready soon and then they could pack up, get back aboard the Al Calipha and move into the attack phase of the operation. They would stay the course here on Peleliu and let the Americans nose around at will. They'd find nothing on the yacht and nothing on Angaur. By the time they started to look elsewhere in the area, it would be too late.

The sun was setting as he walked up the beach back toward their base camp. Soon, the sleeping scientists who were doing all of Dr. Nasuton's grunt work in the sealed structure would be zipped inside their protective suits and another step closer to success. Abdullah just needed to keep things on track and control Ignacio Felodon until he was told what to do with the irritating little martinet.

He was pondering all sorts of mayhem when Felodon came into view strolling down the west road from the direction of Klouklubed, the village nearest their base camp. Despite Abdullah's orders to the contrary, Felodon was still wearing military-style camouflage trousers bloused over well-worn jungle boots. A torn red T-shirt and a baseball cap advertising some establishment that rented scuba equipment did little to hide his martial appearance.

"I thought you were up in the hills seeing to the defenses." Abdullah fell into step with him and pointed at the burlap sack that Felodon was carrying. "Or were you doing some shopping in the village?"

"The shopkeeper said there would be fresh fruit, but it was gone before I arrived." If the Filipino was disappointed it didn't show. "I just picked up a few other things I wanted." He was smiling and bouncing along the shoulder of the road at a brisk pace.

"And what of the defensive positions?"

"Complete. And what of the mission?"

"Dr. Nasuton indicates we are very close...perhaps days. He has ordered some final experiments conducted on the latest strain."

"Yes, I've seen the dogs and pigs he's collected. I hope he isn't wasting time."

"We'll know in a day or two."

"Yes...yes, indeed we will."

As they turned off the road headed for the sleeping tents erected in a grove of coconut palms just inland from the experimental lagoon, Abdullah decided not to tell Felodon about the encounter between the aircraft and the Al Calipha. Felodon seemed to be in a rare good mood and that probably meant he'd crawl off into the jungle somewhere and spend the night sucking on the native beer concealed in the burlap sack he was carrying. It also meant Abdullah might get some sleep.

* * *

Keana Sulukep admired the three fat fish in the bucket of seawater in the kitchen of her home on the edge of Kloukluebed village and decided she'd gotten the best of the deal with the little Filipino from the fish farm. Two quarts of Red Rooster beer and a pint of local whiskey was a bargain for fish that would feed her family for two days. And these were deep water fish, fat and sleek, the kind Peleliu fishermen sold to the local restaurants and hotels. Delicacies were hard to come by with her husband a couple of hundred miles away on the Yap islands working for a construction firm, so she didn't haggle much with the man in the military clothes. He got liquor she never touched and Keana got a feast for her two kids—maybe she'd even invite her neighbor lady—plus a second fish to fillet and put on ice for later. The third fish, that fat one in the middle, she'd take up to the Storyboard Beach Resort where her cousin worked in the kitchen. Twenty dollars was not too much to ask for a fine fish like that.

Keana Sulukep plopped the middle fish in a second plastic bucket, called her daughter to clean the other two while she ran an errand, and went outside to borrow the neighbor lady's bicycle.

Koror, Palau Islands Group

Mike Stokey thought about having a quick beer in what a rusty sign said was the Red Rooster Café, but he was running late. He fought off the temptation and consulted the sketch-map directing him through a maze of ramshackle buildings that seemed to have been scattered at random across a dusty neighborhood near Koror's waterfront. He'd spent a long and frustrating morning in Ngerulmud being passed from one official to another, listening to mind-numbing pitches about mineral mining opportunities and quietly spreading cash around among mid-level bureaucrats.

He didn't get much for his efforts except a strong hunch that the glad-handing, overblown Minister of Cultural, Agricultural and Scientific Affairs was bullshitting from the moment he opened his fat mouth. In about thirty seconds from the time Mike mentioned Peleliu, the guy went from sunfish to shark. The minister said he'd be glad to authorize research anywhere in the Palaus, except Peleliu, where there was supposedly a moratorium on commercial enterprises due to work being done on restoration of World War II battlefields. A light went on but when Stokey pressed the issue, asking about current activities on Peleliu and indicating he'd really like to explore the island, the bureaucrat clammed up and said he wasn't empowered to grant such permission. He'd have to bounce the request off other officials to obtain proper clearances. It was an obvious stall tactic and Stokey didn't like the look he got he got when he said he'd be happy to wait. The bureaucrat eased him out of the office saying permission might take as much as a week to ten days to get the clearances. Stokey's clue phone was ringing off the hook.

Mike gave the man the name of the hotel where he was staying in Koror and immediately made a lunch date with a friendly secretary in the Palau Visitors Bureau. He gave her a good meal and $500 in cash, just so she'd know he was really sincere about doing business in the Palaus. The secretary said if anyone would know about a program to restore the battlefields on Peleliu, she would—and she didn't. The minister must have been mistaken, she said. Her tone told Stokey she thought the guy was shifty dirt bag.

And she knew for a fact there was no moratorium on commercial activities on Peleliu. In fact, just last week some foreign outfit had been given clearance to conduct aquaculture experiments in the southern islands. She wasn't sure if it was Peleliu or Angaur, but she knew a man in Koror who owned a charter boat that regularly took fishermen and divers to both islands. She jotted the name Josh Watkins on the back of one of her cards, ordered a pricey dessert and promised to keep their conversation discreet.

A cabbie dumped Stokey at the commercial slip on Koror's waterfront and pointed to a well-kept motor-sailor moored near a sign that advertised Flying Fish Charters. There was no one aboard and it was getting dark by the time Mike found a deckhand on one of the adjacent boats who knew where Mr. Watkins lived. He couldn't provide a phone number, but for $10 he was happy to draw the map that Stokey was trying to follow through the back streets of Koror. It was almost time for one of his regular update calls to Bayer and the crew out on the Independence but he wanted to find this Watkins and arrange for his own little excursion to the south islands before he got on the horn and told everyone to focus on Peleliu.

Meanwhile, it was apparent that he'd either missed or misinterpreted some of the landmarks on the sketch. There was supposed to be a bicycle shop on the corner, but all he could see was a rusty tin shed in one direction and the Red Rooster Café in the other. It seemed likely someone in the bar would know Watkins, so he turned in that direction and headed down an alley littered with trash receptacles and dotted with oily rain puddles.

"Hey, man, you got a light?" The chunky man with Maori tattoos showing on arms knotted with muscle had a cigarette dangling from his mouth but the look in his eyes told Stokey he wanted something more than a match.

"Yeah, I think so." The entrance to the Red Rooster was still fifty feet distant and the man was moving to cut off that route even as Stokey dug in his pocket for the Kershaw Scallion folding knife that he'd picked up in a local dive shop on the day he arrived. It wasn't much; only a three-inch blade, but it was scary-sharp and had a one-handed assisted opening feature that made it quick. He was closing on the tattooed man with the small blade hidden in his hand as if it was a lighter when he sensed rather than heard movement at his six o'clock.

Stokey flashed the blade open and spun ninety degrees putting the first man on his left and whatever else was in that alley on his right. That side presented the most-imminent danger in the form of bulky figure in a yellow linen shirt bearing down on him with a brutal-looking slapjack raised and ready to strike. He ducked the first swipe and raked his blade across the bridge of the man's nose. There was a spray of blood but the cut didn't keep the attacker from making a vicious backswing. The weighted sap caught Stokey behind the right ear and dropped him to his knees. He tried to keep the blade up and slashing while he fought to stay conscious. The tattooed man was advancing slowly from the left but he didn't appear to have a weapon.

He focused against the pain and when the man with the sap made his next swing, Stokey jabbed straight up and buried the blade to the hilt in the attacker's wrist. Tendons snapped and the slapjack dropped on the ground. As the man backed away trying to stem the flow of blood running down his hand, Stokey snatched at the sap and spun to face his second assailant.

To his surprise, that threat was being handled by a tall, deeply-tanned individual with muttonchop sideburns who had the tattooed man in a painful-looking chokehold. Stokey spun on the first attacker, took two quick steps and laid the slapjack hard into the man's skull just in front of the left ear. The man dropped like a sack of cement into a puddle of his own blood.

By the time he got his breathing under control and looked down the alley, the tattooed man was sprawled unconscious and clearly oblivious to the kicks Mr. Muttonchops was laying into his ribcage. "Looks like you've done all the damage necessary, buddy—and thanks for doing it, by the way."

"Saw these two from the bar and came out to have a look." Mister Muttonchops sounded a lot like Crocodile Dundee. "They're never up to any bloody good."

"You wouldn't be Josh Watkins, would you?"

"In the bloody flesh, mate. I heard there was a Yank lookin' for me. That would be you, right?"

"Guilty as charged, Mr. Watkins..." Stokey shook hands with his rescuer. "My name is Mike Stokey and thanks again for the help here."

"Call me Chopper, mate. We've been back-to-back in a punch-up and I reckon that puts us on an informal basis. You've been up in Ngerulmud, right?"

"Yeah, but how'd you know that?"

"These two." Watkins kicked the nearest form and nodded his head at the other one. "They're a couple of musclemen from up that way. "It ain't the first time they've showed up in Koror and it's always trouble. My guess is you gave somebody a chapped arse up in the capital and these blokes were sent to convince you not to do it again. That fit the profile?"

"Yeah, mostly it does. I've been trying to get official permission for a visit to Peleliu."

"Not usually a problem, mate. I take people down there for diving and fishing all the time. No government permission required. There's something you ain't tellin' me."

"Look, Chopper, is there somewhere besides this alley where we can talk for a few minutes?"

"Beer always goes good after a punch-up." Watkins nodded at the Red Rooster and reached into his pocket for a cell phone. "Just let me ring up the local coppers and report our encounter with these two bastards."

"How about we don't do that?"

Watkins hesitated, glanced at the unconscious thugs and then pointed a blunt finger at Stokey. “I live here on this island, mate. That kind of thing can land me in serious trouble.”

“It could also land you a very lucrative private charter. I’ll go double your regular rate for a trip to Peleliu.”

“Let’s get that beer, mate.” Watkins flipped his phone closed and smiled. “We’ll talk business and I’ll find a couple of local boys to haul away this trash.”

Angaur, Palau Island Group

Whistle Dick Grey checked his GPS more out of habit than any need to know precisely where he was on Angaur. It would be hard for a Cub Scout to get lost on the little island's three square miles, much less a detachment of two SEALS and a shit-hot female black-shoe Navy officer who rode the swimmer delivery vehicle like it was a jet ski. Grey turned and looked to his rear through the green glow of his Gen III AN/PVS-7 night vision goggles. He was barely able to make out LCdr. Janet Dewey and his swim-buddy Petty Officer 2nd Class Chuck Lane hunkered down in a clump of scrub brush thirty meters to his rear.

Clearly visible to his direct front was what remained of Angaur's abandoned lighthouse on the northwest coast. According to the map study they'd done with Gunner Shake Davis out on the Independence that put the village of Ngaramasch off to their right at the base of the island's highest hill. Hopefully, all of Angaur's less than two hundred residents would be sound asleep at 0345 local time. And that should give Dewey plenty of peace to deploy her array of sensors and detectors. If the target turds were here dicking around with chemicals or biologicals, they'd know it in an hour or two, either through gizmo response or direct observation.

He was about to signal his team forward when Lane suddenly stood up looking like some kind of swamp monster with his swim fins and other SEAL gear hanging off his angular frame. "Pack it up, Whistle Dick. We're in the wrong AO."

Grey slithered to the rear wondering if his swim-buddy had lost it somewhere on the long haul aboard the SDV from the helo splash-point to the northeast coast of Angaur. Lane was talking in his usual loud voice and standing up like he didn't give a big rat's ass if anyone spotted him silhouetted against the island skyline. "What's up, douche-bag! Get the fuck down off the skyline!"

"Relax, Dubbya Dee." Lane helped Janet Dewey to her feet and jerked a thumb at the radio on his back. "The Boss just pushed on tac-two and we are operating off the wrong map-sheet. They got word the turds in question are definitely not on this island."

"What now?" Janet Dewey tugged at a point near her thigh where the SEAL-issue wet suit was becoming way too intimate. "Did they say anything else?"

"They said they got some hot intel from Mike Stokey and we're wasting time here on Angaur. Typical shit. We're here and they aren't. Welcome to the wonderful world of special ops."

Grey slung his MP-5SD and stuffed a dip of Skoal into his lip. "Well, fuck me down to parade rest. Ain't it always the way? So where the fuck are the bad guys, or do they know?"

"North of here," Lane turned and started walking back toward the beach where they'd reenter the water, refloat their SDV and then head out to sea toward a designated pickup point, "We extract, recover and do it again on Peleliu."

Whistle Dick Grey fell into a loose file behind Janet Dewey and followed Petty Officer Chuck Lane on their return trip to the same Red Beach where the U.S. Army's 81st Infantry Division, the fighting Wildcats, came ashore on Angaur during Operation Stalemate II in September 1944. The female officer didn't seem to be having any trouble humping the heavy, water-proofed rucksack that contained her sensor gear, but she was doing a weird little kick-step that had Grey concerned.

"You OK, commander? It's gonna be a long ride out to RV with the helo."

"I'm good, Whistle Dick, just a little embarrassed."

"About what?"

"I peed in my wet suit."

"No sweat, ma'am," Whistle Dick Grey laughed loudly and didn't give a shit if anyone on Angaur heard him. "If it feels good, do it. Ain't this SEAL shit some kind of glamorous?"

National Counterterrorism Center, McLean, Virginia

Director Bob Bayer swept his gaze across the heavy-hitters seated around the oval table in the NCTC's secure conference room. The emergency meeting had drawn all the big guns he'd invited and marked the first time heads of all the various agencies involved in counterterrorism efforts had assembled in one place to discuss one topic. It was hard for anyone, no matter what rank or attitude, to ignore a presidential directive that essentially said get with the program or find another job.

Bayer owed that bureaucracy-busting order to Homeland Security Director Jerry Goodall, who had convinced the President to step on some delicate toes and kick the slats out from under a few balky fiefdoms. As a result, Bayer had all the major players in one room and examining the same potentially disastrous problem. Now all he had to do was convince them to take the quick, decisive action he had in mind.

Bayer caught Goodall's eye and nodded his thanks before calling for attention. "Ladies and gentlemen, that list you have contains the names of the people we are convinced are the major players in this biological attack that's being cooked up out in the Pacific." He pointed at the flat-screen video monitor containing the image of Chan Dwyer staring into a webcam mounted on her computer console aboard the USS Independence. "And you've heard Chan Dwyer's excellent assessment of what we believe is the plan for introducing a new strain of very deadly botulism toxin into food sources. I don't need to lead you by the hand to see the consequences if they manage to pull it off."

Bayer paused to sip water and glanced across the table where the National Security Advisor, Secretary of State and the President's Chief of Staff sat mulling the situation and pondering political fallout. He had all the authority he needed to move on the bad guys stirring the deadly soup in the Palaus, but these three would have to handle retribution and consequences for the backers in Saudi Arabia and Iran.

"I'm hoping for a quick and concrete consensus here. My plan, in consultation with Defense, CIA, Homeland Security and the FBI, is to hit these folks out in the Pacific hard. And let me be clear, by that I mean kill or capture—either one will do—to stop this thing before it goes any further."

Near the foot of the conference table, Dr. Joe Jerardi, the presidential science advisor, raised his hand for attention. "I don't want to interrupt, Bob, but do we know how far it's gone already? I mean, are we fairly confident that these guys haven't already done significant damage or run some experiments that could get out of hand? I did my homework on this Dr. Nasuton from Indonesia. He's a brilliant biochemist and geneticist."

"He's also a committed terrorist, Joe. Let's not forget that. Meanwhile, we don't know for sure beyond what the scientists who examined the fish and bird kills out on Wake Island told us. They believe they were looking at experiments gone bad. This was stuff that wasn't ready for employment on a large scale but represented a serious danger if experiments were to proceed. That's why we've got to stop this right now. If there's already been some spread of this toxin into food sources, then we'll have to deal with that as it's discovered. As you know, we've intercepted much of their data and I'm told our best brains are working to develop an effective antitoxin.

"Defense has assets in place right now." Bayer pointed at the image being transmitted from the Independence. "And we will be moving immediately to take down that yacht that's being used as a sort of support ship, as well as hitting their base of operations on Peleliu. That brings me to subjects that will need all of our best efforts working hand-in-glove, with political concerns on a back-burner."

Bayer focused on the Secretary of State who was clearly not happy with being ordered to attend the meeting in person. "Madam Secretary, we need you to handle the situation with the Palauan government in the short term. Someone in their bureaucracy has let snakes into the tent. That needs to be dealt with and we can't have any local interference with the team that goes into Peleliu to take on these guys. In the long run, your people and the White House will have to determine what we do with this Saudi royal that's been writing the checks, with the Indonesians who are providing the scientific support and with the Iranians who are in this thing hip-deep for their own reasons."

The Secretary of State tapped her pen on a legal pad for a few moments and then glanced at the National Security Advisor seated on her right. "Well, the Palau thing is simple. We have significant influence there under the '94 Compact of Free Association. They are independent on one hand, but dependent on us for a great deal on the other. It's no problem. As for the rest, we will take whatever political and diplomatic measures are called for with the backers of this thing obviously." She dropped her pen, folded her arms and leaned back in her chair causing the springs to squeak in protest. "However, you must be aware we can't start pointing fingers or declaring sanctions without solid evidence that nations like Saudi Arabia or Iran are involved. Give us that and we'll take it to the World Court, the United Nations and the international press. That's our best course of action...and that means you need to rethink this dead-or-alive cowboy stuff."

The National Security Advisor caught the hard glare the Defense Secretary fixed on his cabinet colleague and jumped into the conversation. "I think I can guarantee the president will step up with strong international reaction given evidence that the Saudis and Iranians have their fingers in this pie, Bob. But he's got to have solid shots in the locker. I'd advise your people to do everything they can to take the players out on Peleliu alive. We get our hands on these people and we can draw a solid line to their backers."

"I don't think that will be a problem." The Defense Secretary shuffled through a small leather-covered notebook. "We've got a SEAL Team out there aboard one of our new littoral combat ships. That's some of our best operators up against a team of scientists and a handful of security goons from Quds Force. No doubt there will be gunplay involved, but I'll instruct our operators to take everyone alive if they can possibly do so."

"In my view, the most important thing is to contain the stuff they're playing with out there." Homeland Security Secretary Jerry Goodall screwed the cap off a bottle of water and took a drink. "We need to drop a bio-hazard curtain over that island, contain and isolate any experimental materials, and then make an assessment. The best case scenario is to shut 'em down, capture the players and bag up a bunch of evidence concerning what they've been doing. It's gonna be hard for the rest of the world to shrug that off, much less defend it in any way."

"That pretty much outlines what we're planning to do." Bayer fiddled with his mouse and tapped a key on his computer. "I've just sent each of you a bare-bones plan of action that I will order at the end of this meeting, unless anyone has questions or serious objections. Independence will intercept the yacht and detain the crew; SEALs will go ashore on Peleliu and hopefully capture their science guys. Our bio-warfare specialists will contain what's dangerous, and then we'll move our scientific team from the Seascope in to lock it all down for analysis and ultimate containment. It's Friday night out in the Palaus. I expect it all to be over by Saturday night or Sunday morning at the latest."

Peleliu

"I was told that this man brought fish to Missus Sulukep..." The Peleliu Chief of Police pointed at Ignacio Felodon, "and traded for liquor. She eat fish for supper last night and now two people dead. Nurse thinks it was some kind of poison in the fish. Missus Sulukep and her daughter found an hour ago by neighbor lady who reported it to me. She said she was invited to supper but could not go. Thank God for that."

"How can you be sure the fish were from our stock?" Sayed Abdullah struggled mightily to keep his voice under control and his expression calm and reassuring. The little bastard standing off to his left with a smug smile on his face had wrecked the mission. There were no options now. He had ordered the Al Calipha to Peleliu to begin evacuating the entire operation.

"Your man standing right here..." The Peleliu Police Chief pushed past Abdullah and confronted Ignacio Felodon while pulling a small notebook from his shirt pocket. "You were seen in the village of Klouklubed at approximately 6:30 last night and carrying a plastic pail. Were fish in that pail?"

Abdullah caught Felodon's eye and glared. "Tell him what he needs to know, Ibrahim." Surely the man would not be stupid enough to admit the fish he'd traded for liquor came from the experimental stock. "We want to cooperate fully with the authorities."

Felodon nodded and turned his attention to the police chief. "I brought the woman three fish. She gave me some beer for them."

"And were these fish from your lagoon here?"

Felodon hesitated. Abdullah signaled furiously from behind the policeman's back. They had to end this confrontation peacefully and get on with evacuating. It wouldn't take long for word to leak out that there were suspicious deaths on this tiny island. There was a fairly sophisticated cell phone hooked on the man's baggy shorts.

"I bought them from one of the local fishermen..." Felodon gestured toward the docks to the south where locals usually tied up with their daily catch. "He said they were from out beyond the reef."

"And who was this fisherman?"

"I don't know his name."

"You must come with me, sir." The policeman snapped his notebook closed. "We will visit all the local boats and you will identify the man who sold you the fish."

The officer pointed toward his pickup truck and spun to confront Abdullah. "There will be a complete investigation of this incident. I will be calling in support from the National Police on Koror. In the meantime, you must shut down this operation until the investigation is complete."

"Of course." Abdullah nodded and motioned for Felodon to accompany the officer. "As I said, we want to cooperate fully with the authorities. And I'm very sorry to hear of these deaths, but I assure you our activities had nothing to do with them."

"That is to be determined..."

They were the last words the only certified law enforcement officer on Peleliu ever spoke. Felodon stepped up behind the man, shoved the muzzle of a Makarov pistol between his shoulder blades and pulled the trigger twice.

* * *

"*Inshallah*? You arrogant bastard! How dare you quote the book to me?" Sayed Abdullah had a Glock semi-auto pistol pointed at a spot directly between Ignacio Felodon's eyes. It was taking every ounce of his control to keep from squeezing the trigger. "You are no believer and you never have been. You are alive at this moment only because our leaders thought you might be useful once the weapon is deployed. That is no longer a concern."

Felodon shrugged and cut a glance at his own pistol lying in the sand where he'd been forced to drop it when Abdullah drew down on him after he killed the local police chief. What Abdullah didn't know was that the situation in their little bio-weapon task force had changed significantly last night after a conversation with Amin Faraz, the leader of the QF Security Team.

"You may shoot me or not...as you please. Nothing changes. The mission continues as planned with a first strike in the Philippines. I may not live to see it but I will have justice for the killing of my family. Nothing you can do will stop that." Felodon stared beyond the muzzle of the pistol pointed at him and saw the uncertainty in Abdullah's eyes.

"You are wrong about that, Infidel. The Al Calipha is on its way here and Dr. Nasuton's people will be packing for immediate departure. This mission has failed and you are to blame. I may be punished for the failure, but not before I do what I should have done the first time we met."

"And what of the security team?"

"They go where I direct and do as I say."

Felodon cut a glance over Abdullah's shoulder and smiled. "I don't think so. And I would suggest you drop your weapon before Amin Faraz shoots you in the back."

Keeping his pistol pointed at Felodon, Abdullah spun quickly and caught sight of the senior QF security man sighting down the barrel of a Krinkov AK-74 assault rifle. The muzzle swung and pointed directly at the center of his chest.

"What are you doing, you fool?" Abdullah shouted in Farsi. "The council will have you killed for this!"

"It's Plan B, the emergency response," Faraz responded in his native language. "You should know about that. Drop your weapon and kick it in my direction. Let's make this easy."

Abdullah dropped his pistol and sent it skittering across the sand. "There is no Plan B, Amin. We are evacuating as soon as the Al Calipha gets here. The blame for this failure lies with the infidel. You can see that."

"There is always a Plan B in Quds Force, Sayed...and you should know that. I was briefed before we left Tehran. Pity you were not...but perhaps the leadership did not repose as much trust in you as they did in me. Plan B simply said if you should waiver, I assume command. When you ordered an evacuation, we reached that point."

Abdullah watched as Felodon picked up his Makarov and brushed at the sand. He had only moments to salvage the situation. "How can you cooperate with this nonbeliever, Amin? He is only here to be the scapegoat once the mission is launched. That will not happen now. He's killed local people with contaminated fish. He's killed a policeman. We have been compromised. It's over."

"Yes, it's over, but not for the mission. Dr. Nasuton reports that the infidel saved us time and trouble by experimenting on local people. The weapon is ready for use. It works. Now we will deploy it as planned." Amin Faraz nodded once in the direction of Ignacio Felodon who was performing a press-check on his Makarov to be sure there was a ready round in the chamber.

Reassured that the weapon was free of sand and fully functional, Ignacio Felodon stuck the muzzle into Sayed Abdullah's right ear and pulled the trigger.

"You are now in command." Felodon stuck the pistol into his pocket and assumed a position of attention. "What are your orders?"

"You will take Dr. Nasuton and the two scientists with sufficient fish samples and evacuate when the Al Calipha arrives offshore. You will conduct the initial attack in the Philippines with the help of three of my Quds Force men. Once you have made the attack, proceed to Jakarta and await further orders."

"And what happens here? It won't be long before there is some reaction from the authorities."

"We will destroy the evidence here and make our way to Babelthaup. There we will arrange transportation to Jakarta. That is all you need to know."

Amin Faraz, the new field commander of the bio-weapon mission signaled to one of his men. "Destroy the telephone cable trunks, disable the cellular booster tower and deploy to over-watch positions as planned. No one gets on or off this island until the Al Calipha arrives."

Aboard FV Flying Fish, Peleliu Waters

"Something wonky here, Mate." Josh Watkins pulled back on the throttles keeping just enough turns on the boat's powerful engines to hold position against the current streaming along the outer edges of Peleliu's western coral reef. As Mike Stokey joined him beside the wheel in the elevated cockpit, Watkins pointed toward the Camp Beck Docks about five hundred meters off their port beam. "All the local boats are tied up when they should be out here fetching supper."

Stokey reached for a pair of 7x50 binoculars hanging from a bulkhead hook and swept the dock area. "Not all of them, Chopper. There's some guy headed our way in an outrigger and it looks like he's trying to get your attention."

Watkins took the glasses and focused on the boat. "That's Des. He's my local mate and one of the best diving riggers on the island. Not like him to be on the surface of the water this time of day." Chopper Watkins shifted his scrutiny of the distant shore back to the dock area. "Something definitely out of sorts here, Mike. There's a black flag flying on the dock. That's trouble; means no boats to approach closer inshore than the seaward side of the reef."

"Why?"

"That's the money question, mate. Only time I've seen a black flag flying out here was when the Koror cops shut down the island a couple of years ago. They caught some boat out of Papua fueling up on Peleliu with a load of cocaine in the hold. I reckon Des will give us the gouge when he gets out here."

Stokey helped Watkins set an anchor aft while they waited for the outrigger to traverse the distance between the docks and their position out beyond the reef. If his instincts were any guide—and they hadn't failed him in thirty years in and out of dodgy situations—there was something seriously wrong somewhere beyond the idyllic scenery of Peleliu's beaches.

"Des, old son, what's up on the island, mate?" Chopper stood in the bow of the Flying Fish ready to heave his friend a mooring line. Des cut power to a clunky outboard and swung his battered boat to bring it alongside when a gout of seawater exploded in his wake. Stokey recognized the situation seconds before he heard the distant report of a rifle. Someone was shooting at their visitor from the high ground beyond the beach. He made a sprint for the binoculars on the bridge but not before he heard a second shot smack into the seasoned wood of the outrigger's hull. As he climbed the accommodation ladder, he looked over his shoulder to see the islander bail over the side of his boat and disappear underwater. Chopper rushed aft to raise the anchor.

"Pull Des up on the outboard side!" Chopper heaved mightily on the anchor and Stokey felt the boat swing with the current as he jumped down to the deck and scrambled to locate Des and haul him aboard the Flying Fish. Just as he was reaching for the man's outstretched hand he heard a third shot slap into the superstructure. The shooter on Peleliu was putting in some credible rounds at a range of 500 meters or more so he was no amateur and it wouldn't be long before he had the range bracketed. They needed to get out of that range in a hurry.

With very little help from Stokey, Des lunged aboard and with a cursory nod to his rescuer rushed to the bridge where Chopper Watkins was already spinning the wheel and jamming the throttles toward warp speed. The Flying Fish squatted as her propellers dug in and then wheeled into a hard right turn taking them seaward of the shooter on Peleliu.

Twenty minutes later they were cruising on a northerly course five nautical miles offshore. It had taken some strong argument to keep Chopper Watkins from reporting the encounter to the Palauan National Police on Koror. In fact, he had the radio tuned and ready to transmit when Stokey finally convinced him that bringing in the local cops would only complicate matters on Peleliu. If the national police hadn't been notified already by someone on the island, it was best to keep them out of the picture until the situation could be stabilized by real professionals.

Stokey went below to see what he could find out from Des. The native islander was more than a little anxious to tell someone in authority about what was happening. There were four locals and two visiting divers dead on Peleliu and nobody knew why. The islanders were hunkered down in their homes, no one could find the local police chief and the phone lines normally used to communicate with Babelthaup were not working. Des didn't know if anyone had reported the situation by radio or cellular phone to Koror. He'd heard the deaths had something to do with eating local fish, so he'd personally raised the black flag over the docks.

"You've got some people on the island doing science experiments, right?" Stokey handed the islander a cold beer from the reefer in the boat's tiny kitchen area. "Aren't they working with fish?"

Des hit on the beer greedily and nodded until he could swallow a mouthful. "Lots of people sayin' them guys poisoning the fish. My cousin says Keana Sulukep and her girl eating fish from them guys and they dead now. Mister Monoro, the cop...he supposed to shut them guys down but nobody can find him."

Stokey reached for his satellite phone and checked the power status. "Des, you got any idea who might have been shooting at us?"

The islander drained his beer and shook his head. "Nobody on Peleliu got that kind of gun. I'm thinkin' it's the fish guys. Lots of people doin' day work for 'em say they act like soldiers not scientists. And some kids from up by Ngalkol village say they seen people from the fish farm with army-type guns up in the Umurbrogol. They doin' the shooting, you ask me."

Stokey handed Des another beer and stepped out onto the fishing decks with his sat-phone. "Hey, Chopper. Is it worth another full charter fee to get me around the other side of the island and put me ashore after dark?"

When he saw a grin and a thumbs-up from the skipper, Stokey plopped into one of the big fishing chairs and punched numbers into his phone. When Shake Davis came up on the other end of the circuit, Stokey took a deep breath and started the briefing.

"Houston...we've got a problem..."

He was blinded by glare from a descending sun and deep into his plan for going ashore on a reconnaissance mission, so Mike Stokey missed the small dot on the southern horizon. It was the Al Calipha plowing through the Pacific chop and headed for Peleliu at top speed under emergency orders from the team leader on the island.

Aboard USS Independence, West of the Palaus

"Thanks, Mike. Hold one while I check with the mission commander." Shake Davis swept the crowd gathered around the wardroom table where Stokey's sat-phone report was being piped through a speaker in the middle of the mess table. SEAL Lt. Kerry Dale Hunter was standing beside the Independence skipper who was measuring distances on a chart with a pair of navigational dividers. "It's your call, Mr. Hunter. You want Mike to go ashore on Peleliu or hold aboard the boat and wait for us?"

Hunter nodded at LCdr. Janet Dewey and leaned across the table. "I need input here, Janet. If he goes ashore and does a little recon for us, is he gonna be OK? Is this stuff lethal? Or do we know?"

"From what Mike tells us he got from the islander, I don't think it's communicable yet or there would be a lot more than four dead on Peleliu. I'm betting the science guys tweaked it to be deadly if consumed but safe enough for them to handle." Janet Dewey paused for a moment to run fingers through her blonde hair. "I think he's safe as long as he doesn't mess around with any of their experimental stock."

Hunter mashed a button on the console and slumped into a chair where he could be closer to the speaker. "Mike, this is Lt. Hunter. You're good to go ashore for recon. Opinion out here is that you'll be fine if you don't handle any of the experimental stuff—or have a fish dinner."

"No chance of that, Kerry Dale. I'll go ashore on the east side of the island after dark and keep it low and slow. How soon can you guys be here?"

Hunter glanced at Cdr. Doug Bland, CO of the Independence, and saw three fingers held up in the air. "We're about three hours out right now, Mike, but we've got to take down that yacht before we deal with Peleliu. I want to make that a night op to avoid a fight if we can. What time are you planning on going ashore?"

"I dunno, maybe 2300 or thereabouts. Late as I can. They tell me there's gonna be a full moon." Out on the Flying Fish, Stokey checked his watch and did a rapid calculation. "If you guys hit the Al Calipha around that time and it goes fairly easy, you can send the landing force ashore a couple of hours later. I'll set up an RV point and we can tweak your plan. I should have it all scoped out by then. We can hit 'em hard around dawn. How's that sound?"

Shake Davis grinned and leaned in toward the speaker: "You afraid of night ops, Mike?"

"Negative, Shake. I love that shit. But it's been my experience that it goes easier at first light when they're either in REM sleep or just getting up to piss and scratch their ass."

"Copy all. Proceed with the recon and feed us regular updates via sat-phone." Lt. Hunter winked at Shake Davis and rose from his chair. "We'll have someone monitoring the other end twenty-four-seven."

"Roger...but don't call me unless it's an emergency. I don't think this thing's got a vibrate function and my ringtone might piss 'em off. I'll report in hourly from 2300. You guys can expect an initial SALUTE report around midnight tonight. Out here."

Chan Dwyer reached across the table to cut the speaker connection. "Last time I heard that was in Officer Candidate School."

"Last time you heard what?" Tracey Davis stood looking confused as the team began to gather up charts, notes and laptops.

"She's referring to a SALUTE report, Tracey. Don't they teach you Navy officers anything these days?"

"I'm thinking you're not referring to toss the senior officer a highball and a polite greeting. Right, Dad?"

"SALUTE is an old reconnaissance mnemonic thing, Tracey. When you're doing recon by direct observation, you're supposed to focus on enemy Size, Activity, Location, Unit, Time and Equipment. Mike's an old recon Marine. He'll feed us the information we need to plan the attack."

"And we'd best be getting to that right now." Lt. Hunter unfolded a Peleliu map as his SEAL operators closed on the wardroom table. "I'll need Commander Bland and all of my guys to stick around. The rest of you can get back to stations. We'll have an all hands brief-back in an hour. That's your chance to shoot technical holes in what we're planning to do with the yacht and with the assault on Peleliu. Anybody seen Lurch?"

"You rang?" Chief Frank Wiley stuck his head into the wardroom and nodded at his laughing teammates. It was apparently an old joke among the operators.

"Where you been, Chief? We gotta cook up an underway takedown."

"You might want to hold on that for a few minutes, Boss. Comm shack just got flash traffic from PACAF. The Al Calipha changed course. She's headed for Peleliu; doin' forty knots, no smoke."

* * *

Chan Dwyer caught up with Shake Davis as he was headed down to the well-deck where SEAL riggers were working on the rigid inflatable boat or RIB that would be used in the boarding and takedown of the Al Calipha. She pinned him up against a bulkhead and moved into drill instructor range.

"I've got something to say to you and it needs saying right now."

"Uh-oh." Shake grinned down at her and saw she was serious about something. "I have apparently pissed you off."

"No, I could handle that. This other thing has got me confused."

"What did I do?"

"You've flattered me to the point where I don't know how to handle it." She poked a playful finger at his chest. "I had no idea you had serious feelings for me, about me."

"Shit, I'm gonna kick that kid's ass."

"Don't let me hear about it, Shake Davis. If Tracey hadn't told me, I'd never have known that you thought about me that way?"

"What way?"

"Don't be dense. You know what I mean. I had no idea you had, you know, genuinely romantic feelings about me."

"Well, I do. What do you think we ought to do about it?"

"Damned if I know." Chan draped her arms around his neck. "But it's worth exploring."

What Chan planned as a chaste kiss on the lips turned into something much more in a hurry. When they finally broke the embrace she looked up into his clear blue eyes and saw a tear trickle down his cheek.

"What's the matter, Shake?"

"I can't believe you think I'm worth exploring—or anything much else for that matter."

"Listen, Mr. Hard Ass." She smiled and brushed at the tear track on his face. "It's OK to have feelings...but you've got to let me know about them."

Shake pulled her into a hug and felt her body melt against his. "Hell of a deal, ain't it? All this comes out after we haven't seen each other for a couple of years and right about the time we're gonna go kick-ass on some dudes that might just put a round between my running lights."

"No factor, Shake." Chan pulled a piece of paper out of her coveralls pocket and shook it in his face. "Kerry Dale Hunter gave me the assignments for the Al Calipha and Peleliu. You'll be safe and sound right here on the Independence with me."

"Sonofabitch!" Shake Davis unfolded the personnel assignment roster and held it up to a bulkhead light. "We'll see about this shit!"

He stormed off down the passageway looking for Hunter and leaving Chan Dwyer wondering what she was getting herself into with a guy caught somewhere between old warhorse and old horse's ass.

Peleliu

Mike Stokey lay flat on the sand of Honeymoon Beach, letting a rising tide wash over him while he tried to catch his breath and work a few knots out of his hamstrings. It had been a hell of a long time since he'd had to swim a mile in open sea. The mask and fins Chopper Watkins provided were helpful but the jury-rigged waterproof bags for his sat-phone, field glasses, shotgun and ammo had added tiresome drag to his swim from the Flying Fish, now lying blacked-out just over the horizon.

When his legs felt like they could stand the strain, he low-crawled across the sand to a clump of palmetto and took inventory. His binocs, phone and a borrowed Brunton hiking compass looked dry and functional. A press-check on the phone showed full charge, so he'd be OK for his first sitrep in less than an hour. The Mossberg 590 Mariner 12-gauge pump had taken a little water but it was designed for use at sea, which is why Watkins carried it as a shark-killer. Most importantly, the ten rounds of double-ought buckshot—all Chopper had aboard the boat—were in good shape. Stokey slid five rounds into the feed tube and racked the slide as quietly as possible. He was on the opposite side of the island from where Des indicated the bad guys' base camp was, but he knew there were shooters somewhere in the high ground between this beach and the western side of Peleliu, so he wasn't about to get careless about noise or light discipline.

Stokey hand-scraped a hole into the marshy ground and dug around until he had a mud puddle. He smeared goo over the exposed skin of his face, neck and hands, ignoring the swarms of mosquitoes and sand fleas he disturbed, and then oriented his compass. The luminous needle told him northwest was toward his right-front. According to Des there was a paved road that the islanders used to get to Honeymoon Beach, but Stokey wanted to avoid running into any locals. No telling how they might react to yet another armed yahoo running around on their island.

Shake Davis, who knew the terrain intimately from battlefield explorations and an in-depth study of the 1st Marine Division's devastating fight on Peleliu back in 1944, said the bad guys were likely camped about halfway up the island's north-south axis where a pair of sandy promontories formed a natural lagoon. Des had pointed it out on a map. The high ground overlooking that spot was an infamous World War II battle site.

Stokey set his compass bezel and headed for Bloody Nose Ridge.

* * *

Showing only navigation lights as ordered, the Al Calipha lay at anchor in a two-point moor just off the west shore of Peleliu where there was sufficient depth to handle her displacement. The captain had come ashore personally in a Zodiac to see for himself who was giving the orders he was required to follow now that Abdullah, his original mission commander, was dead.

His encrypted email queries to Jeddah had gone mostly unanswered except for a terse directive to check personally with the QF security force on the island. He'd done that directly after coming ashore on Peleliu where Amin Faraz led him into a tent and showed him a piece of paper bearing the seal of his ultimate boss, Prince al-Azizi of the Royal House of Saud. Absent instructions from the prince himself or from the original mission commander, the captain was to submit his ship and crew to orders from the man holding the document under the light of a hissing Coleman lantern.

"Do you have questions—or problems?" Amin Faraz clearly did not expect any. The captain fiddled with his pipe and silently thanked Allah that he would not be taking orders from the little piss-ant Filipino who was outside the tent shepherding the scientists into the Zodiac for transport out to his ship.

"I have no problems." The captain struck a match and sucked on his pipe for a moment deciding how to frame his questions. "Once we are at sea, who gives the orders?"

Faraz motioned for one of his men to step out of the shadows. "This is Ali, my second in command. He will be in charge of the mission as far as the Philippines. You will take your orders from him. Dr. Nasuton and his cohorts will direct insertion of the weapon into the waters off Manila Bay. We have contacts within the fishing fleet that will insure it is properly dispersed. What else?"

The captain fiddled with lighting his pipe again, playing for enough time to cover all his fears. The over-flight of the military drone was nagging at him and he did not want an encounter with warships during the passage from the Palaus to the Philippines. "If we should be stopped or boarded by authorities? What then?"

Amin Faraz flicked flame from a butane lighter and set fire to the letter from Prince al-Azizi. "You will plead innocence, of course. You are simply a rich man's yacht touring the South Pacific. Dr. Nasuton has been briefed, and he has sufficient funds to buy your way out of trouble. My men will deal with anything else. Your mission is to bring the scientists and the weapon into Manila Bay." Amin Faraz laid his right hand on the butt of the pistol tucked inside his belt. "Can you do that?"

The threat was clear and the captain had been on enough missions with Iranian Quds Force *jihadis* to understand that there was no room for debate. The innocent pleasure cruise facade might work with local law enforcement in the Palaus and cash might get them past problems with authorities in the Philippines, but the Lebanese captain was more worried about the U.S. military. He took a last look at the steely glint in the Iranian soldier's eyes and decided it wasn't worth mentioning.

"Of course, we will carry out our orders to the letter." Among men like Amin Faraz, commitment always trumped logic or reason.

A crewman from the Al Calipha stuck his head inside the tent to interrupt: "Captain, we have most of the cargo aboard. Next trip is the Indo's and the Filipino. We'll be ready to get underway in thirty minutes."

The captain nodded and motioned for his boatswain to proceed with the loading. He fiddled with his pipe for a moment and then turned to the QF security force commander. "What about that little Filipino infidel, commander? It would be an easy thing to dispose of him at sea."

Amin Faraz grabbed the Al Calipha captain by the elbow and led him toward the blackout flap of the tent. "I take orders as you do, Captain. Under no circumstances is he to be harmed. He has value to the mission in the long view."

USS Independence

Shake Davis caught up with Lt. Kerry Dale Hunter in a passageway leading to the well-deck where seven SEALs were rigged and ready to launch their RIB toward the takedown of the Al Calipha. The detachment commander was Number 8 in the team chalk and anxious to join his men. Shake Davis was blocking his path in a very determined manner and Hunter realized he was in for a fight before the mission even got underway.

"I know why you're here, Gunner. And the answer is no."

"That's *your* answer, and it's the wrong one."

"C'mon, Shake, don't give me a hard time. Why didn't you bring this up at the brief-back?"

"Wasn't the right time or place." Shake had to bite his tongue at the final briefing to keep from creating a scene and disrupting focus on details of the mission. That and he knew he'd get heat from Tracey and Chan Dwyer if he insisted on a spot in the takedown team.

"Well, now is not the right time either. Jesus, Gunner, we've already had to delay the launch due to the Al Calipha's new position. Be reasonable. We do this shit for a living and you don't. It's that simple. And it's a delicate operation. It takes precision moves and teamwork from practiced guys."

"What if there's a fight?" Shake played the hole card he'd decided on at the brief-back. "You said you're gonna leave two men in the RIB to hold it alongside. You'd be better off putting all hands aboard the yacht. I'll be the guy in the RIB maintaining position for you."

Hunter checked his diver's watch and thought it over while the second hand made one full sweep. Best guess by Cdr. Bland was that the Al Calipha had a crew of at least twenty men. No telling if they were armed, but they probably were. LCdr. Janet Dewey was included on the assault team in case they had to deal with bio-hazard. That left him with only Chief Wiley and two other operators remaining behind to prep the Peleliu assault. Davis had a point.

"You ever handled a RIB?"

"I was in on the formation of the Small Craft Assault Company at Camp Lejeune. You guys trained us until we got our shit together on the RIBs and the other shallow draft boats. I can handle it. And you need me. All I need is to borrow some gear."

"Gunner, I hope I don't regret this. My guys think you've got your shit together and I'm inclined to agree." Hunter checked his watch again and listened for a moment to a transmission coming through his headset. "Chief Wiley is down in the gear locker by the well deck. He'll give you what you need."

Bloody Nose Ridge, Peleliu

According to Shake Davis when he recommended this spot as an ideal over-watch position, Wattie Ridge was named after the man who commanded a platoon of G Company, 2nd Battalion, 5th Marines that wrestled it away from Japanese defenders in a very bloody fight back in 1944. Mike Stokey lay huddled in a coral crevice on the nose of that ridge waiting for his sat-phone to synch up with a bird and wondering if he would have survived the brutal contest for this little stretch of coral high ground just 150 meters above Peleliu's sandy western beaches. Wattie Ridge was just one of several spiky, cave-encrusted fingers of high ground that composed the long, jagged stretch of the Umurbrogol Massif known collectively as Bloody Nose Ridge. It was also the perfect place to see everything happening on those beaches for half a mile in either direction.

And he'd already seen some very disturbing stuff since reaching his position on the ridge half an hour earlier. Surely the people out aboard the Independence knew by now that the Al Calipha was moored right here at Peleliu. They'd have the big yacht on radar but he didn't know if the presence of the luxury vessel just offshore would help or hinder SEAL plans for the takedown.

What he did know was that the yacht wouldn't remain for long. The bad guys below his perch had been ferrying people and equipment out to the Al Calipha ever since he'd been watching them through the binoculars under a shiny-bright tropical moon. Stokey punched the speed dial, listened to some electronic noise, and then heard Chan Dwyer's voice loud and clear.

"We're here, Mike. Send your traffic."

"Can't talk too loud, Chan. Can you hear me OK?"

"You're good. Go ahead."

"I'm looking at the fucking Al Calipha anchored right here offshore. You guys know that, right?"

"We've got her position, Mike." Stokey recognized the voice of Cdr. Bland. "Any idea if they plan on staying around?"

"No chance, Commander. I've been watching for the past thirty minutes or so and they've got small boats shuttling back and forth. Looks like they're pulling out as soon as they've got everything they want off the beach."

"Mike, this is Tracey Davis. Can you tell if they're just taking people out to the yacht? Or are they also moving equipment? We need to know if they're taking any samples with them off the island."

"Got to be taking some stuff with them is my guess. They moved at least two things that look like fish tanks to me. A boat just left that was carrying what looked like buckets for live bait. My money says Hunter and his guys will find a bunch of bad fish aboard that yacht. Better let 'em know right away."

"Janet Dewey is going along on the takedown." Chan's voice sounded cool and professional. "I'll be sure she knows about it."

"Roger. Two more things, and then we better sign off. Thing one: Tell Hunter they've got security positions up in these hills and he'll likely be facing some serious firepower. I hope to have more detail on that in my next sitrep."

"So they're leaving some people behind? Why would they do that?"

"Beats me but they're recovering the shuttle boats now out on the yacht. And there's still a bunch of guys with guns milling around down on the beach. Here's thing two: I can't be dead certain about this, but tell Shake I think they're taking his little Filipino buddy with them out to the ship. I'm pretty sure I recognized him boarding one of the shuttle boats. Updates on the hour. Out here."

USS Independence

"Captain...CIC."

Commander Doug Bland stood in the ladder-well three levels below his normal station on the bridge and watched as his chief boatswain supervised the flooding of the ship's well deck. He reached for the portable radio clipped to his horse-collar life vest and talked to the watch officer in the combat information center.

"This is the Skipper. Send it."

"Sir, radar reports target is moving. She's on a north-westerly course at about twelve knots and accelerating. We have a constant track."

"Copy all. Stand by." Bland jumped down from his perch and splashed his way toward the 35 foot rigid hull inflatable boat that was already bobbing in the chilly seawater streaming into his ship. Five of the nine raiders including Shake Davis and Janet Dewey were already aboard kneeling next to the gunwales. Four other SEALs of the assault team were stabilizing the boat and steering it toward the launch ramp at the rear of the ship. Bland waved his radio in the air and pointed at his ear. Lt. Hunter caught the signal and came up on the net.

"I've got you, Skipper. What's up?"

"Radar reports Al Calipha is on the move. She's heading northwest away from Peleliu. Looks like we do this underway. You OK with that?"

"No problem, Commander. We briefed it either way. If she doesn't heave-to, we'll do it the hard way. Just keep their attention focused on you."

"Gunner Davis, you up on this net?"

"Send it, Skipper."

"We just talked to Mike Stokey on Peleliu. He wants you to know he thinks the Filipino is aboard the Al Calipha."

"Copy. We'll be looking for him."

"Good luck, you guys."

Cdr. Bland watched the RIB and its complement of raiders disappear into moonlit waters aft of his ship and mashed the transmit button on his radio. “Bridge...Captain. Bring us onto an intercept course and sound general quarters.”

Aboard Al Calipha

"Al Calipha, Al Calipha, this is United States Navy vessel Independence. Be advised you are transiting territorial waters under protection of the U.S. government by agreement with the Republic of the Palaus. Heave to and stand by for close inspection."

It was the third time the message had been broadcast over VHS Channels 13 and 16. And for the third time Ali, standing next to Ignacio Felodon on the yacht's enclosed bridge, ordered the captain to ignore it. The captain checked his radar repeater and did a calculation in his head.

"We are just over five kilometers off the coast. Under maritime law, the order is valid."

"The order is nonsense." Ali stood staring at the dark shape looming off the yacht's port bow. "They won't shoot at an unarmed civilian vessel. Continue on your course."

"They might not shoot but they can bring unwanted attention. I'd suggest you hide what you don't want them to see and we let them approach. They may just want a closer look. If they see nothing suspicious, they go away."

The captain was prepared to provide further argument when a blinding spear of light stabbed into his eyes. Ali reeled away from the windows as the warship's high-power xenon searchlight swept over the bridge nearly blinding the sailors on watch at the yacht's conning stations.

"Al Calipha, Al Calipha..." The radio erupted and the voice that boomed through the bridge speakers sounded ominous. "This is your last warning. If you do not heave-to immediately, we are prepared to fire."

Ali grabbed at the captain's elbow. "Buy us some time to hide the equipment and samples. Send a signal. Tell them we have radio failure." Ali and Ignacio Felodon scrambled for the exit to go below as the Al Calipha's captain called for a hand from his communications section to mount a blinker-light and send a message to the threatening warship.

At a point in the second deck passageways where a transverse corridor led to the yacht's kitchen, Felodon cut a sharp left turn and headed for his shipboard contact. He had $5,000 in his pocket he had stolen from Dr. Nasuton's stash. The Filipino cook's helper in the yacht's crew had agreed that was enough to buy his silence and cooperation should Felodon require it.

* * *

Five hundred yards aft of the Al Calipha and gaining on her under the powerful thrust of two muffled 300-horsepower outboards, Lt. Kerry Dale Hunter watched the cone of brilliant light play across the yacht's superstructure. The bridge crew had to be blinded. Carefully avoiding the searchlight beam, he hit the power to his night vision goggles and swept the after weather decks for movement. There were two men scrambling on the starboard side who appeared to be messing around with one of the davits used to lower small craft or cargo from the deck into the water. Whatever they were doing clearly wasn't critical. Both men quickly headed forward and disappeared through a hatch. The decks were clear as far as he could see. They needed to remain that way for another few minutes. He nodded for the coxswain to increase speed and keyed his radio.

"Skipper, we're closing fast. What's happening on your end?"

"They've slowed to around eight knots. I think the xenon scared the shit out of them. There's some douche bag on the bridge sending blinking light. Says they're having radio trouble. We just repeated the heave-to message with our own light. Whaddaya think?"

"Can you see anybody out on the decks? Anybody aft? It looks deserted from here."

"Doesn't mean there isn't a bunch of 'em on the interior getting ready to repel boarders. How about I put a shot across their bow? Jesus Christ, I've always wanted to do that."

"We're right behind 'em now. Fire away."

The SEAL coxswain turned the wheel over to Shake Davis and shifted his bulk to a position just behind teammates holding grapnels that would hook four aluminum boarding ladders onto the yacht's starboard quarter. Hopefully, they'd get up those ladders and aboard the yacht while everyone on watch was focused on the Independence looming on the opposite side.

USS Independence

"Weps, you hot to trot on the Mark 110?" Cdr. Doug Bland watched the turret mounted forward on his littoral combat ship traverse smoothly as it swept across the Al Calipha's bow. The barrel of the 57mm weapon depressed and then elevated slightly as the gunner in CIC searched for the right trajectory.

"We have a solution, captain. Round should pass right over their bow chains. And we're firing tracer element to be damn sure they get the picture."

Bland grinned and keyed his intercom. He was feeling like a high seas buccaneer about to halt a prize on the bounding main. "Very well. Two rounds, fifty-seven millimeter, stand by. Fire!" The weapon barked snappily and Bland's smile widened when he saw the long tongue of flame leap from the muzzle. Firing the MK 110 in weapons quals was one thing, but this shit was way cool.

"XO!" Cdr. Bland was on a roll as he turned to his second-in-command and jerked a thumb toward the flight deck on the fantail. "That ought to get their attention but I'd like to *keep* it, at least until the SEALs get aboard and in control. Let's launch the helo and have the brown shoes buzz around for a while. Tell 'em to keep to the port side of the Al Calipha."

Al Calipha

"Their intentions are clear." The captain turned to Ali, who had rushed back to the bridge when the American warship opened fire. "What are yours? You know they will come aboard. And when they do, they will find the weapon, and we will all wind up at Guantanamo."

Ali thought for a moment, running over his diminishing options. "Allah has shown us this path. We follow it. Have every crew member that you trust locate a weapon and be prepared to use it. When they come aboard, we fight."

"You can't be serious." The captain stared incredulously at the QF operator and pointed at the Navy helicopter now buzzing around off their port side. "They will either open fire on us from the ship or that helicopter will launch some devil weapon that will sink us."

"*Inshallah*. The main concern now is to protect what remains on Peleliu. If they kill us they will believe they are safe and call off any further effort. But there will be another time and another mission."

"Increase speed." Ali started for the bridge door and a ladder that led below. "Make them chase us. I need time."

That was all the captain needed to know before he died in service to the faith. There was no need to tell him that packed in one of the equipment cases down in the spaces where the contaminated fish were stored was thirty kilograms of Semtex high explosive and the necessary detonators to blow the bottom right out of the Al Calipha.

One deck below the bridge, Ali encountered two of his men passing out weapons to a clutch of crewmen. He estimated about eight of them looked capable of putting up a credible fight. "Finish here quickly, and then get the launcher ready. I want to blow that helicopter out of the sky."

* * *

With seven SEALs plus LCdr. Dewey safely aboard the yacht and stacked up along the starboard superstructure, Lt. Hunter made a hand signal and the pre-briefed takedown plan kicked into high gear. All hands had carefully and critically studied the diagram of the Al Calipha's physical layout obtained by the CIA through the ship's builders, and each member of the four two-person clearing teams knew the drill.

They would gain the interior of the vessel and work in quarters from the bottom of the superstructure to the top. Hunter and Petty Officer Grey would head directly for the bridge, eliminating any resistance along the way. Petty Officer Chuck Lane would escort Janet Dewey below decks to search spots where contaminated fish or any other bio-hazards were most likely stored. All hands would report progress and keep chatter to a minimum on their personal radios.

Hunter was pounding up an interior ladder directly behind Whistle Dick Grey when he heard the first burst of gunfire. The radio report was terse and tense.

"Contact main salon. Two down. No friendlies. Charlie Mike." So much for quick and easy.

* * *

Ali bolted through the portside access hatch leading to a balcony off one of the yacht's upper deck staterooms. He had the RPG-7V launcher in hand and the QF man following him carried one rocket round ready to load and fire plus a reload that could be ready in seconds. Ali didn't plan on needing a reload. He was an expert with the finicky weapon and had fired it accurately in attacks all over the Middle East. A moving target and a rolling platform as the Al Calipha gathered speed made the shot difficult but well within the capabilities of an accomplished RPG gunner.

He knelt by the balcony rail where a thick steel plate provided cover and a colorful awning helped with concealment. He handed the launcher to his assistant and kept his eyes on the helicopter's flight pattern. In seconds, the warhead, motor and propellant combination was loaded and the launcher checked for firing contact. Ali's assistant clicked the launcher off safe and propped it onto his leader's right shoulder.

Ali squinted through the amber lens of the sight and picked up the reticle marks which would give him the necessary lead on the American helicopter which was cutting tight loops less than 200 hundred meters off the ship's port beam. He focused on one of the aircraft's navigation lights mounted near the engines just under the rotor fan and waited for the pilot to complete a left turn to commence a run parallel with the ship's course. When the helicopter stabilized, he placed the second hash mark to the right of the sight's vertical index on that flashing light and squeezed the trigger.

* * *

Shake Davis was having a difficult time fighting wake turbulence and keeping the RIB close as the Al Calipha rapidly picked up speed. He saw a flash from the other side of the yacht followed by a blast that sent the UH-60A Seahawk helicopter spinning toward the sea. The radio bug crammed into his right ear exploded with distress calls from the helo crew and orders from the bridge of the Independence. He keyed his radio with one hand, spun the wheel of the RIB hard left with the other and jammed the throttles to the stops.

"Break, break! This is Davis in the RIB! I'm heading for the splash point now. Give me some light on the water."

As he bounced and bounded across the Al Calipha's wake, Shake saw two gouts of muzzle flash from the Independence and heard the deep boom of its .50-caliber machineguns. Apparently, the sailors had spotted the shooters. Ma Deuce times two ought to keep their fucking heads down while he searched for survivors of the helicopter crash. Two search-light beams swept across the dark water and then froze onto a flight helmet that was glowing with reflective tape. Shake adjusted course and keyed his mike.

"I see him. One in the water and he looks OK." He glanced to his right and saw a body floating face up in the pool of light from the second searchlight. "There's another one to his right and he looks out of it. I'll get him first."

Shake maneuvered the RIB alongside the survivor and cut the throttles. The airman was either dead or unconscious. There was no time to determine which right now. He reached down for the rescue loop on the man's inflated life preserver, braced his feet against the gunwales and hauled him aboard. He was just back at the controls, ready to head for the second crewman when his radio warned him of another problem.

"Gunner, heads up! There's a couple of them shooting at you. Portside, main deck level." Shake maneuvered the RIB to put it between the floating survivor and the shooters on the Al Calipha. As he cut the throttles to make the pickup, he heard rounds crack into the hull and scrambled for cover behind the cockpit. The man still in the water had latched onto the boat and looked to be in pretty good shape. Shake grabbed one of his hands and hauled back to pull him aboard the RIB. It was the pilot. Shake had eaten with him aboard the Independence.

"You OK?" The pilot seemed as good as could be expected as Shake shoved him toward cover and heard a couple more rounds impact the RIB. "We need to get the fuck out of here."

"Where's Sandy?" The pilot pulled the helmet off the unconscious man as Shake scrambled to keep a low profile and get back on the steering controls. "This is Macintosh, crew chief. Where's Sandy?"

Shake whipped the boat into a tight turn away from the shooters on the Al Calipha and keyed his mike. "Independence, I've got two aboard...one OK and the other will need immediate medical attention. How many were aboard the bird?"

"Three. Two pilots and a crew chief. Who have you got aboard?"

"Crew chief and pilot. He keeps asking about Sandy. That the co-pilot?"

"Roger that...Lieutenant jay-gee Sanderson. Look to your right. We've got him spotted. We're putting another boat in the water now."

Shake glanced over his right shoulder and spotted reflective tape on a flight helmet. He also saw muzzle flash from the Al Calipha deck and water spouts erupting around the floating crewman.

"Hunter, this is Davis. You got anybody aboard that can deal with a couple of shooters? They're amidships on the port side and cranking rounds at one of our guys in the water."

"We're a little jammed right now, Gunner. We'll get to it soonest."

"Independence, hold that boat. I'll get him."

* * *

Lieutenant Commander Janet Dewey and Petty Officer Chuck Lane hit paydirt in an after compartment one level below the weather decks. Among crates of rapidly packed scientific equipment that were first clues they were in the right place they found two aerated fish tanks brimming with Pacific salmon. In another corner was a stack of specimen pails that sloshed seawater in reaction to the steady vibration of the Al Calipha's churning engines one deck below.

"This is it." Janet Dewey stared at the deadly fish churning around in the tanks. "Don't touch anything. Let's just mark it and then you can go help the guys up forward." Janet pointed at her earpiece. "It's sounding like they could use a hand."

"Oh, shit!" Lane had just cracked a crate with the Hooligan's tool he carried for breaking down doors. He clearly didn't like what he'd found. "Commander, we've got a problem."

Janet Dewey joined him and pointed the beam of her flashlight inside the case, which was layered with plastic-wrapped blocks of what looked like clay or plumber's putty. Blasting caps protruding from several of the blocks and a tangle of wires made it obvious they were looking at a serious demolition charge. "You're the expert, but I'd speculate that's plastic explosive."

"Check." Lane carefully lifted the tangle of wires and took a closer look. "It's Semtex or an equivalent. And it looks like it's rigged for command detonation."

"What's that mean?"

"It means somebody aboard this fucking barge has got a little switch at hand which sets it off whenever he's ready." Lane keyed his mike while trying to trace the wiring, looking for a wireless receiver unit. "Boss, Lane."

"Send it, Chuck." Lane could hear small arms fire in the background as Lt. Hunter answered on an open-mike circuit. It seemed like a hell of a time to introduce a serious mission glitch but there was no option.

"I'm with Commander Dewey in a compartment on the second deck aft, starboard side. We found the fish. And we also found a fucking big bomb rigged for command detonation. Better get Whistle Dick down here in a hurry."

"Copy. You guys lock it up down there. Dubbya Dee is inbound."

"What now?" Janet Dewey had her sensor kit open on the deck and was dunking strips of chemical sensitive paper into one of the fish tanks. "Can you defuse it?"

"Maybe." Lane was still tracing wires with his fingers and talking around the Surefire high-intensity flashlight gripped in his teeth. "But Whistle Dick is not only a chick magnet, he's also a certified EOD Tech. Trouble is..."

Chuck Lane never got a chance to explain what the trouble was beyond the obvious. The shot from the compartment doorway blew past the flashlight in his mouth taking out four teeth and the back of his head.

Janet Dewey reached for her M9 pistol, snatched it out of her thigh holster and ducked behind one of the large fish tanks. Through the churning seawater and milling salmon she saw a man in civilian clothing and clutching a semiautomatic pistol duck into the compartment and put his back to the bulkhead. When she saw him reach inside his jacket and come out with a device that looked like a TV remote control, she didn't hesitate. She stood straight up from behind the fish tank and began to empty a magazine of 9mm ball ammo in his direction.

Two of the ten rounds she fired hit Ali before he could drop and roll out of her line of fire. One round caught him in the right chest area and collapsed a lung. The other hit his left shoulder causing him to drop the remote detonation device which went skittering across the wet deck. Fighting against the pain in his torso, Ali saw the shooter scramble toward the detonator, pick it up and toss it into one of the fish tanks. As she turned the pistol back on him, Ali squeezed off two shots. One missed. The other tore through LCdr. Janet Dewey's throat killing her instantly.

Ali was on hands and knees, bleeding profusely and crawling toward the fish tank to retrieve his detonator when Petty Officer Chris Grey charged into the compartment and pumped two rounds from an M-4 carbine into the back of his head.

* * *

Shake Davis scrubbed at the blood streaming down his forehead into his right eye and tried to focus on the bobbing flight helmet that the current was carrying ever closer to the Al Calipha's hull. One of the shooters on the deck twenty feet above the surface had some kind of small-caliber submachine gun. He was spraying and praying to little effect. The other one had a rifle and was firing deliberate, well-aimed shots, one of which had struck the uprights of the RIB's canopy and ricocheted to gouge a bloody crease in Shake's scalp. They were both impediments to Shake's efforts to rescue the last helo crewman, but he needed to deal with the rifle shooter before the guy put one through him or his two passengers. They'd been through enough for one night.

"I'm gonna need a hand here." Shake cut a look toward the two helo jocks curled up behind the steering console. The crew chief was conscious but hurt too badly to help. If the pilot couldn't cut it, they were screwed. He steered the RIB into an outboard turn away from the yacht and grabbed the pilot by the arm. "I need you to steer this boat. You up for it?"

"Show me what to do." The helo pilot laid his crew chief's head down and crawled over to Shake. "I can hack it."

"I'm gonna get us over to the other side of the ship where the assault team left their ladders rigged. Once we're in position, you've got to hold her steady and match speed so I can get hold of one of the ladders and get aboard. It's the only way to save your buddy's life and we'll only get one shot at it."

The pilot grabbed a stanchion and pulled himself upright. "If it'll help somebody kill those bastards, I'm good to go."

Shake keyed his mike and whipped the RIB into a power turn heading for the frothing wake of the Al Calipha at full throttle. "Independence, Davis. I'm gonna need some covering fire from your fifties. Have your gunners turn a light on those two deck shooters and beat the shit out of their area. When they see me start across the deck...for Christ's sake shift your fire to overhead, way overhead."

"Independence copies all. We'll be on it in a heartbeat."

The Al Calipha seemed to be slowing and Shake hoped that was because Hunter or one of his guys had taken over the bridge. He crossed the wake, whipped the wheel to the left and pulled the throttles back to match the ship's speed. "You take it," he shouted to the pilot and pointed at the aluminum boarding ladders banging against the yacht's hull. "Just jockey these throttles until we get next to one of those ladders and hold it steady."

The pilot took over the wheel as Shake snatched up an MP-5SD submachine gun and mounted it to his body armor with a three-point sling. He checked the chamber for a ready round, tapped the bottom of the magazine and then let the weapon hang across his chest. He clambered up to the bow of the RIB, nodded at the pilot to hit the throttles and keyed his radio.

"Independence, light 'em up!"

As he eyed the nearest boarding ladder just coming into reach he heard the chug of two .50 calibers booming across the water and saw the deck above him bathed in bright light. He lunged and nearly went overboard on his first try as the pilot let the RIB drift to the right.

"Hold it steady! Jam this fucker right into her!"

The pilot did as he was directed and this time Shake got a hold on the ladder with one hand. With the other he signaled the pilot to bear away and began to climb. His legs and arms were screaming for relief by the time he reached deck level and he could hear the big machinegun slugs thumping into the yacht's deck and superstructure. He grabbed his weapon by the pistol grip, raised it into the light spilling across the deck and waved it three times. Hopefully the gunners aboard Independence had seen that or he was about to climb into a hailstorm. Either way it was go big or go home.

Shake Davis saw the two shooters immediately when he scrambled onto the deck. They saw him at just about the same time. Fortunately, the rifle shooter was reloading and the subgun guy was the only one to get off a burst. It was high and to his left. Shake shouldered the MP-5 and closed the range, methodically putting three-round bursts into each man.

He picked up both of their weapons and tossed them over the side making room for him to slump down next to his victims. He watched .50 caliber tracers streak overhead for a few moments and thought aimlessly about Tracey and Chan Dwyer. He'd likely have to cease and desist on this sort of cheap shit if he was going to have any peace in a new family.

"Independence, cease fire. And thank you. Better get a boat in the water and police up that last crewman."

* * *

Lt. Kerry Dale Hunter was holding a SOCOM modified M1911A1 .45 caliber pistol on the captain of the Al Calipha and three other men of the yacht's bridge crew. He had a good sight picture on the captain's face and was pondering whether or not he could get away with killing the man. He could probably skate a murder charge, but it would be cold comfort for the loss of Chuck Lane and Janet Dewey. More importantly, he thought as he slowly lowered the muzzle, it wouldn't be the honorable thing for a naval officer to do.

He released the pressure on the trigger and ordered the captain to bring his vessel to full stop. "Just keep enough turns on the engines to hold position, Captain. And please believe me I will kill you where you stand if you do anything I don't like." Hunter watched as the captain punched computer keys that sent orders to the automated engine controls and then switched channels on his radio: "Bridge is secure. Send somebody up to help me hog-tie four. Leading petty officer, say status..."

* * *

As SEALs continued to clear the interior, Ignacio Felodon and his ex-pat countryman, the yacht's assistant mess cook, were working feverishly on the starboard side of the yacht, away from the action and prying eyes aboard the U.S. warship. Fuel, a few extra weapons, Dr. Nasuton and his precious laptop computer containing all the experimental files were aboard the Zodiac that was being lowered into the water. Felodon jumped aboard and tossed a packet of money to his new-found friend.

The Muslim money-men and their various toadies might have been planning to make him a patsy but things had changed drastically. He was in charge now. The Al Calipha plan was destroyed, but he had the brains with him and all the money needed to launch another attack. He could buy a boat somewhere in the Palaus and there were plenty of contaminated fish in the lagoon back on Peleliu. Amin Faraz would understand and support a new plan as long as there was life in his body. Ignacio Felodon would have his justice. And maybe even live to see it.

He could still hear random shots aboard the yacht as the boat eased onto the surface of the water and settled. Felodon unhooked the lowering lines, handed Dr. Nasuton an oar, and they began to paddle. In fifteen or twenty minutes of rowing, they'd be far enough away from the Al Calipha and the American raiders to start the engine and head for Peleliu.

* * *

"Boss, I've got a count." Whistle Dick Grey ducked inside the wheelhouse just as Hunter finished cuffing the Al Calipha's captain.

"Zip-tie these other three shitbirds and let me have it." Grey pulled a sheaf of flex-cuffs out of his gear and began to secure the bridge crew with their hands behind them and one turn of the plastic running through their belts. He patted them down for weapons as he gave his OIC the butcher's bill.

"Chuck Lane and Lieutenant Commander Dewey are kilo. The guys have got 'em laid out down on deck. Bat Kybat took one through-and-through just above the right knee. He's mobile and pissed off. Gunner Davis caught a ricochet and got a big-ass gash in his gourd that looks worse than it is. We got twelve tangos down hard. Three more wounded who will need patch jobs plus some plasma."

"Noncombatants?"

"In a manner of speaking, I guess. We've got thirteen of 'em who swear to Allah they didn't know shit about shit and yada, yada, yada. We're pretty sure two pencil-necks are the Indonesian science guys. There's one Filipino in the crowd, but no way is he Felodon."

"Where the fuck is he?"

"Beats me, Boss. We need to get some swabbies over here from the Independence to help us do a clean and sweep down. If he's aboard here, we'll find him."

"Check. We all good on that bomb deal?"

"Disarmed and colder than an Eskimo's asshole. Thirty keys of Semtex rigged and ready to go—until Janet Dewey killed the guy with the detonator switch. She blew his ass away and then tossed the detonator in one of the fish tanks. He got her with one round just before he died, I guess."

Whistle Dick Grey didn't mention that the man with the detonator was still alive when he arrived or that the detonator might still have worked if it had been recovered from the fish-tank before he killed the man LCdr. Dewey had wounded. "There might be a decoration write-up for Janet Dewey in there somewhere, Boss."

"Damn sure is. I'll take care of it right after Peleliu."

As they shoved the bridge crew down the ladder to the weather decks where team, casualties and captives were mustered, Hunter switched channels and sent a message to the Independence.

"Independence, Hunter. Vessel is secure and holding position on autopilot. Send your boarding party. And tell Chief Wiley I need him to come over with the rest of my guys to help us search this pig."

* * *

Shake Davis sprawled on one the Al Calipha's luxurious deck chairs feeling like the class dummy while a chief hospital corpsman gleefully stitched a row of sutures into his scalp and his daughter stood glowering over his shoulder. He reached for Tracey's hand on his shoulder and patted it. "Maybe I'll take to parting my hair on the other side."

"Dad, goddammit, I knew something like this was gonna happen. When will you grow up and start acting your age, your real age, not your imaginary age."

"Folks who sail in harm's way get shot up no matter how many birthdays they've had. Ain't that right, Doc?"

The salty corpsman glanced up over his bifocals and nodded. "I've stitched 'em up from sixteen to sixty, Lieutenant. Your Dad's gonna be fine. Wish I was in his shape."

"I know he's gonna be fine, and I'd like him to stay that way." She was about to continue but Chan Dwyer ducked under the awning and cut her off. It provided no escape for the patient being tended to on the deck chair.

"How many Purple Hearts does that make, Shake? Seven, eight?"

"Who's counting? If there's a decoration to come out of this it ought to be Janet Dewey. Did you talk to Hunter about that?"

"He's way ahead of you. I'm gonna help him draft a Silver Star recommendation soonest. I think I still remember how to do that."

"Do your best, Chan. From what I hear, she deserves it."

The corpsman was tying off a final stitch when Lt. Kerry Dale Hunter stuck his head out an access to the salon deck and interrupted. "Doc, I need the Gunner in here."

The Corpsman tied a dressing over the wound and secured it under Shake's chin. "That ought to hold you, Mr. Davis, but you're gonna have to walk around uncovered for a week or so. And be careful in the shower."

"Thanks, Doc." Shake got to his feet and headed for the salon where Hunter and his SEALs had mustered the surviving crew of the Al Calipha. "Let's go, you two." He motioned to Chan and Tracey. "I think Kerry Dale's got the line-up ready for inspection."

The SEAL team had all upright crewmembers lining the teak walls of the plush salon. Several of them were sporting dressings over minor wounds after being treated by the corpsman. Hunter's guys were in the middle of the ornate deck area with fingers near the triggers of the weapons strapped across their chests. The SEAL Detachment Commander pointed at two bearded individuals who looked ready to have a heart attack in the next couple of minutes and turned to Chan Dwyer.

"Recognize these guys?"

Chan cracked open a folder and paged through to the pictures she'd downloaded from a CIA file. When she found what she was looking for, she approached the men and compared photos with faces. She pointed at the first man. "Galan Wahid, geneticist, Islamic University of Riau." She glanced at another sheet in her file and pointed at the second man. "Ahmed Suharto, microbiologist, same pedigree. If Mike Stokey's report is good, we're missing one Indonesian scientist."

Hunter stepped up and put a hand on her shoulder. "He's not aboard the ship. We've turned it ass over tea kettle. Nasuton either didn't come along on this expedition or he's elsewhere, like back on Peleliu." They both checked the Indonesian scientists for reaction but got none. These guys were *jihadis* as well as scientists. If they were going to give up anything about Dr. Nasuton, it would come later under professional interrogation.

Hunter walked across the salon and confronted a short Asian man leaning against the bulkhead with his hands bound behind him and a stunned look on his face. "Gunner, this guy's a Filipino obviously." He held up a wad of U.S. dollars bound with a rubber band. "He had this in his pocket. Five grand that he says is his savings from salary and shit like that. You buying it?"

Shake grinned and shrugged his shoulders. "Ignacio Felodon he ain't. Let me talk to him outside—alone. And let me have that cash."

Whistle Dick Grey shoved the Filipino mess attendant toward the door where Shake Davis grabbed him by the arm and pulled him outside. Tracey Davis followed, keeping her distance but curious about what he had planned. She was hoping it wasn't sticking the muzzle of a weapon into the man's ear but she'd learned long ago never to underestimate her father. Shake led the man to a deck chair, shoved him into a seat and scrounged in his pocket for a pack of Marlboros. He lit two and stuck one between the man's lips.

"*Salamat*, my friend. "*Ang aking mga kaibigan. Kailangan namin upang makipag-usap. Nagsasalita ba kayo ng Ingles?*"

Tracey watched in awe as her father plopped down into a deck chair beside the captive. She had no idea he spoke

Tagalog. The Filipino relaxed visibly now that he was away from the rest of the crew. "I speak English."

"What's your name?"

"Carlos. Carlos Jesus Quintero from Olongapo."

"Carlos, you know the rest of these guys are going to jail for a long time." Her Dad plucked the smoke from his mouth and flicked ashes into the wind. "I can keep you from joining them. I know you had nothing to do with all this. But that money puzzles me. Where did you get that?"

"A man gave it to me."

"A Filipino man? Ignacio Felodon?"

The crewman cut a glance toward the salon and nodded. Shake looked at the wad of cash for a moment and then stuck it into the man's shirt pocket. "As far as I'm concerned, this money is yours. What did you do to earn it?"

The Filipino sucked smoke and exhaled gouts through his nose. "I helped him get off the boat. We had a deal. If things went bad, he was to get away in the motor launch. I helped him do it while everyone else was fighting. I swear to you by all the saints, I just helped him get away. I never shot at anyone. I don't want to go to jail."

"Relax, my friend. I'll take care of that. You have nothing to worry about as long as you don't lie to me. Ignacio Felodon got off the ship, yes? And did he have anyone with him?"

"The Indonesian...I don't know his name."

"OK, that's good. No problem. What did they have with them?"

"Some guns. And the Indonesian had a computer. He had it wrapped in plastic. I saw that clearly."

"Do you know where they were going?"

"Where else?" The Filipino shrugged his shoulders and puffed on his smoke. "Peleliu is just five or six kilometers. They had plenty of fuel."

The White House, Washington, D.C.

Bayer slid the last of the photo packets across the polished surface of the conference table in the Situation Room and dropped back into his chair. The President, seated at the head of the table, had already seen the report and the pictures from the takedown of the Al Calipha in a private briefing, so he didn't open his folder. He simply stared at the ceiling, hiding his emotions and waiting for assembled members of his National Security Council to get a good look at what Bayer's strike force had encountered in the South Pacific.

When sufficient time had passed and Bayer felt certain everyone had a chance to absorb the images, he cleared his throat and got everyone's attention: "The Al Calipha is currently being sailed to Koror, where the ship will remain anchored well offshore and under strict quarantine. We're assembling reps from all the appropriate agencies to fly out there right now. To keep this under wraps until you decide how to approach an announcement or make the necessary complaints to the parties involved...or whatever the President directs as the appropriate course of action. We'll be keeping the crew and the scientists involved under wraps aboard the ship. I understand Interior is dealing with the Palauan government. An FBI team is already on the way to Koror. They'll be conducting the interrogations and compiling the evidence."

Bayer grabbed a packet similar to the ones he'd just passed out and held it up. "As to the what and why of the effort, much of that information is speculation at this point, but our best opinions are included in your packets along with the photos. There's a good, plain English report in there that describes the danger these contaminated specimens could have presented if they had been introduced into the food chain. You won't have time to read it now, but I urge you to do so at your earliest convenience. It's some scary stuff."

The Secretary of State tapped one of the photos with a polished fingernail. "And you believe the initial target was the Philippines? Why the Philippines?"

"Who knows for sure, Madam Secretary? There are likely two factors involved. The Philippines are nearby and maybe they wanted to conduct a test. You know, see how this thing would work in a population that relies heavily on seafood in the diet. And one of our people out there who used to know Ignacio Felodon believes the man was looking for revenge against the Philippine government. Details on that are in the report from Chan Dwyer, our DIA rep on the team. That's also included in your packet. She believes, and I agree with her, that the people involved at the highest levels thought Felodon would make a perfect fall guy and take the heat off of them when we started looking around for culprits."

The President leaned forward and put his elbows on the table. All eyes turned to him and he swept the room, looking at each face before he spoke. "Let's not get distracted with speculation just now, folks. They may have been going to conduct a test attack in the Philippines, but Bob Bayer believes the ultimate target was the United States. I'm inclined to agree, given what we know about the backers in this thing. The Saudis and the Iranians don't give a damn about the Philippines, but there are zealous factions in both of those countries that would dearly love to kill a bunch of Americans with a credibly deniable biological weapon. It's twisted but I believe it's true. We'll deal with those nations as evidence is developed over the next couple of weeks.

"Meanwhile..." The President stood and leaned over the table. "The threat is still out there and we need to deal with it forcibly and quickly. I'm talking about what's left on Peleliu and the surviving players who are likely still on that island guarding their stock of biological weapons. And let's be clear about this: They may be just a bunch of fish that these guys have genetically altered, but they represent a serious biological weapon if deployed or introduced into the world food chain. We are not going to let that happen."

The President started toward the door of the Situation Room and then paused. "That's all for now, but I had better not hear one whisper about this outside this room. No leaks, period. None at all. No backgrounders. No nothing with the press in any way shape or form. I'm deathly serious about this. If word about this threat gets out and people start to panic, heads right here in this room will start to roll."

He checked his watch and pointed at several people around the table. "Sidebar in one hour in my office: National Security Advisor, NCTC, State, Interior and Press Secretary."

Peleliu

It was nearly four in the morning when the Quds Force foot patrols returned and reported to Amin Faraz. The northern sector around the island's main settlement was quiet, but if they weren't off the island by sunrise, they'd have to do something about the population when locals and a few tourists began to stir. Faraz planned to be gone off Peleliu by full dawn. It was their best bet and the southern patrol had located a boat that would likely be able to get them to Koror. The four QF security men Faraz had held back to disassemble the base camp had nearly all traces of their presence either buried in the Umurbrogol foothills or burning in the bonfire they'd lit in a clearing just across the island's west road.

The eastern sky was showing pale light low on the horizon as the QF mission commander walked toward the high water mark and decided they were nearly ready to extract, escape and evade, always the most difficult part of any mission. All that remained to cover their tracks on Peleliu was to pull the anchors on the containment net at the mouth of the lagoon. That would release the remaining contaminated fish to the open sea. Amin wasn't sure what effect that might have but he sincerely hoped some of the deadly creatures would wind up on infidel dinner plates.

He was about to issue the order when he heard the growl of an outboard engine approaching the lagoon. His men were piling into defensive positions when he recognized the two men approaching in the Al Calipha's Zodiac. Dr. Nasuton and the Filipino were returning to the island and that meant something had gone seriously wrong.

"Hold your fire!" Faraz waded into the surf and waited to hear the bad news.

When the boat was close enough for beaching, Felodon cut the engine and jumped over the side to help Faraz haul it up onto the sand. Dr. Nasuton remained in the boat clutching a laptop that was encased in bubble-wrap and waterproof plastic.

"What are you doing here?" Faraz grabbed Ignacio Felodon by the elbow and led him further up the beach while his men helped Dr. Nasuton out of the boat and began pawing through a stack of weapons that seemed to be the only cargo. "What happened to the Al Calipha?"

"What I'm doing here is saving the mission," Felodon shook off Amin's grip and pointed out to sea beyond the horizon. "We were ambushed. The American Navy stopped us about five miles out. They put people aboard Al Calipha. There was a fight. I escaped with Dr. Nasuton and his research material."

"Abdullah was right." Faraz was rapidly running over options and there didn't seem to be many.

"About what?"

"The Al Calipha was spotted by a drone aircraft. We ignored it."

"Why was I not informed?"

"Abdullah's decision. It was a mistake."

"No matter. We have Dr. Nasuton and his research. Now we get off this island. We live to fight another day."

* * *

"Are you guys coming or what?" Mike Stokey mashed the sat-phone to his ear and stared down from his perch at two QF men tending a bonfire less than a hundred meters below him in a clearing just below Wattie Ridge. "These dudes are getting ready to split. I trailed a bunch of 'em about an hour ago and they were checking out boats down around Camp Beck dock. I'm watching two of 'em burn their trash right now and it's less than an hour to dawn."

"Took us longer on the yacht than we figured." Shake Davis stood aboard the USS Independence steaming southeast at flank speed for the most southerly tip of Peleliu. He was watching Chan Dwyer draw weapons and equipment for the assault on the island. Shake was not at all happy about it but she'd been pegged to go along on the assault in place of LCdr. Dewey to handle immediate bio hazard threats. "We lost the helo so we had to tap dance. New deal is we come ashore by surface craft on the southern tip of the island and then work our way up toward you."

"How long?"

"Launch time is zero-five." Shake checked his watch and shook his head vehemently when Chief Wiley tried to drape an H&K MP-5 over Chan's shoulder. He pointed at the shoulder holster attached at chest level to his body armor indicating that was all the firepower she needed. "That's about thirty minutes or so and we'll be underway."

"Sun will be up by then. Why don't we just let 'em scoot and police 'em up at sea?"

"That's been suggested. Hunter ran it by PACOM as soon as you reported Felodon and Dr. Nasuton were back on the island. No dice. They want those two breathing and talking at the end of the day. Hunter thinks they wouldn't let us take 'em alive out at sea...and I agree with him. Plan is to pinch Nasuton and Felodon out of the fight while we deal with the QF shooters."

"Copy. You ready for updates?"

"Send it."

"My best count is twelve shooters. One of them is the honcho. Short guy built like a fireplug with a goatee and wearing a dark green or black sweatshirt. Plus Felodon and the good doctor that makes fourteen, give or take. They've got an arsenal with 'em. Usual stuff...I saw two RPDs and a sniper rifle. There was an RPG and a bag of rockets in the boat with Felodon. And there's assorted handguns plus a mix of AK-47s and 74s. I didn't see any other high-explosive stuff or grenades but that don't mean they haven't got 'em."

"Roger. I'll pass the word. We should be ashore in an hour or less. Sit tight."

"You guys better hurry. I see two goons out on the beach and it looks like they're getting ready to drop the containment net."

"Shit! Mike, anything you can do to buy us some time would be helpful. Out here."

Shake found Lt. Kerry Dale Hunter up on the bridge conferring with Cdr. Bland and fed him the updates from Mike Stokey on the island. The skipper of the Independence checked his watch, his navigation chart and the brightening horizon. "Kick out the jams, people! I want us doing Mach II right now!"

Shake felt the deck below his feet vibrate as the ship's engines strained and the trimaran hull lifted higher in the water. "You got anything else for me?"

"You up for this?" Hunter eyed the plaster patch on Shake's scalp just visible under a knit watch cap. "You were a damn fine hand in the takedown and we appreciate it but there's no call to stretch..."

"Save it, Kerry Dale. We covered that ground at the briefing. Nobody knows that island like I do. If these assholes disappear up into the Umurbrogol once they know we're coming for 'em, you'll need a guide to all the scenic locations."

"When you're right, you're right, Gunner. Better get below and stake out a boat space."

Tracey Davis caught him in CIC and stood blocking his exit. "You've heard this a time or two from me before, Dad, but please be careful."

"No sweat, sweetie." He smiled and gave her a quick kiss on the forehead. "I'm just a tour guide on this one."

"Yeah, right..." She tapped the submachine gun strapped across his chest. "Got your tourist maps stored in here have you?"

"Relax, girl. The SEALs are doing all the heavy lifting. I'll just point 'em in the right direction and keep an eye on Chan."

"Do that, Dad. It would be nice if both of you survived to spend some time together—other than when you're killing people and breaking shit."

* * *

Two of the Quds Force operatives were struggling with the left-hand cable anchor-point for the lagoon containment net as Mike Stokey slowly and silently made his way down from Wattie Ridge. It looked like difficult work getting the thick cable loose and they had to free both ends before the net would drop completely. That gave him a little time to do something about stopping them.

Stokey knew from experience that it was in the nature of human beings to crowd around a fire and stare at the flames. It was probably something in the genes that stretched back to cavemen in awe over the miracle of fire. More importantly it was enough distraction to allow him to approach the bonfire tenders to within shotgun range. He settled into a thicket at the edge of the clearing wishing the two men would move about six feet closer to each other to put them both inside the spread of one round from his 12-gauge. With these guys he probably wouldn't get a second shot. He wanted their weapons. Both men had folding stock AK-47s slung from their shoulders that would give Stokey the range and firepower to drive their buddies away from work on the containment net. They'd be after him in a hurry, but Stokey would be so deep in the heart of Bloody Nose Ridge it would take time to chase him down. And that was the objective of this little exercise.

He was mentally mapping his escape route, aiming in on the back of the man nearest him when the fortunes of war cut him a break. He wouldn't need a second shot. A commanding voice from across the west road on the other side of the clearing caused one man to take off at a run. The remaining QF man mumbled something in Farsi and began poking at the fire with a bamboo pole. Stokey shifted his aim, thumbed off the scattergun's safety and squeezed the trigger.

The full load of double-ought buckshot caught the fire tender full in the chest and slammed him to the ground. Stokey sprinted to the bonfire, grabbed the victim's AK and then used the little Kershaw folder that served him so well on Koror to rip through the man's equipment. In thirty seconds he was thrashing his way up the face of Wattie Ridge with the shotgun, an AK-47, a Sig-Sauer P229 and a knapsack full of what he hoped were magazines full of ammo.

* * *

Neither Amin Faraz nor his veteran QF men were foolish enough to rush into the open toward the bonfire after they heard the boom of the shotgun. They squatted in the bush near the edge of the clearing, forming a ragged crescent and staring at the body of their comrade lying lifeless near the fire. There was no one else in sight, but it was clear that whoever did the killing had stripped the dead man of his weapons and equipment. "Probably one of the natives…" Faraz mumbled to the QF man at his shoulder. "Or perhaps the local policeman had a deputy. Wait a few minutes and then toss the body on the fire."

Faraz was on his way to the left-hand promontory where two of his men were still struggling with the containment net anchor cable. Apparently, the weight of the water-logged net was making it difficult for his men to unseat the anchor spike. A hacksaw would be helpful but they didn't have one of those. He'd either have to leave the containment net in place or put more men on the job. They were wasting valuable time.

He was considering what to do when the first burst of fire tore into the promontory spraying his men with sand and seawater. Both of them went prone and hugged the ground. Faraz sprinted back toward the clearing to deal with the shooter.

One hundred and fifty meters above him, Mike Stokey cursed the shaky folding stock of the AK-47, adjusted the leaf sight and sent another burst of fire toward the men hugging the sand out on the promontory. He watched the rounds impact low and left of his intended targets and decided it was time to move. He could hear people slipping and sliding on the coral slope below him as they tried to climb in his direction. Stokey took off, heading for Hill 140, part of the Bloody Nose ridgeline about 200 meters to the southwest.

Dawn was breaking; he'd eliminated one shooter and bought Shake and the SEALs another very valuable fifteen minutes. If these guys persisted in dicking around with the containment net, he'd take another shot at them from Hill 140.

* * *

Hunter and his SEALs flowed into a security perimeter like an expanding oil slick moments after the RIB ground up onto the sand. Shake stepped ashore, took a knee and handed Chan Dwyer the rubberized sensor case. "Wait here." He pointed at Chief Wiley who was securing the RIB with a sand anchor. "Stick with the Chief when he moves up." Shake spotted Hunter and sprinted up beside him to go over the plan they'd developed from a map study.

"This is what they called Scarlet Beach back in '44. We go direct north from here past the Camp Beck Docks. That's where you drop Chan and a security detail off to guard the boats, right?" Hunter nodded without taking his eyes off the huge green wall of the Umurbrogol Massif looming at the other end of the old abandoned Japanese airfield just visible to their direct front. "We go by the original landing beaches, Orange and then White. You'll see some old bunkers off to the left and parts of the old airfield off to your right. There's a little finger that sticks out in the water at the north end of White Beach. That's where the Japs cut up the 1st Marines when they landed. You'll know why once you get a look at it—perfect enfilading fire across the beach. At that point, the coast line bends hard right. About 200 meters farther up the road is the lagoon where these guys set up their base camp."

"And Stokey's pretty sure they're gonna head south to pick up a boat?"

"That's what he said." Shake reached for his sat-phone and punched the power switch. "I'm gonna try him right now to see if there's any updates."

"We'll stick with the plan." Hunter motioned for his team to move and the SEALs took off like a tidal wave headed north on both sides of Peleliu's west road. "We put security on the boats at the dock and set up an ambush near that point on the north end of White Beach. Firepower on the left of the road. Whistle Dick and Clutch Blake on the right, ready to snatch Nasuton and Felodon when the shit hits the fan. Join us when you can and push me on tac-one if you get any important updates from Mike."

Hunter sprinted after his men. Shake watched with a grim smile on his face as Chan Dwyer passed his position. And then he hit the speed dial on his phone.

* * *

"Welcome aboard!" Stokey sounded winded and Shake could hear coral crunching under his buddy's boots. "It's about fucking time you guys got into this thing. Where are you?"

"I'm just moving off Scarlet Beach." Shake could see the SEALs disappearing into the green on either side of the west road. "Hunter and his guys are up ahead of me going for that point where Pope and his King Company guys held out on D-Day. You remember that spot?"

"Yeah, I'm just climbing up Hill 140. There's a couple of 'em on my tail...maybe three or four. It's hard to tell. I nailed one of 'em about twenty minutes ago and took his weapons. They were trying to drop the containment net on the lagoon, so I lit 'em up and then split. If they're still out there working on the net, I'm gonna fire 'em up again."

"Nice work, Mike. I'll catch up with Hunter and pass the word. Maybe we ought to shit-can the ambush deal and move on 'em before they can drop that net."

"Well, whatever you do, hurry the fuck up..." Shake heard two staccato bursts of AK fire and then the connection failed. He stood and looked toward the Umurbrogol and heard the distinct, familiar sound of a distant firefight in progress. Orienting himself quickly, he sprinted toward the foothills of the Umurbrogol Massif. His radio blasted to life just as he stepped out onto the crumpled concrete of the old Japanese airstrip.

"Davis, Hunter. You hear that firing? It's up in the high ground to our right-front."

"Check. That's Stokey. He's got tangos on his tail. I'm headed in his direction now. Check that sketch map I made for you. He's up around Hill 140."

"Copy. I'll send you a couple of shooters. Where are you?"

"Save the shooters. Stokey says they're trying to drop that containment net up by the lagoon. We need to stop that. Suggest you forget the ambush and get up there soonest."

"Roger all. We're at the docks now. I'm dropping off Chan plus two for security on the boats. We'll haul ass up the road and deal with it on the fly."

"You're the honcho. I'm headed up into the high ground to see if I can pull Stokey's nuts out of the fire. More follows soonest."

* * *

Amin Faraz was frustrated and more than a little angry. He didn't like to change plans on the spur of any moment in any mission, but there didn't seem to be much choice. They had finally succeeded in pulling up the left hand anchor stake of the containment net by brute force applied by no less than six men. He'd hoped that might be sufficient but it was not. The floats on the top edge of the net were keeping it firmly in place. If the poison fish were to swim free they'd have to deal with the anchor on the right side of the lagoon. He had four other men chasing some idiot up on the high ground and time was an enemy. Faraz had no doubt the American Navy knew by now that they were on the island. The critical concern was to get off Peleliu with Dr. Nasuton's research material.

He heard the rattle of gunfire from the high ground and pressed the transmit button on his radio. “What’s happening up there?”

“We have one man pinned inside a cave. He’s going nowhere. We have an RPG with us.” His pursuit team leader sounded calm and confident which simply added to Amin’s irritation.

“Deal with him quickly. And then join us at the boat docks.” Amin mentally wrote off his pursuit team up in the Umurbrogol. They would survive or not, but there was no room for them in the Peleliu lawman’s stake-bed truck that would carry them on a high-speed run to the docks. He did a quick head count and then ordered his remaining fighters into the vehicle. The sun was a semicircle of blood-red light on the horizon when he stuffed Dr. Nasuton and Ignacio Felodon into the back of the truck and decided they had done all that could be expected of them on Peleliu. Amin Faraz jacked a round into the chamber of his Krinkov, poked the muzzle out the passenger side window and nodded at the driver.

* * *

Shake Davis’ combat-tuned ears told him about the nature of the firefight even as he scrambled up the coral slope leading toward Hill 140. It was mostly 7.62x39 but being pumped from two different directions. Heaviest on his right and that would be the bad guys. The return from his left would be Stokey. Apparently Mike had acquired a small-caliber pistol somewhere along the way as the sounds from his left occasionally included the short, sharp pops of a 9mm.

Shake took a knee, sucked on the mouthpiece of his Camelback hydration system and tried to decide on an approach that would take the heat off Stokey. To his right-front was a spike of coral that might put him behind the shooters but it would be a tough, noisy climb. Lots of jungle had grown over the area since it had been blasted to scorched stumps by naval gunfire, artillery and Marine airstrikes back in 1944, but the footing was still treacherous. He decided the noise of the firefight would cover his movement and began to claw his way up the hillside. How in the hell World War II Marines, wearing torn-up boondockers with empty canteens and humping M-1 rifles did this under Japanese machinegun fire he had no idea, but his respect for those veterans kicked up a notch beyond slavish admiration.

Shake spotted two of the shooters rattling away with AKs as he reached the crest of the finger. They were shoulder-to-shoulder behind a boulder that faced a cave, firing at muzzle flashes that had to be Mike returning their shots. Stokey was deep enough in a coral cave to keep from silhouetting himself, but there was no escape when he eventually ran out of ammo. The shooters keeping him penned up inside that little fortress understood it was only a matter of time.

Pausing to catch his breath and settle into a steady firing position behind a large rock, Shake de-focused his off eye and concentrated on the ACOG sight affixed to his M-4 carbine. It was a hell of a lot easier when he only had iron sights, breath control and trigger squeeze to worry about but that was then and this was now. Range was no factor, so Shake flipped the weapon's selector onto full-auto, put the sighting dot on the first man's left shoulder, squeezed the trigger and swung the weapon to the right. Both shooters caught at least four rounds in the back and collapsed out of the fight.

"Mike, you're clear! Get out of there!"

Stokey's wide-eyed, mud-crusted face appeared at the mouth of the cave.

"Shake? That you?"

"Yeah, up here to your left. Haul ass out of there!"

Just as Stokey cleared his hideout he was blown off his feet by the exhaust of a rocket-propelled grenade that disappeared into the cave and detonated sending gouts of coral chips zinging through the air. Stokey tumbled down the face of the ridge, arms and legs flailing for purchase. Shake bobbed up to spot the rocket gunner only to be driven back down by a burst of AK fire. He was spotted and pinned so he decided to cede the initiative, wait it out and see what happened next. Shake couldn't spot Stokey but he was likely out of the fight—if he was still alive.

After about a minute, he heard someone scrambling over rock and thrashing through bush to his left-front. Shake peered cautiously around the left side of the rock and spotted an RPG gunner carrying his launcher and heading for the cave entrance. It was a dumb move making for an easy shot. Shake shifted the M-4 to his left shoulder and picked up the target in his sight. He never got a chance to squeeze the trigger.

Something hit his back like a sledgehammer and drove him breathless into the ground. He felt as if he'd been stabbed him with an ice-pick, deep and hard between the shoulder blades. Shake heard someone moving behind him through the loud ringing in his ears and a shout in what sounded like Farsi or Arabic. Slowly and cautiously, wanting the approaching shooter to believe he'd nailed his target, Shake slid his right hand under his body toward his shoulder-holstered pistol. The M-4 was within easy reach but if he went for it, the shooter would likely put another couple of rounds into him. He didn't know how badly he was wounded, but there was no way he could absorb any more punishment and survive. If the bastard thought he was approaching a corpse, there might be a chance.

Wrapping his fingers around the butt of the Kimber .45-caliber pistol he'd borrowed from Hunter's stash of special operations weaponry, Shake slowly pushed at the Velcro retaining strap and credited years of experience for always carrying an M1911 pistol in Condition One, ready round in the chamber, cocked and locked. He'd only get one chance and there'd be no time for fumbling or slide-racking. Shake thumbed the safety off and tried to slow his breathing.

The Quds Force shooter shouted something to his buddy letting Shake know his target was very close. Any closer and the man would likely put a couple of insurance shots into him so Shake made his move. He rolled to his right and drew the pistol, shoving it toward a man with a bushy mustache and a very startled look on his face. He pulled the trigger twice and saw the man crumple as both slugs slammed into his stomach. Crawling painfully to his knees, Shake put two more rounds into the man's head and wondered how he'd fight through the pain in his back and chest to deal with the RPG gunner who would be charging in his direction any moment.

That question was answered as he drew a long, painful breath and staggered to his feet. He winced and ducked at the sound of gunfire on the other side of his rock: four small-caliber shots, two double-taps with just a tick between pairs.

"Shake, you OK?"

He pulled himself upright and peered over the coral rock. Mike Stokey was standing over the RPG gunner keeping the muzzle of a Sig-Sauer semi-auto pointed at the prostrate form. "I'm what passes for OK after taking a couple of slugs in the back. Did we get 'em all?"

"Looks like it." Stokey shoved the pistol into his waistband and began to climb toward the rock that was holding his friend upright. "How bad you hit?"

"Won't know until you can help me peel off this body armor. Feels like I might be bleeding some down my back." Shake had bitched a bit out aboard the Independence when Chief Wiley insisted he wear body armor with heavy SAPI plates covering his chest and back. Once again he'd been shown the value of keeping your suck shut and trusting the wisdom of senior enlisted men.

Stokey helped him shrug out of the body armor and raised his shirt to get a look at Shake's back. "Two big-ass bruises, no blood. You're gonna be hurting for a while. And you're gonna need a new Camelback." The water bladder was blown open in two places and flat empty, which explained the liquid Shake had felt flowing over his butt and thighs. Mike spun the protective vest and pointed to two ripped and frayed bullet holes leaking Kevlar threads.

Shake stuck his finger into one of the holes. "Feels like the round is still in there. Remind me to write a glowing letter to the manufacturer."

Stokey walked over to the man Shake had killed in the close encounter and kicked at the Krinkov short assault weapon lying on the ground. "You're lucky he was carrying a 74 instead of a 47. SAPI plate might not have stopped a heavier round."

A distant outbreak of gunfire from the base of the Umurbrogol stopped the speculation. Someone was engaged down by the west road and it sounded like a serious fight. Shake shrugged and stretched to see if his throbbing back would support the effort and decided he could continue. "We'd better get down out of these fucking hills and see how the SEALs are doing."

* * *

His SEALs weren't doing as well as Lt. Kerry Dale Hunter had hoped. Halfway to the original ambush position a panel truck roared past him and forced his guys off the west road to keep from being run over. Before anyone could recover to take a shot at the tires or engine block, shooters in the back of the vehicle opened fire wounding one of the SEALs and driving the rest to the deck. Petty Officer Hal "Clutch" Blake caught a round in the left hip that made him immobile. The team corpsman tending to him threw a hand signal toward Lt. Hunter that said both of them were out of the chase.

Hunter eyed the truck carefully as it roared southward past his position. Through the cloud of dust and exhaust smoke he was fairly certain he had spotted Ignacio Felodon and the missing Indonesian scientist. They were too late to do much but turn around and chase the speeding vehicle, but he had backup at the Camp Beck docks where the bad guys were obviously headed.

"Chief...Boss." He keyed his radio and took off down the road waving for his men to follow. "You're about to have company. There's a white panel truck headed in your direction. It's full of shooters plus the two HVTs in the back. Do what you can to stop 'em. We're hauling ass on foot in your direction."

Shake Davis and Mike Stokey were struggling up and down the Five Sisters group of ridges when they heard Hunter's call to the dockside security team. Shake pointed to his earpiece and described what he thought was happening. "Looks like they split before Hunter and his guys could reach the lagoon, blew past 'em headed south on the west road."

"They're headed for a boat. He got anybody by the docks that can stop 'em?"

"Yeah, goddammit. He's a good hand. Smart officer. He put some people on guard at the backdoor. Chief Wiley and one other SEAL, plus Chan Dwyer. But it sounds like they'll be outgunned if it comes to a fight."

"He's headed in that direction, right?"

"Yeah, and so are we. If we get down off these hills and head for the old airstrip, its open ground all the way. We can make some time." Shake faced down slope and took off at a trot with Stokey stumbling behind him. Ten seconds later both of them were sliding on their backsides and plummeting down toward what the Marines of 1944 had labeled Death Valley where they'd hit open ground and sprint for the dock area.

* * *

Chief Petty Officer Lurch Wiley slid a 40mm HE round into the tube of the M203 grenade launcher slung below the barrel of his M-4 carbine and took a look at their hasty ambush position. He could hear the truck banging through gears as it headed in their direction and there wasn't much time to adjust. His swim buddy, Petty Officer Guy Cornwell, was settled into a solid firing position on the east side of the road. Chan Dwyer was back by the boats lying prone behind a dockside piling. She had her M-9 pistol out and was using her sensor kit as a firing platform.

"Chan, switch to tac-two and push the Independence for me. Tell 'em to close on the island and put a landing force ashore near the lagoon. Get some people in here to be sure that area is secure." He glanced over his shoulder to see her thumbs up then turned his attention to Cornwell on his right and slightly behind him.

"Aim for the tires. I'm gonna try to put a round of HE right in front of that truck when it comes into range. Boss says our targets are in the back of the vehicle so for Christ's sake don't take any chances on nailing those guys. What we need to do here is stop the truck and pin these guys down until the Boss and the rest of our guys get into the fight. Max firepower...minimum impact after we stop the truck, copy that?"

Chief Lurch Wiley got two squelch breaks in response and rolled prone waiting for the truck full of Quds Force shooters to come around the bend.

USS Independence off Peleliu

Commander Doug Bland understood clearly and unequivocally for the first time in twenty years of service as a naval officer why he'd remained a surface warrior in spite of several career enhancing opportunities to go for submarines, aviation or special warfare. He was in a fight and in command of a warship. It wasn't Nelson at Trafalgar or Bull Halsey in the Solomons but Commander, by God, Doug Bland out of Ceiling, Oklahoma, via the U.S. Naval Academy, was large and in charge of a no-shit sea-based combat operation with nary a gravel-crunching soldier in sight.

Standing on his ship's bridge wing and watching his heavily armed and highly motivated sailors scramble to launch two small craft for the trip to Peleliu where SEALs had requested backup, he wondered how many officers would sell their souls to do what he'd done in the past 24 hours. First he'd actually fired shots across an enemy's bow, then he'd engaged an enemy vessel at sea, and he'd just punched up on his vessel's 1-MC announcing system to issue the hoary old sea command: "Away the landing party!" Maybe he'd write an article for Naval Institute Proceedings. Or there might be a book in here somewhere. The first boat hit the water when he noticed someone standing and begging for attention.

"What's up, Lieutenant Davis?"

"Sir, the landing party is heading for that lagoon and I'm the fish expert. Request permission to join the landing party."

"Lieutenant, don't take this the wrong way, but I think we're gonna need shooters more than we need scientists over there on Peleliu."

"I get that, sir. But my Dad is on that island. I can handle myself, but I'm not sure he can. My father has a tendency to...well, to do more than he needs to do in situations like this. I'd really like to go ashore and check on him. And, well, we're dealing with fish in that lagoon, sir. That's my specialty, for what it's worth."

Commander Bland took a close look at Gunner Shake Davis' daughter and decided another Navy cliché worked in this encounter. He liked the "cut of her jib." And she had a point about the fish deal. What could it hurt?

"Permission granted, Lieutenant Davis. Draw a sidearm from the master-at-arms and tell the bos'n I said to put you in the second boat. Good luck. And tell your Dad..."

"Semper Fi, sir?"

"That's it. Good luck, Lieutenant."

Peleliu, Camp Beck Docks

At the same time the 40mm high-explosive round detonated just in front of his right front fender, the QF driver felt the steering wheel begin to shake violently as if someone had shot out his front tires. He discovered in an instant that must be the situation as he jerked the wheel to the left and got no purchase on the pavement. The engine died as the vehicle staggered to a shuddering halt, so the driver grabbed his weapon from the front seat and began to bail out of the truck. Two rounds sailed through the open driver's side window and killed him before his feet touched the ground.

On the opposite side of the truck, Amin Faraz rolled out of the cab and kept rolling until he fetched up near a concrete cistern that gave him some cover from a hail of bullets being fired from the dock area. He glanced over his shoulder to see two of his men lying on the asphalt leaking blood. The others were being chased to cover on both sides of the road by an unknown number of shooters. The only bright light in the situation was that whoever was doing the shooting wasn't very good. Most of the incoming rounds chasing his men away from the truck either went high or smacked into the road sending up gouts of pavement.

They'd either hit a mine or someone on the other side of this engagement had an RPG or maybe a grenade launcher. That was trouble, but he had sufficient men left with sufficient firepower to handle it. The most pressing problem right now was to locate the shooters and eliminate them. Amin Faraz stuck his weapon up over the cistern, triggered a burst and then caught the eye of one of his men on the other side of the road. He signaled for that part of his remaining force to move left into the bush and probe for a flanking position. Then he motioned for two of his men on the right side of the road to move up behind the cistern where they could provide covering fire.

When they arrived and opened fire from either side of the cistern, Amin Faraz crawled to the edge of the water and slid out of sight behind some dock pilings covered with a thick coating of green algae. The old wooden dock and the moored fishing skiffs would conceal his movement while he felt for another flank and found the shooter with the high-explosive weapon.

Ignacio Felodon and Dr. Susilo Nasuton huddled behind the beefy differential casing of the wrecked truck cringing as rounds continued to tear through the vehicle and dig long gouges out of the hot asphalt on either side of it. Gasoline from a ruptured fuel tank was beginning to pool under the dual rear tires and Felodon understood escape was no longer in the cards he'd played for so many years since the death of his family and the cruelty of his native country. He had been in enough firefights in his life to recognize the situation for what it was. The shooters were Americans, probably Navy SEALs, from the warship he could now see approaching the island. And they were launching landing craft. There could only be two outcomes and both were terminal as far as Ignacio Felodon was concerned. When the Americans finally overwhelmed the Iranians, he would either die in the fighting or he would live out the remainder of his life in some prison cell where the memory of a murdered family and the rage he felt for the country that rejected him would destroy his soul.

Felodon decided on the first option, gathering himself to stand and step out into the line of fire when he saw something in the bed of the truck that might present a third course. There was a bundle of emergency flares in a metal can and he reached up to grab two of them. As he pulled the caps off the flares and prepared to strike them into life, he nudged Dr. Nasuton with his foot.

"When I light these flares be ready to run." He pointed at a path on the other side of the road that led through a patch of dense bush. "Be sure you've got the computer and don't stop for anything. Just follow me."

Felodon struck the first flare into light and held the sparking tip well away from the gasoline pool on the road. Dr. Nasuton eyed it warily. He was on the verge of panic.

"It's no use. We should just wait—and then surrender."

Felodon retrieved his AK-47 from the ground and shook it under Nasuton's nose. "You have a choice. You go with me or I will kill you right here and take your computer. Decide!"

Nasuton indicated his choice by rising into a crouch as Felodon tossed the first burning flare into the pool of gas. He struck the second flare for insurance but it was unnecessary. The entire truck exploded into a sheet of flame roiling with thick black smoke. Dragging Dr. Nasuton behind him, Felodon sprinted across the road and disappeared into the bush. They wound their way through thirty or forty meters of scrub brush and then broke through to open ground near the old Japanese airfield. Felodon stopped to think until he spotted two men on the other side of the old airfield, carrying weapons and running in their direction. To his right were the docks and a deadly hail of incoming fire. To his left were the craggy, jungle-covered foothills of the Umurbrogol. The choice was simple and obvious.

* * *

"Chief! Right-rear!"

Lurch Wiley scrambled to check that direction and saw PO Cornwell cranking rounds at muzzle flashes that exploded from a line of warped coconut palms. It looked like his swim buddy was bleeding but he was still in the fight. Wiley dropped another 40mm HE round into the launcher and blooped it toward the tangos trying to hit them in the flank. The detonation reduced the fire from that direction, but it was clear they'd have to pull back and tighten the perimeter.

"Fall back. Go when I open up!"

Wiley flipped his M-4 onto full-auto and whipped half a magazine across the road to his front as Cornwell broke cover and ran toward the docks where Chan Dwyer was guarding their rear. Cornwell had only covered about fifteen meters when he went down hard. This was going rapidly from substandard to shitty, Lurch Wiley thought as he sprinted toward the rear, heading for the docks and waiting for the burst that would cut his legs out from underneath him.

He was shocked to discover he'd made the run in one piece when he slid behind a bundle of thick dockside bollards where Chan Dwyer was calmly reloading her M-9 pistol. "Wish Shake had let me take that damn assault rifle you offered," she muttered. Wiley gave her an encouraging smile and handed over his own pistol. He pumped out two more HE rounds from the M-203 and did a quick check. They were close to Winchester, the SEAL radio code for lack of ammo. Rounds were still pounding in from the right-rear and the shooters were still active on their left front. He'd just about decided their best bet was to get in the water and swim out to sea and he was wondering if the former Army intel officer crouching at his side had passed her swim qualification.

Chan Dwyer had other things on her mind. She was trying to figure out which gun to use with her strong hand, the reloaded 9mm or the harder-hitting .45 the Chief had just handed over, when she sensed something big and close moving in the water near the edge of the dock. She glanced in that direction and saw a face, dripping water from a bushy mustache rise from the water. The man's dark eyes snapped open wide as he fumbled to stand and bring a weapon up into firing position. Chan pointed with the hand containing the .45 until the muzzle nearly touched Amin Faraz' nose. And then she pulled the trigger.

The boom of his own pistol nearly blew out Chief Wiley's left eardrum. He winced and snapped his mouth open, trying to equalize the pressure. When he looked in her direction, he saw Chan Dwyer staring at a headless corpse that was floating near one of the dock pilings and leaking gore in a spreading pool.

"You see any more of 'em?"

Chan stared at the corpse for a moment then shook her head. "Just that one, but he was way too damn close." Wiley realized it was decision time and keyed his radio.

"Boss...Chief. How far out are you?"

"We're just around the bend, Chief. I can see the smoke." Hunter sounded winded but anxious to get into the fight. Chief Wiley understood that just around the bend might not be close enough given their situation at the docks and the bad guys closing on their final position.

"Boss, here's what you're gonna find. There are two or more in the bush to your left of the docks in some palm trees. Cornwell is down dockside of those trees. Don't know his status and I can't reach him. There's a couple more behind a cistern on the right side of the road just ahead of the truck. There's probably more but that's all I've spotted so far. They're closing on our position."

"Copy all, Chief. Can you hold?"

"Better not, Boss, we're back-to-back on the docks and nearly Winchester. And I've got Chan here with me. We're gonna exfil via the blue."

He began to strip off his body armor and reached for a drag harness inside one of the attached pouches. "Dump your gear but keep the weapons, Chan. Put this on." He showed her how to fit the harness, flopped onto his belly and led her slithering through the sand toward the water beside Camp Beck docks. As they slid into the brackish water, Chief Wiley grabbed the drag loop of Chan Dwyer's harness. "Just roll over easy and don't fight it. I'll tow you all the way. You're swimming with a genuine Navy SEAL."

* * *

Lt. Hunter held his panting team behind the smoke-screen provided by the burning truck and took a knee. It looked like taking the remainder of the Quds Force shooters alive was a no-go. He could see the Independence holding position out beyond the reef and two small craft full of armed sailors making for the lagoon. The Iranians were trapped. He knew it and so did they. He reviewed the bidding and decided the key was to capture the Filipino and the Indonesian scientist. The rest of the assholes could surrender or die. Either option was acceptable, but he wasn't going to lose any more SEALs.

He reviewed the brief from Chief Wiley and keyed his radio. "You all heard the Chief's estimate. Dubbya Dee, take your team across the road to the left and get behind the shooters in the palm grove. I'll take my guys to the right and handle the others on this side. They get one shot at surrendering. The next shots are double-taps. I'm tired of fucking around with 'em."

"Boss...Dubbya Dee. What about the Chief and Chan Dwyer?"

"We're closest to the water. I'll keep an eye out for them. All set?" Hunter looked around one last time and saw his guys bunched into their designated assault teams. "Let's do this."

Hunter led his SEALs toward the sandy beach and then made an abrupt left turn. As he cleared a clump of palmetto he saw two Quds Force shooters sprinting toward the docks, triggering bursts from their weapons as they ran. He shouted in the Farsi they'd memorized from an on-line language tutor aboard the Independence, but the shooters were in no mood to comply. One of them hit the deck and scrambled for cover. The other spun into a crouch and triggered a burst of AK fire in the direction of the assaulting SEALs.

The team sniper nailed the guy on the ground and Hunter emptied a magazine at the crouching shooter that doubled him over and dropped him hard. The assault team was on line and moving cautiously toward the bodies when an incoming rocket from somewhere to their left-front blew Hunter off his feet. The warhead detonated against the cistern, showering them with water and concrete shards. Hunter found himself cross-eyed and flat on his back being dragged to cover by Petty Officer Chris Christofferson.

Hunter shook his head to clear it and saw two of his guys take out a shooter that was firing in their general direction from a position in the tin roof shack local fishermen used to clean their daily catches. Just before Christofferson dumped him into a drainage ditch at the side of the road, Hunter saw one of his men toss a flash-bang through the window. He didn't see the blast but he heard it followed almost immediately by the rattle of a weapon hosing the shack and the shooter.

He was doing the math based on his observation of the dockside battlefield and trying to figure out how many remained in the fight while his head cleared and his hearing gradually returned to a ringing version of normal. He was fairly sure neither Felodon nor Nasuton were among the casualties he'd seen. That likely meant they were somewhere among the shooters in the palm grove to his left-front.

He sat up carefully, reached for his radio and came up with a tangle of loose wires. The mini-transceiver was gone, probably ripped from his gear by the rocket detonation. Hunter turned to Christofferson and pointed at the man's headset. "Push Dubbya-Dee and tell him the HVTs are likely in his area. Be damn sure he doesn't blow 'em away."

Whistledick Grey and two SEAL teammates had a dead drop on four shooters who were bunched up in a school circle where it looked like they were trying to figure out what to do next. One of them was muttering into a hand-held radio but apparently getting no response. Grey heard the transmission about the HVTs and peered around the area trying to locate them. Neither man was anywhere in sight but they might be hunkered down somewhere close by in the tangle of tree roots and scrub brush. He decided not to take the easy shots and yelled the Farsi equivalent of "drop your weapons or die."

His Farsi wasn't worth a damn but one of the QF men got the message. He stood, dropped an RPG launcher at his feet and raised his hands. The QF man with the radio triggered two rounds into his unmotivated comrade's chest and took off at a run. The SEALs in covering positions squeezed triggers and dropped the two fence-sitters before they had time to stand.

"Check 'em out and search the area for the HVTs. Then go see about Cornwell." Whistledick Grey took off at a run on the track of the escaping man. "This other guy looks like he might be a leader. I'm gonna try to run his ass down."

Whistledick was following the runner along a narrow path leading toward the water's edge when the Soviet F-1 hand grenade hit the trail and bounced along headed in his direction. He spotted it immediately and took a flying leap toward a fallen coconut log to his left. Unfortunately, his ass and lower legs were still exposed when the frag detonated. Whistledick felt hot shrapnel dig into his backside and pulled himself to the other side of the log where he took inventory and decided that while war was hell, *combat* was a motherfucker.

* * *

Shake Davis and Mike Stokey stood panting and hurting at the base of an overgrown trail that led from the edge of the old airfield up toward a portion of the Umurbrogol known as the China Wall. Stokey crouched and peered upward trying to catch sight of the two men they'd seen climbing in that direction. There wasn't much to see through the tangle of lush vines, leaves and palmetto bush that had overgrown the track.

"Whaddaya think, Shake?"

"I recognized Felodon in the lead." Davis crouched beside his buddy and listened to the diminishing sounds of the fight off to their left. There were only a few desultory shots being fired and they were all from M-4s or MP-5s. Apparently, Hunter and his SEALs had the upper hand in that situation. "I'm betting the guy on his ass has to be the Indo geek, Dr. Nasuton."

"Well, we better haul ass if we're gonna run 'em down."

"Here's a better plan, Mike." Shake peeled the radio headset off, jerked the mini-transceiver out of the pouch on his gear and handed it over. "Let's let the pros from Dover handle it. Take the radio and see if you can pick up their trail. I'll send Hunter and some heavyweights up to give you a hand."

Stokey squinted at his older buddy and smiled. "It's a plan...but not the one I was expecting from you." Stokey donned the headset and clipped the transceiver to his belt.

"Does this have anything to do with the lovely and talented Miss Chan Dwyer?"

Davis shrugged and began walking in the direction of the docks. "Let's just say I'm anxious to find out if she's OK."

"You heard the radio transmission, Shake." Stokey began to climb into the foothills heading up the track leading to the China Wall. "She's with Chief Wiley."

"I'm just gonna confirm that, Mike. It's important to me. Stay in touch."

After ten minutes of fast walking, Shake Davis emerged from the bush beside Peleliu's west road and scanned the aftermath of a serious firefight. Hunter was shaky on his legs but holding his own, making radio transmissions while his SEALs stacked bodies and tallied the score on what looked like a very bloody encounter. There were seven dead QF fighters lined up next to a stack of captured weapons. Two more were bound by flex-cuffs and having wounds tended by one of the SEALs.

Some distance away in the shade of a warped coconut palm, some combat lifesaver had plugged a liter of blood expander into the arm of an unconscious buddy. Shake knew the man by sight but couldn't remember his name. Beside the unconscious SEAL and keeping an eye on the IV was Petty Officer Whistledick Grey who was basically naked from the waist down except for the shredded remnants of his trousers and a swath of battle dressings. Grey waved and shouted for Hunter's attention. "Boss! Gunner Davis is inbound."

Hunter looked up from his radio and staggered in Shake's direction. "Hey, Gunner, looks like we got 'em all...but no sight of Felodon or Nasuton."

"They got away." Shake pointed toward the Umurbrogol rising at his back. "We saw both of 'em heading for the high ground. Mike's tracking 'em now. He's got a radio."

Hunter immediately switched channels on his radio and tried to raise Stokey. He got a quick response. "He's up on tac-two. He hasn't spotted 'em yet but he's on the track." Hunter called for four of his men, did a quick ammo and gear check, and then turned to lead off toward the airfield. "It's the trail just to the left of the old Japanese admin building, right Gunner?"

Shake nodded and caught at Hunter's elbow. "What about Chan and Chief Wiley?"

"I've got some sailors from the Independence looking for 'em." Hunter pointed at his radio headset. "They're gonna patrol the whole west side of the island close inshore. We'll find 'em."

"No radio contact?"

"They're swimming, Gunner, and nobody's better at it than Chief Wiley. Look, he probably just dragged Chan out toward the reef and he's lying low. Chances are we'll find 'em both walking up the beach hand-in-hand in a little while."

Hunter led his SEAL assault team into the bush at a trot headed for a rendezvous with Mike Stokey up on the China Wall. Shake walked toward the docks trying to decide which of the little island fishing skiffs would be easiest to handle. He was exhausted and hurting down to the bone, but he intended to find Chan Dwyer before he rested. And he was praying—for the first time in a long time—that he'd find her alive.

He was about to launch a little outrigger canoe when a rattletrap pickup truck came roaring into the dock area, swerving around the burned out flat-bed with a grinning Peleliu native driver at the wheel. Sitting next to him, hanging halfway out the window and waving wildly was a naval officer. The truck slammed to a dusty stop near the pier and Tracey Davis jumped out wearing body armor and a holstered pistol.

"What in the hell are you doing here, girl?"

"I'm just checking on my Dad. And also supervising security around that damn lagoon up the road. So, how you doing?"

"I'm fine; Tracey. And you shouldn't be here."

Tracey ignored him and stared around at the carnage. "Where's Chan?"

"I don't know. She's somewhere with Chief Wiley. They got crowded during the fight and apparently swam out to sea. I was just gonna go looking."

"That explains it." Tracey shaded her eyes and stared out toward the reef. "They detached one of the boats and sent it down in this direction. I thought they were sending sailors to reinforce the SEALs." She nodded at the dead bodies lining the road. "Looks like the SEALs didn't need any help."

"Focus, Tracey. I said you shouldn't be here."

"I heard you, Dad. And I ignored you because you know damn well I need to be here. There's a whole bunch of really bad fish penned up in that lagoon." She pointed north up the west road. "And I'm the geek that knows what to do with them. Somebody who knows what she's doing has got to keep a lid on things until the science team from the Seascope gets here. They're on the way but it's gonna be well after dark by the time they arrive."

"And then you're back in the science biz, right? Promise me, Tracey."

"All in good time, Dad, there's a lot to do here on Peleliu. They've got Palauan police on the way from Koror along with a bunch Feds from a bunch of agencies. They're gonna lock this island down tight. Plus they need help dealing with a big bunch of very frightened and confused locals." She indicated the pickup driver who was cautiously examining dead QF terrorists. "That guy is a village chief. He finally came out of the woodwork when we got ashore and I talked him into giving me a ride down here. I think he likes me."

"Tracey, it isn't over yet by a long shot. Mike Stokey and Lt. Hunter with a team of SEALs are up in the hills chasing Felodon and Dr. Nasuton. And we don't know how many QF guys were on the island, so we don't know for sure if we got 'em all. It could still get ugly." Shake shoved the outrigger into the calm water beside the pier and jumped aboard. "I've got to see if I can find Chan. Do me a favor and stop trying to be a line officer."

"The sailors will find her, Dad. Give it a rest."

"You know me better than that, Lieutenant Davis. I'll rest when I'm dead."

Shake Davis fumbled with an oar and rocked the boat a time or two to get the feel of the outrigger. Then he paddled out toward Peleliu's ring reef in search of the woman he'd decided to spend the remainder of his life with, assuming she was alive—and willing.

* * *

Three quarters of a mile south of where Shake Davis was paddling away from Camp Beck docks, the last member of the Quds Force security detail was paddling another outrigger and trying to decide on a course of action. He'd found the small boat hauled up on a deserted stretch of beach just after he'd tossed a grenade to stop the man pursuing him. He'd slipped the boat into the water and paddled as hard as he could to put distance between himself and the scene of the firefight with the Americans.

He'd tried the radio for a while but there was no response to his repeated calls, so it was likely Amin Faraz and the others in his team were either dead or captured by the infidels. His first duty in support of the mission on Peleliu was done. Quds Force doctrine said his duty now was to escape and survive. Somehow, someway he would find a way to get home and report on the action. As a survivor who had done his duty to the best of his ability, he might even be declared a hero of the *jihad.*

But first he had to escape and evade and his QF training had prepared him for that. He let the outrigger drift with a southward current for a while and tried to work out details. He'd once been involved in a horrific raid on Zionists in Gaza during which all but two QF fighters were killed. The other survivor was captured, but he had escaped and made his way through the Bekaa Valley of Lebanon, into Syria, across Iraq and finally home to Iran. He had nothing but a weapon and his wits and the trek had taken six weeks, but he made it.

He was mentally planning a route and wondering how long it would take to get from the South Pacific to the other side of the world when he felt something bump against the hull of his boat. He peered over the side and spotted nothing on the right. On the left side of the outrigger, the side closest to the beach, he thought he caught sight of something large and dark in the water. Shark, he thought, and reached for his AK-74 assault rifle. He was leaning over the left side of the boat, aiming the weapon at the water and searching for a marauding target, when the boat suddenly rocked violently. He heard something that sounded like a very large fish jumping and suddenly his field of vision shifted from the surface of the water to the scudding clouds in the sky over Peleliu.

CPO Lurch Wiley pulled himself out of the water with his left hand on the gunwale of the outrigger and clamped his right arm around the neck of the Quds Force shooter. The outrigger on the other side of the skiff splashed down loudly as Wiley pulled his catch into the water and dunked him hard and deep. As expected, the man struggled and thrashed but Wiley had him in a rock-solid grip. He'd let the man swallow a little salt water just to correct his attitude but this guy was a sand-rat and no sailor. A close encounter with a SEAL combat swimmer was well out of the guy's comfort zone.

Wiley finally surfaced with his captive under control, letting him breathe but keeping steady pressure on the man's carotid artery. In less than twenty seconds while Wiley floated on his back and waited for the inevitable, the QF fighter passed out cold. He rolled the unconscious captive onto his back and kicked for the opposite side of the boat where the outrigger would provide some stability and then shoved the sodden lump aboard. He pulled himself into the boat and with a quick stroke of his survival knife; Chief Wiley cut the outrigger's bow line. It would serve to hog-tie the QF fighter and keep him out of trouble after he regained consciousness.

"Hoo-ah, Chan!" Chief Lurch Wiley stood in the gently rocking boat and waved at the shore. "What we got us here is a water-taxi. I'll be right there."

Chan Dwyer stood up from behind the coral rock where Chief Wiley had beached her after their long swim along the southern edge of Peleliu's shoreline and waved. She was soaked and exhausted even though the Chief had done all the swimming but nothing sounded better to her at this moment than a boat ride. As Wiley paddled toward her, she marveled once again at the man's facility, comfort and skill in the water. He had to be part fish. They'd covered at least two miles while he swam strongly, towing her along like a toy boat in a bathtub, and he wasn't even breathing hard when they'd spotted the outrigger canoe being paddled by a man with an AK-74 strapped across his chest.

"Sit tight right here," Wiley whispered as he pulled her ashore and shoved her behind a big coral outcropping. "I'm gonna take care of a little business and then get us back into the fight." Her legs and arms were cramping badly as she watched the SEAL chief slide silently and strongly back into the water. It was like watching an aquatic animal slip from a rock or a rest back into its natural environment. Regardless of the Navy acronym, there was a reason these guys were called seals.

Thank God, Chan Dwyer thought as she tumbled into the outrigger and picked up a paddle, that I did my time in the Army, where swimming was a recreation and not a tactic. She was due to help Lt. Hunter write up a medal recommendation for Janet Dewey but she'd also provide a statement that she hoped would lead to something similar for Chief Lurch Wiley.

Chan was holding a water-logged pistol on the recently-revived Quds Force fighter when the boat rocked and Chief Wiley stood in the stern waving his paddle over his head.

"Ahoy, Gunner! Stand by to come alongside."

Chan Dwyer turned to see Shake Davis paddling furiously in their direction. She didn't care a bit if the bastard staring into the muzzle of her pistol heard her sobs or saw the tears streaming down her cheeks.

Peleliu - The China Wall

"If there's one cave on that slope we can see, there's gotta be forty buried under the bush." Mike Stokey stood next to Lt. Kerry Dale Hunter glassing the rugged east face of the China Wall. "It was probably a lot easier back in '44 when they had 16-inchers and airstrikes to burn off the vegetation."

"Digging people out of crap like that was never easy, especially if they're determined to stay put." Hunter stared at the dark mouth of the single cave they could see and figured a former soldier like Felodon would never pick such an obvious spot. "You sure they're up there somewhere?"

"Don't see how they could have gotten much farther. Nasuton's in no shape for bush-bashing so I caught up with 'em fairly quick. Last good sighting I had they were headed for that cave."

"My bet is that's not where they are now. Too obvious."

"Yeah, Felodon's too good for that. You got any brilliance you want to bring to bear on this thing?"

Hunter turned to look at the four SEALs he'd brought along up to the China Wall. "Maybe we get up onto the high ground along the ridge line and sweep downward. I could get some people to form a line at the base of the hill and we might flush 'em out that way."

"Might work, but sure as hell there'd be gunplay. Way I see it, Felodon's not interested in being taken alive. But it's important to take Nasuton in one piece. We need to be more precise."

"I'm sure as hell open to suggestions if you've got any."

"Shake Davis has been all over this area doing historical research. He probably knows where the best hidey-holes are. Let's get him up here and see what he thinks."

* * *

At the Camp Beck Docks, a line of native pickup trucks was being pressed into service to haul survivors and stiffs up the island's west road toward the former Quds Force base camp where the Navy contingent from Independence had set up a sort of expeditionary headquarters. As senior officer present, Cdr. Bland had come ashore to take charge and his first orders were to consolidate forces, isolate the experimental lagoon and deal with a curious—and increasingly furious—native population demanding to know what was happening on their quiet island home.

Tracey Davis was gone when Shake returned to the docks with Chief Wiley and Chan Dwyer. One of the officers from the Independence told him she'd been called away to supervise the isolation and subsequent handling of the people on the island who were presumed to have died from ingesting poisoned fish. She was apparently the duty expert on such matters until the scientific team from RV Seascope arrived or until a haz-mat team from the States arrived in the Palaus and could be rushed to Peleliu.

Chief Wiley hauled his prisoner toward the other two surviving QF fighters sitting defiantly beside the road and directly past Whistledick Grey, who eyed the man suspiciously. "Hey, Chief, where'd you find that turd?"

"He was dicking around south of here in an outrigger. Looked like he couldn't figure out whether to shit or wind his watch, so I helped him decide."

"That's the asshole that fragged me." Grey struggled to his feet and stuck an extended middle finger in the man's face. "You gotta do better than that, dipshit!"

The first loaded pickup rattled up the road with the wounded SEALs and Chan Dwyer, who thought she might be of some value helping Cdr. Bland deal with the natives until the national police arrived from Koror. They were due shortly, with one contingent coming by small aircraft and a larger element following by boat. Shake was about to climb aboard the second truck loaded with dead QF fighters when the Navy officer supervising the loading waved a radio at him.

"Gunner, Mike Stokey calling for you on tac-two." Shake took the hand-held radio and pressed the transmit button."

"Davis here, Mike. Send your traffic."

"We're up on the east face of the China Wall, Shake. I'm fairly sure our two birds are holed up here but you know what this place is like, right? There are probably a hundred caves up here that the Japs dug in Dubbya Two and they could be in any one of 'em. You better come take a look."

Just under twenty minutes later, Shake Davis stood with Stokey and Hunter scanning the face of the China Wall with field glasses. He reached into his gear for the tactical map he'd marked up during his last visit to the island the previous year. It was covered with all sorts of symbols and scribbled notes along the margins. He spread it out on a nearby coral rock and oriented the map to the terrain it depicted. "I spent four days up here last year poking around in the caves and crevasses." Stokey, Hunter and his SEALs all gathered around the map and watched Shake tap a location with a pen.

"That's the cave we can see from here. I found some old Japanese gas masks and some rusted rifles in there. There are probably ten more like it above that one and maybe a dozen more below it. He pushed the pen across the map from the north to the south. "They stretch all along the China Wall from about here to here."

"It's never fucking easy." Hunter shook his head and glanced from the map to the tangle of green covering the coral and dirt of the China Wall. "No wonder they called this place Bloody Nose Ridge."

"The good news is that Felodon and Nasuton won't be in any of them." Shake moved his pointer about two inches to the right of the spot that depicted the cave they could see from their vantage point. "They'll be right here."

Stokey slipped a pair of reading cheaters onto his nose and took a closer look at the map. "Just looks like heavy bush to me. I take it there's something under there."

Shake pointed at a scribbled note above the spot on the map. It read "BAT CAVE."

"There's a hole in the China Wall and the opening is right here. I found all kinds of stuff in there including some live mortar rounds and a few skeletons plus a whole shit-pot full of bats. The cave winds up and down and around and has some pretty tight passages at places. It also leads to an exit that's just above the west road." He tapped another location on the map. "Right about here, north of the lagoon they were using and south of the village."

"And you figure Felodon would know that?" Hunter was using his fingers to measure distances from the China Wall to the west road. "How would he know that particular cave goes all the way through the ridge?"

"He's used to caves like that. We used to crawl around in 'em when we were stationed in the Philippines and get ourselves covered in bat shit. Strange thing about South Pacific bats is they always nest up where there's more than one bolt hole. If he sees bats, he'll know the place has more than one exit."

"So we go in up there." Hunter pointed up toward the slope of the China Wall. "And we keep pushing from this side. Maybe we toss a flash-bang or two to let him know we're on his ass. And he runs for the other exit where we have some people to snatch him up."

"That's the general idea, I guess." Shake stood and folded his map. "Remember he's got a weapon and he'll use it, so don't get too close. We need to take both of those guys alive and you get into a gunfight in a coral cave like that, there will be a lot of ricochets."

Stokey seemed unconvinced. "You thinking Felodon is gonna let us take him and Nasuton alive?"

"Don't underestimate this guy, Mike. If he thinks there's a way he can escape and use Nasuton's work to stage another attack, he'll take a shot. He's got a lot of hate built up over what he considers some serious insults. Filipinos are like elephants over that kind of shit. They never forget."

"I'm gonna call up some of my guys and get 'em set up around that exit point." Hunter reached for his radio. "Shake, can you get down there and show 'em where it is?"

"On my way." Shake handed over his marked up map and grabbed Stokey by the elbow. "Radios probably won't work inside the cave, so we'll be out of touch until you guys get near the exit on the other side."

Hunter motioned his SEALs forward. "How much time have we got?"

"It's better than five hundred meters to the exit from here. Add in all the twists and turns, the tight passages—he's got no light that we know of—call it an hour, maybe more."

* * *

Dr. Susilo Nasuton was crouched in a near panic swatting feebly at a number of large bats that were swooping and diving all around his head. Two hands would have been more effective against the curious animals so recently roused from their sleeping berths all across the ceiling of the coral cave, but Nasuton was unwilling to let go of his laptop computer. And the little Filipino who led him into this level of hell had promised there was a chance to escape with his precious research.

"They won't hurt you!" Ignacio Felodon grabbed at the scientist and pulled him to his feet. "Just ignore them and let's move. We will find an exit soon. Where there are bats, there is always an exit. We just need to find it."

"And then what?" Nasuton pulled a bandana from his pocket and tied it around his head. "There are Americans all over the island. They will find us."

"They will not find us." Felodon steered his reluctant companion toward a tight opening that led deeper into the interior of the cave. "We get out of this cave and then we hide in these hills until the Americans leave. You've got money. We will find someone to help us."

Dr. Nasuton prayed fervently and followed the Filipino into the inky darkness. He had well over one hundred thousand U.S. dollars in the knapsack he'd carried with him off the Al Calipha, but it was small comfort. Only Allah could save him and Susilo Nasuton very much wanted to live through this nightmare. If he wound up in some infidel gulag...*Inshallah.*

* * *

"I've been thinking..." Shake Davis sat staring at the long dark slit in the western face of the China Wall. For the past half hour Shake, Stokey and a detachment of SEALs had been staring at the cave exit and listening to occasional loud detonations mixed with the rattle of gunfire. "Suppose that little shit and his Indonesian butt-boy just hole up in there once they see we're waiting for them out here."

"We just wait 'em out, I guess." Mike Stokey passed a canteen of fresh water and shrugged his shoulders. "Either that or Felodon decides to kill Nasuton and swallow the muzzle. That could happen."

"Mike, I think we need to take a lesson from the Marines that fought for this island back in 1944. What we need is a special weapon designed to flush rats out of holes. You keep an eye on things here. I'll be back shortly."

Shake Davis clambered down onto the west road and began running south at a steady pace. If he could keep it up, he'd be at the lagoon in less than fifteen minutes.

* * *

Tracey Davis was helping a crew of Independence sailors load dead civilians into the back of a refrigerated truck borrowed from a local fish market when she saw her father running down the road streaming sweat and breathing in time with his footfalls. She'd seen him run long distances like that at morning PT when she was a little girl living with her parents on various Marine Corps bases. For an old guy, her Dad was in great shape.

"Tracey!" Shake spotted his daughter and waved. "Secure whatever you're doing and find me a sailor—an engineering rate." She cut a look at the clutch of sailors milling around at various chores near the lagoon. There were only about ten left here. Cdr. Bland had sent most of them up to the village of Klouklubed to help with reassuring the local population. The first contingent of Palauan national police had just arrived and mustered the population to issue explanations and instructions.

As her Dad huffed into the beach area just behind the lagoon that constituted her first official command since she'd been in the Navy, Tracey saw a sailor approach and salute. "I heard that guy yelling for an engineering rate, ma'am. My name's Rick Grimm...machinery repairman first class. Maybe I can help."

Tracey grabbed Petty Officer Grimm by the elbow and steered him toward her father who was bent over and catching his breath on the edge of the lagoon. She made a quick introduction and watched her father look directly into the sailor's eyes. She'd seen it before many times. Shake Davis sized a man up in a hurry and he was rarely wrong in his conclusions.

"Grimm, I need to make a flamethrower. And you're gonna help me do it in a hurry."

"I've made a lot of weird shit out at sea, sir, but I've got no fucking idea how to make a flamethrower." Grimm glanced nervously at Lt. Tracey Davis. "Pardon my fucking language, ma'am."

"It's basically a source of compressed air that passes through a source of fuel and then the stream gets ignited. Simple really. You got any tools?"

"Yessir." Grimm pointed at a large red metal container sitting near the refrigerated truck. "I never go much of any place without 'em."

"Check. So here's what we're gonna do." Shake turned to Tracey and pointed at the refrigerated truck. "I'm gonna borrow that truck and then me and Petty Officer Grimm are gonna blow down the road to the docks. I spotted some scuba tanks down there and they've got all kinds of fittings we can modify. There's plenty of boat fuel available. And we'll figure the rest of it out as we go."

They took off toward Grimm's toolbox while Tracey waved the sailors loading cadavers away from the truck. "I signed for that vehicle, Dad. I'm coming along,"

Tracey Davis jumped behind the wheel and cranked the engine. She had a little trouble with a slipping clutch, but had them rolling south in seconds after the engine caught.

When the truck screeched to a stop near the Camp Beck Docks, Shake Davis jumped out and ran to the shack where he'd seen the scuba equipment. There were tanks labeled full among a bunch of empties. There was an air compressor and a box full of fittings nearby. He waved Grimm over and pointed at the tanks.

"Figure out a way to run a hose off of a valve so we can turn the air on and off. We'll run that hose into a fuel tank and then another hose from the fuel tank becomes the launcher. Get the picture?"

"Yessir." Grimm was already grabbing for wrenches and pawing through a parts bin. "See if you can find me hoses and a fuel can that can be sealed. They got lots of worm clamps here. We'll get it done."

"Find the fuel can, Dad." Tracey ran toward the air compressor. "I see some hose that might work."

By the time Shake returned with a bright red boater's fuel can, PO Grimm had one of the scuba tanks rigged with a bayonet valve. He pushed on the valve lever and grinned when he got a rush of compressed air. Then he grabbed a hose from the selection Tracey had found and worm-clamped it onto the valve outlet. Shake plopped the full fuel can down next to Grimm and asked what he could do to help.

"Sit tight, Mr. Davis. I eat this shit like candy." Grimm was clearly a talented hand with jury-rigging. In minutes he had the air tanks connected to the fuel tank and a secondary hose clamped tight to the fuel can spout. He handed the hose to Davis.

"Point it somewhere and let's see if she works."

Shake pointed the hose out the window of the scuba shack and nodded at Grimm, who cracked the air valve. They were rewarded by a high-pressure stream of fuel that looked like it had a range of about twenty feet. "Out-fucking-standing, Grimm! Now we need a source of ignition."

Petty Officer Grimm grinned like he'd just been awarded a Nobel Prize and reached into the pocket of his coveralls. "Just flick my Bic, Mr. Davis."

"Hit it." Davis held the lighter near the end of the hose as Grimm once again cracked the air valve. When the stream was steady, Shake thumbed the lighter into flame and they saw a huge spear of burning fuel shoot out the window. It was a scary weapon—and just what he needed.

"That gonna get it, sir?" Grimm stood and started collecting his tools. "We can modify as required now we've got the basic working model."

"Damn near perfect, Grimm. Only thing missing is something to thicken up the fuel."

"What did they use for that, Dad?" Tracey stared at the Rube Goldberg gadget relieved that the whole thing hadn't exploded in their faces.

"I don't know for sure...some kind of stuff to thicken the fuel. This will have to do. Let's get up the road..."

"Wait a minute..." Tracey began to rummage around on shelves at the rear of the scuba shack. After a minute, she turned smiling and holding a box of laundry detergent over her head. "If my college chem courses were worth what they cost, this ought to thicken the fuel."

"Perfect!" Shake Davis unscrewed the cap of the fuel can and pointed at the opening. "Pour that stuff in here and let's go. Bouncing around in that damn truck will mix it just fine."

* * *

There was a one-sided fight going on up above the road when Shake Davis arrived in the truck with Grimm and their homemade flamethrower. He needed Grimm to help him carry the ungainly rig but he insisted that Tracey Davis return to her post at the lagoon. She bitched a bit, but Shake won the battle of wills by pointing out that she was officer-in-charge at the lagoon and that was her duty station until officially relieved. When his daughter wheeled the reefer truck around and headed south, Davis picked up the front end of their weapon, motioned for Grimm to pick up the scuba tank and they began to climb.

The shooting up near the cave exit was from only one weapon and Shake was fairly sure it was Felodon trying to clear a path for his escape. Fortunately, none of the SEAL gate-guards had opened up to return fire. Stokey met them just below the crest where the SEALs were hunkered down in covered positions and pointed at the contraption they were carrying.

"What the fuck is that?"

"Flamethrower, Mark II, Mod B…and this is Petty Officer Rick Grimm who made it."

"Tell me you're not planning on burning those two out of the cave. Weren't you the one saying we need to take 'em alive?"

"I'm not planning on a barbecue here, Mike, but I think I can scare the bulldog shit out of 'em. Everybody hates flame weapons. Squirt a little napalm at their ass and they rapidly lose motivation. Marines learned that right here on this island during World War II. What's happening up topside?"

"Felodon poked his head out of the hole about ten minutes ago. One of the SEALs yelled at him to surrender and he emptied a magazine. He's got a Krinkov but I didn't see any other weapons."

"Did you see Nasuton?"

"I didn't, but one of the SEALs said he saw another guy in the shadows just after Felodon ducked back into the cave. I figure they're both in there and fairly close to the exit." Stokey pointed at his radio headset. "We're back in contact with Hunter and his guys are pressing from the rear. They can't back up."

"Check. We're in good shape. Let's get up there and see if we can end this thing."

When they reached the level of the China Wall where the SEALs had a tight security perimeter, Shake borrowed a radio and contacted Lt. Hunter.

"Hunter...Davis. How copy?"

"Lima Charlie, Gunner. You outside?"

"Affirm. Where are you?"

"Maybe twenty meters behind our HVTs. He tosses a few rounds our way every once in a while, but we're in covered positions."

"Sit tight. I'm gonna see if I can talk him out."

Shake told Stokey and Grimm to stay down in a defilade position and crawled up toward a coral crest where he had a good view of the cave exit.

"Ignacio! Come out of there. We need to talk."

There was silence for a long time before a voice shouted out of the shadows. "Who is that?"

"Shake Davis, Ignacio. You remember me from the mobile training team on Mindoro. You've got a lot to be upset about, Ignacio. But I was once your friend. I can help you out of this situation."

"I don't believe you. Gunner Davis is dead."

"Not by a long shot, Ignacio." Shake slowly and carefully got to his feet and walked toward the exit of the cave. He held his arms out to his sides so Felodon could see he had no weapon. One of the SEALs yelled at him from behind a nearby rock.

"Mr. Davis, that's not a good idea. If he shoots at you, we'll have to blow him away."

Shake kept his eyes on the inky slit in the China Wall that marked the cave exit. He thought he could see something moving in the gloom. Just to his right was a long, slick ditch that had been eroded over the years by rainfall cascading off the China Wall.

"Ignacio Felodon won't shoot an old friend. Will you, Ignacio?"

* * *

Crouched behind a vertical spit of coral just inside the cave mouth, Dr. Susilo Nasuton thought maybe Allah had finally answered the constant, fervent prayers he'd been saying since they entered this horrible place. He glanced across the way where Ignacio Felodon was staring fixedly at whoever was approaching the cave. "Who is it?"

"Someone I used to know." Felodon didn't look at his fellow fugitive. "It was a long time ago—in another life."

"Maybe he can help us. He said he's your friend."

"I have no friends, and I have no family!" Felodon yelled at the approaching figure and glanced at Nasuton. "And neither do you, doctor. Don't be fooled. I have no family and you have no future. There is no escape. We will die here. Set your mind and make peace with your God." Felodon unfolded the stock of his weapon, tucked it into his shoulder and squeezed the trigger. Doctor Nasuton cringed and hugged his computer, barely aware of the urine soaking his crotch.

* * *

The burst of four or five rounds ripped into the ground at Shake's feet. He jumped for the ditch on his right screaming as loud as he could.

"Don't shoot! Hold your fire!"

"They damn near blew him away and you too, Shake!" Stokey peeked from around a coral outcrop and watched Davis shimmy backwards toward cover. "He's not coming out of there."

Shake slithered down next to Stokey and reached for the radio headset and transceiver. "He wasn't trying to kill me, Mike. At that range, he'd have dropped me like a bad habit no sweat if he really wanted to. He was trying to commit suicide—by SEAL in this case." He slipped the headset on and keyed the radio.

"Hunter...Shake. You hear those rounds?"

"Yeah, I heard 'em. And I heard the conversation before he fired. You OK?"

"Missed me by a mile, intentionally. Look, I've got a plan here. Move your guys back another twenty meters and stand by."

Davis tossed the radio set to Stokey and issued orders. "Pass the word to the SEALs. No matter what happens in the next few minutes, hold fire. All these guys look like they played a little football. It'll be open-field tackling. When they come out of there, just knock 'em on their ass like a defensive safety snags a running back."

Shake turned to his assistant flamethrower operator. "Grimm, you got your lighter?" The sailor nodded and picked up the scuba tank. "Let's go see if we can make this thing work a second time."

As Stokey crawled from position to position briefing the SEALs, Shake led Grimm to the right of the cave exit and began climbing. Grimm struggled to keep up without breaking the delicate hose connections. His Navy issue deck shoes weren't made for purchase on slippery shale covered with jungle undergrowth.

"Where we headed, Mr. Davis?"

"When I was here last year, I noticed some of the cave bats disappearing at night when they came out to hunt, but they didn't exit through the hole down there. That meant there was another exit. I found it one night by watching the bats. It's just up ahead here."

"What the fuck, sir? Are we going into that fucking cave?"

"No we are fucking not, Grimm. We won't have to if this contraption works. The hole is about ten or fifteen meters behind the exit if I remember right. We'll just punch a little of our homemade napalm down there and they'll come running out the exit where the SEALs will knock 'em on their asses and take 'em prisoner. That's the plan, son."

"What's gonna keep us from turning 'em both into crispy critters?"

"That's why we thickened the fuel, Grimm. If we hadn't done that, burning crap would have splashed all over everything, them included. With the thickened fuel, there's less splash. At least that's what they told me in boot camp."

* * *

Just inside the cave mouth, Ignacio Felodon snapped the magazine from his Krinkov and checked his ammo supply. He had only three rounds remaining and no spare magazines. It was decision time. He decided to put one round into Dr. Nasuton's head and a second into his computer. That left just one for him but he was confident that was all he needed with the muzzle placed just under his chin. He glanced at the Indonesian on the other side of the cave mouth and was disgusted by the sight of a coward. So much for Allah and all the militant Muslim bravado, he thought. And then he dashed across the opening to close the range and be sure he couldn't miss when he brought all this to a bloody end.

* * *

"There it is." Shake pulled at a clutch of jungle vines and pointed at a hole in the coral at their feet. He could feel cool air blowing up through the crevice and tried to decide how far the hole was from the mouth of the cave below the ledge. Probably about ten or twelve meters, he figured and turned to Grimm. "Put the tank over there and let me have your lighter."

"How we gonna do this, sir?" Grimm handed over his lighter and maneuvered the tank next to the hole as ordered by this old jarhead, who he'd decided was one crazy sonofabitch. As he waited for instructions, Grimm wondered how come his U.S. fucking Navy didn't have more fucking guys like Gunner Shake fucking Davis wearing bars and stars.

"Just like the test down at the docks, son. You stand by on that valve. I'll poke the nozzle down near the hole with the lighter at the ready. When I give you the nod, you crack the valve, I'll flick the Bic and we're in business. Got it?"

"Aye-aye, sir. Weapon is manned and ready."

* * *

Ignacio Felodon pointed his weapon at Dr. Nasuton and raised the muzzle as the man struggled to his feet with abject fear in his eyes. "It is time, Doctor, time to stand before God—yours and mine." He was just taking the slack out of the trigger when he was blown off his feet by a blast of intense heat and a wall of virulent flame that rained down from the roof of the cave. A blanket of fire hit the ground of the cave and rolled toward them with an intense roar.

It was a scene from the depths of hell and Dr. Nasuton thought for a moment the scathing heat would boil his skin and melt the meat off his bones. And the fire was charging toward him like a broiling, burning tidal wave. For just a second he thought he must be dead. The Filipino must have fired and he was now in hell suffering for the sins of his life. But Felodon was cringing on the floor of the cave and Allah would never consign an infidel to the same hell as a True Believer. He must be alive. Dr. Susilo Nasuton gripped his computer like a shield and sprinted for the cave exit. He was chased by two shots but both of them missed as he emerged into the clear air and ran toward the cool green of the surrounding jungle.

He had taken barely five steps away from the inferno when something hit him from the left side and knocked him off his feet. Nasuton felt his precious computer snatched from his grasp. He found himself staring up at the jungle canopy as a grinning devil dragged him across the rough coral and dumped him into a ditch. There was another devil waiting there that quickly bound his hands and then dropped one of his padded knees onto Nasuton's chest.

"Got the geek—and his computer."

Shake Davis motioned for Grimm to shut the air valve, dropped the hose nozzle and sprinted for the ledge overlooking the cave exit. It was about a six foot drop to the ground directly in front of the cave mouth. He grabbed a thick clump of roots and swung himself down to the cave level. He landed less than three feet from the cave mouth. Lit by flickering flames from the interior he spotted Ignacio Felodon rolling onto his back and struggling to get the muzzle of a Krinkov tucked up under his chin.

Shake lunged with his arms outstretched to knock the weapon away from his intended target and was nearly blinded by the flash of the shot. He hit Felodon like a wet sandbag and wrestled the Krinkov from his hands. He expected the man pinned beneath him to be headless but he saw tears leaking from his former friend's eyes and nothing more than an angry flash-burn on the man's cheek. Ignacio Felodon was finished and he knew it. There was no more fight left in him.

Shake Davis pulled him to his feet and shoved him out into the cool air. A SEAL sprinted up and quickly and lashed the Filipino's hands behind him with flex-cuffs as he shouted into his radio. "Boss, we got 'em both. Come on out of there." He jabbed the muzzle of his weapon into Felodon's spine and prodded him roughly toward the trail leading down off the China Wall.

"Take it easy, son." Shake shoved at the muzzle of the weapon and grabbed Ignacio Felodon's elbow. "We're the cops, not judge and jury." Then he smiled at the SEAL and pointed toward the ledge overlooking the cave exit. "I got this. Why don't you go up there and bear a hand. There's a sailor up there name of Rick Grimm who did a hell of a job in this thing. He'd probably like to hear a SEAL tell him so."

By the time Shake got back to the lagoon on Peleliu's western shore, the island was coming alive, crawling with Palau National Police and sailors from the Independence. Before too much longer, he realized, this backwater idyllic limbo in the broad expanse of the Pacific would be crawling with cops, journalists, U.S. Feds, political agents and investigators of every ilk and stripe. In a week or two, once the word of what nearly happened out here got around, Peleliu would be infamous once again—a blood-stained battlefield for a second time in its history.

He caught sight of Cdr. Doug Bland standing in the shade of a coconut palm and eyeing the green wall of the Umurbrogol where it rose to rocky heights across Peleliu's west road. "I was just thinking," Bland muttered as Shake slumped onto the sand at the base of the tree, "what it must have been like for those Marines back in 1944 having to climb up into that and pry the Japanese out with nothing but bullets and bayonets."

"It was one of the bloodiest fights of World War II, Commander." Shake picked up a handful of sand and let it trickle through his fingers. "Nearly ten thousand casualties between the Marines and the Army before it was over. The 1st Marine Division lost nearly a third of its combat strength up in those hills. And the historians are still arguing about whether it was even necessary in the overall scheme of things."

"There won't be any argument about that this time, Shake. We dodged a serious bullet by taking these guys out here on Peleliu. Ten thousand casualties is a hell of a price to pay for an island, but you've gotta imagine how many would have died all over the world if we hadn't stopped this thing."

"There it is..." Shake fell back on the familiar phrase grunts used throughout Vietnam when someone stated the obvious. "What worries me ain't this bullet. It's the next round in the magazine. World War II wasn't over when Peleliu fell. I'm wondering what's next, Commander. And I'm wondering how much longer our luck's gonna hold."

Iwo Jima, Volcano Islands—One Year Later

Shake Davis draped an arm over his new bride's shoulder and hugged her close against a chill wind blowing up off the black sand below their perch atop Mt. Suribachi. The orange ball of sun descending on the horizon lit the surface of the rolling sea with brilliant light that stretched toward them in lengthening spears. It was a spectacular sight, as if a drowning man was stretching desperate fingers toward the island in a last effort to keep from slipping beneath the Pacific waves.

"Hell of a place for a honeymoon," Shake mumbled into Chan's silky hair and hoped yet another time since the wedding that she was really happy to be here with an old warhorse on yet another desolate South Pacific island haunted by specters of World War II.

"It beats the hell out of Niagara Falls or Honolulu, Shake. We've been there and done that." Chan snuggled into his embrace and decided there was no other place on earth she'd rather be than right here with her man. "And Tracey warned me..."

"About what? When?"

"Just before the wedding when we had a little female bonding session. Tracey said the only thing I could expect by marrying you was to expect the unexpected. It wasn't news but it was sage advice from a smart woman, if you ask me."

"She did a hell of a job on the Peleliu deal. I'm proud of her."

"You should be. She played a big part in stopping what could have been a real worldwide problem. It was a close-run thing, Shake. The world dodged a serious bullet when we stopped those guys."

"Thought I was gonna lose it when the Secretary of the Navy pinned that medal on her." Shake held a digital camera out in front of them and spun his new bride around so the brilliant sunset would be background for a snapshot. "How many medals did he wind up giving? I lost count."

Chan took the camera and adjusted the angle for their self-portrait. "Jan Dewey and Chief Wiley, Lieutenant Hunter and one each for all his SEALs, plus a unit citation for Commander Bland and the Independence. And Mike got a special decoration from the CIA. It was quite a haul."

Shake smiled at the lens wondering if he really deserved the delight he was feeling locked in physically and emotionally with the woman at his side. "I can't help wondering what would have happened if we'd screwed the pooch out there on Peleliu. Those Seascope people said the assholes were a whisper away from coming up with a communicable disease deal."

"Don't go borrowing trouble, husband unit." Chan shivered in the cold air as darkness descended on Iwo Jima. "If the President did nothing else, he threw a serious hissy-fit on a worldwide stage."

"We did get a pretty good outcome." Shake thought it over. The President had a pot-full of evidence to present because of their success. For the first time in a long damn time the United Nations stepped up and imposed sanctions on Saudi Arabia and Iran. The Philippine government pushed a serious task force down onto Mindinao and Abu Sayyaf is running for cover. Diplomats shut up and got serious about bio-war threats.

"Yeah, and the folks at home are back in a 9/11 mindset." Chan scrubbed at her arms to ward off the wind chill. "I wouldn't be surprised if Felodon and Nasuton wind up hanging from a yardarm. Even the ACLU lawyers won't touch that case. There's a lot of PC crapola that's no longer valid. That's a good thing."

"And so's this." Shake leaned over and kissed Chan, warming them in the dark sulfurous air.

Chan clicked on a flashlight to help them negotiate the track down off Mt. Suribachi to their base camp and a double sleeping bag inside a tent near Hill 362-A. "You know I love you, Shake, and I'm a believer in vows. So, whither thou goest, I will go." Chan grabbed his hand and gave it an affectionate squeeze.

"But can we have a little peace for a while...say, at least until our first anniversary?"

"At least a year and no killing people or breaking shit, I promise. And you get a real honeymoon any place you choose—except Peleliu—as soon as we find Bill Genaust and General Kuribayashi."

"I'm gonna hold you to that, Gunner Shake Davis."

"Aye-aye, sweetheart."

Shake Davis followed the love of his life down from Mt. Suribachi toward the ghosts waiting for them on the desolate plains of Iwo Jima, He was happier than he could ever remember feeling in a long, passion-riddled life. And it occurred to him that maybe that's as it should be.

About the Author

Dale Dye is a Marine officer who rose through the ranks to retire as a Captain after twenty-one years of service in war and peace. He is a distinguished graduate of Missouri Military Academy who enlisted the United States Marine Corps shortly after graduation. Sent to war in Southeast Asia, he served in Vietnam in 1965 and 1967 through 1970 surviving 31 major combat operations. Appointed a Warrant Officer in 1976, he later converted his commission and was a Captain when he deployed to Beirut, Lebanon with the Multinational Force in 1982-83. He served in a variety of assignments around the world and along the way attained a degree in English Literature from the University of Maryland. Following retirement from active duty in 1984, he spent time in Central America, reporting and training troops for guerrilla warfare in El Salvador, Honduras and Costa Rica. Upset with Hollywood's treatment of the American military, he went to Hollywood and established Warriors Inc., the pre-eminent military training and advisory service to the entertainment industry. He has worked on more than fifty movies and TV shows including several Academy Award and Emmy winning productions. He is a novelist, actor, director and show business innovator, who wanders between Los Angeles and Lockhart, Texas.

www.ingramcontent.com/pod-product-compliance
Lightning Source LLC
LaVergne TN
LVHW022158010925
820009LV00015B/1317